A NOVEL
TO EQUAL

"ROSE GARDEN"!

"The setting is the office, the desk, the telephone; the action is the repeated confrontations; the pace is dizzying. . . . [Ralph Oakland is a man] passionately involved in his calling. . . . He never lifts his nose from the grindstone, and the reader never does, either.
Nor does he want to!"
The New York Times

"So packed with realistic case histories that one cannot fail to appreciate the role of the social worker among deprived and handicapped people!"
Library Journal

Also by Joanne Greenberg

THE KING'S PERSONS
IN THIS SIGN

THE MONDAY VOICES

Joanne Greenberg

 AVON PUBLISHERS OF BARD, CAMELOT, DISCUS AND EQUINOX BOOKS

AVON BOOKS
A division of
The Hearst Corporation
959 Eighth Avenue
New York, New York 10019

First Avon Printing, June, 1972

AVON TRADEMARK REG. U.S. PAT. OFF. AND
FOREIGN COUNTRIES, REGISTERED TRADEMARK—
MARCA REGISTRADA, HECHO EN CHICAGO, U.S.A.

Printed in the U.S.A.

THE
MONDAY
VOICES

1

Ethwald Kittenger

Ethwald Kittenger and his aunt were coming in this morning and Ralph hadn't even received Ethwald's medical report; John Kroll from Boys' Shelter was sitting out front playing with a book of matches, striking them one by one and dropping them to burn out on the floor, and the telephone was ringing—an average day. He might get on top of it by noon, but his stomach would be grinding by then. He picked up the phone.

"Mr. Oakland, I'm Elmo Nagy, Ross Business College. There's a girl in my typing class, a good student who's never going to be able to find a job . . ."

"Since you're calling us, I gather she has a physical handicap. What's the trouble?"

"She's deaf. You see the problem; she couldn't hear instructions from an employer—uh—take dictation. I called you because there might be *someplace* . . . I hate to train someone where there is no hope."

"If she's ready for an interview and things work out, she could be working by two this afternoon. There's a place that has a standing order with us for deaf typists."

"Not the asylum, or someplace like that."

"Not the asylum, the airport. They used to have a problem keeping typists; that infernal din of takeoffs and landings and messages on the intercom. Our office has been staffing out there for almost two years."

"That's *fine*. I'll tell her today; we can make an appointment with you."

"Good. I'll look forward to your call."

"Mr. Oakland, this is Mark Foster. I was talking to my uncle and he says that typewriter repair is a bigger field than camera repair."

"Look, Mark, if you change your mind again, it will be the third time. I think we ought to talk about this in your next counseling session. And in the meantime, please don't make any decision ..."

"But my uncle says ..."

Ethwald was sitting next to his aunt, wondering—no matter what they would do to him—if his fear could be any worse. The door had been opened because it was hot and a breeze was going through the office from the hall and out the open window at the back. A train of noise went with it. DEPARTMENT OF REHABILITATION, shining in printed letters looked back at him. His aunt had brought him here through the terror and hatred in the streets, through all the dangers, making him walk out in the merciless daylight of Outside.

The secretary said: "Do you have an appointment, ma'am?"

"Our doctor told us. His name is Ethwald Kittenger. I'm the aunt."

"Are you his guardian, ma'am?"

"Sedges. His mother died. He's our ... responsibility. We mean to find out if there's something for him to do. We're not made of money. My husband gets nervous with him sitting around the house all day long, a big ... big ... *boy* like he is."

A man came out of one of the offices. "How do you do, I'm Ralph Oakland. Will you come in."

"Sedges," the woman said. "It's about *him*," and she motioned with her head toward the bench on which the bewildered-looking boy was sitting.

Ralph Oakland saw a plain woman, almost aggressively plain. She gave the immediate impression that life was a grim business to her and not to be softened or lied away with perfumes or pleasures. "Well, Mrs. Sedges, if you'll come in ..." He looked over at the boy on the bench as the woman began to talk. The boy's face was gray and he stared out of it, but his body was held with great tension, as if he was sitting on a delicately wired bomb. The immediacy of Mrs. Sedges' need seemed to have evaporated. She was talking about background matters.

"Martha, my sister, died and the boy is with me now."

8

Ralph kept trying to move her toward the office, but she was too involved with her problem.

"He got sick when he was about five years old. Then he couldn't move his hand or foot like it's normal."

"The doctor who referred you to us . . ."

"My sister Martha was a pretty girl, I always said so, but she had a giddy nature."

The "waiting section" of the office was filling up with clients to be seen. Ralph glanced again covertly at the boy on the bench, whose eyes were going from one of them to the other as if he was expecting either one of them to trigger that bomb, and now his mouth was wavering in a frightened, apologetic smile.

"Uh, Mrs. Sedges, I think it would be better . . ."

"She never thought to die!" the woman said bitterly. "She never thought to die and leave a twenty-year-old baby boy to me!" Her voice had risen, and a sudden hush of the others answered her wave of sound, and she realized how loud she had gotten. "He isn't going to be normal, not ever, but we can't keep on like this. It's just too difficult, the three of us, without him doing anything. Don't you have stands where crippled people sell things, newspapers or something . . .?"

"We'll have to find out a good deal more about your nephew before we go into a job placement for him. I know that you had him examined, but the doctor hasn't sent in his report."

"That doctor wouldn't tell me anything. You know, it's not the easiest thing in the world to go dragging him around. He puts up a fuss about walking in the street where he can be seen . . ."

The boy hadn't moved. That kid is severely retarded besides, Ralph thought, or mentally ill. One of the tough ones—and he sighed. There was an indefinable sense of illness and invalidism about the boy that underscored the loud martyrdom of the aunt. Perhaps he was too ill to be helped. Maybe she knew it and was just going through the motions of trying before committing him to some institution or other. Well, people used the agency for many purposes—sometimes its judgments were a salve for stricken consciences.

"Mrs. Sedges, I will call when the reports come in, and then we can make more realistic plans with Mr. Kittenger." For a moment she didn't know whom he meant. While they talked, John Kroll, Ralph's ten o'clock client, was lighting his endless matches and dropping them. When Ralph went into his office with Kroll, Ethwald was still there, sitting as forlornly as a lost child.

Ethwald Kittenger

Two plums were ripening in the afternoon window. The woman reached over the sink to feel them. They were warm with the late sun and ready. One for each of them. Ethwald's mother called to her boy. "Sonny-bee!" There was an echo-sounding emptiness in the house. Sighing, she went to look for him.

When Ethwald was five he had been very ill, and when the sickness had drawn away, his arm and foot were horribly twisted. She had protected him through the years from the relentless progress of his brothers and sisters and from the unconscious cruelty of their successes. Ethwald's father had left—he had always been a stupidly selfish man, crying to her that there was no room in the house for him with Ethwald taking every moment of her time and every scrap of her concern. Soon the healthy brothers and sisters grew up and went away. They couldn't seem to realize that they could fend for themselves in the jungle of the world and that Ethwald could not.

Take the paper boy for example. He used to go by on his bicycle, throwing the evening paper up on the porches with great sweeps of his arm. Ethwald used to watch him from the upstairs window with such an intense look on his face that she had felt a need to make light of the silly boy and his silly job. Maybe it looked interesting, taking papers up and down all afternoon long; it was really only ordinary work. Still, she found Ethwald waiting for the paper boy to make that long throw, and hanging behind her when the boy came for his money. It was no use for Sonny-bee to go on sorrowing after that boy swinging his good arms. She had the paper stopped entirely. After that, he had started in with those silly magazine subscriptions. *Mechanical Science* or *Scientific Mechanics* or some nonsense like that. He was up there with them now, probably, scratching around among the piles of them. Well, it passed the time for him, poor boy.

She went up, sighing, to the second floor. He was in his room, in the shadowy corner away from the window, picking over them. "Ethwald Kittenger, there are two chairs, the best

10

in the house put here for you to sit on, and there you are bundled up in that corner." She saw he wasn't listening. "It's four o'clock, Sonny-bee, and look what your mama brought you."

She had always brought him something just at this time. Routine was best; people could always look forward to the next thing—supper or bed or the church program they listened to every Sunday morning. He got up docilely, but he had hold of one of the magazines and he was marking the place between his fingers, so that he had to grab for the other one that fell, going after it with his wrong hand, the crippled, offending hand. A second and then it flew to safety behind his back and he looked down. The foot, too. Ugly. Ugly and ruined. It made his walk into a ragged limp with a little sh—h sounding before each long stride. They were both deeply embarrassed. They stood motionless and silent until she looked toward him again and said, "I've brought this all the way up here for you, Sonny-bee," and handed him the ripe plum.

Late in the afternoon Ethwald's mother decided to hang some new white curtains at the parlor windows. Because she considered herself a mother first and last, and shied away from "professional" experiences, she used the combination of chairs, pillows, and mail-order catalogues favored by some housewives when they wanted height. It was somehow "more feminine." She raised the odd-weighted rod flowing with the new curtain over her head. Sun, late and long-slanted, burned suddenly in back of her eyes and then blurred there. Off-balance. She was falling before she realized it, and no more.

Ethwald heard her light cry and the fall, and came down to see, but he stopped halfway down, a place of habit to stop when salesmen were at the door. She lay all swathed in white curtain, like a very strange old bride. She was very still. He went back upstairs and sat down again, and in a little while he went to the window of his room and called for help from a passerby.

Things seemed to happen by themselves after that, and Ethwald had no more to do than sit in the comfortable chair in his room. The aunt who came to take him away did not recognize him. This was not odd because, although Ethwald was twenty years old and not at all undersized, he had not spoken to or known anyone but his mother since the age of eleven.

"Mr. Oakland, this is Praylo at the probation office."

"Yes, Mr. Praylo. I'm sorry I didn't see you at the meeting last week. I hope you're over that flu." (Don't throw me fifty cases at once . . .)

"I'm a little dragged out, the way you get. I just wanted to call and introduce myself formally, now that you'll be taking the referrals from our department. I know your work. I did student work with Hobson, a man with one arm. Do you remember him? It was about three years ago."

"Yes, surely. I didn't think anyone else remembered back that far." (What does he want?)

"I know how loaded the rolls are. I just wanted to tell you that I'll try to keep the number of referrals down."

"Well, I do have five other agencies to service . . ." (Why am I so cynical, always looking for the hitch? Why am I so damned cynical?)

"That makes two of us who are overloaded. You know, sometimes I think we spend too much time on hopeless cases, just shuffling them back and forth between agencies, hoping there'll be someplace—well—I won't keep you. I just wanted to say we're glad you're with us."

"Thanks for calling, Mr. Praylo."

He turned back to the sluggish delinquent lying flaccidly in the chair. "Well, John?"

John Kroll

It was a tough day so I take out a cigarette and light up and stand around and wait for the guys. The outside of me is resting, easy, waiting and smoking and looking up the girls' legs to make 'em feel like they don't have no clothes on. They giggle and go by, but they say, "Who's that?" Then somebody says, "Oh, that's Badges Kroll!" They got a lot of admiration for me, but they don't know what I'm really thinkin' about inside my mind. I'm with the fellas who are making the breakout now. I fixed everything for my boys, made the plans, slipped some dough to the right people, wired the switches at the main gate, set up the times when everything would be workin' just right to the minute. I ain't so dumb though that I don't know somethin' could happen. I sweat it out with my guys all the way, one by one, like I set it up. Now I'm waitin' for my guys. Around nine Petey comes, first one off in the breakout. I'm leanin' back, just

hangin' easy. He comes up close. I say: "Good work, boy."
He says, "Thanks, Badges." It means a lot to him when I say
that. One by one, right on time, my guys come, all of 'em
cool and tough and strong. I'm their leader and they show it,
like they check in with me. Sometimes somebody goes past
our corner and says to somebody else: "See them guys?
That's Badges Kroll's gang. They're fast and tough and
they're all together." That's what they whisper. When all my
boys are there, a few of them say: "Hey, Badges, where should
we go? They'll be out lookin' for us." I know right what to
do—there's lots I know—lots. I say: "I got a place. My old
lady's waitin' home for us with a ice box full of beer and a
zipper on her lip. She'll hide us out while the fuzz. . . ."

"Kroll—next!"

The dreamer rose from his bench and moved as if through
water, slow motion, into the social worker's office.

"You've reported to the Conduct Captain?"

He made assent with his cold eyes. Then he turned back to
his own story and let her go on without him. After a while he
tuned her in again to see where she was in the talk.

". . . in the old days we used to whip runaways," she was
saying. He looked at her, thinking that she was fat. "Now we
try to find out what they want to prove by running away."
He tuned her out again.

Three days, we're out. I go out on a stick-up job alone. I
got lots of money, even some jewels for the old lady, and
best of all, another cop's badge to add to my collection.

The damn, stupid——social worker broke in again. She was
trying to get on the right side of him by proving she cared
about him.

"If only you would tell us why, when you were so sure to
get caught. . . "

John Kroll knew that it was no good to wonder too long
about that question, or any question about what he did or
thought, but he had found out how to act with everyone
behind a desk from the director (not warden—director) on
down to this old lady social worker. Clam up. If you say
nothing, they got nothing to bring out against you later or fix
up to make it seem like something else. Sometimes the bosses
got mad enough to want to slug you. Sometimes they did.
You could see the hate on their faces, but it made you bigger
with the other guys, just clammed up like that. See, even this
one. She was going to let him go. He stretched luxuriantly, a
little extra touch, something for Badges.

13

The social worker sat back and sighed; a difficult boy, John Kroll. He was fifteen now, undersized and retarded mentally, a bully, a liar, a cheat, and a thief. He had never shown a single sign of a single moment's concern for anyone but himself, and, most painfully hard for every public health nurse or social worker who had ever seen him, he was almost entirely a state product. If she looked through all his voluminous file, adding up all his time in various institutions and foster homes, what would the time be? She went for his file. Even if his institutional time was less than she'd thought, she knew that he had been a state ward for practically all of his life; and so, technically, the state had concurred in all the decisions made for him and about him through all of these years.

Here it was, KROLL, JOHN. She pulled the file. Age two to four at the State Home for Children. Mama's boy friend must have left then; she rated a line where she had taken her son back with her again for two months. Back to the orphanage for another year, and then to a foster home. There came Mama again, another line, this time for three months, and then she sent him to the Sisters of St. Joseph, who ran an orphanage near where she lived. "This would enable her to visit him on weekends," the report said. But she had never come. One year. Back again, there she was, back again to take her boy, full of repentance. Six weeks. New man, new agency. New foster home. The "behavior problem" notes began.

"Foster care impossible," and the yoyo spin between the slum of the drunken and promiscuous mother, the chagrined Sisters of St. Joseph, and Boys' Shelter (which had as its full name, Boys' Shelter and School of Correction, and was called B.S. by the boys.) What was the box score? In all: mother three years; Sisters three years; state nine years. All the workers and teachers and guards who had seen this boy and handled these case sheets were the state. *She* was the state. Why didn't we ever fight for him? We could have proven that mother unfit and given him a decent home when he was three, and stopped the wrenching back and forth from place to place, emotion to emotion, promises that were never kept and remorse that was never lasting!

So, here he was, the fruit of the state's social experiments that had fought generation after generation of public vengeance or apathy. She looked around her office. Thirty years ago, when Poverty was *the* Cause of Crime, a whole new set

14

of showers had been installed on the main floor of the gymnasium (1940: Idleness Is the Cause of Crime). Now there were rumors of dope being smuggled in and passed out through those showers. John Kroll. Who else would try with him? Where else could he be sent before the state would claim him in wardship forever? Maybe something could be done. Maybe someone different.

She picked up the phone. "I want the State Department of Vocational Rehabilitation." She had to say it three times to the girl at the switchboard. "I want to speak to a Mr. Oakland there."

"Mr. Oakland, this is Georgia Burns, the social worker for Boys' Shelter. We have a boy here by the name of John Kroll, and we would like to refer him to your agency. I've heard about your work on the Valdez case from a few sources, and, frankly, I think you might be this boy's last hope."

"I gather that he's a juvenile and has been in trouble with the law, but he's got to have a physical or mental disability, and he's got to be at least potentially able to train for a job and hold it."

"But Valdez . . ."

"I know, Valdez was suffering from acute and chronic anger, anemia of the expectation, fracture of the family, collapsed hope, and a bad squint. The state doesn't recognize any category of his real handicaps, but luckily we were able to get him through on the squint."

"My boy, Kroll, is retarded. He has an I.Q. of 60."

"Well then, at least I could see him and try to get some idea of what his potential is."

"There's something else; it's kind of personal. I don't know how long you've worked for state agencies, Mr. Oakland, but, well, this boy is a real source of heartache to me because he's a mess and he's a state mess, and he's been the state's doing since he was small. He's not what you'd call a likeable kid, but if he ends up in the chair, well, it will be more than a little bit our making and our fault—the state's, I mean."

"Well, what's his name?" "John Kroll." "I could see him on the 23d. Let's give it a try."

"Ralph, this is Etta. We still haven't gotten your share of the office present for Elizabeth's baby shower, and the baby is six weeks old aready . . ."

"Are you John Kroll? I'm Ralph Oakland," and Ralph put

15

his hand out into the social no-man's land between them, watched it die there, and let it drop again. "Will you come into my office please?" He went ahead, and when he turned around to sit down he saw the boy standing at the doorway of the little office, surveying. Ralph watched him a little in wonder at a posture that at the same time could show aggressiveness and boredom. If ever a kid was "going the route," it was this one, and the route ran in Ralph's mind like some old mnemonic chant of childhood: Boys' Shelter to Boys' State and Boys' State to State Pen. Boys' Shelter to Boys' State again, again, again, again. The Rhyme was counting out this John Kroll and Ralph looked at him and knew that he was being counted down unaware and unwary, all bravado and boy-blind pride.

"You are John Kroll, aren't you?"

The kid blinked once, affirmative without giving anything. Ralph motioned him to a chair. He didn't go to it but stood nursing his slouch, his face showing only a vast vacuity and boredom. Ralph wondered if the elaborate care he took to guard his thoughts was meant to show how mighty they were and how savage, as if clearing his throat would doom the world. He was just barely beginning to shave. His jaw circled slowly over a thick wad of gum. After a while he began to move in dreamlike underwater motions to a chair, not, of course, the one which Ralph had pointed out to him. Then he sank into it, not in obedience but only because he seemed no longer interested enough to resist the downward pull of gravity. We're all of us, all, out of our minds! Ralph thought. Who would want to hire this boy under *any* conditions of training or talent? He already works full-time being a punk—and, God, he's good at it; he damns himself without even opening his mouth!

Ralph began by asking some of the standard questions. Usually they helped the client to frame his thoughts as to where he stood and in what direction he might wish to move. The boy was silent and motionless except for the measured milling of that patient gum. Sometimes his eyes moved over the objects in the room, one of which seemed, pointlessly, to be addressing him. He was elaborately wasting his time.

It was a good job of punking, Ralph thought, angry and amused at the same time. He could freeze kindness into animosity and elicit hatred without even calling anyone a name. It was a beautiful technique, but what a terrible cost to the master of it. It was this cost, this waste, that drove

16

Ralph from his clinical objectivity into irritation. The bonelessness of the baby-man-hulk in front of him was suddenly intolerable.

"Men sit in that chair. Sit up like a man or get out!"

It amazed Ralph himself that so much vehemence was carried by his sudden voice. They heard it outside even over the ground tone of the typewriters, and the secretaries' heads flipped up and so did John's before he could catch it. Woman behold, thy son liveth! The mind got the words and half began to respond, but the other law caught up with it and the boy stopped himself from obeying until he was able to look again at the man who had said them without making a commitment. Ralph saw the eyes dull themselves, but the glance came back and back again, as if in passing, to size up Ralph's chest under the white shirt and the suit jacket. It was the most basic of studies between savage strangers: Could I beat him? Could he beat me? Ralph found himself thinking it also. Could I? Yes. The answer seemed to come to both of them together. The boy covered his embarrassment and relief with a sneer and straightened in the chair by barely perceptible degrees. It was a relief. There was an urge to back down, but magnanimity in victory is misunderstood by someone who never "played the game," and Ralph dared not follow the wish.

"Okay," he said, "come on. Maybe we'll work together, maybe not. Maybe something will come of this and maybe not, but when you come in here, it's got to be like a person. Forget the zombie slouch. Sit up—I mean all the way—and leave the gum at home."

The boy was asking—What if I don't—with his eyes.

"This is a service," Ralph said, "and if you don't want it, don't come back."

Then the boy sat and Ralph sat.

The silent minutes gathered, filled like water drops, burst and bled away, wasted. Outside, there were people waiting to be seen; here, there were letters to be written, phone calls to be made, work; but they hung there together in the vacuum of John's pride and anger until abruptly he got up and, without a word, left the office. After he was gone and when Ralph was getting ready for the next client, he discovered that the back of his shirt was damp with sweat.

2

Alan Devereaux

He was sitting on a bench at the Union Hall, waiting to be seen. In the large room, which was a meeting area, there was now a slow drone of cardplayers at one end, the coarse, easy male camaraderie, punctuated every now and then by a gust of laughter. The other two men on the bench beside him leaned toward the sound, attracted by the warmth of the scene and the friendliness of the easy and comfortable nicknames. But Alan Devereaux was two days out of the state prison, where he had been Devereaux, Alan B. 18662 L for almost two years, and a hunger for the company of men had been sated to the point of anguish, and the friendly ease and slowness only grated on his nerves. These men had no catching up to do; they weren't running to get back into the rhythm of working and living. He tried to relax and wait, but the voices droned on and the day seemed to be spilling away—one more into the number he had wasted, into the number lost from the rhythm. Well, at least his prison time hadn't been a complete waste. He stretched up a little and felt the papers in his inside pocket. There was his high-school certificate from the prison's education division and a certificate of completion from the Trades Training division. He would have to present these papers; there wouldn't be any way to get around that. The man would look up and say: "State prison—is this your training?" However the man said it, it would be a bad moment, a hanging moment, hot and stifling, and Alan would sweat even more than he was sweating now in his jacket and tie. But the moment would be over then, and he would be able to tell them that he had a high-school education and a trade, too. I hope he won't call me an ex-con—and he looked around to see if he had really

18

said it out loud, but the others on the bench were still looking straight ahead, patiently, in the heat. It was the last day of June. He had been out two days already, and though the warden had laid it on a little thick about how lucky he was to have been sentenced to a "modern prison with all the advantages for training and self-improvement," he was glad for the papers that at least gave him a place to sit and be seen and interviewed and a way to begin to get back in. This Certificate Is to Acknowledge that Alan Devereaux, Having Satisfactorily ...

At last the office door opened and men walked out, laughing and talking. The petitioners on the bench quickened a bit, but the men walked by them and out the door. Time passed. The men at the card game were talking about sending out for beer. Alan got up and went to the table, hesitant, looking into the faces of disinterest.

"Who do you see around here about getting a job?"

The men laughed.

Finally one said, "You seen him, kid; he went out with the others. He's gone for the day."

"Now there wasn't much to see after all," another man chuckled.

Laughter.

"It ain't funny, mister," Alan said, and some of the old anger made his face go rigid so that the cardplayers remembered that they were soft and heavy and they looked again at him more gravely, seeing the taut muscle of his neck and the competent hands and strong wrists coming from the white shirt.

"You come in tomorrow and I'll see you get to see The Man. You got your card?"

"No, sir." (Oh, damn that prison "sir"!)

"Oh, well, that's what you got to do first. You got to go before the Board and get your license."

"Where do I do that?"

The man looked around. "Charlie?" He turned back to Alan. "Why, hell, the damn Board only meets once a month at one of the boys' houses. Hey, Charlie, who's on the Barber Board now?"

Other men began to move around, waiting for something interesting. Names came out of the group over the heads of the kibitzers. "McCorcle—what's his name." "Hey, whyn't you call Jimmy Page; he knows all the latest." "Bemis is on the Board this year, ain't he? He used to date my sister." At last, the first cardplayer, nodding wise comfort, said, "Yeah, you call Jimmy Page. He'll get you fixed up." And they turned back to their game.

On the street he found he had a pounding headache. Maybe it was prison, ruining a guy's chances, like everybody said it did. It didn't happen the way the guys said or thought. In prison you got your jobs and numbers and clothes and eats just be being on the right line. That cellblock number takes you right through the day and on and on right through your time. Soon you get to know the good jobs from the bad, the good guys from the bad. Maybe he'd done wrong, going in and asking like that. Even now he didn't know who The Board were or where they met.

Better get those names down before they just faded away. He went into a post office on the next block and scrawled out the names on a piece of scrap paper. McCorcle (what's his name . . .). Jimmy Page, Bemis or Bemish—all the way into town for that! No, wait. If he looked under the barbers in the phone book, it would be easier to get these fellows. From the way the men had talked, it seemed that this Board was made up of barbers who had their shops right in town, that it was informal and changed every year or so. Today could still be okay, even carrying the weight of that expensive set of barbering equipment that the folks had given him. The gift had been waiting for him by his bed when he woke up this morning, a whole set of instruments, complete. His parents were slow, quiet people. It must have taken them all night to come to decide on this gift for him, piece by piece, complete. It had made a weight more than their love and hope and forgiveness. He stopped at a phone booth and looked up the names in the yellow section of the phone book. He found a James Page right under Downtown Barber Shop, and a McCorkle also, and somehow the way seemed clearer again. So he called the Downtown Barber Shop and asked to speak to Mr. Page. The affable voice reassured him, and so when Mr. Page asked him what he could do, Alan said simply, "It's about getting a license to work." There was a slight pause and then the other voice said abruptly: "I don't know you, do I?"

"No, sir."

"Then you're not from our barber school here . . ."

"No, sir."

"Hmmmm, out of state, well then, drop around sometime

this week and we'll talk it over. The Board won't be meeting till next month anyway."

Alan hadn't wanted to press, but the awful oppressive sense of time and loss and hunger for place drove him against his better judgment. "Well, I'm free tomorrow. Could I come then?"

The pause did come, acknowledging his mistake, and then, "Sure, sure, if you want to—any time."

He hung up and started home. At least he could say to the eager faces over the supper table, "I'm seeing a man tomorrow."

At 2:20 exactly, Alan Devereaux went into the Downtown Barber Shop. He had timed his entrance carefully for the lull in business after the lunch hour and before the mid-afternoon rush. On the three chairs the spotless and dapper barbers were sitting themselves, and when he came in there was no alacritous rush, no too conspicuous "service." All ease, the youngest man got down to wait on the new customer. It was quite a trick, running a barber shop. There had to be a careful balance between medical precision and cleanliness and old-world relaxed ease and comfort. The young man coming toward him just missed the mastery of it in his smile.

"I'm here to see Mr. Page—uh—I spoke to him yesterday . . ."

The second man along the line got down. "You wanted to see me?"

"Mr. Page—uh—I called you yesterday. I'm Alan Devereaux—about the licensing board . . ."

The face opposite was still politely blank, but the voice said, "Oh, yes—you're the one from out of state."

"Not exactly," Alan said.

The man went on. "Well, fella, here's the way it is, see. We're an independent union, and we recognize only the licenses we want to. Guys in this state take training at our own barber school and then we certify them and that's that. A guy from somewhere else, it's just up to the Board if they let him in or not. Where'd you have your training?"

"Well, it was in this state, all right." And he took out the certificate signed by the warden and Mr. Colcis, the head of Trades Training, and others whom he did not know. The barber looked at the certificate for a long time. Alan was ready to show him where it said it was set to the national standards, but he saw that the barber was reading the small print, the whole thing about how it was state training and accredited and how the standards had been set up and approved by the major unions in the country. He was reading right down to the bottom, State Division of Correction, Department of Prisons, name of the warden and members of the board of prisons, and right off the bottom of the paper where there was a red-and-green framing design that had little swirls in it and the motto of the state in Latin. When he was all through, he smiled and tossed the paper back. "Buddy, we aren't going to admit you."

"But all the states . . ."

"We only license graduates of our own barber school. I told you that."

"But you said . . ."

"I said, our *own*. That's all."

"Look, Mr. Page," desperation was burning out the shame in Alan's face, "if I went to the school and showed them, they could tell that my certificate is good. Let me prove that I'm trained. Let me pass *their* test."

"You got an awful thick head, boy. I'm telling you you'll never get to flick a scissors in school or out. Not five minutes."

"But . . ."

"You know, you got a hell of a nerve coming in here with that paper of yours. What's Latin for jailbird? We've got a morals consideration, see? No undesirables in the union and the union is the Board and the union is every shop in the city and in the county and in the state!"

How had he angered Page? Was it his youth or vulnerability or innocence—or hope—as he passed the precious document for the barber to see? Maybe it was the maddening perseverance in hoping.

Jimmy Page waved him out the door. "Get another trade, fella; there's nothing here for you!"

The boy went out the door, dizzily, and the barber went back to his chair and sat down, affecting ease and failing.

"Damn jailbird!" he said to no one in particular. "He comes in here like anybody. Well, the union is a brotherhood! Says so in the name and by-laws too. We got a right not to have a jailbird for a brother!" He grunted. The damn jailbird had spoiled his whole afternoon.

3

Alan Devereaux

It was July. The streets and store windows glared. In the streets the people were limp and the toilet water that women used to excuse themselves for sweating made him a little dizzy as he stood in the crowded downtown busses or at store counters where he wandered to escape the white-hot noon hour. Alan Devereaux had been in solitary four times in the early days of prison. Solitary was dark and hot, but he was less lonely there than he was on these streets. All around him in the jail the cells had echoed with the voices of men speaking pain like his, laughing, crying, praying without apology. When the bolts slid back on the main door everyone's teeth were on edge, and, neighbored in darkness, men sometimes called and answered one another.

In this solitary, burning with sun and buzzing with people, there was all of the hell of the prison punishment and an added separateness that made him stop sometimes, finding that his eyes were full of tears. Jail makes you mean, little mean. Jail makes you see insults in the way a guy holds his spoon or scratches his cheek when you go by. It makes life and death arguments over who got more chicken in his stew, who rumpled a letter when it was getting delivered. You have enemies in jail. In the outside-solitary you have nothing.

("Well, Devereaux, your records show you've done well here—high-school diploma, barber training—you've completed your course, too. By the way, I've never seen that diploma; you wouldn't have it with you, I suppose. . . ." "No, sir, it's with my things. Mr. Carrol says it ain't no fake; I mean, it isn't no fake. The tests they give you's what they give all over the country.")

He had asked at every single barber shop between his

23

home and the city: great big emporiums, air-conditioned and impersonal, and little two-chair neighborhood places, father-and-son, where they'd tell him: "Forty years we've been here . . . ," before they knew why he had come. Forty-six shops. In all the city and all the suburbs around the city there were two hundred places. He would have to try all of them, every one.

("Devereaux, when you came here, you weren't set on straightening yourself out; then you seemed to take hold. What made it happen?" "Well, sir, it was Bo Martin." "Bo Martin! Why, he's hardly a human being. If he is anybody's model, no prison can hope to reform its men!" "That's just the point, sir. Bo Martin was tough, sir, tough and smart. The smartest guy I ever knew and he was dying in jail. Dying ugly. Hey, if I tried all my life I couldn't be as smart as Bo. Even being that smart he was still out of jail only six years in the last thirty. I knew I didn't have a chance in the world to be . . . big. I . . . I would have to do it straight or not at all.")

Not all the places had slammed the door in his face. Some of the men seemed sorry, some were embarrassed and took his name and number and said they sure would call him if they got an opening. Then he realized that they were just hiding and would not call.

("I'm proud of you. Devereaux, you've pulled yourself back; you've worked hard, gotten up early, fought the ridicule of the others—I know that too, and what it must have meant—you've given up your leisure time to work on your trade, put by your own scorn and even the scorn of some of the guards. Well, this isn't the nineteenth century. You've paid your debt and done your time, and now you're going out with a trade. Good luck, Devereaux!")

One or two really seemed to want him, but they said that hiring him would mean boycott for them. Sorry . . . sorry.

Every day a clean shirt. Every day the big "workingman's" breakfast that was supposed to send him out righteous and honest into the world. The month was thirty-one wheels, and every day he rose, bound to the wheel of that day, bound to the law, bound to the endless excuses he made and his mother and father made, and the faces made behind the doors. Each day he heard the sounds of clicking, like the step of a mechanical man, like the turning of the wheel, like the closing of all the doors of possibility.

He went to his parole officer, who was harried and impatient, and he told him about the whole useless thing.

24

"You did try to get in contact with the Board . . ."

"Sir, they won't let me near it. This guy Page is on it, and he just gave me the word: no work now; no work ever. No work without that license and no licenses for jailbirds."

"Well, you won't have to worry about our regulations because your training certificate is in lieu of a job guarantee, so you're straight with us. You keep out of trouble and you won't be in violation."

"I didn't take training just to get out! I took training to be—to be a . . ."

("To be a man! a man, you blank-faced, you uncaring dead face!")

". . . a barber. They promised, in a way. They tested and trained me and made me proud of doing a good job. . . ."

"Well, why don't you find another line of work, that's all?"

"Doing *what?*" The angry hand could no longer be disciplined. It slammed down on the desk making the scattered paperclips jump and the other heads in the hive jerk up for a moment. "You don't understand, do you! I mean, I'm coming here with some information for you. When I go, you aren't going to pick up the phone and call the Joint and say: Stop the damn Trades Training! Stop the eager jerks in the barber school!" He looked at one of the case folders on the officer's desk. "The law is satisfied. I got my training."

"Parole is a privilege, not something that's coming to you," the officer said. "It's your promise, not ours; it's your responsibility, not ours."

"You don't understand at all, do you?" Alan said.

(It's hot here; I'm so tired and it's like shaking the door in solitary when you can't stand the darkness or the time that's stopped passing any more. The guards don't hear, and these guards don't hear, and the men guarding their places behind their glass doors don't hear; and I'm going to have to keep asking until I've asked them all!)

"You just don't understand," he said.

Now the man at the desk was angry. He shoved open a drawer and pointed to a thick folder. "Names," he said, "just names. Current cases, past cases. A hundred and fifty men now on parole for me to make a report on every month; thirty men who are going to call me to 'make it okay with the judge' when they go on a bender; ten men to come in with their pregnant girl friends and ask me to write the four forms in triplicate it takes for them to get married so they

25

can start the whole blind circle over again! Is your wife on narcotics or booze? Are your kids old hands down at juvenile court? I got a dixie cup held up under Niagara Falls, mister, and no time to fix your little leaky faucet." He looked up at Alan, coming back again from his own anger. "I can't *make* them hire you, after all. Look. . . . ," and he began to write quickly on his pad. "If your job had given out on you, you'd have to get another. Go to this office. Tell them you're from here. They might be better set up for your kind of problem."

Alan glanced briefly at the slip: State Department of Vocational Rehabilitation. Another meaningless mouthful of syllables, like the collection on his diploma or on the door of this office. Was the lucky, job-holding, unfrightened sonofabitch behind *that* desk any more able to help than this one? Did he care any more than this one cared, or was it all a hot-potato game to pass him and his agony around and around until it lost its meaning to all of them and to him? Bo Martin, out in the exercise yard, he had a name for it: Square John's Tango. He told it; he told it: Decent men in their decent suits all lined up and dancing the jerks along in the unending rhythm; a minute more and out the door and back where you came from twice before.

Alan folded the slip vaguely and put it in his pocket. His voice sounded sick and far away in his own ears. "Yeah. I got a big day. I got a hundred and twenty jobs I got to go for."

He got up to go. (Whose scheme was this: Give the Cons a Trade? Some vine-covered professor's probably. Sleep well, professor.) He heard the phone ring behind him on the parole officer's desk. (Sleep well, you sonofabitch.) He heard the man's voice tighten and found himself listening.

"Look, keep him there, tell him anything. If he goes out in that shape the cops'll pick him up and it'll mean a lifetime stretch for him. No. No, just keep him there. I'll be right down."

In a moment the things were swept into the desk, desk locked, man gone; a row of reporting parolee faces gaping after him.

Alan's mother had made him take lunch money every day. It shamed him and he had never used it, always giving an excuse, but today, because he had not even been permitted the luxury of hating purely, he decided to eat lunch after all. Over his coffee he opened the slip again.

"Hey, Mr. Oakland, this is Clement Soames. What the hell is holding up everything down there? I put in my application down there almost two months ago and I haven't heard a damn word from you birds since, and every time I call you aren't there. If I didn't need help bad, I wouldn't have asked from the State."

"Mr. Soames, I have been completely unable to get your doctor to send me the medical reports I need. I've called him many times and I've told him that we are prohibited by law from going ahead with testing and training until we get the medical evidence to satisfy our requirements. I'm hamstrung, Mr. Soames, until your doctor sends me those records."

"He told me he thought all these agencies were leading to socialized government. Every time I ask him, he tells me you guys are just a bunch of paper-shufflers. . . ."

While listening to a phone voice, Ralph opened Ethwald Kittenger's medical report, which had come at last. He read two lines and stopped in amazement.

"Mr. Oakland?"—the voice at his ear.

"Yes, yes, I'm listening." (Is it possible? I *saw* the boy) and he flipped the page back to make sure that there was no mistake. There it was: Kittenger, Ethwald. When the caller finished, Ralph put the report in front of him and began to read in earnest: "This patient was examined for evidence of neurological or neuromuscular damage involving left lower arm, hand and left leg and foot. All findings negative."

What did that mean, "all findings negative"? Ralph turned the report over and was glad to find that the doctor, in his own amazement, had included a note in the never-used box labeled *Remarks*.

"This male patient, 20 (?), was extremely hesitant to use either foot or hand, even to show them. Whole demeanor one of very weak or ill person, but all evidence was of normalcy. Because of manner of patient, made elaborate tests, but found nothing to indicate physiological or neurological cause for weakness, lack of tonus in arm or leg. Believe this individual has practised misuse of limb." Practised was underlined three times in the doctor's unemotional and precise hand.

Ralph sat back, defenseless against the doctor's certainty. But what about the mother, the aunt, the look of the boy himself? Were they so certain that Ethwald could never be "normal" without any actual evidence? Perhaps the mother had hidden the true illness, a mental illness, out of shame or guilt. He would have to look at Ethwald again. It didn't seem possible; he was so obviously ill. . . .

Ethwald Kittenger

They were sitting straight as strangers, nothing touching, Ethwald and his aunt. He was in the same strange position, with his "bad" foot behind his "good" one and his "bad" hand behind him, but it was something much more than that that made Ralph wonder again if the doctor had been mistaken; there was the kind of resignation and dullness which one sees only in the very old or very ill. His childlike face made the expression seem all the more incongruous. The boy was an invalid. Ralph felt it strongly.

He went toward them. "Hello, will you come in?" But he was somehow warned away from putting his hand out to Ethwald.

Mrs. Sedges got up and followed Ralph, who had to turn back to the bench and say again, "Oh, Mr. Kittenger, will you come in please?" They went into the office and sat down, but Ethwald didn't follow.

"Mrs. Sedges, would you . . ."

"*Ethwald!*" she called through the open door. Then she turned to Ralph. "He's shy of that hand and foot." And her own hand involuntarily assumed a little gesture, his hiding. It was the only slightly sympathetic thing Ralph had seen her do, and it comforted him. Difficult as it was, and painful, too, ordinary people still feel for one another. It was not all agency-involved, duplicate and triplicate.

"My sister—she set great store by looks. That was why she married that—that Kittenger. He was no good. Ethwald was about five when he got sick. Eth*wald!* Get in here!—He took off when the boy was maybe eight or nine, just took off one day and never come back. He left her the house though, and the car and all, but he wasn't any good. I used to go over there and visit, but then . . ."

The boy was coming. Mrs. Sedges talked on, but Ralph's attention was on Ethwald. He was coming slowly, his face contorted with effort and terror. Brutally vulnerable, he sidled and stumbled, having to lead with the right shoulder and leg and at the same time keep the enemy world on his right in order to defend that "bad" left side. Surely the doctor was wrong! Ralph could almost see the uncompleting and dysrhythmic nerve impulses warping along spent nets, muscles releasing without the complementing pull from the other side. Anyone could look at the boy and see that he had very severe neurological—and then Ethwald sat down, stopping at the chair, left leg folded under, left arm back, balance and control, all as gentle and disciplined as a dancer coming to rest in position. Oh, boy! Ralph thought, oh, boy. I saw it, but I can't believe it. Neuromuscular damage doesn't just shut off at a signal. The doctor was right and I have one honey of a case!

Aunt was still talking. "Yes, I stopped going to visit them. I don't mean to speak bad of the dead, Mr. Elkin—" (The boy's eye twitched slightly. Ralph saw him looking over the fence of his terror, listening to his aunt as she castigated his mother, listening passively, except for that twitch, the involuntary twitch of a slapped face)—"my sister, she just let the other children run around the whole day, like orphans, all but Ethwald here. Him and her would be inside the house. She used to fix all the food for him herself and cut it up and feed it to him from a spoon. She did it until he was maybe ten years old, and all the time the others just had to do for themselves."

(How they must have hated the spoiled baby brother; how they must have shown that hate when no one was watching!)

"Well, Mrs. Sedges . . ."

"I'm just giving you the facts you need, Mr. Elkin."

"Oakland."

"Yes, well, I wanted to say this for the kids; I mean, I'm sure you're wondering why the sisters and brothers didn't come forward, because, you see, they left, which was why we had to come forward . . ."

The left eye flickered again in Ethwald's dead face. Ralph shifted his weight in the chair. (I don't give a good Goddamn why they didn't come forward, lady, don't you have any tact at all?)

"Well, Mrs. Sedges, the medical report has come in, and . . ."

But she was still worrying and pulling at her defense. "I want you to know, Mr. Elkland, that I didn't just go off and leave them alone. I tried to visit after the others left, but I felt funny, like I wasn't really wanted there, and it was that that made me quit going. Now, Martha . . ."

"Excuse me, Mrs. Sedges, I have some questions for Ethwald."

The eye twitched at Ralph again, and Ralph tried to smile at the boy (Look—nothing in either hand, no whip, no hose. See, I'm not even wearing a monocle.) "Ethwald, how much schooling have you had?"

Ethwald's eyes opened wider. "Uh—well . . ."

Mrs. Sedges said, "At least Martha wasn't entirely stupid there. She got him a high school certificate, too; they get it by correspondence, you know. I found the certificate going through her things."

Ralph looked back at Ethwald for the twitch of his eye that signaled The Wrecker walking across his landscape, but the eye was still. Maybe it had beaten Ralph's look. He would have to tell them soon about the medical report. How does a person tell someone that his whole life has been lived on a mistaken premise. Wake up, Rip, you've made a fifteen-year detour into fields of mother-poppy-dreams. See that arm?— Jackie Robinson. See that leg?—Fred Astaire. Okay? Case closed. The direct approach to rehabilitation. I must save it for the next convention discussion, but Ethwald's dawn—and Aunt Sedges' too, for that matter—would have to be as gradual as time and pressure would permit, as steady and constant as retraining after a stroke. But start now, start now . . .

"Well, we've gotten the medical report back from Dr. Strauss, and the report is very good."

Their faces were impassive. Ralph was suddenly struck with the difference of his voice and gestures in the two latest interviews he had had this morning. With John Kroll, his "normal" voice was resonant and varied in tone. With Ethwald, the whole range of "normal" was narrowed and softened; gestures and words were slower and less emphatic, and it had happened as a response, without his thinking about it, to account for—for what? It was for a timorous quality in Ethwald. He was like some soft, young, nocturnal bird caught in the hot stare of naked daylight. John Kroll was fighting a world in which he had never really doubted his membership. This boy seemed only to peer out at passing shadows to which he had not given names or values.

"Ethwald, have you ever thought about some job that you would *want* to do, some work that you would *like*?" The shadows flickered in the deep for a moment and then were gone. Silence—and the quality of this silence also was very different from the thrumming, virulent but vital muteness of John Kroll's hate. Ralph felt himself amazed all over again at

30

the variety of even the simplest forms of expression. Kroll's silence was everything unsaid. Ethwald's seemed empty, hollow. Mrs. Sedges was going to answer again. She couldn't stand Ethwald's silence, but even her irritation and disgust were muffled, like anger at the undertaker's. Let the doctor say there was nothing wrong with this boy; the world knew better.

"Oh, he got a desire in his life. That's to set in the living room all day with every one of them two hundred twenty-five magazines and look at the pictures!"

"What kind of magazines do you like?" Ralph asked, looking at Ethwald and not his aunt. She would have to remember that Ethwald was the subject of this interview. There was another silence, but Ralph could see that Ethwald was venturing toward it very slowly. As he began to take possession, just as he began, Mrs. Sedges swept him away.

"Engines, that's what it is, just engines," she sniffed. "Build your own locomotive! Can you imagine that!"

"Do you like to think about motors and engines?" Ralph asked, looking at Ethwald again as if no one else were in the room. He hoped for some little way toward the hiding wish, and he was answered with Ethwald's little "yes," creeping out of the silence so tenuously that it seemed almost a whisper, but it had been yes and Ralph smiled. "Fine," he said. "Why don't we give you a set of tests then . . ."

The boy winced and shrank back into himself, and Ralph, realizing his mistake, said quickly, "Oh, this isn't a physical endurance test or anything like that. No, the test I want you to have will be a lot like the quizzes they have in the magazines, you know, pictures of gears and wheels that you might be able to answer questions about. These tests are to help find out what you can do best." He looked at the miserable Ethwald who was trying to pull assurance out of the air. How desperate that fear was, how convulsively he was leaping to his own defense!

The word *test* had only suggested to this sickly, ruin-minded boy some agony of weight-lifting, muscle-flexing, or distance-running. He saw himself lost and hopeless immediately. Was hope so hard to endure? Ralph sighed. Apparently it was. He suddenly knew that Ethwald couldn't wait a week or two to have his tests. Distance-running! And there would be his aunt ambushing him with his certain failure. With luck—maybe—he could get Ethwald tested right now. It was Tuesday, and Tuesday was usually Martenson's light day. He

31

picked up the phone and called Martenson. Ethwald was back in his world again.

(What are they going to do to me? Can they hurt me if they want to? That Dr. Strauss, he knows what he needs to know. He says hmmmmm and writes an answer down. God, he hurt me, making me walk and show my hand and swing it and lift it again and again. I know he didn't like me when I cried. He didn't like me—in the same way Mama didn't like those black beetles that used to come up out of the old drain—I wish I could stop being afraid. I wish Aunt Louise would let me come with the magazines. Men like this one—they call up and say—even when they ask things it's like saying. They say and they do and make things and break them and they *know*. Outside is filled with men who—oh God!) The hand was shaking again, fluttering behind him against his back, like a ghost tapping quickly, quickly at a door.

"You're free now? Fine, fine, we'll be right over." Ralph put the phone down and said, "We're in luck. Mr. Martenson is a counselor here, and although we all do testing, it's his specialty, so when we can, we want all our clients to have top service."

Ethwald had gone a dead white in front of him. For a minute Ralph thought that he was going to faint. Even so, this was better. Auntie's scorn would be kept from permeating this try, and for once in his life, Ethwald Kittenger would see straight, simple action going forward in his behalf with no undertones to read and trace, no confounding reasons of help given from quicksand.

Martenson was better with some kinds of people than he was with others. He and Ralph had locked horns many times about cultural factors in the tests and about how completely they could be trusted; but with Ethwald, Martenson shone.

Ralph went in with Ethwald, leaving the stone aunt waiting outside. He saw again the agony and shambling, the same brutal vulnerability in the boy as he stood erect, and again the graceful and controlled descent into the sanctuary of a chair. Martenson was deft and tactful in allaying the fears of his test subjects.

Ralph left, saw a client, looked in again, and got Martenson's signal that they were doing fine and would run as many as Ethwald could take. Ralph went out to Mrs. Sedges and told her that it would probably be a matter of hours before the boy was finished, if she wanted to leave for some shopping or go home, but she was adamant and stayed waiting grimly among the flowing and slackening tides of the office's afternoon clients, refusing to leave even for coffee. When Ethwald emerged, punchdrunk and dazed at the end of the afternoon, he did not hide his "bad" side with quite so much anguish. He had come, exhausted, from an ordeal from which all others also came exhausted, and he was proud. Ralph was looking for space for their next appointment when the telephone rang.

"Mr. Oakland, this is Miss Burns at Boys' Shelter . . ."

"Oh, yes," he sighed, "I was expecting your call."

"I'm sorry to bother you; it was John's oversight not to ask when you wanted to see him again."

"What?"

"John Kroll . . ." Suddenly the voice hardened. "Mr. Oakland, he *did* report to you this morning, didn't he . . ."

"Well, he showed up, but he didn't do anything more than sit in my office and glower. Frankly, I don't see him as a candidate for job training."

"I know how hard it is to get through to John. Please, Mr. Oakland, just give him a little time. He's been a 'hopeless case' for so long that he's given up . . ."

"All right, we'll try again. There's an opening for half an hour on the 23rd at three o'clock."

"That's fine, Mr. Oakland," she said, "and we're so happy that John has found somebody who will work with him."

He hung up the phone. Someone who could work with John! How desperate they must be! Why the hell hadn't he said that training and testing were hopeless with someone who was too busy being a battleground. What did they want him to do, set up his delicate surveying tools in the middle of John Kroll's world war? Ask the bloodied fighter at the vital gun whether the red was below the green on a traffic light? Well, they weren't all deluded. Ralph knew he wasn't mistaking a teenage boy's grab for a little change of scene for "the beginning of a sense of vocation," as the big books put it.

He stood up to say good-bye to Ethwald Kittenger, and the wildest sense of the extremes in people made him smile. Would anyone really consider taking on an employee like the raw, vulgar tough guy John Kroll tried to be? He held out his hand to Ethwald, saying that he would see him on the 21st. Confounded by that extended hand, Ethwald gaped and writhed, and Ralph was suddenly a little annoyed. You're *not* an invalid, damn it, there's *nothing* wrong with your *right!* It was embarrassing to stand there like a fool with a hand out, but Ralph knew that he couldn't put it down now. Then Ethwald's trembling and flaccid fingers finally came up to meet his hand. It wasn't a handshake really; their hands only touched; and Ralph realized at that moment that it might be the boy's first sharing of that male gesture.

Ethwald's hand dropped loosely and he turned and started to go, but at the door he turned again, a full turn, covering for his left side, and he sealed the good-bye with a little boy's wave.

4

John Kroll

Walking into the office, John Kroll balanced himself with consummate delicacy on the line that Ralph had set for him. He was just barely clean enough, just barely erect enough, just barely responsive enough. The gum had been removed, but the jaw milled on with patient hate, as if it were still there. And he did not speak.

Ralph questioned him again, and then he began to realize that John was daring him to legislate the conversation as he had tried to legislate the dress and behavior. This, of course, he could not do, and he knew that John knew it, so he put down his pencil and waited. Unknown to John, his status as a client had many more thorny aspects to it than his silence. There were technical problems to be overcome. John had his pose, his hatred, and his hunger for the return of the Pleistocene and the cave man to the world; but Ralph had a feeling about the quality of that pose and of the anger which disturbed him for reasons other than John suspected. Somehow, the boy just didn't go about all of this in the way that a retarded boy would, and if he wasn't retarded, he wasn't eligible for state help.

The agency, unknown to John, recognized categories of disability: diseases that were chronic or incapacitating, all the physical handicaps, and then social disability of people who needed new vocations after protracted stays in prisons or mental hospitals. Finally, there were the retarded. John Kroll was sound of wind and limb, and was "applying" for the agency's help before the prison system got him. The only category left for him to fit was as retarded. America the Free is the promise of as infinite choice and variety in occupations as it is an opinion. The dark side of this promise was a familiar landscape to Ralph; telling the retarded young man that he could not hope to be a brain surgeon, telling the hungry day laborer that there was more competition for the simplest day-labor jobs than there was for a chemist's job or a counselor's. These encounters with the American Dream were seldom included in the statistics of services to currently active cases, but a hard one could take a great deal of time and suck the joy out of a day until it fell apart like a dry husk. John Kroll might well have been broken by the state, but he had been into the office three times, each time a silent, glowering repetition of the first interview, and it was becoming crystal clear to Ralph that the embittered, "retarded" boy was doomed. This time he walked in and sat down and looked at Ralph and sneered; and Ralph looked back, hoping that there was no pity in the look.

So John Kroll sat in a silence strident with his pride; and boy's intelligence. The time ran slowly away to waste again, and anger was building in both of them. At the back of his head Ralph was seeing pictures of other clients waiting, waiting while this waster played out his scene.

John was trying to get nearer to the TV show he was starring in. The silence was hard for him, too, he could barely hear the voices of the gang members, another night, another getaway in a big, low-slung car, his mother proud and terrified of her son, The Most Wanted Man in the United States.

"What for, John?" Ralph said finally.

John shrugged, but a moment of expression had beaten the careful sneer across his face. It was fear and wonder. Ralph realized that he really didn't know why John was going on with this, taking the long bus ride to sit like a zombie in the little office. He sighed. Perhaps he would never know.

"Okay, John, I'll let you fail in peace. You served your time; you dared me to get to you. Now you can tell yourself that none of us care. Do it now, John. I can use the fifteen minutes we have left over."

The boy shrugged again, unfolded his bones, rose, and moved in slow motion toward the door.

"Tell Miss Burns to get in touch with me, will you? Good-bye, John, good luck." It was said as flat as a plank.

The boy left and the tired old remonstrances of failure began to flow in Ralph. Why was I impatient? Why did she send him here; he wasn't even ready to admit that holding a job is better than stealing. How could I have gotten past that death mask of his? What was I supposed to *do* for him?

He felt a presence and looked up and was surprised. John again in the doorway, and the impatient next client gritting his teeth behind him. John's face gave nothing further. "Hey, that Miss Burns. She told me I gotta give this a chance or I don't get no late pass."

"What am I supposed to do about that?"

"Maybe I could make it one more time, so's I could . . ."

"Oh, no, buddy, not just to let you sit here and waste my time. You want to square it with Miss Burns, you earn that late pass. Three sessions, okay, but three sessions where you talk and you listen and you play it straight!"

John rose into his adolescent hauteur, not seeing it for the tragicomic parody it was. "I'll t'ink it over," Marlon Brando said.

"You do that," Ralph said.

He must have looked grimmer than he thought. The next client walked in very, very carefully.

Ethwald Kittenger

What am I going to tell Ethwald? Not only do I have to break it very slowly—the news that he isn't an invalid—but now I have to tell him that he has strength and competence in the thing he loves. Brawn and now brains—what a disaster! All right, it's hilarious; but what real good are they to him when he's too scared to see beyond the shadows that his mother must have painted for him on the nursery-pastel walls of that prison he was in? I wonder which came first, the aptitude or the magazines. . . .

He came stumbling and writhing behind Ralph and they closed the door on the midwinter of Mrs. Sedges, who sat chilling off the waiting room. Why couldn't Ethwald come downtown alone? Better go into that later, better go slowly, ray by ray, and light up just one thing at a time. Too much will blind him.

Ralph walked to his desk and sat down and said quietly, "Well, Ethwald, your tests are in, and I think you're going to be very pleased with what they show."

The face lay unchanged, like a stone under the moon.

"Of course, you will have to take a lot of training, but here's what I thought we might hope for. The doctor who examined your hand—(And here he saw the boy wince and wondered if he could listen and hear through the shame that the word had caused. He had to say something else to pass the time until Ethwald was free to hear him.)—the doctor's report was quite encouraging, and he says that the thing that will help most now is mild exercise, especially in squeezing and lifting. Ethwald, I want you to learn to use a wrench with that hand, work toward that, because our tests show that you have a good aptitude to be a mechanic."

There was still no response. It was about someone else that the counselor had been speaking, some other Ethwald more fortunate and strong.

Now Ralph called through the empty space between them. "I mean you. *You* can learn and do and be these things."

". . . outside?" the voice answered dimly. "Where?—I mean—in a *place?*"

"Not yet," Ralph answered, "but when you're trained and ready. And you'll be able to use all those years of work on your magazines. You're going to be a valuable man on the job maybe, because of that reading." He looked out carefully to sound his own words in the feelings of the boy. Ethwald showed nothing, but slowly, very slowly, the villain hand moved up across his chest to be seen, to mortify. The damage in that hand might be a lie and a charade according to the judgment of the world of reality and work and people and "places," but so convincing a fact was it to Ethwald that Ralph had to hold his answer back.

". . . and—my—foot." Ralph didn't know whether the tone was yearning or self-pity.

"By the time you start training, if you work hard, the hand will be well enough to carry and lift anything you'll need, and you can go on with the exercising until you get it just as strong as you want it to be." Something moved him to say again, "But you'll have to keep exercising and not give up hope."

The boy motioned with his head hopelessly toward the door, sending Ralph through it with him to where the granite judge sat waiting. Ralph leaned over the desk, wishing he could shout: "Damn it, boy, you're free! Fly a little!" He knew that there could not, really, be joy when there was so much fear, but his own eagerness and expectation were fading slowly under the hesitant look of the boy. Still, he had to go on with what had to be said, the joy was a luxury beyond both of them now.

"Practice in your room or in the basement or even in the

bathroom. Do it all by yourself without anybody's help. Get a wrench or a hammer and work with it. Only five minutes the first day—pick it up, clench it, then raise it high over your head. I want you to come back next week and show me the progress you've made."

For the first time the shadows solidified behind Ethwald's eyes and he was there, present and caring. "Mr. Oakland, you don't mind looking at my hand, do you?"

Ralph answered very gently, "No, Eth, I don't."

He had made the nickname without thinking, a natural response of comfort to Ethwald's anguish. There was a sudden breaking sound from Ethwald's mouth that could have been laughter, pain, or rage, but Ralph looked up intently and saw that the boy was fighting tears. So Ralph got up, trying with elaborate casualness to make it seem natural.

After a few minutes the boy turned a little in his chair. "Mr. Oakland, I—I never told anyone this. I did practice once when I was finishing my school." He was still holding his arm to his chest, but slowly he made the fingers fold together, reaching in, tighter and tighter, until he was sitting there clenching a fist against his chest. "I can do—this."

One single male gesture, so small and secret in the darkness of his mother's imprisoning house. Ralph had forgotten, too, that so easy a thing as a nickname must have been beyond Ethwald Kittenger's wildest dreams. He must have had mother-love names, made of his outgrown baby words, but never brother-names, names of a ring of boys choosing up sides. Ralph had given Ethwald a nickname without even knowing why, and there sat the boy himself answering to it out of his long muteness. The fist was still wrapped, waiting for comment, on Ethwald's chest.

"Well," Ralph said, "you've got your start already. I won't say a word," and he looked toward the closed door and the aunt sitting on the other side. Ethwald's fist flopped open into the old, limp posture.

(He says I can be like a man—Outside. He's a man, an Outside man, with charts and papers, and he's strong enough to make Aunt Louise sit on the bench and wait, and he calls me Eth, who could be—anybody. He says I can be like—men, and Outside, but does he really know? If there was a mistake on that test and they added up the answers wrong, maybe he really doesn't know. I bet if no one was looking, not even me, if it was dark—in a small, dark place—I bet I could hold that hammer—and lift it, maybe lift it, too. He likes me. He calls me Eth. I wish I could stay here and be Eth until I was sure I really was Eth and could lift a hammer. . . .)

Ralph saw him to the door and left him, now using to conscious purpose the new common coin. "So long, Eth, see you next week."

The flabbergasted Mrs. Sedges was left for a moment, all alone, and then she took up her cross and followed.

Alan Devereaux

"Okay, mister, what are *you* going to tell me?"

He had a hardness which Ralph saw wasn't bluff. "My parole officer sent me," he said, and then he stood back and waited for Ralph's polite surprise and anxiety, the familiar after-payment of Paying Debts to Society.

Ralph simply asked, "Do you have a trade?"

Out came the two worn documents, beginning to pull away at the folds. DEVEREAUX, ALAN, HAVING COMPLETED THE TWO-YEAR PROGRAM OF TRAINING ACCREDITED BY THE NATIONAL BOARD OF BARBERS AND COSMETOLOGISTS IS HEREBY . . . "It says I'm a barber. National standards. That's great, just great. See that design on that? That's engraved, see, like money. I mean, they don't run this off on the mimeograph machine; they give it *time* and *trouble*." In the presence of the worn certificate his eyes had gone hard and there was a twitch of anger flicking his lower lip. "Mister, the horse don't take trouble to drop a pile. He lifts his tail and there it is. We take lots of trouble. There are guys workin' in the prisons getting five, six thousand a year, just to test and train. Lots of tools and teachers and barber chairs. Then at the end, the warden compliments you about this engraved diploma. Yes, sir, it's being rehabilitated to society, but it's still horseshit, mister, it's still just horseshit."

Ralph looked hard at Devereaux, and then the phone rang and he cursed it to himself. Alan cut off his words as if the bell had been some final signal to him, and Ralph moved forward to pick up the phone. He had told the switchboard not to let in any calls but those from agencies, because their workers were as busy as he and as difficult to get hold of. The voice on the other end was an "agency" voice, one of his own breed, professional and harried.

"Mr. Oakland, this is Miss Phelps of Juvenile Probation. I understand that you are doing rehabilitation with juveniles now, and I'd like to refer three urgent cases to you as soon as possible. Now one of them . . ."

"Miss Phelps, I'm not taking any referrals of that kind. I don't know where you got the idea . . ."

Her voice was querulous with the urgency of the three cases and her exasperation. "Couldn't you fit them in somewhere? Judge Moonhoven's secretary is a friend of mine and she heard that you were working with a boy from the Shelter. These three of mine are on the brink. It's going to be Boys' State for them if they don't get help quick. We've felt right from the beginning that some trade or job—something for them to be . . ."

"I'm awfully sorry, Miss Phelps, but my schedule just won't permit it," Ralph said, wishing that Devereaux were not hearing him. "You know yourself that they are not ready for training and placement. We don't have the counseling staff to take the kind of time that your people require."

Mutual apologies. When he hung up the phone, he saw that his client's anger was tinged with exhaustion. He turned away from the phone and toward the man, trying to open him again. "You've been to the union, I suppose."

(These funnymen, these con-haters ask the same questions and wear the same clothes and close the same doors—a locked step, eyes front, like the prison walk. If I ever thought I was free, I'm not fooled any more . . .)

He lifted up his head. "Twice."

"What about the non-union places?"

"It's all union. They told me it was, all of it."

"Mr. Devereaux, let me see what I can do. First, I'm going to call the barber school. The agency places men for training there all the time. Maybe we can persuade them to persuade the Board—you've been to the Board, too, I guess."

It all sounded like the old get-'em-out-the-door routine. Alan stood up and then leaned over the desk to where the bureaucrat was still sitting. "I don't want to steal, mister. I know how to steal because I got lessons in jail from the other guys. I don't want to write bad checks because—damn you, damn you, you bastards in the joint and in Trades Training made me want to—" his voice dropped. "Oh, never mind." There it was, forget it. There were still a hundred and ten more places, and he had to do them all, because there had to be that whole, finished answer to the accusations of the fat and satisfied workers in all the agencies who would raise an eyebrow at the second-time offender he would soon be. (Did you try to find honest work, my man?)

And so he wiped his sweating hands on his pants pockets and started to go.

"Hey," Ralph stopped him. (Damn the luck of that blamed phone call! This guy has heard me turn away a whole invisible legion with no more than the usual sorry, they don't fit in our category. If he's got a case here, the agency should go into it.) "I've got your name, but where can I get hold of you?"

"Don't call us, we'll call you."

"Do you want to call me or make another appointment? See the secretary. I'm not deaf, Mr. Devereaux; I've heard you very well. I'm going to do what I can."

"I'll just bet." Alan said. "216-6371."

(Well, I'm down on another list. They keep writing down my name in offices. Those guys yesterday were too inexperienced at dodging; it embarrassed them and they did it stuttering and red in the face. The times that hurt are when the guy who swings the axe just doesn't give a damn, that one with the potbelly: You musta paid plenty for that diploma, Mac, guys in there for counterfeiting; what'd they do, run these off for you? Another list. God, God, God—I'm applying in triplicate! Isn't there anything I can *do?* The wheel is rolling over me, and the ones who lock it are writing my name on another list!)

"Mr. Praylo, this is Ralph Oakland down at Rehabilitation. I saw Alan Devereaux today; I understand from the secretary that he's one of your cases."

"Yes, he is. Funny, I never thought he'd show up. Glad he did, though. I've got some notes on his case that were sent to me from down there. They don't want to see him back in the pen because apparently while he was there he had some kind of a conversion. I don't think he's going to stay straight unless he gets work."

"Have you got the report handy?"

"Just a minute, hang on. Here we are. 'Devereaux, Alan, 18662 L, White Male, age 23. Three-year sentence.' It was passing phony checks, and he served a lot more of that time than they usually do. He was living it up, apparently, when

42

they caught him: flashy car, girls, and a wrist watch that told the time in New York, London, and Paris. No remorse. They don't say what he had to be remorseful about."

"Why did he serve extra time?"

"It shows in the general notes from the psychologist, the work captain, and the block captain. He was a pretty surly punk, arrogant, cocky, a trouble-maker. Then something happened. There was a kind of stopping and then the wheel just started rolling backward. Here, suddenly, we have a note requesting a job change. Here's a note about his request for entrance into the tutoring class. They're a bunch who use the correspondence courses. High-school certification. Use of library after work permit, request for barber training. The most interesting thing, though, are the comments. Teachers call him hard-working, serious, keen, and alert. I've never looked the whole thing over, but it makes you wonder, doesn't it? Is it true what he told me about being closed out of the hiring because of his record?"

"I don't know, but I'm going to find out. He's convincing enough."

"I—uh—I was a little short with him when he reported in. It was one of those nuthuse days down here, and after all of it, his problem sounded like—well—it was just one too many. Looking over his record it seems like a damn shame to drive him away from the trade he's learned. Well do this, will you—when you find out one way or another, let me know."

"I sure will."

"Mr. Oakland, this is Sister Mary Aquinas at the Good Shepherd Home. I understand that you've been counseling one of our boys, John Kroll, who is now at Boys' Shelter. Mr. Oakland, we have twelve boys here who are going to go that same way if something isn't done to help them. Our teaching and practical care leave little time for . . ."

"Mr. Oakland, this is Judge French. I have on a list here the names of twenty-seven adolescent boys whose cases I've continued because I'm not convinced that sentence to the reformatory is in their best interest, or ours. They are first offenders or petty delinquents. Most are school dropouts who need to get decent jobs and earn a little self-respect if they are going to stay out of trouble. They feel the courts are against them, and until I heard about you, we had no place to . . ."

"Mr. Oakland, this is Miss Burns again. John Kroll was in this afternoon and said that you wanted to keep on with him. We're all relieved, and we hope you will be able to take more referrals from us. We get at least eight a month. There are a hundred and twenty now, just like John in that they . . ."

"Mr. Bemis, you're on the Board of Barber Certification . . ."

"Is this the Brotherhood of Barbers and Cosmetologists? My name is Oakland; I'm with the State Department of Rehabilitation. May I speak to Mr. Sanky, please." (From Us and from Them, and Lord, from the lost chasm between eligibilities, deliver us. Amen . . .) "Mr. Sanky, my name is Oakland . . ."

"Yes, Mr. Dawson, I've spoken to Mr. Bemis on the Board and I've spoken to Mr. Sanky at union headquarters; but this isn't a matter of politics or power or influence; it's a simple question of our own honesty and responsibility."
"*I'm* honest. I didn't ask that guy to steal and get caught and go to jail, did I? I think we go easy on these guys and they start thinking they have all of this stuff just coming to them."

"But when we won't let a man back into society after he's served his time, then we're giving him what amounts to a life sentence, aren't we? We're lumping light offenses and serious crimes all together, aren't we?"
"I run a barber school, not a jail. What do I care about crime and criminals?"

"You guys, you management are all the same. This here's a union, a brotherhood, and we ain't gonna be infiltrated by the types of people that's gonna be a detriment to the influence of the union."
"I'm not management, I'm with the State De . . ."
"You ain't labor, that makes you management in my book."
"Mr. Page, I wonder if you've thought about money, the money you pay in taxes. If we deny these men work, if we *keep* them out of jobs, then the state has no choice but to put them and their families on relief. The arrest and imprison-

ment of this man has already cost us thousands of dollars in taxes; isn't it time he started working and paying *into* the kitty?"

"Oh, look, there's plenty of other jobs he could get. You welfare guys are always coddling these jailbirds and winos. Let him get a job on the pick and shovel somewhere, a good, honest job with a little sweat to it."

"Mr. Page, there hasn't been *any* day-laborer's jobs open in this town for three months, and when Carey & Knight advertised for three laborers last season, four hundred men showed up."

"Well, Oakland, that's your problem, ain't it? My part of it's all settled. Union says no, school says no, Board says no. Thanks for calling."

"Mr. Oakland, I'm Dr. Mariani. I'm up here for the National Conference of Hospital Administrators. I don't know if you know this, but we have, at our state mental hospital, a crowded adolescent wing. It's got a hundred and eighty kids, thirteen to eighteen. A lot of them don't belong in a hospital really, and wouldn't have to stay if we could get them into out-patient situations where they could take training in a trade. Unfortunately, those older kids are pretty bitter and antisocial, and the local communities don't really want them back. When I heard that you were doing work with disturbed adolescents . . ."

"Mr. Frailey, this Ralph Oakland at the State Office of Rehabilitation. I understand that you use trained barbers as demonstrators for your equipment. I have a client here with a certificate underwritten by the National Board of Barbers . . ."

"Ralph, this is Herb Vinson. I'm calling about Unwin's tuition check."

"Oh, hell, Herb, I'm sorry; I haven't had a chance to get it out yet. Look, I'll get to it right away and get into billing under the wire. I'm sorry, Herb. Uh—this may be the wrong time, but I was just about to call you about one of my clients. Do you have room in your motor-repair class?"

"Yeah, we have room, bring him down."

"I'll be down two weeks from Thursday, O.K.? The boy's name is Ethwald Kittenger. He's had no experience with working in a shop before, so I just thought I'd bring him in

45

to see the layout, but I expect he'll want to take the class. He might be a little shy about the use of his arm and leg, but it's just the tag end of a childhood sickness. I think it'll be fine. How are Mestrovick and Finley doing?"

When Ralph tried calling the wholesalers of barbershop equipment and the companies who sold products to barbers and might need demonstrators, he seldom got as far as Alan Devereaux' name. He had known that it was unlikely, his finding a loophole in the close cloth of interdependences and favors by which the tradesmen were bound to one another. If the suppliers used Alan to demonstrate their tools, or the manufacturers to demonstrate their products, barbers simply wouldn't buy; and after Alan's attempts to get certification in the city, he would only be a failure as a salesman. There seemed to be only one thing left to do. The state would have to speak out for the man it had imprisoned at great expense and had trained. The state had an investment in Alan Devereaux, and it was time to start protecting that investment. It was time to call a supervisor.

There were five levels of supervision in the agency's chain of command. It was an embarrassment of riches, since the only thing that seemed to define a supervisor was that he didn't work at counseling clients or digging up jobs. The agency had grown, as most agencies do, amorphously, through liberal reactions and conservative reactions and "reforms" by economy-platform legislatures. These periodically shaved from the bottom and left the top. They voted down money to be spent on the clients; they thinned the ranks of the active counseling members and the secretarial help, but the levels of supervision were left to proliferate in the agency seemingly without anyone's noticing. Now and then an inept counselor would be removed from the area in which he could do some harm and made a supervisor. Of the five levels of this supervision, Ralph knew that at least two were necessary.

Ralph's immediate supervisor was Abner Prettyman. Ab was necessary. He supervised the office and was responsible for all the counselors who worked out of it. He distributed the work and he was a good man to go to for advice. Everyone liked Ab, and in spite of that Ralph did too, but if Ab had a fault it was that he took no pleasure in a good fight. He had no killer instinct, no "cause," no bitterness to goad him, and he was an administrator, which made him still more

46

cautious. In spite of this, and at whatever cost to his peace-of-mind, he let Ralph work without hindrances and in his own way.

Now, Ralph would have to see how far Ab's support of him would go. He went up to Ab's office as soon as he could.

"Ab, I've got a problem."

"Only one? You must be goofin' off."

"This one is good size. Do you think the agency could put pressure on a union?" He caught the quick look in Ab's face that said he hoped it was a joke.

"Just a minute there, Ralph," and Ab sat down. "Now, what's that again?"

"I've got a client who has had state training on state money, but the union won't let him get a job and he has no redress at all. I think that the state has a right to defend its investment in this guy. He took training in good faith, passed the national requirements, and is qualified under all the necessary standards. Now, he's being kept from getting work."

"You talked to the union about this?"

"Sure, but it didn't make any dent at all. The Board has no real legal status and that gives them all kinds of power and very little actual legal responsibility. I will say, though, that I couldn't get to the head of the local on terms anything like equality. It would take Marshall, say, as head of our whole agency, to go to him with the leverage that Marshall has. I couldn't make a fight of it, but he could. If nothing else, he could get enough publicity to make the Board see itself with the eyes of the ordinary citizen."

Ab looked up quickly. "Hey, you're not planning to take this to Marshall, are you?"

"Wasn't Marshall a political appointee *because* he was supposed to be able to deal with this kind of thing?"

"He got a nice appropriation for the agency last year, didn't he?"

"This guy doesn't need an artificial leg or a college education. He's been tested and trained to top standards in his field. He doesn't need money; he needs *allies!*"

"Well, you're his ally, aren't you?"

Ralph knew that Ab was getting defensive, feeling that this was worker against supervisor, the kind of thing where everyone lost.

"Help him or change his trade. We can afford the retraining in anything else you decide on. If he's stubborn, just don't accept the case; you haven't signed him on officially yet, have you?"

"No, but . . ."

"Well, then, it's up to you, but don't . . ."

"I know, *don't go to Marshall.*"

The point had been made and Ab relaxed easily into success. "Look, Ralph, lots of occasions come up when the way we look to the community can make or break us. Every time we make trouble, we make enemies. We can't control the unions and we can't *make* people hire. Even you wouldn't want a policy like that. Anyway, state intervention, any kind, makes people think of socialism, and then the legislature votes our appropriations down."

"Oh, Ab, the richest country in the world and we can't afford simple honesty? I'm not talking about control or force or socialism; I'm talking about alerting our community to an inequity in the system. We can't keep talking about reform while we close all the roads to a returned prisoner. Shouldn't the taxpayers know that *they* will have to pay and pay dearly for the 'brotherhood's' hypocrisy?"

"Ralph, your sociology books are leading you into a mistake. They keep talking about *society*. I doubt if even Russia has a *society* into which you either fit or don't fit. The prisons train guys, but they can't make the unions accept trained men for the good of *society*. There's another state agency right down the street here that's having all its bookkeeping automated. We used to supply them with all those typists and bookkeepers. We can't force them to stay inefficient because it's good for our agency, or for *society*. Look at us for a moment. When we try to place a handicapped man on a job when there is a terrific unemployment problem, aren't we competing with the healthy job-seekers *on their tax-money?* This scattered, disorganized tangle of arms working against one another is the price we pay for our *free society*. The kind of philosophical unity and agreement you're looking for is in an anthill."

"But the guy trained in good faith . . ."

"Why don't you tell him to move West. They're more tolerant there with this kind of thing. Look, Ralph, going to Marshall won't do any good; this is the system." He was looking sympathetically at Ralph, conciliating, trying to make everything all right. Ralph kept hearing in his mind—When he

48

asks for bread, shall you give him a stone? He looked up and saw that Ab had stopped speaking.

"Okay, I'll tell him."

"Mr. Oakland, this is Mary-ann Cullinan down at Juvenile Probation. We're so happy that the state has finally set up a Juvenile Vocational Training program!"

5

John Kroll

When John Kroll came in again, Ralph couldn't help feeling a little grim. There they stood: the Juvenile Vocational Training Program and its product. Judges were hounding him in desperation; social workers were casting about for someone, anywhere who could end the sense of inevitable defeat with hundreds of adolescents crowding their rolls; ministers and priests were calling, two or three a day; and all of them were lighting here, on this fragile bond between Ralph and John.

John did look a little less intent on making himself the hero of a great failure. When Ralph told him to sit down, he did so almost as if it were not a challenge to his manhood.

"John, I'd like us to talk about what you want to do with the rest of your life."

"Yeh?"

A recital of the inventory of an Egyptian pyramid would have elicited more excitement. "What would you like to do?"

"I dunno," he muttered, "be with the gang."

What gang? Everything Ralph had read or heard about John described him as being a loner with no gang and no friends at all, but there was nothing to be gained by letting John in on this knowledge and stripping away all his pride. One was supposed to belong to a gang. Fine. John would have a gang. "What does the gang do?" Ralph asked.

"Aw, hang around." Suddenly John spurted into vehemence. "You know what them 'mother-friggin' cops do alla time? I mean we're standin' aroun' and them friggin' cops come along and make us move alla time when we ain't doin' a damn thing!" As quickly as the anger erupted it seemed spent. He slid back on his spine in the chair.

He was still playing before the invisible audience in a world beyond this one. His world was very like this one; John was not a reformer. He only wanted the tables slightly turned. The listeners, Ralph sensed, preferred the haughty and sneering silence; but John needed his late pass and so he was being forced to give dialogue and to act. John knew that the talking had caught him up before and gotten him into trouble, and he mistrusted it. Still, this Oakland bum had as much as called him a coward last time, as much as said that he couldn't talk, and he did want his late pass. There was always the bus-trip, too, with chances to bump against the girls getting on and off the bus or to say things to them that made them get red in the face—and old Burns was off his back, so the teachers and monitors weren't always on him about something.

"Are you really just hanging around or are you annoying people who have to pass you on the street?"

John smiled, long and slow, the way he had practiced it in the mirror sometimes, the Western way, as if there were all the room and all the time in the world. You knew when the Western stars did it in the movies they would say something real hard-and-funny—("Draw thet gun an' they'll be some loud singin' and some slow marchin'.")—but he had to let the smile drag on because suddenly he couldn't think of anything to say. He knew that if it couldn't be funny, it would have to be wild and surprising, so out of the grin he murmured, "We like to wait around and rub up the broads." Now that damn Oakland would be so busy putting himself together he would miss the clumsiness of the delivery and the way the smile was put on. Instead, Oakland only looked a little bored and then annoyed.

"And that's a life's work? Is that all, for a lifetime?"

John found himself stretching in his mind, trying to see over the present. He couldn't get the shapes beyond it. A month, maybe two, were lighted up and clear. The place beyond his age of fifteen and the people walking there were hidden by some kind of shadow. He knew the "markers," but he couldn't see himself as he passed them. Every kid in Boys' Shelter "knew the markers." When you were eighteen, you were out of juvenile authority. Age twenty-one could get you the gas chamber if you bumped somebody off. You could drive when you were seventeen, get a learner's license when you were sixteen. He said, "I wanna drive a real fast car, a real fast yellow sports car. Hey, what kind of car you got?"

"Chrysler."

"Yeah? I bet it ain't new."

"No, it isn't," Ralph said. He recognized the question as an old trap, a way to discredit any future opinions he might have, but he also knew that he had to be unafraid and unashamed first and completely.

John said, "Hell, I don't see how anyone could drive around in old cars. How could you do it for your presteedge?"

Great God, where did he learn that one? Ralph had to choke back a laugh. "John, don't you know that prestige is in *here,*" and he tapped his chest with his finger and felt a quick, funny click, as his nail glanced off the shirt button. "A man's opinion of himself is what is important. It matters more than you think—certainly more than some group idea of a man's 'prestige.' "

John had wandered away into his own world. It was too scary to go looking for yourself in the future, to be all alone with what you thought of yourself; all this stuff Oakland talked about was letting the cold in inside him. It made him feel sick. He tried to get back to the familiar places where Badges Kroll was freeing his boys again and accepting their praise and reverence and fooling the cops so they respected him. But it wasn't going easy this time. He had trouble seeing the strong, handsome face of Badges and making out the faces of the followers of the gang. He tried to see his mother, like when he gave her the jewels and she fell down crying for him to be careful. It was too hard. That damn Oakland made him feel like a coward!

Ralph watched John and found his own past with more quickness but no less pain. This boy was reminding him very much of himself, wrestling with a future he couldn't see. Once upon a time, a war-and-a-half ago, there was a boy called 3-Eye Oakland. He was a smallish boy, fighting the law, cursing and hating everything that suggested that there was a freedom in discipline. He got his nickname because he always wore an old miner's cap with a big bulbless headlamp. It was an ill-fitting and presumptuous badge of manhood. The other boys were always trying to take it away, and its very possession was part of his scorn and anger. He was a loner and close to no one, and now a certain older defendant, a Ralph Oakland, would have to answer the bitter questions of the outgrown 3-Eye through this John Kroll. He would have to show just cause why he had submitted to wife and children, old car, mortgage, and middle age.

Ralph hadn't thought of 3-Eye in many years, but now he realized that blind 3-Eye, his judge, would scorn him. Ralph Oakland was just another hard-working nine to five jerk, with a geared wheel inside him that ticked off the time. 3-Eye had measured a hundred men like Ralph, knowing that the worst of getting old was getting gutless. "I'll have to ask my wife . . . ," they said. Jesus Christ! and they weren't man enough to be ashamed to say it!

Ralph moved away from 3-Eye, but his feelings were so mixed that it was a while before he dared take comfort in his newer self, this work, the wife and children and home, his books, his garden, his weekend quietness. He knew that the quality of such experience was light years beyond the knowledge or understanding of his old self and of John Kroll. In his thoughts he looked back on those boys with pity, but perhaps not all pity.

Ethwald Kittenger

The secretary saw the kid with the real bad limp stagger into Oakland's office. Ralph's head disappeared from the upper glassed half. He was sitting down, but you could see the kid, Kittenger, shaking with that trouble in his hand. She saw him go tense and clench his teeth. It made her keep looking and she still watched the trembling boy; and there, riding up in his twisted hand, leading his arm up higher and higher over his head, the terrible hammer. She screamed. The office stopped. Then there was a breath out and the other counselors rushed from their offices—a man had collapsed in the waiting room last year and there were those who got violent when their cases were turned down. The men came quickly, their faces full of astonishment before the fact. The rigid secretary directed with her eyes—*there*. Behind the glass the arm came slowly down. Fatika ran in so that he was standing in the picture also. The boy's face tightened again, the hammer arm rose, and there was Fatika laughing in the picture, and then leaving it to come out laughing. "Muscle-building! So help me, only one of Oakland's clients could manage a thing like that!"

"Where does he dig them up—kooks like that?"

"She saw my hand, didn't she, the woman who screamed," Ethwald said, with his eye twitching and his little-boy voice, "through the glass."

"I don't think that seeing your hand made her scream," Ralph said, lost in wonder at the self-centeredness of Ethwald's world. "I think it was the hammer."

"But, Mr. Oakland, what's ugly about a hammer?"

"Ethwald, as far as I'm concerned today, nothing at all. It was beautiful, just fine."

The boy's eye flickered again under Ralph's praise, but he smiled. "I worked in the attic like you said. I been working real hard on it."

He came back the next week and showed Ralph again. In the office he would lift his hammer and clench and release his fist and hold his hand less and less like a criminal thing, but as he left the office most of the old wretchedness would fall back on him as if it were being dropped like a net from the door sill. Ralph had to persuade him to leave Aunt Louise at home permanently, but since then their sessions had been much more direct and free. Now he told Ethwald that on Thursday it would be time to go out into the terrifying great world of fast-talking, fast-handed people.

On Thursday Ethwald came in without a tie. Of course, he told Ralph, he didn't want to start by making a poor impression; and then this eye twitch had gotten worse since Monday, and the man at the motor school would think he had something wrong with his brains or something, "and, you know, my leg is worse because of the damp weather, so maybe we shouldn't go today . . ."

But it was today. Ralph hardened and he could see Ethwald getting pale, as if an impenetrable wall of air was stifling him. Today. Now. Even with Ralph leading him, Ethwald was terrified. They would go out the office door to where the world coiled and slid in its complexities, ready to strike. He could imagine being fixed with its paralyzing eye. As they went into the street together, Ethwald felt as if he was being squeezed through an opening barely large enough for his good arm and leg to wiggle through. Then he closed his eyes and took a step and he was enveloped by the coil, this day, this place.

They drove in Ralph's car out to Herb Vinson's Central School of Auto Repair, one of the very few in the state and almost the only one that Ralph could recommend. Ethwald would be able to start in a basic class and go as far as he was able, from Body and Fender to advanced machine work. He could learn and do as much as he was able, and if the Sedges' couldn't pay for the training, the state's funds would. All that was needed now was Ethwald's own courage and his faith in Ralph—and no mishaps. (If there's anyone around here who has robbed a bank and is going to shoot it out with the cops in the street, please, please wait until we're gone.)

They walked up to the building. They took a breath and went in. It was cool and dark inside after the glare of the summer street. The secret, nocturnal part of Ethwald was comforted, even though they had to pass the gauntlet of the downstairs corridor, where students loafed and smoked, where there were coke machines and men's rooms. They mounted the stairs successfully; they passed the rooms of men and boys working, machine hums in different keys, great carapaces of car parts skeletal and helpless, boxes spewing black lengths of hoses and wire entrails. Finally, they were at the office, and then inside. Herb Vinson was a large, shirtsleeved man. He greeted Ralph, smiling, and getting up quickly to come and shake hands. "Well, how've you been?" and Ethwald was glad and grateful for the worldliness and power of his intercessor in the strange places of the world.

"Fine, Herb, I've got a man here for you," and he introduced them, hoping that Ethwald wouldn't go pale at the word "man" and would put a little into the handshake. He cursed himself for not teaching Ethwald how to shake hands. 3-Eye Oakland, den mother. Now that John Kroll had raised 3-Eye from his unlamented resting place beside the tough and cynical infantryman he had also once been, Ralph felt the presence of him coming and going sometimes at the oddest moments.

Ethwald was making a valiant effort to imitate the sophistication and freedom of his model. He had put his hand forward as he had seen Ralph do, but as the handshake met across his vulnerable left, he flinched and the shameful left hand and foot dove for cover. Instinctively. That was worse. He felt as if he were twitching somewhere. He was getting hot in the face and his skin seemed to be crawling tight over his skull. A cripple. No good. He looked down, hoping that he had not left his hand in Mr. Vinson's. At least he hadn't done that. He was surprised then to hear Ralph talking and Mr. Vinson answering. He hoped it was over, failed and over, but they were beginning to go through the door together to see the shops and the new equipment. "Come on,

Eth," Ralph said, and he stumbled forward, guarding his left, to follow them.

As they went through the shops where the various classes were doing repair and rebuilding, Herb Vinson asked questions of the limping boy and got comments from him about the things they were seeing. His youth and innocence gave him a sort of removed quality that looked good in a shop where there were more than a few teenaged smart alecs. The agonized embarrassment spoke for a kind of eagerness in him and the hesitancy, which would have gone against an older man, was in Ethwald's favor. Slowly, as they went through the building, Ethwald began to breathe a little more comfortably. After a while Herb turned to Ralph and Ethwald, and they began to make arrangements.

So, Ethwald Kittenger became a student, and Ralph began the elaborate paperwork, means tests, eligibility checks, and statistical forms by which the state would free his services and its money in Ethwald's behalf. The boy would need a great deal of counseling as he went on in training. He was lacking the simplest knowlege of common life experience. He was sure to have trouble with some of the other students, the youngest of whom was more worldly than he. The arm and leg were still only well theoretically, on a doctor's chart, and when his training was over, there would be placement to face. But the first crisis seemed to be past, broken over the back of one long moment in Herb's office. Tomorrow, Ralph would call Mrs. Sedges. If he could give her hope or pride in her nephew, well and good, but if martyrdom was what she really wanted, "Well ..."—(as he wrote the notation)—"I might have to become an expert in nice, clean rooming houses."

6

"Mr. Oakland, we're grateful about your calling."

"Well, Mrs. Devereaux, I thought you would want me to call even if there hasn't been anything. I thought it would be good for Alan to know that I haven't given up or put his problem aside."

Ralph was facing Alan Devereaux' mother, a quiet, tired woman whose scrubbed look might have been her statement to the world that she was clean, decent, and hard-working. She had scrubbed herself gray also.

"I've tried all the places I know, but, well, there's a labor squeeze in this community lately and it's going to take time."

Mrs. Devereaux hesitated a little and then said, "He would be angry if he knew I was here. We know how you've tried to help in this—trouble—of his." Then she smiled because she was embarrassed, and started again. "Any time anybody tells me about you office people not doing any work, I'll just tell them straight out it isn't true."

Ralph moved his chair a little bit toward her, but he couldn't seem to help her express herself.

She went on. "I don't know why we have to keep asking for help from the same people all the time. It isn't fair, when there's others who are supposed to help and don't . . ."

He began to feel uncomfortable, sensing something and not being sure enough of what it was.

". . . only he's getting angry now, Mr. Oakland, and mean to himself. I talk about being patient and going to church to ask God for help, but that only makes him angry. Last night my husband and I—well, Mr. Oakland, we know that sometimes there's too many people to help all at once and you have to make a choice. We want you to know, his father and

I—we want you to know that we're not lazy people or drinkers or anything like that. We are working people and we want to help our boy get what he needs."

And then she opened the hands that she had kept folded while she spoke and unwrapped what she was keeping in them. And on Ralph's desk she placed the twenty-dollar bill.

"You see, it's all scaled down," Ralph muttered to his sandwich and Ab Prettyman. "The forty-thousand-dollar-a-year man can get graft, maybe fifteen hundred. The man making twenty has to satisfy himself with a simple five hundred smackers. You and I are modest men, Ab; we work with the poor. What can the poor pay? Twenty bucks! When I think of the graft I *could* be getting!"

"Is this the first time somebody's tried to bribe you?"

"Well, it's the first time I didn't see it coming in time to head it off."

"What did you say to her?"

"I wanted to say thank you and then take it and pass it all the way up the chain of command, all the way up to the governor so that everyone could feel as crummy as I did. When I told her I was really trying my best, Ab, did she really believe me, or had there been someone earlier in the day with twenty-two-fifty?"

"Oh, don't get so upset, Ralph. This is a money economy and people are used to paying for services with money."

"Sight unseen, Ab? No. It wasn't an order; it was a plea, and that's what hurt. I told her we were paid by the state through taxes. I pushed her money back at her and told her to go home and not to worry. I told her I was trying my best. The hell of it is that I'm up against a stone wall on this case, Ab, I told you how when I asked you about going to Marshall on it. Without Marshall and a fight, I don't think there *is* any 'best' for me to try, and that's why the damn thing is hitting me so hard.

"The guy has been going to every shop, *every shop*. He's like a zombie or the man with the albatross, and he's like that because the prison, for once, did what it was supposed to do, started him going straight. When straight is all used up, right down to the last man saying 'get out, jailbird,' he'll begin to steal again, and this time not as a punk kid who wants to impress some broad, but as a tough, bitter destroyer, a man I could be afraid of."

"Have you tried placing him at a non-union shop?"

"There aren't any. I called all the wholesalers, all the jobbers, all the products companies. It was no go; they depend on keeping in good with the union. I called every private place I could think of: social clubs and the old men's homes and the city jail and the vacation hotels out of town. Nothing. I'm not looking for a cause, Ab, but if we can't get work for Trades Training graduates in this state we'd better damn well tell them up at the pen, because this kind of thing is diabolical, Ab, to do that to a man . . ."

"What about the Federal system; have you tried the Air Force, Fort Carey Field?"

"I never thought about that. Are the shops out there civilian?"

"I don't know, but I remember seeing a barber shop out there when I was out looking for a training set-up."

"It can't be any more hopeless than it is now, Ab. Thanks a lot; I'll give them a try."

Hans Marshak

"Hello, Hans, how are things going?"

"Okay, Mr. Oakland, is anything the matter?"

"Well, I'm calling because I need help. I remembered, of course, that you worked out at Carey Field, but that you weren't in the Service. I wanted to know under what sort of arrangement that was."

"Oh, I was a civilian hired by the Air Force. See, when they need men and can't get them through their own channels, they hire civilians. With us in the airplane mechanics section it was about fifty-fifty, civilian and military."

"Hans, do you know anything about the barber shop out at the field?"

"Yeah, the barbers are the same way; they're Federal employees, but they're not Air Force, at least not when I was there."

"Thanks a lot, Hans."

"Mr. Oakland, I was going to call you about changing my appointment."

"You're not back in school, are you?"

"Yes, my wife takes me. It's tough making the steps and all that with the wheelchair, but I just can't waste any more time."

"Just be sure you get that condition really cleared up before you rush over to the Limb Shop again."

"I can't keep waiting for my legs; by the time I get them it'll be time for my retirement."

"Remember, if you rush, it'll only cost you more time in the long run. I'll change your appointment, and thanks for the word about Carey Field."

"Wings Barber Shop, Al speakin'."

(God, why didn't I think of it before? I could have saved him weeks of misery! I'd better not go off half-cocked; it's only a chance, nothing to bank on, except that the wall in front of him has been getting longer and higher every day and there's been no light and it took me this long to find Al, standing in his little window, Business as Usual. God, I should have remembered Hans Marshak; he was a civilian working on a military base—a Federal employee.)

Ralph wrote the name down on a slip of paper. The barber had said; "We're Federal here, the local unions don't run us."

"Can you use another man?"

"Oh, well, I'd have to talk to him first. If his diploma is good, and if he works out, we'll use him as stagger man, filling in for guys on vacation or as outside man until he can come on permanent. Like I say, I'd have to see him first."

In the afternoon Ralph called Mrs. Devereaux, and they took and gave the specially delicate etiquette of people who have much to lose. There was no great gush of hope from Alan's mother, and Ralph's voice was softer than usual. He often called this kind of dialogue The Great Stony Courage Game. Once alone, he knew that this mother might weep or dance or clap her hands. She would suffer waiting an eternity until her boy came home to be told, but over the phone, with a stranger, they had to throw and catch by the old, cold formula. He gave her the address and the name of the head man at the barber shop and she said, "Well, thank you, Mr. Oakland. Good-bye." It was barely a victory, and tempered because it was made possible not by breaking down Page's stone wall but by circumventing it. For Alan's sake, at least, hope was still possible. He sighed and rose to meet the wave in the waiting room. The phone rang.

Every year there were about fifteen hundred people coming to the agency to be interviewed, tested, counseled, trained, and placed on jobs. The laws concerning who was acceptable for vocational rehabilitation were clear on certain

60

definite points. The agency had been created to get jobs for the physically, mentally, or socially handicapped. The physical condition of the applicant had to be stable. Progressive, deteriorating diseases made their victims ineligible. The program was also solely for vocational, not avocational, placement and many hundreds of married women with grown children and a wish to work had to be turned away. Social handicaps were narrowly defined as those arising from prolonged detention in prisons or mental hospitals. Within these three boundaries was an infinite number of choices. Each counselor accepted the clients he felt he could succeed in helping. For some, this spectrum was very narrow; for others, it was as wide as the furthest limits of the laws. Some of the counselors put their emphasis on testing, some on deep counseling, some on a big turnover of applicants.

The counselors were, for the most part, adequate and dedicated men, but the intricacy and difficulty and pressure of their work exposed and cystallized their weaknesses as well as it declared their strengths. The pressure made some counselors and broke others, but usually it did both at once. Looking at Martenson, for instance, Ralph saw a top-drawer testing man, diligent and humane, but Martenson's lack of hope for the emotionally disturbed or alcoholic clients made him turn them away sight unseen. He had a nagging grain of race prejudice which he fought with varying degrees of success as the pressures waxed and waned. Lou Dobbs had a marvelous gift with retarded children and their parents, infinite patience and a quiet reasonableness that calmed the most anguished Phi Beta Kappa father coming in with his dull child. But Lou's strength was his weakness also. He had no anger and therefore no righteous wrath. He did not fight for his clients' rights or interests, and he looked on in a kind of wonder at Ralph's confrontations with the laws and the employers, the schools and the doctors. Ralph respected Ernest Martenson and he liked Lou, even though they all had radically different ideas about what their jobs were about. Then there was Bill Fatika, whom Ralph disliked personally and whose every motive and philosophy seemed to be in direct opposition to everything that Ralph held as a value.

It had once seemed to Ralph that a commitment to anything was better than a commitment to nothing. It was Fatika who made him grateful for the saving, commonplace wonder of simple, sincere apathy. Fatika was a Christian in every sense that made Ralph wince. He hated the "undeserv-

ing" and he told them so, and he told Ralph so. Those
without the ideas decreed by his synod deserved whatever
handicaps God wished upon them, and when Ralph reminded
him that their agency had been set up to serve taxpayers
rather than tithers, Fatika simply quoted a passage from the
single Book he had read since college. Without this saving
complacency, Fatika would easily be the fastest rider in a
holy war, and Ralph couldn't forget a vision he had once had
during one of Bill's genially self-serving comments on The
Right. Ralph's imagination had clothed the proud Fatika in
the Nazi uniform that belted itself *Gott Mit Uns*—God with
Us—on the buckle, a bonus, something for one of the van-
quished to see as he went down. It was a hard vision to
forget, because it made sense to Ralph. By some supreme act
of separating himself from his intellect, Fatika had learned
the numbers and the definitions necessary to get a degree,
and he could parrot the psychological terms by which he
earned a living, but he believed not one word of it. This he
told Ralph also, not without a certain pride, one day when the
subject of Ralph's agnosticism came up. He had said that
Ralph was lost and damned no matter what good he had done
in his lifetime. Ralph had called him a hypocrite and was
unreasonably and foolishly impatient with him, because he
couldn't see it; but after one of their clashes Ralph had begun
to wonder how he himself might look to a spectator. First,
there was a kind of militancy in his agnosticism—Onward,
Unbelievers, Marching as to War—and he didn't get along
too well with priests and ministers or with medical men
either, if they were too doctrinaire. He knew that he made
no sense to Fatika; that Lou, in his easy-going way, wondered why Ralph, who could be a nice guy if he would only
give himself the chance, always made trouble, kept
scrambling for perfection, trying to level to fairness all the
cliffs and chasms of luck and birth. Still playing the spectator, Ralph went home and made a list of people who annoyed him. There were about eight names, but the reasons
why they were annoying were not as varied as Ralph thought
they would be. All of the people on the list had one major
fault, an opinionated and narrow view of life. Ralph saw then
that he had a prejudice against those who "knew," as subtle
and renewing as Martenson's feelings about Negroes and
Mexicans. To this extent, Ralph was one of them. He wrote
his name at the bottom of the list and tore it up, and Fatika's

next serene dictum was destroyed with a cold, slashing logic that made Ralph feel both guilty and triumphant for a week.

Except for occasional blow-ups or personality clashes, the counselors and supervisors got along well together. They were generous with their time and good will, and they were kindly, decent family men, men of modest dreams and therefore not cynical; but there were two subjects about which, by subtle, unsaid agreement, no one ever spoke. Everyone stayed away from talk about the basic principles underlying their work. No one ever argued or defended his reasons for understanding the job as he did. This was probably because the men had to work together—Ralph and Fatika, meticulous Lonigan and disorganized Melchior. It kept peace among the counselors and gave an illusion of unity, but it also standardized their conversations, so that when they talked over coffee they could have been any group of middle-class, middle-aged men. Then there was the unspoken subject which gave Ralph far more anxiety, as if the agency, well meaning enough, was collaborating in silencing the history of its worst mistakes. These were not concerned with the clients, but with the counselors. No one ever discussed Those Who Had Left.

In Ralph's first year at the agency—a year during which he would sometimes come home and tell his wife Mary-Ann in awe that his work was as close as an agnostic could come to a holy act—Paul Durant quit. For a long time Ralph tried to understand why; Paul was the best counselor in the agency, humane and perceptive and intelligent. His written reason for leaving was that his father had left him the family business which he felt morally obligated to continue. Ralph knew this to be a lie. He had gone to Paul and asked him, and Paul had only said, "The pressures build up and after a while they overwhelm you." Ralph had answered with the lovely logic of the "new boy," "But you regulate the number of your clients, you regulate the pressure." Durant had smiled a little and said, "Don't you leave, Ralph, you're very good at this work, you know. Stay with it."

Every so often Ralph would find a case in the records with the small scrawl of Durant's handwriting on it, but no one ever spoke of Durant at all; and when Ralph would say, ". . . reopened a case yesterday, a cerebral palsy, one of Durant's boys," there would be a silence around it so that soon he stopped mentioning Durant. Cliff Murphy went into the limbo about a year after that. He, too, was one of the better counselors, but whatever the rest thought of him, he wasn't spoken of again. The next big losses were Howland and Koveny, and after a while Ralph began to be nagged by an awful feeling that it was the best ones who left, the brilliant, original, ambitious ones, the ones who had most to give. He had long since solved the problem of what pressures Durant meant when they had spoken together, but were the pressures lighter anywhere else? Wasn't there something wrong with a system that could lose a Durant and not care at all? Then Ralph would look around at his co-workers and wonder if they ever felt diminished by the lack of great talent among them: Durant and Murphy and Howland and Koveny, and whoever next would disappear and be too assiduously forgotten.

New men came in, too, and the plodders seemed to stay. Lonigan and Rumpell were new and not yet sure where their weights and weaknesses would fall. Larson and Ogilvy were the special counselors for the blind, in another office. Covington took referrals from the high schools, and Anson was down at the State Hospital, another one-man paper cup held against another Niagara Falls. Buono at the State Prison had somehow missed the Trades Training section, probably because the state had considered trainees such as Alan Devereaux as being already rehabilitated.

In philosophy, ideals, and methods of work it was a varied group, but the members of it were all subject to the pressures of those who fight other people's battles. Every one of the counselors had ulcers, angina, or some other outward and physical form of an inward and spiritual strain. They joked now and then about their rate of attrition, so much higher than that of their clients. But as the new men, one by one, came down with these complaints, it gave the older hands a strange, cold feeling, a kind of quiet loneliness as they each turned back to the endless task of digging in a separate desert with a sieve.

John Kroll

The sneering, gum-grinding John Kroll arrived at his appointment with a new alertness. He's in a good mood today, Ralph thought, and was pleased. But as John began flicking edged questions here and there, Ralph knew that it was only round two of the bout. Ralph had won the introductory circling part by forcing John's hand. Now it was going to be an exploration of weaknesses, jabbing to guage speed, parrying, and jabbing again. John would be hoping to tire the older, less angry opponent, who had to carry the weight of the civilization he was attempting to justify. But John was incapable of knowing that Ralph had a secret source of help. 3-Eye Oakland would be there. If the new Ralph could remember hard enough and true enough, 3-Eye could tell him what part of John's attack was truly attack and what part really defense.

"Hey, Oakland, you married?"

"Yes, I am."

"What's her name? Is she good lookin'?"

"Her name is Mary-Ann and to me she's very good-looking."

"Oh, brother! that don't sound good-lookin'."

There was a pause.

"Hey, Oakland, how much do you make in this racket?" (An attack with little danger.)

"Enough to get by on."

"Enough to, like if you walk down the street and see something you want, you just go in and buy it?"

"Yes, I think so. I'd have to give up something else, though. If the thing was very expensive, I'd have to save for it."

"Oh boy, that's great stuff. Ham and eggs with no ham and no eggs. I know who gets it, mister, your old lady gets it, and she gives you coffee money ten cents a day and you gotta go back and ask her if you can save up for a pack of cigarettes." (Defend yourself, stupid, 3-Eye said in him.)

And Ralph thought, this kid's retarded like I'm Queen Marie. "It's not as grim as all that," he said. "Sure, we can't spend money recklessly, but nobody has that much; and if he did, he would get tired after a while, buying things he really didn't want or need. The point is that we can *choose* how we want to live and what we want to buy."

"You *choose* that? You gotta sit here all day for peanuts and then you take it home and your old lady sits home losin' her looks and havin' kids and you *choose* that?"

"John, you're leaving out the half that lets the other part make sense." (3-Eye groaned in Ralph's darkness.)

"You're just stuck with it, bein' square, re-spec-ta-ble."

"Respec*ting*. Caring. (3-Eye relaxed. The damn jerk had almost said *loving!* That would have done it, but good.) John, you can't test another person's life, because you only know it

65

by what you see on the outside. The part inside, the secret part is something else. Until you really know that part, you don't know the person or the life he leads, and there are some parts that the outsider can never see."

Not by a change of expression on the boy's face, but in another way, some way he didn't know, Ralph found that he had struck some sort of blow, and the blow had told. He didn't know how or where. John was sitting in front of him, trying to come through it without showing anything.

John felt his ears burning on the sides of his head. Those rotten bastards! Did they know anything? Maybe he had spilled something in his sleep, about Badges and the gang, and somebody was listening and took it down. He covered as fast as he could. "You can't fool me," he said, "I never seen a dirty baby diaper that looks as good as a new yellow sports car, even to *you*."

"You're right there," Ralph said, "but I do have a car and it's paid for and it gets me where I want to go. It may not be yellow or new, but it's not a dream either." (One-up, said 3-Eye.)

The tack turned. "This job here, what's in it for you?" John was smirking a little because he had gotten free of the discovery of Badges Kroll. "I mean, what's in it if it don't *pay.*"

Ralph was going to answer that the pay was actually quite good, but he stopped himself. It would boil down to opinion then, and whatever his idea of good pay was, it would automatically be penny-ante to John. "It's a good job, besides the pay."

"Aw, you work with a bunch of nothin' bums . . ." John had caught himself badly, and they both saw it, so he tried to unhook gracefully. "I mean them damn social workers and them. The ones at the Shelter's always talkin' about *my problems,* and they're the ones with the problems cause they're scared I'll pull a knife on 'em someday." He wondered for a moment if he really ever would. Why not? He smiled.

"Well, I like the job," Ralph said, "I like to help people find the right work, work that they're good at. And, sometimes, I'm working to protect my interests."

"What's that mean?"

"Well, you're the one who's been measuring money and the price for everything. Why should *I* pay *your* way through life? Who do you think pays for Boys' Shelter and Boys' State
66

and the state pen and the guards that guard it and the cops and the courts and the judges? Do you know how much it costs to keep somebody in jail? If I can help you get off your duff and get some decent training and get a good job, then you'll be paying your own way. You'll pay taxes too, see?"

It was a little square and self-righteous, but it seemed to give Ralph a purpose that John could understand.

"Yeah, well, I ain't in no hurry to get re-ha-bil-i-tated, so, uh, I'm gonna go. I'll check with that big broad outside," and he motioned with a finger toward the secretary.

"That's right," Ralph said. "There should be time, a week from Thursday." He felt very tired as he always did after a session with John, who was standing at the office door smirking.

"You really are—I mean trying—to turn me into a jerk like you."

This was meant to be the parting shot that would bring Ralph to violence. You want it long and slow, Ralph thought, I'll do it in your own style. So he opened a long, very slowly spreading grin and said out of it, "That's right, John, that's exactly right."

It was a strange thing, trying to show still pictures of his middle-class existence to this blind and angry boy-man. John was a hostile and bitter product of "society's" vacillations, civic and personal corruption, and loveless charitable institutions. He thought he knew the nature of the mountain that was upon him. Its power was money and its purpose was impersonal hypocrisy. John envied the power and detested the hypocrisy, but Ralph realized that for all his frankness with John, he couldn't be honest with him either. Only the bitter, crudely self-interested parts of the truth would be admissible to John, only those parts would be believed. All the more personal underflowing motives: generosity, love, a sense of vocation, a talent for the work he did, a need to share his life—these were not distinguishable in the half-light of John's half-experience. People had lied about their love for John and their befriending of him, and therefore love and friendship were lies. Now Ralph found himself pressed into service as nothing more, for the present, than a liar telling a new kind of lie.

But now more than ever he had to check again on what Miss Burns had told him. He called the Shelter and asked to speak to her. "You did tell me that John Kroll was retarded . . ."

"Oh, yes, we gave him the whole battery of tests when he came in. I have the breakdown of the results in his file, but none of the scores was anywhere near the average. Totaled up, it was in the 60's, a full 30 points below the normal . . ."

"Interesting," Ralph said.

"Do you want me to look up the exact scores?"

"No, I just wanted to make sure. I'm going to try to get him to take another series."

"But why? It'll only come out the same."

"No, ma'am, I don't think so. Our boy has made a hypocrite out of me and a weakling out of you, and I have a strong suspicion that he has also made liars out of the Messers Binet and Wexler."

"But the tests, they're standardized."

"I beg your pardon, standardized liars."

Alan Devereaux

"Mr. Oakland—uh—this is Alan Devereaux."

"Hello, Alan, what can I do for you?"

"I'm calling from the base. I—uh—well, I thought that—I mean . . . Jesus, Mr. Oakland, *I got the job!*"

"Say, Alan, that's great news!"

"I start tomorrow. He talked to me and looked at my papers and asked me about the time I served, how long and was I free or on parole. I was sure it was gonna fall through. I started to feel like all the other times, and all of sudden he's talking to me about how the guys around here like their hair cut closer and neater than the usual civilian cut. A guy comes in and he says: 'Let's see you work.' My hands were shakin'. I mean I was so scared of goofin' the whole thing up. The guy says: 'You're new here.' I start to think he's going to ask me about where I was before, you know, it's funny how you get that way from jail, like that's the only real subject to talk about in the world and everything's going to come down to that. I said yes, I was new, and then he started kiddin' the boss. It was okay; I give him a real nice cut. Afterward the boss just says, 'Okay, Devereaux, you start work in the morning. We rent the jackets so I'll need your size.' Then he sends me to the office to make out the forms. I'll have to go for the physical and write up the Federal forms, but the guy up there said it's just formalities."

"That's great, Alan. Oh, do you have transportation out there?"

"Oh, yeah, there's good busses. Uh—Mr. Oakland, I don't know if you know how close I was to chuckin' the whole business, but I was. I know I sounded pretty bitter when I first came in and I'm sorry about that—I just wanted to tell you. After a whole lot of guys take your name and stuff just to get rid of you, you just don't believe anyone gives a damn. Like, in the joint, they call you a crumb. It's like you really are, after you get out; like you are just extra, left over, and you fall down and get brushed off and into the garbage and that's it. So I wanted to thank you, Mr. Oakland, that's all."

"I'm just glad that you got in out there, and I hope it'll go just the way you want it. I'm glad for you, Alan. Thanks for calling."

How could Durant have left a job like this? He must have been crazy!

"See, what did I tell you, Ralph? You go around stewing over these cases, but eventually everything comes out right."

"It came out right by dumb luck, Ab, after we had all passed the buck just as hard and fast as we could. It was intra-agency co-operation at its most skillful from the carefully set-up Trades Training program down at state, through the eager-to-forget-specifics parole board, the probation department, and right down to us, Ab. It was our blunder, too, and we expected the client to pick up the pieces himself. We never faced the problem; we just sidestepped and went around it, but that's not going to make it go away next time. I still think we sold damn far short. Aren't you ever afraid for the poor saps who happen to fall between big Us and big Them?"

"What did *we* do? We weren't even part of the problem as I see it."

"He had a gripe against a big organization and no redress. Nothing but another organization equal in power could have tackled the problem, a behemoth to talk to a mastodon. And we didn't want our agency 'involved.' "

"Say, Ralph, you ever seen the ground after a 'talk' like that? Why kick and scream? It's another case closed for you. Bang goes the stamp: Closed. Rehabilitated."

"I'm afraid not. He was never on the rolls; he'd already been tested and trained at the prison."

"Ralph, you're a guy that's asking for it. How long did you

spend trying to calm that guy down and calling up places for him and listening to his old lady—she was the one that offered you the twenty bucks toward your Florida vacation, wasn't she?"

"Oh, I don't know, I tried lots of places whenever I had a minute to call."

"And you didn't see that as taking time away from your regular cases, the ones that will go into your books as closed and will be counted to you at the end of the year?"

"Hell, Ab, we're in the Pain, Trouble & Failure business. Do you see a man bleeding to death in front of you and ask him whether his hemorrhage is authorized or unauthorized?"

"You do, if you're smart. You go for the numbers because the numbers give you the personal praise, and the numbers impress the state legislature which authorizes the money, and because the numbers have to spread to cover all the men in this here organization who never go near a client."

"It's a *service*. We're supposed to give *service*. Oh, Ab, why am I wasting my breath pleading it to you? When the Ballantine kid came down with leukemia, you didn't do a damn thing but stay up half the night with the parents figuring out how they could go ahead with training part-time and counseling her so that she wouldn't know she was off the program! Thanks a lot for the good advice, Ab, but I know too many of your secrets."

Ab looked at Ralph very seriously. "I wasn't blowing off to hear myself blow. You're a good man, Ralph, and if you go on doing extras it's going to come from somewhere. It's going to come out of you. The fights cost. Before long, the cost is going to tell. I'm not a fighter, Ralph, I think you know that; but I feel things too, and that costs. It's probably worse if you feel you have to *do* something every time you see a wrong. Play it the way it's supposed to be played, Ralph, with no extras. It's tough enough that way."

"I'm only human, Ab—the summer is almost over."

Ralph meant that soon another autumn would be cutting away at his work time. The geese would fly south and the sound of the gavel would be heard from the rostrums. Conferences on Rehabilitation of the Handicapped, speeches before the Associated this and that. Chicken salad in front of the 260 ladies of the auxiliary; panel discussions with other counselors on problems that everyone knew couldn't be solved in the next 150 years. *Hiring the Handicapped*—six versions of this before six businessmen's associations where there wasn't a personnel man in the place. Ralph believed that one competent client in a factory was better public relations than a hundred of these Agency Images sculpted in aspic. It was partly this that wore out Durant, and it was in this that Ralph resented spending himself. Alan Devereaux would never appear on his books, but neither would the speeches and the regional dinners. The difference between them was that in Ralph's random day dreams, where Alan did appear, his name and shadow rode a rail that shone away to infinity, a rail that sang with the weight that it carried: Justice.

Ralph went back to the office after his coffee break and there was John Kroll, looped over two chairs in the outer office. It was not his regular day and experience had taught Ralph to be on guard against doing "favors" by seeing his people whenever they happened to drop in. When he was new on this job he had wished to keep spontaneity by being "on call," but it was one of the earlier dreams to die; too many fearful and dependent clients used the open door as a subtle form of domination, and Kroll was quite capable of using the method to show his contempt. Besides, Ralph had an appointment over at the welfare office.

"Aren't you supposed to be here on Thursday?" he asked.

John rolled his shoulders back in an approximation of the sinuous, slow Western style. "I just came in to tell you you could tell Miss Burns we could do all that junk you said, that training and junk like you wanted."

Ralph was dumfounded. He said, "Okay, John, sure," and then he went on to his appointment at the welfare department, wondering what the sudden decision meant. A change of heart? Hardly. Some kind of deal, most likely, or something to get "old lady Burns" to let him out of some unpleasant job or other. But the joke, perhaps, would be on John, because his reasons, whatever they were, might be strong enough to drive him on through testing, schooling, training, and even into a trade. He might even fool himself into a paycheck. Ralph smiled as he walked into the welfare office. And they called Fulton a dreamer! Nevertheless—nevertheless . . .

Hans Marshak

Ralph went forward and shook the hand of the man in the wheelchair. "Hello, Hans." He was thinking that his world

71

teemed with the halt and the lame and the sick. It had few heroes. But here was one of them. "Come on in."

Hans wheeled himself into the little office, which now seemed crowded, since he wasn't using the chairs already there. Ralph was glad to see him; Hans seemed sure that his pain and trouble were not the size of the whole world, a rare thing in a man who had not finished with his suffering.

"Have they gotten it, Hans? Have they gotten it all, at last?"

"They think so."

"How long has it been? I suppose I could look it up, but you might remember."

"Oh, about a year and a half. The accident was in March. By May they were fitting the first set of legs. Then, I guess it was at the end of May that the irritation started in the stumps, and then the infection. They didn't find out it was a staph infection until June."

Ralph looked at his brief record of visits and saw the word osteomyelitis written and underlined. Endless drainings and treatment of the infected stumps. Seeming progress and then another outbreak with tissue succumbing again. Cutting, draining, again and again. Through it all, Hans had fought to go on with his training, showing up at the electronic school in his wheelchair. He had a quiet, steady courage that impressed even his doctors. Now the worst of it seemed to be over. The year's training, interrupted a few times for operations, was caught up again in spite of gnawing pain, was going to be over. The latest operation seemed to be successful. At last Hans would be able to get up on legs and get on with his life.

"I called over to the limb company," he said. "They say they have to refit because of the changes in the stumps. The right leg was always better than the left."

"Now, about money," Ralph said.

"I was wondering if they'll charge me the full price for a second pair of limbs—I mean if they have to make them over again—I never even got to wear the first pair."

"I'm afraid so. I know it seems ridiculous having to pay for a pair of limbs which will never be used, but there is the whole limb to be made over again and refitted and read-justed, just as if it hadn't been done before. Hans, I know that you've been trying to keep up with expenses yourself, but it just isn't possible any more. The state has funds to pay for clients' training and also all the prosthetic equipment he needs."

72

"We've always paid our own way. I hate to stop now, but the bills are just too much even to begin on. Helen's working and Dad gives us what he can, but, well, I just don't see how we can manage."

"If you're thinking about this as some form of charity, Hans, you're wrong. It's what your taxes have been paying for all this time, and with your training finished and your condition finally clearing up, it shouldn't be too long before you are *paying* the taxes again. How's the work coming?"

"Oh, I should be finished in about three months. I'm going to try to cut it down, though. I want to be working by Christmas. It would be just the present that Helen and my folks could use."

"How is Helen? Does she like the work?"

"Oh, yes. She's always been interested in designing clothes and stuff, and, well, this last re-infection of mine hit her kind of hard. It was good that she had something else on her mind. Helen wants to be strong and calm about things, but, well, she just can't. Now it's not easy to convince her that the trouble spots have all been cut away and there isn't likely to be a reoccurrence. She and my mother used to sit in the kitchen, I think I told you, and cry over their tea and commiserate with each other all afternoon. I think that's going to be finished soon, too, when I get these legs and get walking."

Ralph remembered one of their earlier conversations, part of the standard probing in which the counselor tried to examine his client's feelings about his injury. If a man thinks of himself as a ruined cripple, he is more likely to be slow in training and hesitant to trust himself on a job.

"I'm not going to be an invalid, no matter what. See, I have sort of a position to fill in life. I worked on those big, beautiful ships out at Carey Field. I worked on 'em inside and out and I worked with a swell bunch of guys. Even if I can't do that work any more, I've got it to live up to."

If only that defeating infection was really over ... Hans had been an airplane mechanic at the Army airfield. That and his years' training in electronic instrumentation would make him a highly skilled man in a field that was crying for trained people.

Now they talked some more. The new limbs would have to be made with special care so as not to irritate the susceptible stumps, and Hans in his eagerness to get going on the new legs would have to be kept from saying that he was com-

73

fortable in them when he wasn't. He would also have to go slow on his training in walking, since any irritation at all was risking a return of the osteomyelitis infection. Ralph warned Hans about working too hard before he was fully ready. It even seemed a little strange to him to be telling someone to take it easy, curb the ambition, don't be too eager to get back to work.

When Hans left, Ralph sighed. There was one trouble with clients like Hans Marshak. Working with them seemed to put a greater strain on his patience with foul-mouthed rebels like John Kroll. The Marshaks made the Krolls and the Kittengers and the dozens of other angry or frightened ones look suddenly weaker, worse, almost a waste of time.

Bernardo Ramirez

They started walking up from the south, bringing its pale dust on their clothes. Mostly, Bernardo rode the mule because of his leg. He thought little because there was little to think of. To the south, the lands were flat. They had been planned by God to bear crops. Here the land went its own way for its own purposes, hills and gulleys and places of bare rock. Four days. Five. The air got cooler in the evenings. At night it was cold now, and all of them had to huddle close together in the blankets they had brought. Another day. Another.

All of this—the leaving a place that was ancestral, the walking into a strange land, the cold, the hunger—it was all because of his leg. Bernardo's leg was like a señor padrón, like a landowner. The leg ordered things. The leg made all things happen. One moment a certain man, Bernardo Ramirez, was working as always. Forever was before him and forever was behind him. Then, suddenly, like a sneeze, before a man could even think what happened, the Señor Chase's machine had caught his leg in its teeth and begun to eat it. Only a moment and Bernardo was no longer himself.

Grandfather had been kicked by a horse and the village had kept him. That was when there were villages and many padróns and many, many people. A village was a big family and it kept its old ones and its hurt ones. The village lost no one, but now the land had lost the villages and the Señor, only one Señor now, was left. This Señor had armies of metal hands and iron legs to do his work. He could not keep

74

a family like Bernardo's. He had been sorry. "Go to the city. The city has jobs." On a certain day he had led them to the end of the land. "Go north. That way." They went beyond the last irrigation ditch, which was the end of the land, up the road to the arroyo, which was the limit of the thoughts Bernardo had ever had in a northerly direction, up and still further to the row of cottonwood trees by the river, which was the northern limit of the world.

Northward, thinking nothing except the idle thoughts of people without homes. This land was bad for beans. Perhaps there will not be food enough. The nights are cold. Sometimes Bernardo got down and walked, and the littlest children rode the mule. All seven of them were quiet under the hot fist of the sun, but at night they would huddle and whimper and have bad dreams. This northern land was not happy for a man.

After many days and many changes in the land there began to be more houses and stores with many things to sell. Then, after a time, they came to where two great black roads met. Lights were over the roads, red and green and yellow, going on and off, and there were many signs, some with arrows pointing and some with words. Bernardo pointed to one, showing his wife sagely, "That is a number." They passed on, still northward, as the Señor had pointed. After the great joined highway had begun to lay down before them the length of a large bean field, they were arrested.

The policeman spoke into a box in his car and the box did not believe him and the box sputtered at him and laughed. "Mule? What wazzat? Urrrrk—we don't have any statute on that."

"Well, there's seven of 'em—no, nine of 'em and this mule . . ."

A crackle and tearing sound in the box. "It's a draft animal, I guess."

The policeman agreed with the box. "What's the name?"

"Ramirez, Bernardo. B as in Baker."

"Baker! Madre de Dios!"

The name of Bernardo Ramirez had been known by perhaps fifty people in all his life, and those who knew his name knew himself also. Now he heard his name begin to ring from bastion to bastion of this world of strangers, from police car to dispatcher, then from jail to legions of strangers in departments and agencies, welfare and public health in duplicate and in triplicate. He had been arrrested, they said, because of the mule, but Bernardo could not see that the mule had done any offense. He never saw the mule again. The welfare people came to see him in jail, knowing his name already, as if he were a famous man. After a while he stopped asking about the mule. The land was no more. God's will be done. And he sighed.

7

Bernardo Ramirez

The welfare caseworker, Miss Jesperson, said, "They're living in that tarpaper jungle down by the new highway cut-off. The name is Ramirez, Bernardo Ramirez. We've got to get him off welfare and working."

Ralph looked at the form she handed him. "Why this Ramirez especially? You've got dozens of families who've been waiting longer."

"Well, he's an embarrassment to the agency, for one thing—seven kids, illiterate, all the rest. We're getting set to support that crew all their lives if we don't get him off right now."

(This Ramirez is an embarrassment to a lot more people than she is counting. Jesperson is a sweet girl; she must agonize sometimes as she budgets her own superresponsible, dutiful, careful, careful life, paying this Ramirez' taxes and sleeping in her single bed. And the parish priest won't be doing nip-ups either, confronted with the birth-control issue between his church and the Protestant community. The antiracist liberals are wincing because they wish the name was Cooper or Jones. The Spanish-American community, too, will want to pull away from the assocation of "another Mex on welfare.")

"Has he got a physical disability?" Ralph asked. "Yes," she said, "he has a game leg."

"Maybe he should stay on welfare," Ralph said. "There are very, very few jobs open that can be filled by one-legged illiterates, and those don't pay enough to keep families of nine."

"I don't know why. In the old days . . ."

"Oh, the old days," Ralph snorted. "In the old days a man could keep goats and raise a vegetable garden down by that

77

junk yard where they live. In the old days a man could send his kids out scavenging; he could get uneaten food at the back doors of restaurants. Now we don't allow *that* kind of poverty, only *this* kind of poverty," and he snapped the application.

"All right, all right," she said, "be that as it may. Won't you even try? Surely there must be *something* ..." She was almost pleading.

Ralph looked at the application again. He was right off the farm in Indio country. If this Bernardo Ramirez was typical, his forefathers had been there since anyone could remember. They had continued to be born and raised as aliens in their own land, living a feudal lifetime in the twentieth century, and now their son was adrift in the city and unable to take the twentieth century for granted. The earnest social worker with all her pleading had forgotten how much complexity was second nature to her. She thought of a man from the Rehabilitation agency taking Bernardo Ramirez and tucking him in somewhere where the industrial revolution and the germ theory and two world wars had not reached. Ralph looked at her and sighed. He had seen these clients before—there was too much to overcome, too much to explain to them, not only simple laws and sanitation and how to cross a street, not only for the body's protection but for the whole spirit. Where was a place where no one needed to tell time, read street signs, work a fixed number of hours, use independent judgment, make a virtue of accuracy, speed, and promptness? All these things were foreign to this man and he was now in an age which extolled them. To what we called our greatest virtue, adaptability, he was woefully blinded by his own culture's call of solidarity, permanence, and personal loyalty to the family. Now, for the welfare agency's inexplicable reason, these differences had to be resolved or waived. "How much does his welfare budget allow him?" Ralph asked.

"Two hundred and ninety dollars a month."

"Do you know anyone who would pay *half* that for this Ramirez' services, sweeping out a store or shining shoes?"

"Couldn't he be a window-washer?"

"With that leg? With that union? Unions are demanding that their workers be high-school graduates, unless there is special pull with someone on the inside."

"But you see—you see, he's taken all this month's check, every penny of it *and he's gone and bought a car!*"

The dimness brightened. Knowledge smiled in the darkness of the mind. So that was it; it was the agency's fear that had to be assuaged, and not this Ramirez' need at all. As much as Ralph hated to accept it, the fear was well-founded. It mattered little that his indigence was not Ramirez' fault, that there was no place for him in the labor market, and that his illiterate self had been replaced by illiterate metal servants needing little food and no holidays. This car and the seven children made Bernardo Ramirez a "relief cheater." It did look bad on paper, although his sin might be nothing worse than poor judgment. Ralph had counseled enough welfare recipients to know that the public brooded over its benevolence like a jealous husband. The acquisition of a single luxury by a single unwed mother or old-age pensioner was enough to ring phones at the welfare office for days, and set off a fusillade of letters to the newspapers. A car—well, that was asking for it!

"You think we can get him into some executive position before the phones start?" Ralph said.

"Can you outrun the wind?" she answered. "We've helped the clients we send to you, haven't we? We give social attention to the cases we refer for training and placement. We give them travel money to and from counseling; we help in every way we can. You know that our budget for these people is minimal. It's written down to the last cent and there's no saving up for a new iron to replace the old one or a new set of dishes to replace the broken ones, not to speak of a new typewriter or set of tools. There's no reward for thrift or for wisdom or for taking in washing, and you know that. All extra income has to be deducted from the following month's check."

"Well . . ."

"Well, Mr. Oakland, we're *still trying* to train and free people, to let money be the incentive it is for everyone else from Joe Doakes to Rockefeller, but we can't afford a scandal! They'll cut us down again—'pork-barrel, 'relief cheaters.' " She was steaming with indignation. It made her look very hearty and young and very affecting, so that Ralph said, "Where did he get the car anyway, one of those bridge salesmen?"

"What?"

"You know, those creeps who can smell a yokel a mile away; they sell roads and bridges and cars. Have you seen the car?"

"I've seen it," she said drily.

"What make is it?"

"Mr. Oakland, we're on the brink of a scandal, as I told you. What make do you think it would be?"

"You win," Ralph said, "bring him over."

"Mr. Oakland, this is Georgia Burns at Boys' Shelter again. I know that you've said you have no room for another boy, but won't you consider Frank Greene, that application I sent you? You will admit that he's a special case . . ."

John Kroll

Ralph was beginning to feel defeated by what had happened because he had taken John's case. He had also begun work with two other very angry and deserted boys, but the clamor of need was for thousands, and the calls alone were cutting into his days. He told the callers again and again that this was a vocational rehabilitation agency. "We don't have the time or the funds for long-term personality counseling. It's not our purpose to breathe motivation, respect for law, and the basic civilized attitudes into institution-broken boys."

One by one, in a hundred different ways, the judges and the parole officers and the social workers and the teachers and the ministers and the doctors had answered: We don't care why you're set up or how your work is done. Train them for Bantu or ballet, if you want, but take them off our files and our consciences. They are a terrifying plague; we want them gone away.

Boy convicts aren't easy to woo, and those raised by agencies and organizations aren't easily convinced by other agencies and other organizations. Facing John again, Ralph wondered who could teach so complicated and cross-cutting a thing as love to boys whose only past rule was the savage and neat expediency of the orphanage and reform school. John was still wearing his fencing demeanor, but he said, "I wasn't kiddin' about learning somethin', gettin' a way to get some dough."

"Well, the first thing is to give you some tests so that we can see what you are naturally best at doing. Then we can train you to be skillful in that thing." He could see John's anger rising in him like a long, slow wave coming up over his head. He could also see that John was having a hard time controlling it. John's hair was very thick and cut in the latest gang style and he was obviously proud of it. Now he took out a comb and began winnowing the whole field, back and back again and again, faster and faster, as his pride, anger, and humiliation took him and left him.

"I ain't havin' none of them stinkin' friggin' tests!" He saw the dictum standing forever, so he gave it again grammatically, to be engraved on the stone slab of Ralph's mind. "I am NOT havin' no stinkin' friggin' test!"

"Why not?"

"I don't want them, that's why. Just give me a O.K. for somethin' to get in."

It was foolish to imagine that a boy with John's intelligence would miss the feeling that the staff at the Shelter thought him stupid and slow. The very dull person is too limited to know just how limited he is; it takes a good grasp of things to gauge the opinions and feelings of others, and Ralph was meeting John's intelligence once again, coming toward him like an enemy on a dark night. The slouch had spoken for John's wariness to play at not caring, the gum for his patient hate, the comb-searching in the tonic-thickened hair for his vanity. So be it, Ralph thought, here goes. He would meet the dark enemy head on.

"John, you know that the school staff thinks you're stupid."

John was measuring Ralph. He made no comment.

"They really do believe you are. I don't. I think you're as smart as the other guys. Who is right, John, are they right or am I?"

"You are," John said. It lacked conviction, but it was his stand and Ralph moved to nail him to it.

"Don't kid me, John. The tests are all against you. Have you been kidding me along here, with these questions you've been asking me? I mean, did someone tell you what to ask to make you look good?"

"No," he said, muttering. He was feeling the nails, feeling 'handled,' but not knowing for what reason, and so he let Ralph go on.

"Then you don't think you're a dummy; you really do think that the people who say so are wrong?"

"I ain't dumb. I ain't no dumber than the other guys."

"Prove it."

"How?" But he knew how; he knew where the nail was biting.

"By taking those tests and showing the scores you should."

John had seen where Ralph was leading him, but to Ralph's surprise, he hadn't pulled too far back. Part of it was the vanity, part perhaps that for some reason John liked him, or at least respected him enough not to want to admit failure to him. Ralph wondered for a minute: Do I like him? No, not at all. He's only familiar, remembered, like 3-Eye Oakland. Could I ever like him? The thought came as a very distant maybe. It was that distance which made Ralph smile.

"Why should I take the stinkin' test anyway?" John said, "just to let you guys figure out who's right and who's wrong?"

"A test is like a dog tag, John. Some people don't think it should be, but nobody has come up with a better way of grouping people for different kinds of training. You take your test and get a certain score on it and unless you can take another test and get a better score, that one grade is on the dog tag and it's just about forever. Low marks keep you from getting training or even being considered for a job in some places. Maybe it shouldn't be that way, John, but it is. It can even change the way people think about you and talk to you."

That rang home. Ralph could see it as if it were a stone striking off the inside of a dark well—down—plink—down—plink—echoing into past years, giving the feeling a name and the name a reason. Then the boy looked up at him. "If the old test says I'm stupid and the creeps at B.S. think so, how come you don't think so too?"

There was no sense in talking about hunches, prickles down the neck, or 3-Eye Oakland. Ralph smiled a little. "I'd like to say it's because I'm the smartest guy in town, but I'm afraid that's not the way it is. I think you did it, John. You opened up a little, just enough to let me find out that what was inside wasn't stupid; it was mean, maybe, wrong, maybe, but not stupid. I gave you your answer, now what about it?"

"This test—what's in it for you, if I'm not stupid?"

"A promotion."

John winked. "Hey, if I take the friggin' test and you get to be a big shot, I could come back and get something fixed up if I wanted."

"Like a job," Ralph said.

"Where do you take these lousy tests?"

"Right down the hall. Two doors."

"You comin'?"

"I'll call ahead; I have to stay here. This is going to be your baby, John, your own baby, all the way."

"Guys with brains make more dough, don't they?"

"Sure they do; look at *me.*"

"Jeeee-sus!"

When he went to lunch Ralph saw John reclining in the far corner of the cafeteria with a sandwich. Martenson came through the line and walked over to where Ralph was opening the lunch he always brought from home.

"Tell you one thing about that kid," he said and sat down beside Ralph—he went through his routine of spooning four spoons of sugar into his coffee, something that always made Ralph feel slightly queasy—"foul mouth. Foulest mouth I ever heard."

"Well," Ralph was irritated at having to defend "his boy," "remember he's grown up with that kind of talk. I think he uses it more for effect than anything else."

Fatika had come up and put down his coffee. He spoke to Martenson, but he was looking at Ralph.

"You're a professional man, Ernie, you don't have to put up with blasphemous talk. It takes away from the dignity of the agency."

"The talk is seldom blasphemous," Ralph said. "Obscene, but not blasphemous."

"I don't think that's very funny, Ralph, because you know as well as I that a moral evil like that is a sin against God also."

"Looking over the Ten Commandments, Bill, I haven't found any orders against taking the name of sexual intercourse in vain."

"You accept this, you molly-coddle these—loafers and delinquents; that's the point, Ralph, and it's very funny, but then you've lost the separation between good and evil, between filth and decency."

"I guess I have, Bill, the line's been drawn and re-drawn so many times."

"Not even you can believe that. Even *you* would admit that there are certain moral *truths,* certain *eternal* truths."

"Oh, but they're all staked out, Bill, those truths are *owned!* The churches tell us what they are and what they aren't. It's a good, solid corporation, the Church, and it wants its interpretation of Truth to last forever; and so it doesn't really want the shares to be bought up by the poor and unfit any more. It wants to be solvent and strong. I don't blame it, but I wish that it hadn't lost its sense of humor."

"What?"

"The one thing that could renew that kid is something he's never experienced: Fun. I think that the Forces of Virtue could win him over if the jokes were good enough."

"Fun or not, Ralph, if you want that hoodlum to get anywhere, he'll have to learn that 'lousy' and 'friggin' are not universal modifiers," Martenson said.

Fatika was on the verge of noting that lessons in manners and speech were not part of a vocational rehabilitation counselor's job, and Ralph could almost see him thinking it, but Fatika had been a counselor as long as Ralph, and he had been inured to the presence of the line, that line past which no one went. Ralph saw this also, and so they both stopped and smiled a little, each one the winner. Ralph thought about Robert Frost's poem, and the line about fences and neighbors. Those fences of silence made agency talks tedious and cautious, but damn the tedious and cautious men; they were right.

Martenson eased the presence of the fence for them. "Well, he's getting along through testing and that's the important thing. Hey, you guys, see the special on T.V. last night?"

A voice, scholarly and hesitating: "Mr. Oakland, I'm Dr. Campbell, pastor of St. Thomas' Church."

Don't tell me, he needs a program for the re-training of wealthy juvenile delinquents! (—St. Thomas was in a very good neighborhood.) He tried to move past the anti-clerical undergowth in his mind as the well-modulated voice continued.

"I've heard of your work. I have had occasion to speak with one of your associates, although only in the most general terms; as I understand, the information which I propose to divulge is to be held in the strictest confidence. Do I understand correctly?"

"What?" Ralph blurted. He could sense an anguish in the voice, but the syntax had trapped him somewhere in the thorn bush of the second sentence.

"I fear I am not making myself clear. Might it not be possible for you to come to see me at my study. I have a matter of some delicacy to discuss."

"I'd be pleased to see you, Doctor, but I seldom make appointments for home visits unless the client is bedridden."

He felt summoned and he didn't like it, nor did he like the implication that the minister's time was more valuable than his, or was the annoyance part of his bias, thickening again?

"Oh, I see," the Pastor said. "I have a full schedule today, but perhaps tomorrow morning . . ."

"I'm sorry, Dr. Campbell, but the earliest open time I have is the half-hour between 10:30 and 11:00 on the 13th; that's two weeks from this Thursday. I could see you in my office then, if you wish."

"Oh—of course—I see . . ." The voice had suddenly gone old. It was being made halt by an anguish that was almost palpable now in the earpiece of the telephone. "This matter—this matter concerns others as well as myself. I will have to—I will have to discuss it with them. Would it be possible to call you tomorrow?"

"Doctor, does this have to do with some of your parishioners or is it a family matter?" The misery in the voice he was hearing humbled Ralph. He realized also that a Pastor of St. Thomas' had easy access to influential people. He could have come to Ralph through the mayor or even the governor, but he had not chosen to take those ways, and Ralph felt better for the directness of the approach.

"It is a family matter entirely and it is for this reason that I wish to keep it as private as possible. A minister is in many ways a public figure, and every facet of his private life is judged and commented upon. Therefore, if you could possibly . . ."

All right! All right! Ralph thought. He couldn't stand to listen to that voice telling and planning as if it were trying to fight an awful moan of pain at the same time. "Doctor, you seem to be in great distress. I'm through here at five. I could see you after that at St. Thomas. It won't be out of my way."

"I will be waiting for you there," the voice said. "We are most—grateful."

John Kroll was through with his tests earlier than Ralph had expected, and the four letters he had to dictate were simpler. Perhaps because of this, he had a sense of foreboding about his little extra trip. Something was coming. Something bad was coming. He left the office five minutes early and found that the flow of traffic was all the other way. His street was almost clear. Something very big and very bad.

The neighborhood was quiet and stable, dignified and green-lawn-tended. The church was square as a tombstone, solid, substantial, and no-nonsense. It seemed to symbolize Christ Ressurected as a Vested Interest. When Ralph went in through the side door, he saw that the area before the sanctuary was part of a corridor and the Pastor's study was to the right, marked by a sign. The Pastor came out then and they looked at one another until the dry, suffering voice asked, "Mr. Oakland?"

Then they murmured the self-easing, situation-easing small talk about traffic problems and the recent turn of the planet into its new season.

But the Pastor's study was his stronghold and the words had to be put. When he stood in the middle of his room, he turned to Ralph and said, "I don't want anyone to know. A minister's questions are weighed by everyone in his congregation and judged as if he stood apart from the common human confusions. My brother-in-law is—is *ill*. I wanted to learn if there is any hope for him in this—this illness.

The waste of time pulled Ralph down like an anchor. "I'm not a medical doctor," he said, "you'll have to take this up with someone who . . ."

"No, you don't understand!" Dr. Campbell said, and gestured the words away from his ear, violently, in the frustrated rage of an eloquent man suddenly unable to make himself understood. "I know that I have been slow—let me tell you, please, what has happened."

Ralph found that he was standing almost in front of a chair. He stepped back and sat down and took his patience away from Time and let go.

"My sister's husband is—was a professor of biology. He was a competent man, very sound always, and proud of keeping up his body. He was forty-six last year . . ." He caught himself in the drift away from due north and the cold regions. "You see, his memory began to fail and it failed so slightly at first and so gradually that we deluded ourselves for a while with pleasant jokes about the abesent-minded professor. But it was not a joke, because soon he began to forget parts of his lectures and then more and more, and then one day I looked at him and heard him speak and wondered how he ever could have been a professor. We got him to see a doctor and then specialists, one, two, three. They were very kind. They told us what the disease *was*, but they couldn't seem to be able to tell us what it *meant* to him and to us. Gerald sits in the house, idle and miserable day after day. He cannot reason or remember as an intelligent man, but could there not be some simple training for some simple job? He wishes still to be of value somewhere in the world. He has begged me to help him. I could not; I haven't the knowledge, but you would know what possibilities there are."

Ralph said very gently, "Did the doctors tell you the name of this disease?"

"Yes, it is called Alkheimer's disease."

If I had met traffic this afternoon, Ralph thought, if John Kroll had cut and run, if I hadn't begun to like this Campbell in spite of myself this afternoon, then it wouldn't have been Alkheimer's disease. What silly thoughts come when you are useless. Now it's going to be my turn to blunder around for a way of saying the thing I have to say, because it's Alkheimer's, a progressive disease. It will get worse and worse and will result in death, but only after a long time of death in the mind, the will, the spirit. The physical death will be the death of a vegetable. There is no training, no job, no hope, no nothing.

"Dr. Campbell, I am not a neurologist. In our work we are not allowed to give medical prognoses, but I will tell you what the books say and what our agency's policy is regarding this disease. The sickness is known by several names, but what it comes down to is that the effects are of those of premature—aging."

"You mean senility, don't you?"

"Yes, Doctor, I do."

"Then he will not recover."

"No, sir."

"But he will get progressively worse."

"The probability is that he will. Occasionally, plateaus are reached in the progress of the disease . . ."

The doctor turned away. "We—we will know what to do now," he said. "You see, we have watched him, waiting for any sign this way or that, which way the disease would go. Why didn't the doctors tell us?"

"Many doctors feel that such information is beyond the scope of their profession, not part of diagnosis or treatment. The labor market or the capacity of a man in that regard isn't their job either."

"They allowed us to live in false hope, waiting for a recovery."

"Are you sure that the hope wasn't your conclusion? There are many doctors who never see people in working situations and just don't know how a disease will affect a person's

87

capacity to do ordinary work. For all we know, your physician might have imagined some temporary, rudimentary job for your brother-in-law."

"Would there be some hobby, some pastime for which he could be trained?"

"I hope so, Dr. Campbell. If you wish, we'll test him in the office. He is ineligible for our program, since it is vocational and because of the nature of the illness, but we will always act as advisors in any way we can."

"You see," the Pastor said, "he still has enough mind to want to . . ." The realization showed in his eyes. He said very quietly, "That will go, too, won't it? Now it is such an awful, such a restless hunger. He knows he's lost a universe; the thought torments him, although he cannot quite remember what was in that universe that he lost. Will the torment go?"

"By all the evidence we have."

"Thank God!" The Pastor was close to tears now, and Ralph wanted to go, freeing him for whatever he needed to do. "Thank you for coming, Mr. Oakland. we suddenly just had to know, and you've given us freedom to make our plans. Good-bye, and thank you again. We won't be in for tests, I think. We will be able to help him here, in our own way, knowing . . ." As Ralph left the room, the voice broke behind him in its last words, "Because, you see, I was so very fond of him . . ."

Ralph went home, having to follow the heaviest traffic. He felt as sad for himself as he did for the Pastor and his family. Why did he stay with this work? Of all the work in the world, this was the most vitiating, the most frightening. The garbage collector sees man's filth and refuse; the surgeon cuts away fetid growths and diseased tissue; but Ralph and his fellows were called to witness, over and over, the ruin that could lay a man low in an eye blink, the mysterious erasure of his identity, suddenly, out of nowhere. Calamity was Ralph's profession, and he was too often frightened, as he went through his days, each one a lifetime of witnessing all of the possible horrors which can descend on a human being. This Pastor's brother-in-law, a man like himself, reduced in a few years to a mindless vegetable—reason: unknown. That was another horror, that there was no way of care or health or wealth or discretion which might prevent so many of these lightning bolts. I am no better than he, Ralph thought, no more deserving or careful. It could happen to me—to me—

88

good God, that disease or any of those diseases could happen to me! Every day Ralph saw a score of men and women on whom these lightning bolts had fallen. There were so many of them that it seemed commonplace, that ruin. How long could his life run on unblasted, and his wife's and his children's? He pulled his car out of the endless beetle chain of commuters, over to the curb, raised his arms on the steering wheel and closed his eyes over his tears.

John Kroll's tests were in. They had been counted, scored, graded, checked, and cross-checked, and the package, garlanded with an extra little ribbon of statistics, was waiting in Ralph's IN box. He picked it up, looked, laughed, and called Georgia Burns at Boys' Shelter. "Our boy's I.Q. tests are here."

"I told you it was just a waste of time," she said, "his scores here were never more than 60."

"You should get that place off the hill, then. Altitude's too high, not enough pressure on the brain. Down here he cracked an 89."

"But that's *impossible*."

"Why, impossible? Don't you think my influence is stimulating?"

"Not that stimulating," she said, "a moron doesn't suddenly decide to stop being a moron."

"That's just the point; this one did. Why do we assume that everyone *cares* about the damn tests as much as we do. We already know that average kids placed in loving and interesting foster homes do better on I.Q. tests than they did in their old environments. We already know that mentally ill people fluctuate all over the graphs from one day to another. Why do we keep saying that I.Q. shows *inherent* capacity?"

"I see I'm treading on an old and cherished corn," she said. "You weren't kidding about the tests, were you?"

"I'm not kidding at all, and I think our boy could do better than 89 when he gets the confidence."

"All right, Mr. Oakland, you've got a normal boy on your hands. How are you going to keep him on your program?"

"I'm going to play your game. He's down on the records as 60, and 60 he will stay until he gets his training and his job. Suddenly, it'll turn out that we were holding the paper upside down and it was 90 after all. All I really wanted this test for was to see just how wide I could open the world to this kid.

We can get him trained for almost any trade on the strength of the second test, but the books will have to carry the first test results temporarily."

"But, that's—well, to put it charitably—it's moving things."

"As long as the laws are arbitrary and the tests entirely too arbitrary, I'm going to try to put as much bend in them as they will take. John Kroll has just flown the twenty-nine points from midnight to morning. I think that's worth something. His choices of job and future have multiplied one hundred times."

"Does it really mean that," she said, "or have we just found out that he's a smarter thief than we thought or a smoother liar or a more well-rounded rapist? You know, he's never shown a sign to one of us that he has any capacity for loyalty or friendship or caring. Mr. Oakland, that boy didn't *scare* me at 60, but he's beginning to scare me at 89."

"Look, Miss Burns ..."

"Call me Georgia."

"Call me Ralph. Look, Georgia, let's face it. No matter what heights he aspires to, he'll never be a Willy Sutton."

Ralph looked at John Kroll's record again. It was petty stuff—shoplifting, truancy, joyriding, picking pockets. He bullied smaller boys at the Shelter and extorted money from them when he could. The frightening thing seemed to be something more than the petty little offenses. It was noted again and again on the official sheets that counted and tabulated the misery of public charges whose bread and beans were given them by the state. It was a quality of coldness they noted, an unfeeling isolation in his own body and mind. Most state boys were impulsive. Most of the time it was their overwhelmingly impulsive acts that landed them under the roof at Boys' in the first place. John was impulsive, too, but without the joy or hunger or passion that makes the sudden act understandable. He seemed oddly removed in feeling from the things he did. It was written of him by some half-legible supervisor at one of the orphanages: "This boy has no pal, no gang, no companion. He seems to wish none. No one has ever expressed a liking for him."

Ralph wondered if training and a trade could matter. The easy clients were those hungering to work. When he read articles in magazines blasting "Modern Middle-class Materialism," he would wonder why people wished to divest the culture of the strongest lever it had to inculcate the hard

90

work and high living standards of which it was proud. Ownership was the trump card that Ralph played to his unmotivated clients. We work to earn; we earn to buy. On this same philosophy the blind tailor could be retrained to earn money for his son's college education and the unwilling gang kid could learn the trade that supported his hot rod. The call that had made John Kroll ask for training was not self-respect, pride in craft, love of honest labor, or the urgings of a secret vocation, but the old, crass call of the good life and the yellow car. If only that want would hold against the hundred sudden assults of sudden urging.

When he saw John again, Ralph gave him the good news and received, as he had expected, no reaction whatever. In order to show John what the difference would mean to him, Ralph had listed the jobs and training programs for a man in the 80-95 group. It was an impressive difference, and the boy had to struggle against his rising pride. "There's a hitch, though," Ralph said. "All the better jobs on the list demand something else."

"What's that?" The guarded tough guy came back, waiting for failure as if its familiarity was loved.

"High school, a certificate that you've had training equal to high school."

"You mean go to school? You know, hey you know they have school at B.S. and what it is, is you sit with kids eleven, twelve years old. Well, the law says you don't have to finish, even if you're in stir, and I just walked out, see. No, man, no more school. Nope!" He muttered something else under his breath.

"I wasn't thinking of that," Ralph said, "I was thinking of another way. The schools have set up a special kind of thing for people who have had to quit the regular school or who never went. It's a deal that works you toward passing the equivalency test and getting a certificate. They have two sessions, a day one and an evening one; and, believe me, you'll be younger than most of the people taking it."

"I ain't goin' to no damn, lousy stinkin' school. I won't take no school."

"Oh, for God's sake, John, look at the difference!" And Ralph shoved the sheet across his desk again. "You've never stuck at anything. Do you think anybody wants to hire someone like that? You're too old for kid jobs and you still do kid thinking. Without that certificate, that promise that you can work your way through *something,* you've got all the chance of a baby in a shark tank. Do you want to leave Boys' Shelter or just make it step one to the big reunion at Boys' State? Aiming for the top spot: Old Timer in the pen? How do you want your time, John, using it or serving it? It's up to you, John, the yellow car or milking cows up at the prison farm."

"Take it easy, Oakland—(That was Marlon Brando, and rather effective.)—what the hell . . ." He got up and took a candy bar from his pocket. "I'll think it over." He peeled the wrapper from the candy with elaborate care—(That was Edward G. Robinson with a cigar, somewhere). He took a large bite and ambled away, savoring the chocolate and the impression he was making.

Two days later Georgia Burns called. "We're amazed at the change in John Kroll. Of course, from the beginning we gave his work with you first priority . . ."

"I wouldn't get excited over any change in that kid," Ralph said. "Did he say anything special to you?"

"Why, yes, I thought you knew. He said that he was going to enroll in the high-school certification class as soon as possible. He even called up and got all the information about it so that he could apply right away. The new class has just started, but it's set up so that he can come in any time and go at his own pace. He told me that he wants to go full time, too, the whole six-day week and from nine to three. Don't you . . ."

"Tilt," Ralph said.

"What? Oh, you think it's too long a day, just starting out. So do I . . ."

"No, I mean *tilt.* You know, lights flashing, bells. Your boy's not hungry for knowledge. He just wants to shake his dough back out of the machine. It just so happens that day classes at the school are *five* days a week, *nine to twelve.* That gives our lover of learning three hours every day and a whole extra day Saturday away from the Shelter on a valid pass."

"Oh, dear!"

"What hurts me is that he didn't even think we would bother to check."

"Well, we both know now, don't worry. Will you break the sad news to John or do you want me to do it, or someone else

92

here at the Shelter? Do you still want him to take training after what's happened?"

"I'll tell him," Ralph said. "Send him in and I'll let him know that we both know what he tried to pull. If he wants to continue on the plan, fine, but it will have to be on our terms. By the way, Georgia, does he have any money? I mean do you give him any extra to come out here?"

"Oh, no, the law is clear on that. We just give bus tokens."

"Then he has no other money of his own?"

"None to be used away from the Shelter without permission, which he doesn't have. Boys are allowed to spend chore money only at the Shelter, but John never worked that hard. Why, is anything wrong?"

"No, just curious," Ralph said.

"Well, I don't hold out much hope that he'll accept the school now, but . . ."

Ralph hung up the phone. Ever since the outlawing of the gum, Ralph had seen John coming and going with a candy bar half-eaten in his hand and one or two on call in his back pocket. It was part of the contest between them. Ralph had vetoed gum-chewing during the sessions, so John ate candy right before and right after. The attitude that prompted this little struggle of the spirit against the letter was one thing, but where was he getting the money for that candy?

8

Bernardo Ramirez

Ralph was sitting opposite Bernardo Ramirez, the car-owner, and he was trying to remember where he had seen him before. When the association came, it had to be forgotten quickly, because it wasn't going to do them any good. Sancho Panza, in the flesh, hardly an asset to any work that Ralph was going to do with this Scourge of the Welfare Department. The great face was gentle, passive, and patient, but the old farm clothes had given way to a kind of Hawaiian-American madness. His shirt was yellow, and on it great orchids were fighting their way around his huge girth in a pattern. His belt was cinched tightly; its leather only a complaining band, barely forestalling an imminent explosion that would burst the black-and-white houndstooth trousers. All the planes of him were rounded and slack, and but for the gravely innocent face that rose from the raucous violence of his outfit, he would have reminded Ralph of a pratfall artist in a comedy show. He had two blood-red handkerchiefs with which he wiped his face from time to time. The welfare worker who had brought Bernardo left and went to sit outside, and then Ralph told Bernardo about rehabilitation and asked him what work he had done before his leg had been injured. The questions were answered shyly, in very slow English and with a very heavy accent. The John Krolls were angry and wouldn't be hired, and this Bernardo wasn't angry, and who would hire him? Every agency got plenty of hopeless cases. Workers wanted to get rid of them in order to get to the cases where they could do some good; and now Ralph feet he was a stop on the route, shoving incapables along helplessly. He sighed and went on with the interview.

Bernardo's clothes were lying about him. He was a gentle,

timid person, respectful and polite, and he seemed not to be bitter about anything that had happened to him. Ralph kept feeling the word *accepting* as he spoke and listened. Bernardo accepted work, no work, strength, weakness, all that was and was not. Acceptance was a virtue, a pearl of great price to all of his feudal generations. It grew layer by layer every year. His people called it wisdom. In this city and time it would count for nothing; it would defeat him, brand him coward, and compromise him in the eyes of his children. Ralph asked him how his leg was, and he looked at it without emotion and said that the doctor had fixed it and had told him that he must keep his weight off it except for short periods. There was no sense of sorrow or bewilderment in the statement, as there usually was when the expectations of men had been changed with suddenness and violence; he was only repeating the doctor's words, like a dutiful child. Ralph asked his "saving" question. He always asked it—often when he did, people were able to look out over their sicknesses and see into a possible world where there were still choices. "Is there anything you ever dreamed of doing, anything you have always *wanted* to do?"

"Oh, yase—keepeen' de family."

"I mean any work that you want to do."

Ramirez said nothing, and Ralph saw that the question was beyond him.

He decided to give Bernardo the intelligence tests himself. There was a test specially made for illiterates and supposedly free of cultural overtones. He suspected that the results would be woefully poor. Culture-free tests don't seem to take into account the many cultures which put no credence in tests or testing. Perhaps Bernardo would do well on it; Ralph looked at him and doubted it. There he sat, passive amid the orchids. Ralph knew that for good or evil he and the everyman in this time and city yearned toward something. The striving, hardworking people about him had been taught to build their desires far out beyond the present reach, and then to extend that reach. Did this man yearn, and if he did, toward what?

He tried again. "Mr. Ramirez, what would you *like* to do here in the city? Have you ever stopped somewhere for a moment and watched a man at work and thought that you would like to be that man and do that work?"

Ramirez looked at him so strangely that Ralph knew it had never occurred to him. How different we are, we two Americans, Ralph thought. Choice had always seemed second nature to him. Somehow he and his friends had spent most of their childhoods casting and re-casting themselves in grown-up parts. He remembered those games and the parents asking and asking again what did he want to be when he grew up. It was a game that had continued with him and his friends, deepening with their experience, so that they began, in a sense, to be job-hunting before they were even in their teens. He could remember even now, looking at the doctor who gave him his shots, at his teacher spelling out a word, at a plumber twisting his wrench against a pipe, and inhabiting their lives for a moment; what would it be like to be a teacher, a plumber, a doctor? Would I be happy doing these things? Was it in such dreams that action began, that dedication began, that choice began? Bernardo Ramirez had never been trained to dream such dreams.

He only looked at Ralph with his helpless unhurried look. "I wan keepeen' de family."

The week coming up was not too heavy. Ralph went to get the social worker to set up time for testing. As he motioned to her, his eye wandered out to the wall behind her. There on a board hung the lists of jobs and job descriptions phoned in to the agency that month which they hadn't been able to fill: electronic technician, laboratory technician, chemist, t.v. repairman, legal secretary. Knowledge and training. Everybody was begging for people with knowledge and training; and on the other side of the scale were as many hundreds of un-skilled laborers clamoring for the ever-shrinking number of simple physical labor jobs.

The social worker came in and they made an appointment for the test. Ralph thought that she gave him a special glance over the head of their charge. One had an idea of what an American was. Words like independent, fortunate, optimistic, and freedom-loving were conjured in the mind with the shocking ease that shows how blind love is. Bernardo's ances-tors had been farming and enduring in this land long before the Battle of Bunker Hill, yet he was a foreigner and his was not the "American way." Magazine writers kept crying for diversity and nonconformists, but Bernardo Ramirez was too embarrassing a reminder of what that diversity might really mean.

"When you come back next week," Ralph said, "we will give you this test to see what you do best and how we can help you."

Bernardo nodded gently. "De welfare pay good" he said, "you cou' fine job pay good like da?"

The caseworker gave a small shrug and sent a quick glance again to Ralph. The hell of it was, of course, that Bernardo was right. His payments were scheduled to the family's barest needs and not to the price his services could bring. He could not compete; he could not hope to find a job in this civilization; and his name was legion.

"Mr. Oakland, the Child Care Conference is lining up speakers for the new season and we wanted to know if you would speak on the problems of juvenile delinquents . . ."

"Mr. Oakland, we want you on the panel next month when the National Rehabilitation Conference has its convention in Houston. It's a four-day workshop on Problems of Vocational Rehabilitation . . ."

"Well, my problem right now in rehabilitation is lack of time to serve my clients. I appreciate the honor, but I'm booked up solid with appointments."

"But—but the national and regional chairmen will be there . . ."

"Then why not ask the administrators of our program? I'm sure they will be glad to go . . ."

"We have all the administrators we need. It was thought that someone actually *working* with the clients *directly* would be able to give another viewpoint . . ."

"I don't think I could bring anything new to . . ."

"Well, Mr. Oakland, your supervisors don't agree. They have cleared your time to attend this conference. It's important we all make a good showing."

"What about the showing I make with my clients?"

"But aren't there always enough of *them?*"

"Hell, Mr. Oakland, it's National Health Week, and we thought you might like to attend our club's luncheon and tell us a little about what you do . . ."

"Say, Ab, I was wondering if you knew anyone who would be free enough to go to that damn conference in Houston instead of me."

"Not me, not Fatika, or anyone I know. You're elected, Ralph old boy, it's orders from upstairs."

"Do any of these workshops, conferences, jamborees, din-

97

ners, luncheons, breakfasts, clambakes, committees, rallies, roundups, and balls do any good? Do they get jobs for anyone?"

"Who knows? I guess they keep the agency in people's minds."

"How much, Ab? As much as a single paraplegic worker doing a good job in a single office?"

"It's part of the way things are, Ralph—and it gives you a chance to swap ideas. It's for you, too; you could get seen by a lot of big people, Ralph."

"It's a cinch I won't be seeing the small ones."

"Mr. Oakland, the National Arthritis Association is meeting in your city for a week-long workshop, whose subject will be The Place of the Arthritic in American Life. We would like you to address our group and also to sit on the panel for a discussion of ..."

To: THE MEMBERSHIP COMMITTEE OF THE NATIONAL RE-HABILITATION CONFERENCE WORKSHOP.

Dear Sirs: (Why do they want *me?* What do these things do anyway?) This is to confirm my attendance at your Workshop Sept. 18-21. (Agencies looking at other agencies, statistics looking at other statistics.) I will also be happy to be on the panel for the discussion of *The Counselor Looks at Rehabilitation.* (What am I kicking about? Houston, they'll pay my expenses. Nice hotel, a vacation.) I am also enclosing the application form in duplicate, containing all relevant material on my education and work history. (Does anyone read those damn things? Why do I hate all of this? "Our boys," local, state, and national—I want to tell them that they care more for the perpetuation of their agencies and the doubling of their benefits than for service to the clients. Service. Isn't service supposed to be the reason for the agency's existence?) I hope that I may contribute usefully to the Conference and also benefit from it. Sincerely (Damn, damn!),

Ralph Oakland.

"Ralph, this is Bill. Say, those posters are in and I wanted to let you know that they're in my office. We're giving seventy-five to each man. They're real nice this year; they're about three feet long and they have a full-color picture of the Handicapped Man of the Year, full-color! That should really get the attention. I always give mine to Doris and she gets 'em in the store windows where she trades ..."

"This is Mr. Selwyn. I'm program chairman for the Big Brothers. About your work in juvenile delinquency ..."

John Kroll

John sat in Ralph's office looking neater than Ralph had ever seen him. His hands were clean and he was wearing the starched white shirt that the Shelter allowed its boys who were taking work or training on the outside. "You said you wanted to see me before I got started in that school dump."

"John, I think there's something you should know. I called the school."

"Yeah?" His face showed no change.

"Yeah." Ralph answered him with a little bit of 3-Eye's quiet archness. "They told me about the classes. Nine to twelve, John, that's three hours. Monday through Friday, that's five days, John."

"Oh, no Saturday? Funny, I thought they had 'em on Saturday, too."

"No Saturday," Ralph said.

"Yeah? Well, o.k., it gives me some time off." A little smile overcame him. He had tried to hold it back, but it beat him to the end of his comment, and hung there after he had finished. Under the smile was a grimace of hate that he had been caught.

Ralph felt impatience rising in him. "Didn't you think we would check with the school? Didn't you think that Miss Burns and I would check with one another? You're not stupid, John"—(the boy's eyes flicked up to Ralph's face and Ralph saw a hard hatred there)—"I'll say it again. You're not stupid. Right now you're sorry you let me prove you weren't stupid, because now I'm not letting you get away with it. It looks to you like a good thing you had going there. You were too dumb to work, too dumb to learn; it was great, wasn't it? Well, remember that along with the soft life and the sweet setup, you had to take a lot of people laughing at you. You had to take being treated like a dummy."

"Aw, hell, you can't blame a guy for tryin'! I wanted to get out sometimes and have some fun. What's wrong with that?"

"Fun is what you earn, John, *after* work. You put in some time on those books and then we'll talk about fun." Ralph didn't want to go picking away at too many things, but he felt compelled somehow to ask about the candy. Even now he saw three chocolate bars stacked in John's breast pocket, where he could get to them without one moment's pause between desire and gratification. "Where did you get those candy bars?"

"Oh, these? They're mine."

"I mean, where did you get the money for them? Miss Burns tells me that you're given bus tokens to get here and back to the Shelter, and nothing more. There aren't supposed to be any extras."

"Jeez, you birds don't give a guy a *chance*, do you. You aught to be in the cops."

John tried to relax back in the chair like James Cagney at his ease. It didn't come off. "I didn't have no money. I stole 'em. You got to steal if you don't have no money, even *you* aught to figger that. I stole 'em off of that blind guy you got outside."

Ralph stopped and listened to his own shocked silence. Across from him sat his client, picking at something under his thumbnail. Down the corridor, the agency's Blind Unit had one of its men set in a candy and cigarette concession, which served the whole office building. Ralph had passed it going to and from his office every day, and he had come not to notice much or to remember the blindness of the man who made change for him so quickly.

"You stole from that man?"

"Aw, hell, he don't know the difference."

Ralph was engulfed in an overwhelming rage. He was suddenly not Society's Representative, a professional man trained in the objective and dispassionate reaches of his science. He was only himself and furious. He got up stiffly and went around his desk to where the dead-faced zombie was posing for him, seeming to wait for nothing more than one of the standard professional responses ("What made you feel that you had to do this?"). But Ralph's rage was not careful. He went toward John with his hands trembling, and he lifted John out of his chair with a strength he had forgotten he had.

"Move."

"Where?"

100

"Outside."

They walked out of the office past the secretaries and clients, tight-faced and rigid, and they headed down the corridor. Ralph still holding John's arm in a tight grip. They headed toward the concession stand where John would put the candy back and make his apologies and be confronted, for once, with his victim's anguish and wrath instead of the indirect and impersonal wrath of police and judges. But the blind man wasn't there. The stand was closed. John looked at Ralph, half attempting a smirk of triumph, and Ralph gritted his teeth and steered John around the corner to another corridor. He was in a cold rage. He turned John against the wall, and in his anger pressed him up against it until the boy was lifted off the floor. Ralph heard his voice coming very low into John's face.

"If I ever see you or hear of you taking anything, stealing from that man, causing trouble for someone who can't fight back, I'm going to beat you to a pulp, you little bastard!" He looked hard into the face, and John's eyes, which had measured Ralph's strength once, did so again. His bravado failed him and left him almost in tears. Ralph let him go and he found his footing and stood. "Now get out!"

John left, going back into the main corridor and muttering in a soft, whining voice.

Ralph felt his anger leaving him and giving way to a tired feeling of defeat at the hands of his professional judgment. (This boy is a *client*. It's unthinkable—that a counselor—that I should threaten a *client* ...) If he believed in anything it was in the aims of his profession, but it had taken only a second to throw all the training and belief and objectivity away without even missing its absence in the movements of his mind and the obedience of his body.

He walked back to his office and sat down in the chair where the clients sat, and felt a little uncomfortable as he realized that they faced him over a desk littered with official papers that catalogued in meticulous detail the agonies of hundreds of others. (To fail—all right, everyone fails sometime—but to fail so easily, to lose so much and not even miss it! Yes, sir, it's my philosophy of life, my whole definition of my life's work, and I just mislaid it around here *someplace*— where *did* it get to? Oh, yes, there it is behind the desk. See, I told you it was right here. . . .)

The phone rang and Ralph picked it up, listened, and

answered. Another call, a letter to write immediately. He knew that if he didn't really believe that people, regardless of their race, creed, or state-of-grace, were worthy of the best efforts of The Department of Rehabilitation and Ralph Oakland, counselor, he'd damn well better get out and get out fast. It was possible, too, that John would take this decision out of his hands. It might delight him to destroy Ralph as hated Authority without even having to lie. On second thought, John wouldn't squeal, no. But not before Ralph had an eye-blink picture of himself facing John down with, "It's his word against mine." Down two. No, John wouldn't report him. The little punk's own personal vanity would keep him quiet. To inform would be to admit that a square, middle-aged pen-pusher could lift him and let him drop without so much as a quickened breath. But—this same pride might make John track him and lay for him with the sawed-off home-made gun he'd occasionally bragged about. They had descended in a long moment of rage, and Ralph was in John's world now, where John's way was familiar. Now his laws, not Ralph's, applied. (I thought I liked this work because of what it stands for—damn it! Can't a man be angry for society, for the blind man, for the waste of all the hours and all the money on this boy? The truth is he doesn't belong on a vocational program; he isn't even retarded. However you look at it, he isn't retarded; he's made me live by his rules, and every time I have a session with him he's made me hold up my middle-class life to him and his cynical judging eye, all my steady, rule-obeying, law-enduring compromises. He's looked them over and called me a hypocrite and the punk has been proven right! When something angers that Lover of Law and Order, when something threatens the little woman or the big mortgage or the lavender-scented beliefs, I am as much an animal as anyone from B.S. or the state pen, and just as quick.)

Ralph went out into the waiting room for the next client, and went on interviewing through the day, looking at test scores, planning with people in other agencies, talking to potential employers. He was working in a kind of trough of drudgery, depressed by the misery and defeat that were the common possession of all his clients, and where the tragic and bizarre were nothing special. In the late afternoon Georgia Burns called.

"I saw John Kroll just now," she said.

"Oh, yes," he said.

"I don't know how you did it; I was sure that your catching him in that lie about the time of his classes would end his interest in education for good. He came in and said that it was all set, and I just—well I just don't know what you said to him, but if you remember it I'd like to have it bottled."

Ralph thanked her and hung up and leaned back, tapping his pencil against his teeth. (I wonder what he has in mind, our eager scholar. I wonder if he's going to try to blackmail me, for money or my influence or extra passes from B.S. for a few hours every week. Or am I wrong? Could he have been trying the whole business in that damn dumb wrongheaded way of his to get something familiar to happen to him? God knows, it's a new self all at once. The truant, the moron, the nothing boy has suddenly become somebody's bright hope. Burns is sure to have told him that their future training plans at the Shelter partly depend on him. Suddenly he's not a moron any more at all. Something about the way he stole that candy—so blatant—four or five bars sticking out of his pocket. Could it be possible that he was trying to find a believable old John Kroll, the punk, the loser, just to get his bearings? As if he were goading me, doing the worst thing or the thing that would get me most angry, so that I would beat him up—no. I'm trying to find the good in what I did, but it won't justify. It won't stand up right. But yet . . .)

The blind man was back when Ralph went out to make an on-the-job call on his way home. Ralph crept up to where the man sat, staring over the rows of carefully arranged cigarettes and candy. He noticed that he was terrified, that his heart was quick and his mouth dry. Trying as hard as he could not to seem furtive, Ralph slipped two fifty-cent pieces on the pile of newspapers that stood in front of the counter. Then he crept away.

Dear Mr. Okeland,

I am writing this to thank you for helping my son, Alan Devereaux to get work where he has been working. He has been there for a month and gets good money and he is not worrying now. He told me it was a big insult to you trying to give you the twenty $. He found it out and he told me it was wrong. So I am writing this to apologize to you and forgive

103

me because I didn't know it was wrong. Thank you for helping us and God Bless you. I remember you in my prayers every night.

Yours,
Mrs. M. Devereaux

Andrea Colvin

Andrea was looking at the sunshine making a square on the floor. Mommy and Daddy were very angry. They were not angry at her, they had told her so; and they were not angry at each other; but they still weren't talking to each other, only a little, every few minutes they would say something about why they were angry so they wouldn't forget it until the man came. Then a secretary came. Andrea remembered that she was going to be a secretary. Secretaries always smiled and looked nice. The secretary said; "I'm sorry, but if you have no appointment he won't be able to see you unless one of his regular clients is late."

"Well, we don't *want* an appointment. What we have to say will just take a minute," Mommy said.

Andrea smiled at the secretary. After a long, long time a man came out. He was getting ready to go away because he walked like it. Then he stopped and came toward them and said, "You're Mr. and Mrs. Colvin? I'm sorry, but I have to go to a hospital appointment and I'm late. If you would make an appointment . . ."

Then Daddy got up and said the same thing Mommy said to the secretary. "Well, we don't want an appointment. What we have to say will just take a minute."

Then Mommy stood up. "We're here to protest the high-handed way this business has been carried on."

Andrea looked at the man's hands. They didn't look high. He was married. She could see his gold ring on his finger. Maybe that made it high, like expensive is high. All of a sudden she remembered the thing; it was about the man and why Mommy and Daddy were angry. She would tell him all by herself. "I want to be a secretary," she said.

"Mr. Oakland, the high school referred us to your office. When we complained to them they said—they said that they *couldn't* train her for secretarial work. Of course, *they* had to defend their decisions. *They* give tests that seem to *show* all kinds of things because they have to back up their incompetent teachers. We're protesting to you, Mr. Oakland, and we are not going to use the services of *this* office."

Ralph wondered what to say and how to break away gracefully. He looked at the young girl who was still sitting. In a place where misery and trouble dug lines in people's faces and weighed upon their bodies, her youth and beauty were almost staggering.

She was like the little green hope among the dark and furious troubles in Pandora's box. Her face reminded him of a face he had seen once as a soldier on leave in the north of Switzerland during World War II. She was one of the simpler Marys adorning a small church. That Mary had no sophistication or wit and none of the noise of war. She was utterly quiet, utterly serene. For a soldier full of doubt and anger, fear and noise, she had been a simple, long breath of sweetness, and he had never forgotten her. Now she smiled up at him from the wooden bench in front of the rehabilitation office. He smiled back.

"Do you give those I.Q. tests, Mr. Oakland?" Mrs. Colvin was saying.

"Yes, we do, and we will test if you think that the school's results are not valid. We do independent testing here."

Andrea and her mother went into the office to make an appointment for the testing. The father stayed behind. "I'm not saying that it's all their fault," he said stiffly, "the school, I mean, but the teachers didn't take time. She isn't dumb. Maybe it takes her a little longer to get the hang of things, but why don't they try to take that little extra time with her so she could be a secretary? She's a sweet kid, too, anybody would like to have her brightening up an office. The school says she's too dumb to be a secretary. Let's face it, how much brains do you need to be a *secretary?*"

Ralph stopped his incredulous answer just short of a word. Then he said, "Mr. Colvin, this is a public agency. Our tests of clients are very long and involved, but they are our own and we won't advise any training at all unless you agree. We test and counsel independently of the schools and anyone else, and if we feel that your daughter is slow, we will counsel her in that way; if we feel that she is not, nothing will make us say that she is. O.K.?"

Abruptly, Mr. Colvin held out a huge hand. "It's a deal."

Ralph left the office with them, late again. If the girl was really slow, it would be hard to convince such loving parents, who hoped to be proud as well as loving. Everybody was after the same dream: an affectionate and dutiful daughter, smart, but not too smart, a "little" job after graduation, to which she was obedient but not dedicated, an easy and conventional marriage with easy and conventional children, affection but not passion. Because it seemed so modest a dream, the dreamers were convinced that it was right, and in that conviction they could go all the absurd, tragic, and unscrupulous ways to have their modest dreams fulfilled. In the sweet smile of Andrea's quiet serenity, Ralph had the feeling that her parents' dream was as meaningless to her as a bird that catches one's eye as it lights for a moment on a branch and then is gone.

"Mr. Oakland, this is Miss Jesperson at the welfare office. Can't you hurry up on that Ramirez case? We've been getting complaints from everyone about him. It seems that the children have been going into school with clothes nowhere near sufficient for the climate here. Their teachers have been calling us to complain about the clothing allowance we give. The P.T.A. found out about their situation and got up a big collection of used clothing which they took down to the family. Well, they saw that car in front of the house, and he said it was his, and . . ."

9

John Kroll

On his first day at the tutorial school, John Kroll had a fight with another boy. On the sixth, he called his teacher a jerk. On the fourteenth, he made references to the questionable paternity of the man in the next seat. He tried three times to make passes at the prettiest girl. His technique lacked everything but directness. He was surly, dour, stubborn, mean, and evil-tongued. He was doing fine. He was learning to read and to add and to name the rivers and the Presidents of the United States. Ralph had to go down to the school almost every week to speak to John's teacher, and there were endless converations over the phone as he tried to win time. In spite of all that John said and did, the other pupils seemed not to be suffering by it, and the teacher let herself be mollified. After a while she too began to see marks and traces made by the inroads of his learning, as it began to wear away the walls of his pride. Fight as he would, he was being helped. Of course, some of his troubles were not as amenable to sweet reasonableness as others. Having been a public charge almost all of his life, John had a wide, first-hand knowledge of civic corruption and bureaucratic apathy. He greeted every bit of the political information presented in his civics class with biting sarcasm, and class discussions of law enforcement brought forth bitter comments which his teachers were ill-equipped to refute. Sometimes his conferences with Ralph had the flavor of bull-sessions, and Ralph could see John's thoughts widening around him. He was still everything he had ever been—impulsive, self-centered, and unfeeling—but there was a new spaciousness in his outlook.

"Hey, Oakland, I mean, what's the use of all this crap? I don't want to be a perfesser, and even, you know what? I

107

found out they don't make beans. I want to have a job that doesn't take knowin' dead Presidents and the formula for crud."

"I'm teling you, John, part of what any employer wants is the knowledge that you stuck with something long enough to get your bill of rights, that little high-school certificate. He wants to know that you can start a thing and finish it, even if it has parts that don't particularly make sense or thrill you."

"And they said *I* was a moron! You know them damn dead Presidents, and it's suppose to help you workin' on a roof?"

"Well, John, then where did you learn to do that kind of thinking?"

"Yeah, yeah, call me perfesser, but it still don't make it right."

"We're in a bind, John. Every kid has a million choices facing him. We can't train him for only one thing any more. Unless we teach him all kinds of things, he won't even be able to begin to choose what he wants to do."

"I'm goin' to get me a photograph of Rutherford B. Hayes and tack it up to the dashboard of a souped-up red Jag, and he's goin' to help me get a girl and the three of us is going to head off together, and that's all the help I'll ever get from Rutherford B. Hayes!"

"Why are you down on Rutherford B. Hayes today?"

"I flunked the lousy stinkin', friggin' test on them Presidents, the dead . . . !"

"Don't worry, John, you'll build your roofs and learn your Presidents, and when you and Rutherford go riding in your car, you'll know why there are speed laws and what those laws are, and you'll know how to vote in an election and measure a circle and write a letter to the gas company. When you're dumb, people take you; you know that by now. Get smart and you won't have to be anybody's fall guy."

"Hey, Oakland, you know any good con games?"

"You're not smart enough yet."

"O.K., Oakland, I'll stick around a while, but if it don't pick up soon, down there, I'm cuttin' out."

"Go back and beat the books, John, and when you look up on a scaffold and see men building, you can start to hope that someday you'll be up there with them." John got up, turned, turned again, and winked at Ralph. "Make sure them ass-faces know what they're doin'. Watch out they don't try me out on the job with the rope and the trapdoor."

Ralph started to leave the office with John in order to meet the next client. These sessions were still difficult enough to make him look forward to stretching his legs a little, and the clients ususaly liked to be walked into the counselor's offices instead of coming into a presence as if Ralph were a bank manager or school principal. On his way out, the phone rang, and Ralph went back and spoke for a moment or two before hanging up and going out to the 2:30 appointment, Mrs. Colvin and daughter Andrea. The waiting section was empty, and so Ralph looked into the hall in case the Colvins were there. Perhaps Mrs. Colvin had changed her mind; she had been angry before, and perhaps she was still too eager for her own vindication.

But they were there, Mrs. Colvin sitting on the bench that was put outside the office for the overflow that sometimes swelled out of the "waiting" section. Andrea was standing a little apart, leaning against the wall, and passing by, again and again, up and down, to delude that world that they were coming and going, there were half-a-dozen boys and young men from half-a-dozen offices and jobs. The boys who served coffee in the lunchroom had obeyed a mysterious call and had come forth from the basement like a risen Lazarus, still wearing his apron. The boy who collected the dust from the halls moved like an athlete in slow motion, in infinitesimal stages past her; and there was John Kroll, transfixed, struck deaf, dumb, and blind, his face alternately red and white, burning and freezing. Ralph had expected to see John in his desire as he was in his other appetites, leering or mulish, but Andrea's real beauty had awed him.

Now Ralph looked more closely at Andrea, wondering if she wasn't flirting or making promises with her eyes or gestures. Her dress was tight, too tight, and its play of gives and takes drew attention to the ripe north and the rounding south. Her face was beautiful, but not stunningly so, and the words that described her beauty described still places, calm havens, quietness. Then Ralph smiled. There it was. To the young and frightened boy-men who hovered around Andrea, a gay and lively beauty would have been too much of a challenge. Wit was too perilous; it called too far into the sharer for answer. Passionate, sensuous beauty put boys on their guard, frightened them because they had not yet been tested and didn't know if they might not be mastered instead of mastering. Andrea's beauty was almost maternal. Her serenity lulled their fears; her quietness called for no display of wit from them. Mother, child, and lover all in one, Andrea was the perfect object for a boy-man's hungers. Ralph asked her into the office and her mother came forward with her. They went in and left the air of the hall behind them heavy with yearning.

He had made an appointment with Martenson for testing Andrea, and after he had explained what the tests would be like, he led her out of the office and down the hall to the testing room. John and some of the others were still outside, very quiet, resting their glands. When they saw her coming they all perked up, like young dogs, suddenly wagging and snorting. Coded impulses throbbed along the netted nerves, enzymes poured and mingled. Adolescence. Ralph bit his lip and steered Andrea down the hall. In the testing room he introduced her to Martenson, waited for a bit until she seemed comfortable with him and unafraid, and then left her and came back to his office where Mrs. Colvin was still waiting.

"I didn't want Andrea's feelings hurt," she said bitterly, "the nerve of that school, telling us she was retarded! Look at her! One look at her and you can see she's no moron!" Ralph began to say something, but she was going on, steaming with the injustices of the last few weeks. "Her marks in school were always passing. I mean, she *graduates* this spring and now the school says they won't recommend her for a job or for secretarial training. Furthermore, they went so far as to tell me that she was *too dumb to be trained* as a secretary! Can you beat that? I mean, *can you beat that?*"

"They didn't use those terms, did they?" Ralph asked, trying to conciliate a little. He knew almost by feeling that Andrea was somewhat dull, but he didn't dare to let the feeling count for anything, especially since Mrs. Colvin was so convinced that it wasn't so. When he was through getting the initial information about Andrea and determining that the family could pay for any training she needed, Ralph showed Mrs. Colvin out into the hall. The outer room had filled again and was overflowing. Even the bench in the hall was full, so Ralph got Mrs. Colvin a chair so that she could wait. As he said good-bye and turned to greet his next client, he noticed that the boys had left the hall.

Ralph looked down at another test. Bernardo Ramirez. It was so bad that it made him sigh. According to the numbers Bernardo would never do anything more than stand before the door of the twentieth century. The one handle, intelligence, was not for his hand. And the eager agencies had better face it. He would be on state rolls all his life. Even if these results were inaccurate, as Ralph suspected they were, it would hardly be possible to justify a great state expense to find out just how inaccurate or to try to get employment for someone whose "official" numbers proclaimed him a man for whom it would be a mental strain to tie his own shoes. Ralph sighed and made a note of the test results for Bernardo's file. The phone rang and he picked it up heavily. (It's somebody calling who's desperate to hire a game-legged illiterate moron with a heavy accent and a car he can't drive. The pay?: $350 a month. I have just the man for you, sir!)

"Mr. Oakland, this is Bill Varro. An awful thing has happened. The compensation board doctor examined me last month and he didn't say anything, but he told the board I'm well enough to work now, so bang, no more compensation. I'm stuck, right in the middle of my training."

"When did you find out about his decision, Bill?"

"Well, this morning. I called them because my check didn't come."

(If he doesn't get training he'll never get out from under. Damn, damn!) "I see the problem. We'll have to figure something out. We might get them to review the case in light of your training. I'll call you back as soon as I find out what we can do."

"He knows I can't go back to trucking. If I can't finish ..."

Bill Varro and Bernardo, the welfare chiseler. There was always an answer for the problems of the unskilled. "Why not make them night watchmen?" "Why not make odd-job men out of them?" Even wise people forgot the obvious— that Bernardo was lost in the machine-age and that night watchman is a job of great responsibility and is kept for long-time employees of proven loyalty. Did they think, these Righteously Wrathful, or did they just want to be rid of all the difficult ones, to write them off the lists and off the welfare rolls and down behind the desk and out of sight? Well, Bernardo would be written off. He was beyond help, impossible. Ralph picked up the phone to talk about Bill Varro.

On Wednesday, Miss Jesperson, Bernardo's caseworker, called again and left a message to have Ralph call her when he was free. When he saw the message he winced. There was nothing to be done and the state would have to reconcile itself to the support of the Ramirez children and the continuation of their squalor. He put the message aside and forgot to call her.

At the end of the week he found himself near the highway cut-off hobo jungle where Bernardo and his family had thrown up a shack. The factory, where he had gone to talk about on-the-job training, was on the outskirts of the city and separated from the hobo jungle by a garbage ditch and car-corpse ravine. On the other side of the wreckage there was a slow, polluted river, Big Stag River. People often joked about staying upwind of the Stag. The whole area was a stinking plague-trap, but it suited its squatters. You paid no rent along the Stag.

Ralph had gotten a look at the whole ruin from the fifth floor of the factory, and when he had finished there he decided to go over and see Ramirez. (God help them when winter comes. Maybe I can talk the wife into nagging him to get rid of that damn car!)

He drove around the dump and parked off the highway. Then he walked down into the ugly jungle that had sprung up thirty-six feet beyond the arm of the city health department. Even if the authorities had been able to raze and burn the hung-together, rat-infested hovels, there had to be somewhere else for the squatters to go, and it would only be some other jungle "out of the high-rent district." He felt odd and out-of-place with his coat and tie, making his way around the fly-swarming refuse piles and broken bottles. He was off poise enough at this visit, which was one of desperation really; society's desperation in the face of its new, swelling caste: the unintelligent. He took off the jacket and tie. At the factory the foreman had worn a tie but no jacket. He had told Ralph that they were automating one of the departments and would try to retrain their own men, but the personnel man and Ralph had exchanged a glance, helplessly. They both knew that only those who could learn to be automation technicians instead of clamp-operators had a chance of staying on. A new form of social recognition was definitely needed: I.Q. 100-110, White shirt; 110-130, shirt and tie; 130-150, shirt, tie and jacket; over 150, Einstein Toga: sweatshirt and sneakers.

He was threading his way around the piles of rubble and

112

past the mounds of former shacks when he saw the car, trash among the ruins. The family had gotten a choice spot; their shack, which was almost dwarfed by the great old car, was close to the lip of the riverbank where three great willows were drawing its brackish water. Bernardo was working on the car. Ralph could hear the sounds coming from behind it. Around the wreck, his children and others came and went, playing their own games and looking idle and happy enough. Bernardo's wife, heavy with wash and pregnancy, was leaning and stretching under a long, sagging clothesline. Ralph stopped and looked, and wondered how hard the happy hobo image dies. It was a haunting image in the phantasy life of men whose days are predicated on responsibility, prestige, and taxes.

Here it was, autumn, and there were the great trees yellowing and taking fire over the shacks and the children, and dropping nostalgia with their whisps of down. The children noticed Ralph first and alerted Bernardo unexcitedly, in Spanish. Ralph came closer and the noise stopped and Bernardo stood up and looked at him over the disputed wreck. The look was without wariness or apology. Ralph envied that look; he felt he never could have given such a look from poverty and strangeness to someone who was coming with the state's power like an aegis over him. It was Bernardo's greatest strength and greatest stumbling block, that acceptance.

The state's representative, so much stronger, could only hope to face down that acceptance. Ralph reminded Bernardo of their meeting and how they had spoken in the office. Bernardo accepted politely. Then Ralph said, "That's quite a car you have there." Among the kids and trees it wasn't hard to keep the slight edge from his voice.

"Oh, yase," Bernardo said, "bu' i' does na go now; I fixeen' it."

"What are you working on?" Ralph asked. It was the kind of question everyone uses a dozen times a day without really listening to the answer. For Ralph, it was a preparation to drop the axe.

"Oh, I'ne workeen' dishere to see if is too loose."

Ralph looked down at what Bernardo was working on and then he opened his eyes very wide. Bernardo had taken the transmission housing out of the car and was inspecting the ridges of the spline. He was working as if he knew exactly what he was doing. Ralph saw that the entire transmission

113

would have to be rebuilt; it was the complicated work of a trained mechanic. "You're doing the transmission?"

Bernardo looked up, now apologetically, "De name of these thing I do na know," he said.

"You mean, you don't know the name in English . . ."

"No, I was never heareen' dem, de name."

"But—how did you learn to do this kind of work?"

"Oh, well, de Señor Chase, he car bad one day. He takeen' me to de station where dey fixeen' his car. De man tell me thin, two thins, I remember. Three month's de Señor Chase his car bad again . . ." He tried to bend the English with his hands to make it fit what he had to say. "I work in my mine what de man say, what de Señor Chase say. I fixeen'. All de time after I fixeen de car."

Ralph felt as if he had been kicking idly at a stone in the road and unearthed a ruby. He turned to the only witness, but Bernardo was innocent of the miracle. "Mr. Ramirez, what is this part here?" Ralph asked gently.

"Oh, dat piece fit just to de flat one here so when de move go from de man driveen' on dat stick in de car; he fit de orders through to de wheels inside dis box, in place one, in place two, in place three dere."

"Who taught you this?"

"It have to dis way because de order have to go back to de back wheel."

"It is your idea of it? Your idea alone?"

Bernardo looked up helplessly. "It is na rie?"

Could it be? Impossible! It wasn't this man, knowing, re-creating the mechanics of the automobile. This couldn't be an accidental revelation: it was only the desperate wish of Ralph's mind and the welfare agency. It couldn't be this one . . . Because for years, Ralph had had a phantasy, a day-dream which he kept for sterile periods in the work when everything was going wrong, when all of the combined brains, skill, training, and dedication of ten agencies couldn't keep one low-grade moron on a dishwashing job. This day-dream was that one morning he would look into a moron's eyes and see—Prometheus; a buried, secret gift, a power, a sense of light. How could it be true?

Yet, here he stood beside the illiterate peon in the ghastly yellow-flowered shirt, watching as Bernardo moved his fingers, articulate in the language they knew, among the parts of his motor. He watched for an hour, for two. The deft, gentle hands went finding and fixing with a strange grace.

114

When Ralph was ready to leave, he knew he had had his vision: Prometheus Amid the Orchids. Now he would have to convince a lot of people, many, many other people that he had not, indeed, been dreaming. Bernardo's looks wouldn't help; his mechanical aptitudes scored on that damn test wouldn't help; his past wouldn't help. People would have to be convinced, convinced enough to start Bernardo on a course of training in spite of the lack of any qualifying papers. Someone would have to see Bernardo at work.

"Mr. Ramirez, would you like to have the chance to see and think about many motors?"

"Well, da's na work to keep de family, is for enjoy, doin' these work." The deft hands moved on.

When Ralph left it was almost six o'clock. There were long streaks of shadow thrown from the branches of the willows and the eastern faces of all the rubble piles were in mellow shadow. It occurred to Ralph, as he walked back up the rise and out of the squatters' encampment to where he had left his car, that his phantasy had never taken into account half of its true message: that these bearers of rich gifts were themselves unknowing. They were more bound than Prometheus, who knew very well what he bore and why he could not withhold it. "In dreams begins responsibility ..." He would assail the forts of reason.

"Hello, Herb, this is Ralph Oakland."

"Hello, Ralph, I've been meaning to call you—about getting those little training reports in a couple of days late. I know you guys want a record of how the students you send are doing, but this has been a hell of a busy month for me. I'll sure get them in by next week."

"No hurry, Herb—there's nothing wrong, is there?"

"Oh, no, the men are doing fine. Holcomb's going to be late getting his certificate because of the month he was out last winter, but the others are coming right along. That Kittenger's started in on some extra work."

"That's fine, Herb, because I want to ask a favor. I've got someone who really shows potential for motor repair. Do you think you can fit him into the transmission or motor class?"

"Well, I think so. We're awfully crowded and transmission is a popular class. Since Chambers retired over in Westfall, we're the only decent auto-repair school within a hundred miles, but, you know, Ralph, you've never stuck me with a lemon, so send him over."

"His name's Bernardo Ramirez. I'll come in with him; there are some special problems. For one thing, he won't be able to read the material in the workbook."

"Oh, blind, huh? Gee, that's too bad, but do you think a blind guy would be able to do motor work . . ."

"Herb, he isn't *blind;* he—well, he just can't read."

"Oh, Ralph, don't you go getting soft. You white-collar guys never learn that motor repair is no job for a moron. You've never sent me a student just to keep him out of the nuthouse or the jail. Sometimes the welfare tried to do that, and there's one nutty dame named Burns at that Boys' Shelter who keeps trying to use my school as a comfort station on the way to the reformatory."

"Bernardo is no kid and he's not a moron either. That's just the point. I want to bring him down to you and let him look over the workrooms. Of course, you don't have to take him without seeing for yourself that he can do the work."

"Well, now, no promises—I'm not promising anything."

"Just take him around, just give him a chance. I'll bring him over on—say, Friday afternoon, all right? I don't think you'll be wasting your time on him. We'll see you then. So long."

"Ralph, this is Martenson. We have those test scores on Andrea Colvin."

"Well?"

"Pretty and sweet: top score. Nothing else. She's dull at the best. She'd never have gotten past fifth grade if she hadn't been carried. I'll send the stuff over and you can see for yourself. Sorry, Ralph."

"Mr. Oakland, this is Mrs. Rapheal Euler. I'm calling to register my son for your program. His name is Danny, and he's sixteen years old. He has cerebral palsy and we can't seem to find anything for him to do. People just aren't patient with the handipcapped, but I guess you know that. Danny is a smart boy, and he can do lots of things."

"Can he dress himself?"

"You mean if I help him with the hard parts? . . ."

"Ralph, this is Georgia Burns. Has John shown up for his appointment with you today?"

"Well, he wasn't supposed to come in until Wednesday; I

had to change the day because of the regional conference. Is anything wrong?"

"I don't want to alarm you—he seems to have disappeared. He left yesterday for his classes, and he didn't come back. I called them, and they told me that he hadn't been there all day. He wasn't in his bed this morning and no one seems to have seen him or have any idea where he went. The problem, of course, is that the Shelter is a correctional institution and his running away is punishable by sentence to the state reformatory. I'm going to have to call the police. When I do, and if they pick him up, of course, it means the end of schooling, training, and everything else."

"You have no idea where he went?"

"I can't think of a place. I called the Sisters at the orphanage to see if they knew. He has no one here whom he really confides in. I'm risking my own position every minute I hold up that call. The head of John's unit came to me to report him missing at the night count, and I said I would take care of the whole thing. If the police aren't called . . ."

"For God sakes, don't go out on a limb for him, Georgia. Call the police now. Maybe he'll come in before they show up."

"I know that he isn't in a hospital somewhere, or dead. They always call us when there's been a boy found with no identification. Oh, I know that he has no idea at all of what this little jaunt is going to cost him, and that's what makes me so sad. And, when I think of all the work you've done, I've done, the school has done, I could just *shake* him. Some movie-hero escapade and it's going to shoot the bottom out of his whole life and all our work!"

"Keep me posted, will you?"

"Of course. Good-bye, Ralph."

Oh, that stupid, stupid punk! Does he think our patience is infinite? Does he think at all? Ralph ground his teeth and picked up a pencil to note John's absence for the records. He would close the case as soon as John was found, and maybe that would end the procession of callers and his unwilling designation as a juvenile rehabilitation agency. There were lots of people on the rolls who were suffering over their futures and willing to work toward goals much, much more modest than the American Dream, and here was John Kroll, giving in to some stupid whim that might cut his life forever to the size of a prison cell.

Bernardo Ramirez

On Friday afternoon, Ralph drove again to the shack jungle down by the highway cut-off where Bernardo lived. The social worker had told Bernardo, and he was ready, dutifully clean, dutifully punctual, accepting the day and the instructions with neither joy nor sorrow. Ralph explained again that they were going to the Central School of Auto Repair to see Mr. Vinson. Bernardo agreed politely. He was dressed in his somber best: a turquoise-and-black-striped shirt and a crimson tie with flames handpainted on it. He also wore a pearl-gray Homburg hat. Blessed are the meek, Ralph thought, remembering that he had seen the hat at the Salvation Army store, for they shall inherit the earth. They got into the car and Ralph started it up. Bernardo sat like a stone. Ralph moved into the traffic, giving and taking with the flow of cars as they headed back toward the center of town.

When he looked over at the unresponding man, he saw that Bernardo's eyes were closed, his face in the expressionless repose of a man accepting death. As Ralph braided the lanes to get over from his entrance on the left to his exit on the right, he saw Bernardo's hand renouncing the world in favor of Christ. When they stopped at the traffic light on ninth, Ralph asked, "Do you hear anything in the motor?" A little of Bernardo's color returned until they started up again, but after a while he said, "De keeper of dis kine of turneen is na keepeen' rie."

Ralph asked Bernardo to describe the keeper of this kind of turning, and after Bernardo's long explanation of wheels is turning far and wheels is turning near together, it came to him that Bernardo was talking about the car's differential. He looked over at his passenger again. The welfare department could have gotten that car away from him by the simple expedient of taking him for a drive in a modern city. No one had thought of it. Well, maybe the luck would stay where it had been. Maybe Herb would be able to see in Bernardo what Ralph knew was there. (And I've got to stop in and have that differential looked at.)

They drove to the school and parked in the lot. The students' cars were lining the lot, ancient wrecks and hot rods, monuments to makeshift.

118

Bernardo looked at them with interest. "My car fineesh now. I ga' no gas, bu i' run."

"Right this way," Ralph said drily. "Mr. Vinson is waiting for us."

Ralph went a little ahead to introduce Bernardo and keep him from breaking on Herb's vision all at once. He saw Herb's face freeze with disbelief as Bernardo came toward him. The gentle, innocent look under the Homburg (International Cartels) and over the flame-painted tie (Carnival Sideshow) was damning Bernardo even before he opened his mouth (which wouldn't help either). Herb turned his astonished face toward Ralph so that Ralph said to Bernardo, "Mr. Ramirez, would you mind sitting out here for a moment?" Bernardo went to a bench outside the office and Ralph and Herb turned inside. The door closed and Herb exploded. "Tell me you're kidding, Ralph; *you've got to be kidding!*"

"Herb, you're looking at the wrong thing. I don't kid with people and this Bernardo is a somebody. Maybe he doesn't have any 'face value . . .'"

"Where did you *find* him? He looks like a character in the funny papers!"

"Sancho Panza."

"Sancho who? Don't bother telling me; he's not staying that long."

"Herb, just take him through, let him see the machines and the motors, let him see them work. Just take him around for fifteen minutes."

"You're really serious about that guy! Ralph, he's a moron. You can tell that just by looking at him. When you told me he couldn't read, I thought you meant complicated stuff or something. I bet he really *can't* read! I bet he barely even speaks English!"

"He speaks machine, Herb. Go with him; let him show you."

"But he's right out of the beanfield . . ."

And then the second little miracle began to happen. Ethwald Kittenger must have seen Ralph go by the workshop rooms on his way to Herb's office. Now he was pacing up and down in front of the glass door, waiting to say hello. Herb saw him and his face began to soften. He had seen Ethwald first come into his shop with that invalid way of his, looking like a beaten kid. Under the influence of the work and Herb's encouragement, Ethwald was beginning to stand taller and hold his limbs more normally. His whole demeanor was changing and Herb was experiencing the same satisfactions that fed Ralph in this difficult work, almost the joy of a Pygmalion whose act of creation became a living being. Herb was proud of Ethwald. He opened the door and Ralph shook hands with the student. The handshake was firm and manlike. Ralph greeted Ethwald and promised to look in on the clutch repair class where he was working. Ralph was pleased to have Ethwald show off to him a little and Herb was pleased also.

When Ethwald left, Herb turned to Ralph, "He's a good boy. He'll make a first-class mechanic." Then his hand came up helplessly. "O.K., O.K., I'll take Pablo around."

"Bernardo."

"O.K., O.K.."

They went out to where Bernardo was waiting and Ralph saw the balance almost change again, as Bernardo came toward them with that meek, mute look of his. How well that same look had sat on Ethwald Kittenger's face. Well, Ethwald had paid the debt he owed for it; Herb had given his word.

He muttered something and Ralph said, "Why not take Mr. Ramirez around by himself. It would probably be easier, and I want to look in on Ethwald and Mestrovick and Finley." Actually, it was only a hunch, a vague intuition that it would go better if they did the tour without him.

Ethwald and the others were fine and Ralph watched them work with one ear cocked for the approach of Prometheus and his Judge. The wait seemed endless. Machines cried and hummed, motor parts were raised and lowered from worktables, instructors circulated checking the steps of the work, and still Ralph waited. The longer he waited the more hurt he felt. How could Herb doubt him after so many students of such high caliber? Maybe Bernardo would fail on this; perhaps he wouldn't be able to show what Ralph knew was there. The chances were that he would fail.

Here they come at last. Ralph looked from face to face for the signs of ruin or hope.

Herb's eyes were lowered and Bernardo was sweating from every pore. He seemed exhausted. The incredible tie was askew, his eyes glassy. Herb led him back to the bench in front of the office and motioned Ralph inside again. He turned around the door he was closing as if he couldn't bear to let a moment be wasted. "Who is he?"

120

"Well—he's just a car-owner."

"He's—he's *beautiful!*"

Ralph lost the humor in pure relief.

Herb let excitement overcome his embarrassment at standing so steadfastly in the wrong. "I took him to where we had some of the new equipment, special power tools for machining very complicated parts. I could see he'd never seen them before. He just stood and looked a while at them, and I was getting disgusted, and I asked him what he thought of them and he said he thought they were good, and then he told me about them—how they worked and what they did, every one of them. I could see his mind kind of moving over the thing, learning it and understanding it."

They looked through the glass partition to the stolid back bulging a width of patient turquoise cloth.

"I want that guy in school," Herb said.

Something a little bit mean and small in Ralph wanted Herb to have to plead. "He's illiterate."

"He talks machine; you said so yourself."

"Low I.Q., dresses badly, right out of the beanfield . . ."

"O.K., Ralph, O.K." And then they smiled at one another. "How did you find out?" Herb asked.

"Saw him working on his car."

"He worked here, too. I gave him one of the simple motor problems to diagnose and fix. Those great big paws of his, and I just couldn't believe my eyes. He works deft and clean, like eye surgery. It's the kind of work it takes years to develop, and it's raw, waiting for us to bring out plain."

"Prometheus Amid the Orchids," Ralph said.

"I don't know who *that* guy is," Herb said, "but I did know somebody like that Ramirez once before, just once, a long time ago. It was the guy who got me started in motor work myself. His name was Magnusen and I think he was a genius."

"I think maybe so," Ralph said.

Hans Marshak

Hans Marshak was standing before Ralph on two legs. He smiled and said, "Well, I'm up at last."

"You look great. How are they working?" Ralph strode toward him, smiling, and they shook hands.

"Well, they told me down at the Limb Shop that there was

going to be a limp for a while, and then even that would disappear. I've been practising on them, going all over; up steps, curbs, bending and stretching, and trying all kinds of things. You never realize how many different kinds of movements there are until you have to learn to do them again."

"Remember," and they walked to the office together, "please remember to take care of yourself, Hans. I know you're eager to get on with your life, but if that stump gets irritated again it's going to be bang, right back in the hospital."

"Okay, but I feel fine, really."

"And if it starts to get sore, just go right to bed and call the doctor."

"I will. The whole crew told me last time about letting it get irritated. I know I was impatient, but Mr. Oakland, my training is almost over and well, I'm up. I won't do anything to jeopardize that."

"When are you going to be finished?"

"Well, I've made up all the time that I was out for treatments and the operations. I've got about three weeks of lessons left, but I hope to finish a little before that. They let me stay late there, you know. And, Mr. Oakland, something happened down there that made me feel, well, funny. So I'd like to finish as soon as I can."

"What was that, Hans?"

"Well, I walked in there today, for my class, and nobody—nobody recognized me. All they'd been doing all that time was looking at the wheelchair. I had to wait and wait at my table and they were looking at me, like, who's that guy over where the wheelchair guy works. It made me feel creepy. I know they were embarrassed because I said, "Hello, fellas, remember me, Marshak?" And they all sounded too glad to see me and it was too big of a laugh to everybody. Mr. Oakland, I never want to be in that chair again."

"I don't think you will be, if you get along all right, but a wheelchair isn't the worst thing in the world either. Believe me, Hans, when you've got a good mind and it's healthy, an awful lot can be done with the rest. Well, tell me, how is it going otherwise?"

"O.K. My wife has cut down on the 'Brave' sessions she was having with my mother. After I get a job, I hope my father will retire, and then Mother won't have to be alone so much. She gets pretty morbid, just working herself up sometimes."

122

"As long as you don't let her morbidity get you down, Hans. I don't know if you know this or not, but the doctors tell me that even infections of the kind you've had are easier to bring under control when the patient has a good attitude. I'm sure yours has helped a lot."

"Well, I'm up now, and soon I'll be working. It must seem funny to you, a guy so impatient to get back to work. It's not only the bills, Mr. Oakland, it's—well—it's being a man again."

"I'm not laughing, and don't kid yourself, a man's job is a good part of his life really; it's all day for him. That's why the agency tries as hard as it does to get clients placed in jobs where they fit in well and are happy. Now, here's a point I want to make to you: You've got your limbs and so, when your training is over, you won't be handicapped any more. There's a demand for the work you do, and I don't see any reason for you to run into the first thing that's offered because you aren't sure that you are the equal of other applicants. It's not true. When we come to the point of placing you on a job, be sure you're satisfied. I don't tell this to everybody, but I'm telling it to you, because—well—because you're one of the people who is able to have a top-grade job and because you want to work so badly. Just don't rush, Hans."

They made an appointment for the day after Hans's training was due to end. He was going to make it, his deadline of working by Christmas; at least, he would if the remorseless infection was really gone. Such an ambition would seem impossible to anyone who didn't know how stubborn Hans Marshak was. From the very beginning he had been determined not to let himself be handicapped one instant longer than he had to. He had called the agency from the hospital, which was a rare thing in itself. A person with such a loss usually takes time to mourn it, sorrowing until his sorrow is dulled, fearing until fear is exhausted, examining all his hopes in the diminished light. Then he slowly begins to search out the limitations and later the choices that are left to him. The rare visits that Ralph had made to prospective clients still in the hospital were usually failures, but a person so changed needs a point of stability in the ebb and sway of feeling, and Ralph never refused those hospital calls.

He had gone to see Hans, he remembered, in an afternoon he told himself was being wasted, really. He had spoken to the desk nurse and been led by another nurse toward the men's convalescent ward, marveling how much the recovery process had been speeded up in these last few years.

"Are you a relative?" the nurse said.

"No, I'm with the Department of Rehabilitation."

"That's not relief, is it?"

"No ..."

"Well, I mean if Mr. Marshak has to go on relief or something, and you need a reference, anybody on the ward would be glad to give it to you."

"Oh?"

"You see, we come to know the real person, not the face he puts on to impress people, and the worst in a person usually comes out sooner or later when he's sick. People drop their pretenses here, so, when you get a real man, like Mr. Marshak, well, you know it isn't just some kind of pose. I'll tell you another thing. If he goes on relief, he *needs* it. I mean, he won't be the usual welfare case."

Ralph thought for a moment of asking her what the usual welfare case was like, but it would serve no purpose. She had a clear vision of them in her mind, formed and fed from a hundred untrackable implacable sources. He followed on.

They came to the ward and went on down to where a young man was lying in bed. It was the visitors' hour and many friends and relatives were standing by the other patients. The unobtrusiveness of Ralph's coming pleased the man—he could tell as they shook hands. Marshak had a strong hand. The nurse left and they began to talk.

"I got a lot of bills to pay, and I'm going to need a job as soon as I get out of here. Mr. Oakland, I found out about your agency from a doctor here. I hope you can help me."

"I hope so, too. What did you do before your accident?"

"I'm—I mean, I was an aircraft mechanic. I did repairs on all kinds of craft when they were on the field, and also in the hangar. I worked at Fort Carey Field."

"But that's an Air Force field. I didn't know they used civilians for that, isn't it a military job?"

"Oh, yes, but sometimes they can't fill all their needs with their own trainees, so they hire civilians."

"Did you like the work?"

"Oh, yes. They give you a good deal, too. It was a good job, and I don't mean only the pay and benefits and stuff. It was a good crew we had, and the work, well, it was really *man's* work, you know? We climbed around on those big

124

babies and got inside 'em and tickled 'em here and tightened 'em there and really made 'em purr . . ." He had caught his strong sexual allusion and it embarrassed him so that he stopped, almost stammering.

Ralph said, "And the pay and conditions—were they good?"

"Oh, sure, we were all buddies down there, all the mechanics. It's what I meant about its being man's work. We were all together; we used to kid around, and well . . ." He looked down at the smooth bed where there were no legs resting. "There's not going to be anything like that for me now, so there's no point in going into it."

"That's not true," Ralph said. "I don't think you realize how far we've come in the last ten years, in the last five. You're still in bed and you're not ready to talk about testing or training now, but I came here to let you know that with modern prostheses, limbs, and with a skill like yours, you aren't going to be handicapped in any real way. What you liked in that job may not be gone at all. If you want to do mechanics, we'll set up training for you to go as high as you can. If you want to do something else, well, we can look into that, too. What I'm trying to tell you is you have lots of choices to make about training and jobs. In the center of your life, your work and recreation, you're not going to *be* handicapped in any real way. Sure, it'll take guts and a lot of adjusting, but we're coming of age in being able to help with this kind of problem."

"You mean I won't have to work from my home?"

"Hell, no! You'll be able to drive a car and work in any one of a hundred shops or plants, and you'll make good money. You'll be able to walk and dance and fish and hunt and all the rest of it."

Hans's face was changing in a very slight way, while Ralph was talking. The attitude of his body was less—resigned. For that moment he looked as if his fight might be for bigger stakes than bare survival. "You're not just kidding me along . . ."

"I'm not kidding about the work it'll take either. I don't want to minimize that. The point is that *with* work, the rest is possible."

The visitor's bell rang and Ralph got up and held out his hand, and said, "Keep in touch with me and let me know how you're coming along, and when you're ready we can set up an appointment and start in to work. O.K.?"

That had been a year and a half ago. Neither of them had dreamed the nightmare that was to happen when osteomyelitis set in to infect and re-infect and re-infect the stump of Hans's left leg. He had come in to the office as soon as he was able, and he had been tested and put into training as an electronic-instrumentation technician. It was a two years' course, but with his airplane mechanics' experience, he would be able to do it in a year and a half. It had taken that full time, but only because of the eternal and endless re-infections, treatments, operations, and drainings. Hans Marshak had gone on studying under surgical sheets and saline drips, in the hospital and out. When he was thought to be cured at last, he was measured and fitted for artificial limbs.

During the process of adjustment, an irritation developed and back again he went, more tissue breaking down, more cutting and scraping and draining. Today, he had walked in to see Ralph on his new legs. It was their regular, monthly meeting (only monthly because Hans was not a "problem" client), but Ralph suspected that this surprise had been planned for him, by Hans, a presentation that had taken hours of work. Ralph was moved by what Hans had done, and was proud for himself and his client. The doggedness and the stubborn courage had paid off. Of all of his 150 active cases, Hans Marshak was the client he respected most. And now, there would be more than just checking up on progress in training. Ralph could begin to help Hans to work and live much as he had before. The purely physical disability was the rarest kind in Ralph's work, and its victims were also the easiest to train and place. The modern world—which could set itself squarely against a Bernardo Ramirez, which wanted to forget a John Kroll, or break an Alan Devereaux between two great sets of bureaucratic gears—was running in Hans Marshak's favor. Technology had given him legs while it was reducing his need for legs in doing a day's work. Earlier in their sessions together, Ralph had asked Hans if that first visit he had made had helped. "Oh, yes, I needed somebody to tell me it wasn't the end. My mother was crying all the time; my wife was crying all the time; and we were all as brave as hell; but nobody really believed it wasn't the end of everything until you came and talked to me."

Ralph got up to go and see the next client. Bernardo had been taken up, and now Hans. It was good, this work, and today it was wonderful.

126

10

Andrea Colvin

"... Mrs. Colvin, there's more to do than argue with the results of the tests." (And she'll never believe that her beautiful daughter is retarded after all.) Ralph knew he had to convince her how dangerous it was to deny the facts. That beautiful kid was walking around with her unknowing, gentle virginity and without enough understanding to keep it. What was she going to say when it was too late? Probably what Hester Ivorson said last year, 'I just wanted to make him feel good, and he said if I did that with him he would feel good.' Oh, brother!

"What you're doing, Mr. Oakland, is spoiling Andrea's reputation! Who will want to marry a girl who's classed as a—a moron! What nice, quiet man will propose marriage after you've convinced everyone that Andrea is some kind of imbecile!"

"But, Mrs. Colvin ..."

"You may not understand why her father and I wanted secretarial training for her. It would be just the right thing to get her to meet the right kind of man, a nice older man, perhaps; somebody who is settled and wouldn't always be wanting his own way; someone who wouldn't move all over the country every time he makes up his mind to. She should have a husband who doesn't have too much family of his own to worry about. Still, they're set in their ways, the older ones. A young boy—no, they're too restless. They want one thing and then something else."

"The point is ..."

"The point is that we had a reason to want Andrea to be a secretary and your meddling and the school's meddling has persecuted her. Now there won't be anything for her!"

"Oh, no, Mrs. Colvin, that's not true. The fact is that there are lots of jobs that Andrea can train for and learn to do and be good at, if you and your husband would just stop focusing on this one idea of Andrea's being a secretary. I want to tell you frankly that she will never find success or freedom in that job; it's just beyond her capacities, and the worst of it is that there are rewards and successes right in front of her, if only we could work for *them*. I want to help Andrea, too. Why won't you let me look into something that will suit her better?" (Such a quiet, beautiful girl—he remembered with tenderness how vulnerable-looking the back of her neck was, all those little downy hairs and the small curl. Somebody is going to see that too, soon . . .)

"Well, it's got to be where she can meet the right people. I don't want her associating with any kind of riffraff. Andrea is a fine girl and that's why her father and I wanted to see her in some nice office . . ."

"Well, then, there's something else that I've been wondering about . . ." (It would have to be accepted right. He would have to stop reddening.) "It's a—well—a delicate thing and I want you to take my questions in the way they are meant, not as prying but because I'm trying to be helpful."

"Well . . ."

"Mrs. Colvin, it's about Andrea's clothes . . ."

"Her clothes? What about her clothes?"

"I wonder if they're not—well, a little tight, perhaps a little too—uh—provocative." He saw the woman's face freeze. He was drowning but there was no way to avoid it now.

"What are you trying to tell me about Andrea?" Mrs. Colvin said.

"I'm trying to help and I'm certainly saying nothing in criticism of Andrea. It's just that she is vulnerable, more vulnerable than most girls. She doesn't have the fears of—uh —more experienced girls, and she's very *trusting*—uh—because she doesn't have the experience . . ." (Oh, God, he was making a mess of this, as if there hadn't been enough shocking things and tragic things to tell people, now he had to attack this simple problem with all the delicacy of a cavalry charge!)

Ralph sat back for a moment, and suddenly he was just thinking about the luminous serenity in Andrea and of the stone Virgin's quietness in the midst of war. Perhaps it was shyness that was making him stumble. Didn't that silly mother realize what she was asking for? He had to try again. What if Andrea's mother-child voice did call to him also; he couldn't let it kill her need to be protected. He sat up. Against the mother's frozen face, Ralph knew that he had no weapon but directness.

"Mrs. Colvin, Andrea attracts boys, all kinds. She's a sweet, gentle girl and she's going to get hurt unless we make sure that she knows what she's doing. How much does Andrea know about sex?"

"Nothing! nothing. Mr. Oakland, I just couldn't find it in my heart to—to go into all of *that*. She's so innocent, and—well—she's *not* as ready as the others to start thinking about *that* kind of thing."

"You feel, then, that she isn't as quick to learn as the others, don't you, Mrs. Colvin?"

"You're saying she's a dummy! She isn't. She's just more *innocent,* that's all!"

"Exactly, more innocent, younger. And here we are, trying to force her beyond her strength into a grown-up world. Some school will train her or pass her out with some sort of diploma, and it'll take years and years, and she'll be laughed at by everyone. Andrea is gentle and kind—why do we have to force her to be hurt again and again, to fail again and again?"

"Well, Mr. Oakland, what's the answer? Have her sit home all day and twiddle her thumbs?"

"I don't think she has to do that. We have a training center here that's just recently been started. It's called a sheltered workshop. It teaches skills to people who learn slowly, and it teaches them work that they can *do* and succeed in."

"What things?"

"Switchboard work, power-sewing, toy assembly, and they've started classes in selling, too; they train girls to be salesladies, to fill out forms and make change and how to handle customers in a shop. The teachers there won't have to push Andrea and she won't be the laughingstock of the class. Why don't we give it a try?"

"I don't know," Mrs. Colvin said, grudgingly, "I'll have to talk to my husband about it. You know, he's got his heart set on her being a secretary . . ."

"Fine," Ralph said, "and call me when you've made up your mind. I'd like to see Andrea try this sheltered workshop. I think there might be a job in which she can succeed. I imagine high school was pretty tough for her, with everything and everyone going so fast."

"Mr. Oakland . . ." The woman sat back and her forehead puckered and there was a hint of Andrea in the look. It moved Ralph a little, to see that similarity between the calm, uninvolved retarded girl and her "normal," suffering mother. "I never realized—you know—it used to puzzle me, why Andrea had so few friends to the house and why she didn't have her bunch of girl friends the way I did. We supervised her parties and fun very carefully and she was so sweet and agreeable that it never came to me until just now how few girl friends she ever had. Every weekend we'd all go to the zoo or the movies or visiting relatives. Well, you just never think about—friends. She never complained or seemed sad, though . . . Would she be less—well—less lonely, do you think, in that place?"

"Talk it over with your husband. We certainly could try it out and see. I wouldn't recommend it if I didn't think it would be right for her."

Mrs. Colvin got up to leave. "I'll let you know," she said. "But about that other matter, that sex talk—well, of *course*, I won't tell my husband what you said. He'd be enraged at your even *suggesting* such a thing." Then she turned and left.

If someone would only give that woman a good shaking! What was an innocent, innocent retarded girl doing in that tight, tight dress? What was her mother defending in that anger of hers? Ralph sighed and got up to stretch. He had seen the boys clustering around Andrea; surely the mother had seen it too. Hadn't she wondered? Hadn't she been afraid? It was she, not Andrea, who would have to be made wary; and now the mother would be too busy defending her point of view to look again and see the danger in it. Well, at least he had tried.

The phone rang. "Ralph, this is Nancy Sprague. I just called up to let you know that your boy, John Kroll, was spotted by the police down on Vandalia Street, coming out of a whorehouse. He saw them first and got away from them. They think he's been hiding there in one of those gin mills with 'bedrooms in the rear.' "

"How do you know about this?" Ralph asked, wondering again how the news about an escaped reformatory boy had gotten around to quiet, patrician-faced little Nancy Sprague, a public-health nurse.

"Well, Georgia Burns and I work pretty closely on some of

130

the families of her Shelter boys. She asked me to keep an ear open, and since we're down at Vandalia Street all the time, and I know most of the officers down there, I just managed to pick up the word. See? It's very simple."

It was the other side of the coin of the pestering he'd gotten from every public agency and half-a-dozen private ones since he had started with the miserable case.

"Do you know what he was doing down there? He has no money that I know of and that means he'll have to steal or beg to keep going. . . ."

"I don't know why he was down there, but I'll tell you this. He's been spotted around town more times than a re-from school kid has a right to be. This isn't the first time on Vandalia Street either. I think you're going to find out that your boy has been leading a little bit of a double life."

There was a word in Ralph's mind, suddenly and certainly. It was a deductive leap that would have put Sherlock Holmes to shame, but he felt very sure of it: narcotics. He knew that Boys' Shelter was getting it somehow; why not through that scholar, that bon vivant, that booster of Rutherford B. Hayes!

"Stop calling him my boy, will you," Ralph said. "I've got an awful funny feeling that I've been had by that boy. There's a cold, cold wind blowing around my legs, and I don't want to look down because I'm scared my pants are gone."

"He isn't making a fool of you," she said gently. "He probably can't even think about anyone else at all now."

"Who said anything about *his* making a fool of me. You don't send a boy to do a man's work." Then he thanked her and hung up.

Damn that lousy little punk! He would get that Kroll off the program the moment he was picked up. Well, it would be taken out of his hands anyway. The juvenile authorities would have to sentence John for running away from a correctional institution. He was on the road now and there was no help for it: Boys' Shelter to Boys' State and Boys' State to State Pen. The other two cases that Ralph had accepted from the Shelter were going ahead with infinite slowness, yet Georgia Burns and the rest of the Shelter people never questioned him about the slowness or seemed to wonder at the lack of progress. It was probably because they expected nothing to come of all this; they only wanted to be able to say that they had done all they could. If John Kroll had really been bringing narcotics into the Shelter all this time, the authorities would put him in a cell so far back that he would never see the sky except in six-inch cuts. Maybe it was just as well!

Bernardo Ramirez

At any rate, Bernardo Ramirez was studying motor repair and was going to have a chance to see into the twentieth century, but for Ralph, Bernardo and his hidden gift were one big headache. Unnecessary people—the old (above 40), the machine-displaced, the uneducated, the slow and the sick and the poor—were so many mounting thousands that people, and agencies, simply stopped caring. Any agency opening a door was inundated with thousands and tens of thousands. Some of these could be saved to become part of "society," to contribute work and dreams to the ongoing nation, but it was harder and harder to train them, counsel them, and fit them in somewhere in the overcrowded world of daily work. Efficiency favors machines above men, and let no one, anywhere, accuse us of being inefficient. Even the dreamed-of miracle man, the one-in-a-million, Bernardo would be difficult to work through the wheels without those precious numbers on an I.Q. test.

Ralph was going to have to convince Bernardo's caseworker, Miss Jesperson, and her supervisors and his supervisors that a statistically moronic and illiterate peon with broken English was going to make good as a skilled motor repairman. Bernardo himself would have to learn it. There might be a lot of fighting to be done; Bernardo would have to learn to make a way and not merely witness, to hold and argue for his rights, and shape the present by his own efforts. That would have to come gradually, and later. The first bastions were bureaucratic.

Ab came first. He should know about Bernardo right away; it would be bad tactic for him to find out somewhere else and conclude that this insane placement of a "moron" in high-skill training was some new social experiment on which Ralph had gotten hipped, the outcome of somebody's Letter to the Editor. Ralph should convince Ab that this was a conscious and defensible plan. Agency regulations gave him the freedom to set up objectives, test, and train independently of anyone else in the agency; but he was open to being

132

"called up" to defend any case that seemed to show questionable judgment. He made his appointment to see Ab, wondering what he really could say when he got to the office with Bernardo's incredible statistics and a tale about hidden genius. Howling taxpayers would never remember that he and Ab paid taxes, too, and that they hated incompetent public servants even more than the average citizen. It might calm the constant public anxiety about some subtle kind of fraud being put over on it, if the laws didn't have to demand the reduction of all human experience to so rigid a set of categories. Then perhaps the agency might stop being so defensive that it defied statistics and preferred incompetence to scandal. Without that defensiveness, the agency might be able to engage the attention of the community about its real problems—there it went again, Ralph's perfect world; perfect agency, built to contain all the wretchedness that no other place could number or name or mark in the books. We're perfect, I know, I know. We live with laws that call irrelevant anything that they can't explain. Our new third commandment: Thou shalt not fall between categories. The new fourth: Thou shalt not suffer in strange ways. Ralph went up to Ab's office, told him about Bernardo Ramirez, and showed him the damning report. Ab's answer was exactly as Ralph had predicted.

"We can't accept this man for skilled training. Are you telling me that this—this moron can do the work of a mechanic, a machinist? The man's illiterate. He has an I.Q. of 60, which means that he will always *be* illiterate. Can he learn to read a simple gauge, no less a tolerance calibrator or a blueprint or a wiring chart or a slide rule?"

"I'm not saying we can train a moron to be a genius; I'm saying that with Bernardo our *tests* are wrong."

"But you gave him the culture-free test, didn't you? Those scores are standardized throughout the country."

"When they're standardized on rural Spanish-American tenant labor, I'll bet Bernardo lifts the lid off."

"But we're *here,* Ralph, we're *now.* The world doesn't run on his time."

"Ab, if you saw a man wearing a sign saying BLIND, and he called out to you, 'Hey, you in the gray felt hat!' What would you say?"

"I'd say he wasn't blind."

"Exactly. And when a moron goes through a machine shop

133

and tells the function of machines he's never seen before, when he understands those machines, he's not a moron then, is he?"

"Does it matter, if the world thinks he is? Who'll hire a guy like that anyway?"

"I've been giving that a lot of thought. I wouldn't be surprised if Herb Vinson down at Central Auto hires him. He wants to train Bernardo, and when that's finished, it's possible that Bernardo can be a trouble-shooter in the shop. If not, I think I can convince other people to look beyond the surface. There's plenty of value there to make the extra effort worthwhile."

"How do you know this for sure? How do you know that machine business isn't just a fluke?"

"Well, we can let him take the first course, if it doesn't work out, we can pull him out of the class and there will only be one semester's fee involved."

"Remember, if he doesn't work out, it'll look bad for the whole agency."

"You know my work, Ab," Ralph said, hoping that his irritation didn't show. "I've never started people on programs that I didn't think they could succeed with."

"Okay, Ralph," Ab said. "See John, and if it's all right with him, well . . ."

Ralph thanked Ab and left. He had won a chance for Bernardo and he didn't want to seem pushy; it would hurt Bernardo's cause. It was hard to be a discoverer—

As he ate lunch, Ralph wondered what else might help. He could get Herb Vinson to call Ab and the immortals higher up and be enthusiastic over the phone; no, something more dramatic was needed, something that could be seen and believed the way he had seen Bernardo's hands, easy and deft in the engine. Statistics are what they want. Very well, Bernardo, too, would have his statistics, a lovely little bouquet of fragrant numbers; and Ralph would see that he got them. Statistics. Ralph went into the bathroom where he wouldn't be bothered. He took out a little notepad that he carried and began to write his plan in it quickly. Oh, God, I hope we haven't refined our techniques of probing thought and feeling just to tell people why we can't help them! Bernardo, pleading in person, would only ruin his own case. Ralph began to make a chart. It would be a whole statistical garden:

RAMIREZ ON THE CITY		RAMIREZ TRAINED	
7 children, 2 adults on welfare $320 per mo. x 12 mos. until majority of oldest child	$26,880.00	Initial training outlay $1,000 maximum of 2 years	$2,000
Thereafter scaled down until majority of youngest child	$15,020.00	Welfare support during training: 2 years	7,680
Great probability of at least 3 children added to family	$22,680.00	TOTAL OUTLAY	$9,680.00
		Auto-mechanic's salary per year	8,400
Ramirez and wife after majority of youngest child and up to age 65	$14,280.00	Age 36-65	$243,600.00
Statistical probability of delinquency 3 out of 7 children on welfare, 3 delinquency prosecutions		TOTALS: Primary and secondary taxation:	
		Savings to state	$19,800
		Outlay	—9,680
	$12,000.00	Total saved state	$10,120
	$90,860.00		

Bernardo Ramirez saves the state $90,860.00 and earns the state and Federal governments $10,120.00, if he is trained.

The numbers were all true and valid and according to the well-loved average or modal abstracts. Let the numbers talk.

Two days later, Ralph handed a clean, freshly typed copy of his hypothetical prospectus to John Hatfield, Ab's superior and number two on the hierarchy (the rest were otoise). He watched John's face as he went down the list. Some of the statistics were familiar. John read the sheet through and then laughed.

"Ralph, you left out about how the second kid runs over a couple of old ladies, thus saving the state their old-age pensions!"

"I was very fair. After all, I could have included prison terms for the delinquent Ramirez kids and a couple of hospitalizations and all the medical bills. Oh, hell, John, I know that none of this is really new to you—how much money the state can save on a person who is working instead of drawing welfare. Ramirez is a gamble—and I know that, too, but look at the stakes. Seven kids, soon to be eight! I don't think we have much to lose in backing this try for him. Can we *not* try at these odds?"

"Maybe you've left something out of this funny little rundown. I don't see your time noted in. The work you've put in already and the terrific amount of work you'll have to do. If this guy falls through on you, it will be that much harder for you to get approval on some other doubtful case that might come along. Are you willing to face the odds on *that?*"

"Don't we all face odds somehow? Look at Fatika's client, Thurlow. Everything seemed sure as could be with that one. We invested in his last two years of college only to have him die of embolism at the end of his senior year."

"Yes, my point. Even the surest ones aren't sure. I'll give my O.K. on it, but if it doesn't work out, get out of it quick. Don't try to save your mistake." He wished Ralph luck, but the tone was very dubious, and Ralph left the office seeing for the first time how dearly some future client might have to pay for any mistake that he might make now with Bernardo.

The administration hadn't questioned Ralph's cases for a long time. If he messed this up, he would have to defend every borderline consideration for a long time to come. He sighed. Finding buried treasure was no picnic after all. Damn those expensive daydreams!

Andrea Colvin

In session after session Ralph was trying to get the Colvins to relinquish their great dreams for Andrea's future. He had gone over all the different trades that could be taught to her in a slower, less demanding "reservation" within the bigger world where speed and accuracy were kings. After a long while Mrs. Colvin grudgingly let Andrea be taken to the sheltered workshop for a look. When she stepped into the big, noisy shop where the power-sewing classes were taught, she was home. Her eyes brightened at the noise and bustle and the girls chattering over the chatter of their machines. When the instructor came to take them around, she left her mother and Ralph without a word and followed the instructor, her quiet, Madonna face now smiling.

Mrs. Colvin backed out of the pandemonium and moved closer to Ralph. "What am I going to tell her father? It's all very well for me to see her and know that this is right—I haven't seen that smile in years, so many that I forgot it was part of her. But power-sewing! Oh, he'll never approve!"

"Mrs. Colvin, why not let Andrea do the convincing? Your husband may well be missing that smile himself without realizing it."

"I doubt if she could convince him. She gets confused so

136

often and forgets the points we've gone over time and time again when she's to tell things."

"Were they things she herself wanted?"

"I don't know any more. You see, Mr. Oakland, until this last year when that secretary business came up, she was always so tractable that I guess we just assumed that whatever happened was what she *wanted* to happen. We got into the habit of expecting her to agree—I remember going to the P.T.A. meetings at the school and wondering what all that talk about adolescent rebellion was about. How could we realize that she was pulling away what she had from us? Still, I wonder if she can convince her father about *this*," and she motioned to the machine-clatter, tongue-racket going on in the power-sewing room.

"Let her try. Let her describe it to him by herself. I think your girl could charm a stone."

Andrea came bursting through the door. "Mommy, can I? Please, can I?"

"Well . . ."

"Mommy, all the girls are so nice. There's this one girl, Mollie, and she's from Lincoln Wells, and she wants me to sit with her and she said she'll help me and everything! *Please*, Mommy?"

Mrs. Colvin looked at Ralph and shrugged. "All right, honey," she said, "you go on in to the lady in there and find out what you have to do to start. I'll wait for you here with Mr. Oakland."

Andrea flew back into the noisy hive and the mother flinched. "I can't imagine anyone *begging* to go into *that*."

"I think she'll find friends there, and, most amazingly, there are going to be some girls who are slower than she is, girls whom she can help and be big sister to. Those girls are not all retarded, but most of them are slow. It may be nice for her to be the smart one, the quick one somewhere."

Andrea came out soon, full of news and instructions, and they went to register her for training and then back to the rehabilitation office to arrange for further appointments and sign the forms. While Andrea's mother was in with the secretary, the girl wandered out in the hall where the blind man presided over his carefully piled packages of cigarettes and chocolate. When Ralph went out to motion her back into the office, he saw that the cub lions were hungry, wounded-eyed, moist-nosed young stags had gathered around their watering place, pacing and stretching with elaborately casual gestures of indifference. Andrea's docile face, now lit with her new joyousness, was irresistible, and the new smile that came and went with theirs was a great big beautiful Yes. Her clothes *were* too tight and too provocative; Ralph saw it clearly from his place down the hall. He had thought before that he might have been wrong; he saw now that he wasn't. Her young breasts fought against the thin cloth of her dress, her hips were limned in every single contour, and over these presided the welcoming, uncomplicated face of the child-Madonna. That virgin, like his stone Virgin in France, was one to whom all men were drawn. She promised no casuistry, no reasons, only love. And this sweet virgin was not robed for a medieval niche. Ralph wished that somehow he could tell Mrs. Colvin and make his message plain. Was the woman crazy? Did she know what she was asking for? Some other woman should warn Mrs. Colvin. Maybe he could get a social worker or one of Andrea's teachers to do it. He remembered the terrible start he had made, and he blushed for it. Then he motioned to the young girl down the hall and with a lovely little hesitating gesture, she recognized him and then came toward him while the pack behind her rose and shook and scratched and began to drift away reluctantly.

"Well," Ralph said, "we're almost done. You'll be able to start school next week."

"School ..." Her eyes filled with the dim evocation of trouble.

"You remember, where the sewing machines were ..."

"Oh, I didn't know you meant that place!" The mist passed; the brightness appeared again.

Mrs. Colvin came out and they got ready to leave. "I hope you're right about Andrea telling her father," Mrs. Colvin said.

"Well, let her give it a try, and call me in any case. If he doesn't approve, we haven't lost anything. If you call me, we can set up some times for counseling, so that I can help if I'm able."

They left, and Ralph went into his office. As he passed by the switchboard, the telephone secretary smiled up at him. "Sweet kid, isn't she? In this office a little doll like that is like a quick vacation in the sun."

"She is lovely, but don't you think she dresses a little—well, aren't her clothes a little—uh—*tight?*"

"Oh, you men!" and the secretary waved him off. "Your minds are all on *just one thing!*"

138

"Maybe so," Ralph said, "maybe you're right."

The phone rang. "Mr. Oakland, this is Captain Sutter. I work with the Salvation Army, the branch down at Twentieth and Vandalia . . ." (Ralph went over the roster of his alcoholic clients. Who was it, who was it this time?)

"Yes, Captain Sutter."

"I heard from one of the health people, who serves this area, that you were worried about John Kroll. I just wanted to let you know that he's all right. I talked to him this morning."

"John Kroll? Is he still there? Do you know where he is now?"

"No, he's not here now. Sometimes he comes to us first; sometimes he tries places by himself. It depends, of course."

What was the man talking about? "I've heard that he's been seen there before. Do you know if he goes to any place regularly down there?"

"No, Mr. Oakland, it isn't a regular thing. He's been here about four times, but he's been to the other places more often, probably. I think he was shy of us at first."

Ralph's strange feeling was increasing. He and Sutter were speaking in two different contexts, he was sure of that, but he still wanted to pin down that suspicion about narcotics. Perhaps John was using a number of the skidrow facilities or even the Salvation Army as a front. He might as well wise Sutter up. "Captain Sutter, you know that the police are looking for John Kroll. He's an institutional ward and he has run away."

"Oh—I see. I never knew that, but it puts a whole new light on the thing. It certainly explains his hesitation to come here. I always did think it strange, since sooner or later we get to know most of what goes on around here. I had assumed that it was the sordidness of all of it that had made him hesitate to confide. It fitted in with my assumption, you see, and so I . . ."

"Do you mean he didn't want to go to you for food?" Ralph was at sea, paddling along with someone who seemed absolutely sure of what he was talking about.

"Oh, we gave him food and shelter occasionally, but of course he came for the other thing first."

Now Ralph knew that he couldn't go on blindly. "Captain Sutter, *what* other thing?"

"Surely you knew—oh, Mr. Oakland, he came here for *information*."

The slightly pedantic manner was making Ralph feel as if he were going to have to drag the ocean. "Information about *what*, Captain Sutter?"

"Why, about his mother. But he's been doing it for several years, off and on; I thought everyone knew. It's a sad case, a case that has given us all many things to wonder about. You see, the mother is—well—a lost woman. Every six months or so she finds her way back here, spends a week or two begging or selling herself for money to buy liquor. She goes on a great orgy of self-degradation. She's usually jailed afterwards, sixty or ninety days, depending on her condition. After that she disappears for four months or five or six, and then she is back and the cycle begins again."

"How does John . . ."

"Ah, that is the strangest part of this. I don't know how he finds out. I suspect that he has some contacts here and there who inform him, but sometimes it seems almost as if John had had some secret feeling or signal in himself. He finds her unconscious or trying to become so or with some man, and he takes her home. The first few times it was relatively easy for him to find her, but lately it seems as though she's been trying to elude him. This time he'd been looking for over six days. She never leaves the area—something keeps her here, on these streets—but she manages to slip away from him, always leaving some little, little clue, as if it were, well, a game! I saw the boy this morning, as I said. Mr. Oakland, he was suffering terribly. I had no idea that the police were looking for him as an escapee. I know that they were asking after him, but I surmised that it was in connection with the mother."

"Captain Sutter, I—uh—do you think you could find him? If the police have to arrest him, it will mean a sentence to Boys' State until he's twenty-one. He has to give himself up to the juvenile authorities if he is to have a shadow of a chance."

The elderly—he sounded elderly—pedantic voice went on. Ralph's mind was spinning. Could his judgment have been that wrong? Wasn't there surely some very clever ruse here, some trick? No, John wasn't clever enough to set up a scheme like that, or to fool more than one person on Vandalia. No one else would use him; he was too undependable, too much of a loner.

"Do you know Mrs. Kroll? Have you met her?" Ralph asked.

140

"Yes. It's Williams now, or Wilson. She's been married several times since John's father. She's come here now and then for food or a bed. Mr. Oakland, I want to say something to you, something I have wanted to say for a long time. I have spoken to the woman many times, especially since I came to know John slightly. I have never known hatred such as the hatred she expresses to that boy. What I have heard her say to him—Mr. Oakland, something must be done so that she doesn't make him suffer any more."

When Ralph hung up the phone, he sat in his chair and looked around at the familiar office objects. It was the office of a rehabilitation counselor, a trained psychologist who had spent years mastering his subject and who had, in addition, some years in the working world, in factories, in mental wards, as a soldier and a social worker. Could he have worked and studied so long and yet misjudge a person so completely?

The crux of the whole case of John Kroll was that he was supposed to have no feelings. It was in the records, and they went back practically to his cradle, that he had not the slightest concern for anyone else. He had stolen from a blind man, lied, bullied, resolutely refused to show any feeling whatever for the rest of the world. Yet, he had jeopardized his freedom and his future to track down a drunken prostitute of a mother through every beer joint and brothel on skid row. John Kroll was impulsive; his impulsiveness was one of his hallmarks. He had no dependability; no stable, long-lasting discipline of any kind; yet he had endured his mother's hatred time and time again. He had tried to rescue her against who knew what obstacles. Of the cold and emotionless boy, a source of terror to Georgia Burns at 89 points I.Q., Captain Sutter had said, "He is suffering terribly."

The more Ralph thought about John Kroll and that double life of his, the wider the case seemed to grow. Ralph's whole strength and usefulness was based on the ephemeral and intangible qualities which he brought to this work, his judgment of people and their potential, his gift for seeing beyond the surface presented by his clients and into their deeper wishes, needs, and fears. How could he have been so mistaken? How could he have been so mistaken and still be valuable to anyone who was not quite the person he seemed to be? The more reasonable part of Ralph conceded the mistake, reminding him that there had been many times when his perception was true and right against all kinds of surface

141

evidence to the contrary. But each of these decisions was a human life, or part of it. If the right answers weren't there for him, what use was all the good will in the world? The next client was there, waiting. He called a few people and went out to her, but through the interview he found himself wondering if he was truly seeing what was there. . . .

Hans Marshak

Hans Marshak sat quietly while Ralph looked over his record. He had been first in his class in spite of having to drop back and make up work time after time, as the stumps of his legs became re-infected. Now, his co-workers on a job might never even know, unless he wished to tell them, that he walked on limbs which were not his own. He probably wouldn't tell them—he had been particularly sensitive to anything that hinted at pity from the very beginning, and lately there was a certain reserve about him which would discourage the personal kind of give-and-take in which the subject might come up. Ralph felt drawn to that reserve and dignity. As often as he had felt frustrated by the pioneer stone stoicism which was the ideal American response, he couldn't help being held by it. It was only for a man himself to know what he was and how deeply he felt.

In a way, Marshak's dignity and strength reflected on both of them. Ralph looked at his competent, independent client and felt a rare pride that he had helped someone for whom he would have respect and admiration anywhere. Most of his clients were inept or weak or dependent, and sometimes he felt that his own dedication was weakened by the quality of the people with whom he had to work. The attitude wasn't right, not scientific, not professional, but it came to him sometimes and he had to face it. Thus, Hans Marshak brought, all the more powerfully, a resurrection of the joy in his work for which Ralph often waited through long periods of tedious detail and resigned compromise with the harder facts of life. Hans's training had gone so well and his capability was so plain that Ralph had to pause in his talk about job possibilities so as not to seem casual about the hard work that Hans himself had done. Ralph didn't wish to sound too flip and sure by telling Hans how easy employment would be for a man of his youth and training. He studied the record again, and said, "We have three or four plants in this area whose

142

work is especially interesting. They always need good men. Carter, for instance, has an electronics components place. They turn out precision stuff for rockets and missiles. Then, there's Lambert Company. They make precision medical machinery. The exciting thing about these places is that their product keeps changing. There's a new wrinkle or a whole new series of parts produced every few months to keep up with the advances in that field. I think we should start with the top places.

"Well, I think I've had all the medical machinery I can use for a while, but the electronics outfit sounds good."

"O.K., I'll start there and let you know. If they need someone, you can go down for an interview and know pretty well what to expect in terms of pay, hours, and so forth. If one doesn't come through, another will." Ralph looked down the list of dates on the right side of the report. "You've been pushing pretty hard," he said. "From what I see here, you've never given yourself any time off. There's been training and your physical health to keep up with; now, this job-hunting may take a little time, so you might as well just relax a little. Take a break. You haven't given yourself time to"—he was going to say "adjust," but he stopped—"enjoy anything. Give your wife a break." He saw a flash of fear move across Hans's face. "I don't mean months, and I'm not stopping you from trying to find something on your own, if you don't overdo it and irritate that delicate tissue. Whatever happens, I just don't want you to start worrying if you go one day without work. By the way, how are things at home?" He remembered what had disturbed Hans at their last conversation. "Your mother stopped moaning and groaning?"

"I guess so. She and my wife don't get to see each other too much now that Helen is working. I know Helen is glad about me having this chance, I mean school and all. That's why I want to get going on a job right away. And then, well, there are still bills to pay."

"I'll try to get calling on these places as soon as I can. Don't worry: It won't last too long; and you might see what they have in the paper and keep up with that. I just didn't want you to go so fast. You should let down for a while, but I guess that isn't really easy with the bills piling up."

"I'll be waiting for your call, Mr. Oakland." And he stood up with a neat flick in adjustment on the sides of the artificial limbs.

They said good-bye, and Ralph made notations about calling Carter Electronics and two or three other places. Hans was trained; he would be a top man. But Ralph had still wanted to make the calls himself. There were companies who hired handicapped workers because they could get them for wages much lower than normal. Hans was too good for that sort of thing, and Ralph didn't want him to be exposed to it. There had been rumors going through the grapevine that Carter Electronics had been guilty of that kind of cutting. It might be only a rumor; he would call them and see. He flipped over the pages of Hans's case file to the last page of the school report. "Training: second year." Scrawled in pencil at the bottom was a comment which Ralph hadn't noticed before: "We are particularly proud to have worked with this student. His single-minded dedication to his studies has advanced him very rapidly and his spirit and morale have given all of us a lift." It was signed by the head of the institute. Then a little p.s. followed. "If you get another one like that, send him over." Ralph laughed. It wasn't that easy. Still, the note pleased him, even though he recognized its slightly guilty and patronizing tone. It wasn't fair to have to be an amputee; everybody knew it, and felt somehow that the unfairness was too private a thing to be worn so openly and brazenly. Men's private struggles should be kept from others, their single facts and selves held aloof. Cripples were stared at in the street sometimes—he had seen it himself. There was a guilty sort of fascination in the looks they got, as if the spectator were saying: I know something about you. It was this false feeling of knowledge, perhaps, that had formed the paradoxical stereotypes: bizarre and sinister cripple, saintly and forgiving cripple. Actually, the good stereotype was as dangerous to the victim as the bad. Ralph knew that his visibly different clients had as much trouble trying to free themselves from the model of saintly acceptance, which the world tried to fit to them, as they had with the pains and limitations of actual handicaps. Hans Marshak was eager and ambitious, but he was not accepting and not particularly grateful. He didn't fit the image, and it would go hard with him when people found it out.

The telephone rang. "Ralph, this is Georgia Burns. They picked up John Kroll this afternoon. The police called me right away. They have him down at Juvenile Hall . . ."

"How is he?"

144

"I don't know how *he* is, but I know that *it* couldn't be worse. They found a switchblade knife on him."

"Oh, no!"

"Did Captain Sutter speak to you?"

"Yes, and I gather that you know all about Mama now, too. Somehow I guess I just assumed she was dead."

"I never had an idea, no idea at all," she said. "I kept thinking that I couldn't have been that wrong about him, so I went down there and got hold of some of those people. They were reading a different soul, Ralph. They said that he was tough, sure, but not mean. They said that he was angry and bitter and a loner, but not cruel. I know that Vandalia Street standards are not ours—they call you kind down there when you hit a dame with an open hand, and they don't consider you cruel until you break her face—but still, Ralph, *still* . . ."

"Will that part come out? Can we go down there and speak up for him somehow?"

"Well, I've called down and what they'll do is to keep him in Juvenile Hall until his case comes up before Judge French. Then, well, we'll be informed, they told me, and we can come in."

"Do you have any idea when that will be, I mean, what day?"

"No, why?"

"I'll have to clear time; I'm booked up solid until the 15th of December. That's almost three weeks away and every day, of course, it moves further; in other words, I'd like to have about that length of time to know, if I could."

"Okay, Ralph, I'll try to find out for you. I have pull down at the courthouse."

"Really?"

"Oh, yes, I'm very big down there. My brother-in-law is bailiff."

11

Bernardo Ramirez

If Bernardo Ramirez looked around, he would see that he was in the motor-rebuilding class at Central Auto school. The background was in, colored and real-looking, but Ralph's next job was to get him to know that he really belonged there. In counseling sessions, Bernardo was still the polite and accepting witness. He answered as if he were sitting in absentia for someone else, someone whose delicate decisions and subtle choices were beyond him. Part of this was because of their laboring over language. *Real* speech was Spanish, although Bernardo was too polite to say so, but every time they blundered on to a common word, the look on Bernardo's face would proclaim his patient despair and plead for Ralph to come to his senses and speak the speech of human beings. His definition of English seemed to be: That in which I shall never be understood. Well, that would take time. Ralph called the welfare office and made appointments for counseling sessions with Bernardo.

"Oh, Mr. Oakland," Miss Jesperson said, "I wanted to tell you that we're having the meeting on the first and the Ramirez case will be presented as well as the others. There will be nine in all." There were usually about nine referrals a month from the welfare office. Ralph was free to take the ones he thought he could work with, usually three or four, and he had five other official sources of referrals.

"I'd like to see Ramirez before the meeting, if I could. I saved a half-hour on Tuesday from 2:30 to 3:00. Do you think someone could bring him over then?"

On Tuesday they faced one another and Ralph tried to tell Bernardo Ramirez about being Prometheus. (You know, there aren't too many people who can work well with motors ... Motors is a good work and it will pay well ...")

As Bernardo was polite, unfailing in patience, and gentle, he nodded yes and no dutifully, as the sentences directed, followed the course of the explanation with slight rhythmic inclinations of his head and carried his face before him in such a way that Ralph knew he did not understand one single word. Ralph might have been explaining archeology. It was an interesting subject and Ramirez was grateful to know of it, but it bore nothing that was going to impinge on his life.

At last Ralph said, "Would you care to make what you do in Mr. Vinson's school your regular work?"

"I don't know if I cou' do dat ..."

"Well—Mr. Vinson thinks you can. You've been working there for a while and it's going well for you, isn't it?"

"Well—Mr. Vingsong, he's a goo' man, bu' he don't speakeen' Spanish, and I'ne na' sure sungtines wha' he sayeen', you know?"

Bernardo sat quietly, without changing a single, patient fold. His yellow shirt threw a butter-colored shadow against the billowing chins. It made Ralph think of how kids used to see the butter in buttercups blooming in the Paleozoic springtimes of his youth. He went on to tell how good it was to have a trade that was needed by the world. He knew that Bernardo had never really had such a trade. He had always been on the losing side of the battle between the machine and the human arm, part of a penumbra of men whose work was fading away. The exhilaration of choice between a good job and a better one had never been his, and it strained his imagination to conceive of it. Ralph knew also that Bernardo was afraid he couldn't really learn from a mouth that spoke no Spanish. He blundered here and there, trying to find a hook that would hold Bernardo's faith. In the middle of a rambling sentence, he found it, right at the point where his and Bernardo's worlds met. He ended his thought and began again, very slowly.

"A man has children ... He holds them and he dreams that they will always see him as proud and strong in his own house. When a man's children walk in the streets, he dreams that the thoughts of his neighbors will be well toward them. If you work to learn this trade, then, as you were strong and good on the farm of Señor Chase, so you will be strong in the motor places of the city."

"You thin' I cou' learn thes theen?"

"It will be difficult. There are other parts of city learning that will be long and hard for you, but I am very strong in my thought that you will succeed. It is *you* who will have to believe this and be strong in *your* thought of it. You will have to speak with strength for yourself."

Ralph had set up a myth and he knew it, and Ramirez knew it, too. The admiring neighbors of the future were cardboard characters in a stylized tale of success and happiness, but at least it was a myth, a tale, a dream that they both shared; it reached to cover them in English and in Spanish, over middle and low income, over twentieth-century America and seventeenth-century Mexico.

Bernardo said he would keep trying at the work. He said that he would try to believe in the work. His look did not change. No little technique or pep talk would wipe the blank look of generations of patient acceptance from his face. If, someday, he could attain even a small glimmer of hope or choice or will in his manner, it might weigh for him, even a little, when he needed it.

When Bernardo left, Ralph checked over the paperwork on the case quickly. The agency would pay the tuition at Central. That was already going through, but since the family was being maintained on welfare, there might have to be some changes in the budget to allow for extras. He made a note on the record and went out to the next client. He would have to think out the needs of Bernardo Ramirez, student, quite carefully before his meeting with the welfare workers.

There were regular meetings between Ralph and the people from the welfare department and between the interested parties on the medical, legal, and psychiatric staffs of all the social agencies in the city. At these meetings, the toebone was connected to the footbone, the footbone was connected to the legbone, and the piecemeal man was resurrected and set before the meeting whole. In Bernardo's case there were no legal or psychiatric problems and no remaining medical problem, so that the people meeting over Bernardo's past, present, and future in duplicate and in triplicate were to be only his caseworker, a welfare supervisor, and Ralph. Other workers would be coming to discuss the progress of their people in training. As they were about to start on Bernardo's case, another worker joined them. Ralph had often worked with her, but he wondered for a moment why she was there, since she handled only the hard-core, chronic dependency cases. Then he realized that welfare must have been making its own plans for Bernardo, based, reasonably enough, on the results of Ralph's own tests which had been sent to them. The department must have felt that since Bernardo and his family were going to be one of the unending ones, the "hopeless" workers might as well be in on the proceedings from the start. Ralph wanted to smile and be triumphant, but he knew the rigidity of agencies, his own no less than this one. It would be just another move that would have to be unmade, one more plan to be unthought.

They all sat down, and Ralph took a deep breath toward his unbelievable news. The caseworker misinterpreted the breath. She began to fight to keep it from leaving in words of a definite refusal. She, too, knew that once Ralpph had spoken, his "position" would have been stated, and all the inertia of "professional status" would be there to keep him from changing it. It would take a tremendous amount of force to displace him from that "position."

". . . you know, we haven't really given this family time to adjust . . ."

"Well . . ."

"Mr. Oakland, I know that you had him go down to Central Auto—we thought probably for handyman or night watchman. Couldn't you try him somewhere just once more?"

"Uh—(There went that night watchman again. Watchman, what of the night?)—and there might be room for this man over at the Industries for the Blind. He may be a moron, but he can see. Don't they hire some sighted to do quality checks or manage certain machines?"

"I don't see why *something* can't be done," the Supervisor said, "it seems a shame to give up when so large a family is involved. And there is the *car*. It's already been such an embarrassment to the agency—of course, we could *force* him to give it up one way or another, but we want him to *learn* why it's foolish to have—why . . ."

"Excuse me," Ralph said quietly, "but I think you'll be happy with our agency's plans for Mr. Ramirez."

"Oh?" (A polite, questioning lift of three sets of eyebrows.) They were only half-listening for whatever scheme of part-time make-work this could be.

"Well, Mr. Ramirez was taken down to Central Auto, as you know. He is not working there; he is registered there as a student. Mr. Ramirez has been accepted for advanced training at Central. He's going to be an auto mechanic and motor repairman."

The silent moment hung about them for a moment, and then fell in embarrassed laughter. "What, not brain surgery?" "What, not fashion design?"

The Supervisor looked a little annoyed at the waste of time and at the ridiculing of One of Society's Major Problems. "Please, let's be serious about this. We have work to do."

"I am serious," Ralph said. "I was down at Central yesterday. He's been with them for about three weeks now on a trial basis. Mr. Vinson told me that he wants Ramirez in his second-year class. I wanted to tell you about this sooner, but I've been swamped with work and I just didn't get around to it. I know it's a surprise; it was to me, too—before I got used to the idea ..." He realized that he didn't have anything more to say, and so he just stopped.

"This *is* Ramirez, Bernardo Ramirez you're talking about ..."

"Isn't it a surprise? I couldn't have guessed. He's the one-in-a-million freak genius that everyone of us hopes for in that half-second of every new client's coming in."

"But—but that's *impossible!* Look at his tests, his records. If he had *any* mechanical aptitude, it would show up on the test scores."

"*You* look at those tests," Ralph said. "They show gears and the taker is supposed to trace the direction of the gears; they give spaces and the taker is supposed to fill them in most economically. The tests never say why; they never show the context of those gears or the purpose of those squares; and they never explain why *time* is made so much of a factor. *We think* only this or that is relevant! Well, here I go on my pet crusade. I can only say that where Bernardo sees no need, he sees no meaning. Where he sees no urgency, he feels insulted by speed. Why is this so hard for us to accept?"

"But how do you know that he can do the work then?"

"By a stroke of dumb luck I saw him do it." There was a long pause while the words sank in. Then Ralph followed up hard while they were still in shock. "He can benefit by this training, but only if welfare follows up with the training that Central Auto can't give."

"What do you mean?"

"Well, he's going to need some basic things: enough reading and numbers to get around in the city without getting into trouble."

150

The Supervisor and the worker exchanged looks of annoyance. "We've been trying for years to get funds to set up little classes in basic health and nutrition and cleanliness and money and numbers; reading a street map, basic laws, and the need for literacy. We've been voted down every time. The state legislature is made up of very few welfare recipients. For some reason, unknown to me, they think that it's cheaper to send a trained social worker *with* every illiterate client, who has to change houses or budget his money or go to a new stop on the bus. Now don't get me started on *my* cause."

"Bernardo Ramirez has got to be taught enough to add change on the bus and stay out of ladies' rooms. That is a job for welfare," Ralph said, knowing that without basic knowledge Bernardo would never be anything more than a stranger and an oddity. "Aren't there some service clubs in town that would jump at the chance to show an affable, polite, ex-peon how to get from 17th and Lacey to 16th and Grand?"

"Well, I don't know," the Supervisor said.

"Why not? I've got to talk to women's clubs and the various lodges of this and that and the other; I'd love to tell them that there *is* something they can *do*. It would keep me from feeling that the damn talks are just wasting time, and it would give the members an understanding of just what our problems and needs are."

"You forget, Mr. Oakland, that welfare's first principle is confidentiality. It's why we never let anyone but professional workers help. Your clients, fortunately, do not have the same—well—stigma attached to their receiving help as ours do. We don't want anyone but the professional workers even to *know* who is or is not receiving a welfare grant."

"But Bernardo couldn't care less who knew, and with someone working with him on these practical things his whole future could be more secure."

"It just isn't agency policy to bring in outsiders to work directly with welfare recipients. Besides, Mr. Oakland, how well could we screen such volunteers? Could we really search into their motives and prejudices? Haven't we failed many times to train our own workers not to be condescending—and your Ramirez, more than anyone else, would come in for his share of prejudice. Imagine, seven children and one on the way!"

Ralph saw her point. Some service-club volunteers aren't far past the poverty from which they have climbed in cold

151

desperation. Some blow so frigid a wind of self-serving complacency and humorless, asphyxiating righteousness, that they take a toll in morale twice what they give in service. A domestic Peace Corps would be fine, but confidentiality would swamp them in Springfield as it never would in Senegal.

"Mr. Oakland ..." It was the caseworker, Miss Jesperson. "Do you really think that he can learn these things? He's so—so *mañana.*"

"Aren't we the ones with the *mañana*?" Ralph asked.

"You mean always bigger and better?"

The Supervisor shook her head. "I won't buy that. *They* always say it: Tomorrow. The job? Tomorrow."

"Maybe they do," Ralph said, "but I have the strongest feeling that Bernardo's *mañana* means, if not yesterday, then never."

"He didn't resent his Señor Chase down in Indio county," Miss Jesperson said. "I thought to myself when I first interviewed him: at least there's no hate here."

"We always assume there will be resentment between master and man," Ralph said, "because with *our* tradition there would be. Bernardo's 'señor' was señor from the beginning of time. Perhaps, in Bernardo's view, the señor is no more deserving of praise or blame than Bernardo himself who was bending his back in the world's first sunrise. We always assume bitterness, but I saw Bernardo with Herb Vinson down at Central and he wasn't cheeky or sour or fawning or servile ..."

"All right," the Supervisor said, "you want us to set him up with some basic reading and numbers. I think we can get one of our students to do it or a teacher who is moonlighting. It's going to be a job getting funds to do that, if we have to use someone from the outside. And I imagine you'll want us to pay his bus fare."

"We'll pay the fare if you'll give him fifty cents a week mad money."

"You must have been out in the wind too long. You know our regulations. There *is* no madness on relief. There is no miscellany. It's all been figured out by a trained economist as the basic subsistence in our economy. Everything is taken into account, even the amount of toothpaste used by the average person in a month. It was figured out in 1948 and hasn't been updated since, but it's the law. This year it was cut a flat two dollars per person per month as an economy

152

measure. No allowance for depreciation, no extras, no mad money."

"Nails? Rags? Cigarettes? Phone calls to Tangiers? What about a damn evening paper, for practise?"

"You see, we can't make exceptions, even if he works or wants to be trained to work. Working or studying isn't part of the plan . . ."

"I'll make a deal with you," Ralph said. "If my agency gives him thirty-five cents a week mad money, will you agree not to take it off his grant as income?"

"Sold!" said the Supervisor. "If you swear to me that he won't use it to buy gas for that—that *car.*"

" . . . and thirty-five cents a week, mad money," Ralph said, and wrote it in his notes. The hopeless case worker gathered her books together, caught the eyes of Ralph and the Supervisor, smiled, shrugged, and left. Although she was young and pretty and gentle and kind and dedicated and gifted, Ralph couldn't help heaving a sigh of relief toward her back as she moved through the door. The angel of death had departed in peace without claiming a soul.

"Mr. Oakland, this is Mr. Haye, returning your call. As a matter of fact, there is an opening here for an electronics technician. I was on the governor's board last year myself: Commission for Employment of the Physically Disabled. Did I meet you at the dinner?"

"No, sir, I don't think so; I wasn' . . ."

"Too bad, too bad. You missed a fine spread and even the speakers were good. They gave the award, too. It was a great night. I was glad our group was smart enough to move the thing to the Collegiate instead of having it at the hotel as usual. I tell you, it was a first-rate affair."

"Yes, well, our man here has been trained at Fleetwood; you know, that's the best place in the area. They give a two-year course in electronics instrumentation that's equal to anything in the country."

"Of course, we train our men for our own specialized operation. If he's worked in missile electronics, we can use him right now, and we'd pay him for the time he trains in our operation."

"Fine. His name is Hans Marshak and he's had six months of missile and computer electronics."

"Good, very good. What's his handicap?"

"None, really, he's an amputee."

"Oh, in a wheelchair then?"

"Oh, no, he can walk, drive a car—anything. He has only a very slight limp, which we hope will disappear in time."

"Well, you send him down then. We're always glad to help somebody along that's down on his luck."

"Yes, I see. Well, Mr. Haye, what's the pay scale down there?"

"Well, we'd pay him two dollars an hour and one-fifty while he trains."

"But, Mr. Haye, the standard for electronics men with his kind of training is closer to three dollars an hour . . ."

"But you forget, Mr. Oakland, that your man is handicapped. My insurance will go up, and there'll be other costs: absenteeism and so forth."

"But, Mr. Haye, if you were on the governor's committee and attended those banquets and so forth, you know that the insurance bugaboo is a myth and the absentee record is a myth, too. Mr. Marshak isn't handicapped at all for any of the operations for which you would be hiring him. There's no distance running necessary. Most of all, he isn't a charity case . . ."

"I should think that a cripple like that would be glad to get work at all. You people trained him and what's that but charity?"

"We're a public agency. We hope to be repaid by the income taxes of men like Hans who make a decent wage."

"It's a free country, Mr. Oakland, and if you find anybody who'll take a handicapped for more than two an hour, you'll be lucky. When you're through, call back and I'll still take him at two, without prejudice."

"Without prejudice . . ."

"Good-bye, Mr. Oakland."

"Mr. Oakland, this is Carnegie again. You found anyone yet?"

"I'm sorry, Mr. Carnegie. You know yourself how tough it is to get people with the patience and dexterity and—well—personality it takes to do contact-lens grinding."

"But we're backlogged months on our orders. Please try to find someone. I have calls into the employment office and I place ads every week in all the papers. If I don't get someone soon, I'm going to have to start sending work out."

"Mr. Carnegie, tell me this, will you? Would you mind taking a Negro trainee?"

"No, not at all; have you got someone for me?"

154

"What about a Mexican—what if he's fat?"

"Mr. Oakland, I'll take anybody who can be trained to hand-grind my lenses to prescription."

"I'm not trying to play games with you, perhaps I'm a little furious at the hidden requirements of some of the employers I call."

"Mr. Oakland, I don't care if he has cornstalks growing out of his ears. I wouldn't even care if he was a *Democrat!* Fifty a week for the first three months training, sixty for the second, and on up. When he is trained, a hundred a week, and after a while it'll go as high as one-fifty. And it could be a woman, too; don't forget that . . ."

"It's need, isn't it. Simple need, and you'll even take a Democrat if the need is great enough."

"Please call me if you get somebody . . ."

"Mr. Oakland, this is Mrs. Colvin, and I just want to tell you how happy we are with what's happened. Oh, it wasn't easy to get Andrea's father around to accepting it, I mean *power-sewing!* But she wanted it so, he just had to give in. You see, she still needs us a great deal, even with so many new friends at the workshop. Why, the girls come over here to make fudge. Next week she's been invited to spend the night with her little friends, but they didn't tell her where they lived. I was wondering whether it was a hotel or something."

"No, I think they were talking about Mrs. Mercer's. Do you remember the girls' names, Mrs. Colvin?"

"Yes, one was Marilee Hutter and then the other was a Janice something."

"Oh, yes, they're girls from Kinmount and Deep Ford. They're in the sheltered workshop here because it's the only one in the state. Two or three years ago we found Mrs. Mercer, who runs a boarding house and who seemed to get along especially well with our girls. We send her many out-of-town clients who have no place to stay in the city while they are training. There must be about six girls there now, and they tell me it's a very friendly and nice place."

"Well, then, it will be all right to let her go then. I know that I was against this whole idea about Andrea being slow, but when you said something about her being laughed at, it started me to thinking and remembering. I guess we just forgot what it was like to be young. She laughs a lot now, and she's full of talk about her friends and her work. I want

155

you to know, Mr. Oakland, that we are very grateful to you for what you've done."

"Well, thank you, Mrs. Colvin, but we aren't finished really. I'd still like to see Andrea and you every month or so, at least for a while. Of course, if anything comes up in her training . . ."

"Once a month . . .?"

"Well, for a while anyway, just until she gets in the swing of things; and then, later, if it's possible for her to work outside, I'll be glad to help her get a good place. I can switch you to the secretary and she'll make an appointment for Andrea and for you, if you'd like."

"Well—if you advise it . . ."

"Are you the rehabilitation?"

"This is the office of the state rehabilitation program. My name is Oakland."

"I bet you don't take no epileptics."

"What?"

"I said, I bet you don't take no epileptics."

"We have all kinds of people on our program, including epileptics. Are you asking this for yourself?"

"You don't take me in that easy; I been around, I mean *all* around. They took my money to train me all right, and then come to find out about it, nobody will take me on a job."

"Well, Mr. . . ."

"Never mind who."

"I just wanted to ask if your seizures were controlled."

"What?"

"Are you under medication?"

"I tried lots of them nerve cures, but they don't do no good. Sometimes my mother gives me some of that bay-leaf tea."

"I see. Where did you take training and what did you train in?"

"Harrows. I took tool-making. Now they say they won't let me near them big machines out where I went for work."

"I think we can help you, but the first thing is to see if there is adequate medication to get those seizures under control. If you'll give me your address, I'll send you all the information about how to get to the neurology clinic down at City Hospital. You tell them about the condition and ask for an appointment for testing and evaluation."

156

"I ain't givin' you no address; you just send it to R.P. Avon in General Delivery."

"Fine. Go through the tests and get set up on medication, and then you call me again, O.K.?"

"O.K., but you better not be leading me on . . ."

"Mr. Stinson, this is Ralph Oakland at the State Department of Rehabilitation. We have a man who has just finished training as an electronics technician. I was wondering if there was an opening for him at Carter right now."

"Feast or famine. Where were you last month? I just filled two open positions after we had run ads all season. Who did you say you were?"

"Department of Rehabilitation—we're a state agency. We test, oversee training, and then find jobs for our clients."

"And they are, like, on relief . . ."

"Oh, no. The service is for everyone. If the client can't pay for training, the state pays for it, but the testing and counseling are open to anyone who is phyisically handicapped."

"He just has to be handicapped?"

"That's right."

"I never heard of that. I didn't know there was such a thing. I've got no openings for you now, but I sure will keep you guys in mind. But look—I've got a sister, and her son has a congenital heart diease. Do you think . . ."

Ralph, this is Etta. Your requisitions for—Herbert, Winfield—Kroll, Sanford—and Van Bronckhorst were late this month. They'll have to go under the January budget."

"Did you say Kroll?"

"Uh—Herbert, Winfield, *Kroll*; yes, here it is."

"Well, we don't have to worry about that one. You can just take it out of the file and throw it away."

"I wish you counselors would get those requisitions in on time. It fouls up the whole accounting system!"

"Bureaucracy."

"What?"

"There are things you can't plan ahead for."

"Like what?"

"Like the camera lens that Winfield broke during his training that had to be replaced, like the cab that Van Bronckhorst had to take to work for a week when the fellow who was driving him got sick."

"Well, I just wanted you to know that late requisitions are very hard on we girls."

"I'll keep it in mind, Etta."

". . . who just finished training as an electronics engineer. I wonder if you have an opening there just now."

"As a matter of fact we do. Where did this man get his training?"

"Fleetwood. He was an airplane mechanic before that."

"Oh? Why the switch?"

"Well, he was in an auto accident. He lost both legs. With modern limbs though, he has virtually no handicap; but the other job was quite an athletic one, climbing around those planes. I think that the mechanics will stand him in good stead."

"Sounds fine. Can he come in, say, Thursday at two? We'll want to take a look at him and show him the plant."

"I'm sure he'll be able to make it, Mr. Merton. Oh, by the way, what is the pay down there?"

"We pay two-twenty-five an hour while training, two-eighty for a junior—that's the first six months—and then three-twenty-five after that. There are promotions, too, for good men."

"Sounds good. Let me get in touch with him and check on the time. Let's leave it at Thursday, two o'clock, and if he can't make it, then he'll call. All right?"

"Fine, Mr. Oakland—good-bye."

John Kroll

"Hi, Oakland."

Ralph looked up. Punking. John Kroll was in top form. "Take a seat, John," Ralph said.

Kroll draped himself flaccidly into the chair.

Ralph growled, "Sit up!" And John stiffened with surprise. "How come you're out? I thought the juvenile authorities were keeping you."

"Yeah, well, Old Lady Burns fixed it for me to come here and see you. See, I got a long chain and there's a guy back in Juvenile that's got ahold of the other end. When I get through here, I'm going to snap it in hard and alla way down there, he'll go boiiiiiiing!"

"John, I'm beginning to wonder if my I.Q. test wasn't

wrong after all. You walk out of school in the middle of the day; you're out two weeks; you violate your sentence to the Shelter, toss away your whole training, your freedom, your future; and then you walk in here—Hi, Oakland—like a character in a grade-B Western."

"Yeah, well, I ditched, but I had stuff to do."

"I know all about that," Ralph said, "but that doesn't change a damn thing. Did you find her, at least?"

"Yeah."

"Did she go home?"

"No."

"Well, what happened?"

"I seen her, but she didn't come this time. She—uh—she was—fu—she was with this guy, so I waited—uh—till they was suppose to come out. I thought he was gonna take off, see, uh—but . . ." There was a light sweat beginning to bead on John's upper lip, like the very light beginning of his manhood fuzz. His upper arms, shoulders, and neck were rigid. "He spotted me waitin' and come over and—uh—took me around the building. See, my—uh—she paid him to beat me up, so he was gonna, but—uh—I guess he wasn't too bad of a guy, so he just told me what she said and then said I should beat it, and he give me a shove. I went out of there, and *what the hell!* I was hungry and I went around down 18th 'cause I knew there was cops there."

"Why did you keep the knife then, if you were giving yourself up."

"Hell, you didn't think I could leave it *look* like I was goin' in, do you?"

"John, John, *John!* Do you know how much that damn knife is going to *cost* you? Do you know how much five minutes of movie-tough-guy is going to be paid for in *jail?*"

"Hey, Oakland, I'm sorry about that school and stuff. I mean, I hope you don't get canned or nothin'."

Ralph thought wryly about his great reputation in the juvenile rehabilitation field. His two other Shelter clients were still fighting the world and him, still full of rage and bitterness. What terrible pain he could give John Kroll by telling him that his job was safe not because of his worthiness as a counselor but because the community at large, beyond yearly debates about bringing back flogging, was indifferent.

He didn't want to hurt John, so he said, "It's unselfish of you to worry about that, but it will be all right. What I want to know is why you went off without warning, without letting anyone know. If you'd told me, I might have been able to make it O.K. If you'd told Miss Burns at the Shelter, she might have been able to do something. Now you've lost even that."

"Well, you see, I didn't even know I was goin' to take off. I was on the bus and then it was time to go. There wasn't no time to figure out and go into a lot of big plans and junk."

"What makes you take off just like that? I've heard that this wasn't the first of your little visits to Vandalia Street."

"Well, I know when it's time to go."

"How do you know?"

The head dropped again. A sound from under the greased hair. "Her."

"Your mother?"

"Uh—yeah—her. I—uh—I see her and—uh—that's the time."

"You mean you think about her in some special way, or what?"

"No, I mean like the first time. She used to visit me and then she stopped, and one day I seen her at the gate—that time I was in that orphan home. Then I looked around and she was gone. I seen her goin' down the street. The next time I followed her." (Ralph remembered suddenly in this new context the nun's legible notes—a truant and a runaway.) "Sometime she was at the gate or walkin' by. The time before this I seen her in a taxi drivin' slow past the Shelter. I got out in the night and come back before they even missed me. This time I was on the way to class, and she gets right on the bus, see, and she walks right past me and out the back."

"She didn't even smile or nod to you or say anything?"

"No, she never knows me and that's why . . ."

Ralph wanted to stop him. The little beads of sweat were standing out against his upper lip. Strands of the smothered hair were beginning to break away from the mass. "She never knows me and so I . . ."

"No more, John," Ralph said very quietly. John looked up at him. The counselor had stopped the confidence and John was beginning to be frightened.

Ralph leaned forward over the desk. In their silence they heard the office clatter outside seemingly louder, typewriters clicky-clack to the bong-zip and begin again, phones ringing and the noises of people asking, and answering.

"John, I wish I could let you open up all the way, every-

160

thing you've been carrying inside you. I can't because it isn't fair to you. You're going to have to go back to Juvenile Hall and I don't want your anger to be opened so wide that you can't close it. I don't want you to have to suffer for this."

"I only got mad at her maybe this time, a little," John said.

Ralph looked at him and believed that John thought so. That was good, now. He was going to need every ounce of control he could muster in the next few weeks. Any small infraction and the judge would have the record of it before him as he studied John's case. Ralph believed that there was far more hate in him than John admitted to. How else could a child answer the repeated faithlessness and denial of that woman?

John looked at him and said very quietly, "You think I didn' see them records they got on me? The Sisters and them creeps at b.s.? There's always ways to get to see what they really think about you, and I read that crap. What they never said was how nice she was when she took me home them times and the first couple of times when I took her home and she was goin' to get dried up and we was goin' to be together and stuff. It was great then, honest. She was like them—uh—mothers you're suppose to have. We just use to sit down an' eat and then maybe go someplace. She had special names to call me, you know, I mean like just her and me know."

"John . . ."

"No! (And he was very much alive behind that face. The actors were dead; the passion was pure Kroll.) No. They didn't write it down fair. They never say what really happens in them stupid files. You know, the fifth time I got in that orphan home she tried to visit me, but they wouldn't let her in. I sneaked out. We was goin' to Oregon 'cause she got some relatives there, but the landlord must have called them sonofabitch cops, 'cause they caught her on account of she couldn't pay for the room."

"John, I wasn't trying to say anything against your mother. I just wanted—well, never mind that now. We've got a lot of work to do, because no matter what the reason was, you are down as an escapee from a place of correction and that's bad enough, not to mention the switchblade. The first thing I want to tell you is that you'd better shape up at Juvenile Hall. No fights, no back talk, no slouching around like you're doing the world a favor by being alive. That's very, very important, John, do you understand?"

"What's all the big effort for, Oakland? They know about me already. I'm on more files than the Ten Commandments."

"Okay, but if rehabilitation and teaching have helped you, then you're not incorrigible. If Miss Burns and your teachers at the school and my work have been able to make any difference to you, that difference will have to *show*. If it doesn't show, it will seem to prove that you can't be helped by anything we can do. You know what the other choice is. If you want us to try to help you, John, you will have to work at it too."

"Yeah, me an' Rutherford B. Hayes."

He turned his truculent face toward Ralph, and the counselor sighed inwardly. With a look like that, he wouldn't even need back talk.

"John, you said that Miss Burns arranged this session . . ."

"Yeah, didn' you see her?"

"Where was she?"

"She was sittin' right next to me. I told you she was fat—Jesus, how could you miss her?"

"Why didn't you say who she was?" Ralph got up, leaving John in his chair, and went out into the waiting area where a large woman sat. "I'm terribly sorry," he said, "John didn't tell me who you were and I guess my feelings were pretty mixed when I saw him, and so I . . ." He realized that he was staring at her.

She laughed. "I know—I work in a reformatory and I shouldn't look like this. Everyone who meets me seems to want a tall, gaunt man-woman with sabre scars, instead of a stout old spinster who looks like Mother Rabbit. If I didn't like the work, I'd get myself a rocker and model for Christmas cards." She took a breath. "Well, what are we going to do for John?"

"I don't know," Ralph said. "I hear conflicting things about Judge French. I have the idea, though, that if we talk too eloquently down there, for too long, it may work against John, and the Judge may think he's smelling an ulterior motive."

"I hadn't thought of that," she said quietly. "How strange it must look from the outside: us defending a boy with that record. It might well look as if we were trying to salvage our own mistakes—but we can't let him go again. It took us

162

months to find out about the mind he was hiding, the mother he was searching for, and the suffering he was going through under that slick-talking zombie he had posing for all of us."

"Okay, Georgia, just tell me when the hearing will be, and if I'm not tied up I'll be there. If I can't go, I'll write as strong a letter as I can in John's behalf."

They walked to the door of Ralph's office. Framed by the doorway was their lying, defending, hating, wise, stupid, passionate, indifferent boy-convict, John Kroll, slumped like a wilted vegetable in his chair. As his keepers came on, he slowly summoned his extremities into motion, heaved his whole organism into a slumped standing position, and began to amble toward them.

Georgia Burns said, "Well, we'd better be starting back. I don't want to spoil our chances."

John turned toward Ralph, grinning as he passed.

Ralph went back to his office in wonder. What the world understood of hypocrisy had no relevance in John Kroll's case. People covered up their lack of feeling with manners and their lack of spontaneity with mannerisms, but what word described John, who covered his plain and sufficient intelligence with an outward dullness, who withheld the decent agony and showed only the savage indifference that made people hate him? Judge French would see only the punk, John would make sure of that. It would be for Georgia Burns to remember some look that had crept from under the sneering mask. It would be for Ralph to remember a description from the foul-mouthed boy of finding his drunken whore of a mother. He had kept the street word away from her. Ralph and Georgia together would have to try to shield from John the great and crushing indifference of the world to his agony, his intelligence, and his small brief gallantry.

12

Hans Marshak

Hans Marshak had gotten the job. Before he knew it, Ralph found himself asking Hans to drop in on his way home from his interview if he had the time. When he hung up the phone, he realized that it was because he had been starved for a little triumph; a story that ended in a straight, successful placement, virtue rewarded, the success of a deserving, bright, hardworking man.

He had, that morning, gotten a job for a retarded boy on whose case he had been working for six months. The severely retarded are handicapped in an especially cruel way, because they haven't enough intelligence to gauge their own limitations. The job, a rare and beautiful Godsend, was to unload cases at a liquor store and to keep the shelves replenished. No reading or special talent was required. He had taken his client over and the boy had worked all morning. In the afternoon a customer had come in and gotten into a conversation with the owner of the store. He was the same age as the retarded stockboy, it turned out, and he was a precision machinist making exactly triple the stockboy's wages. The owner had just called Ralph to tell him that the stockboy had worked for five minutes after the affable machinist had left and then had taken off his apron, hung it up, and gone forth into the world to be a precision machinist.

Never mind the failures, Hans Marshak was going to go to work, and he was going to work as a competent, trained man, one of an industrial society's pampered darlings. His taxes would keep Ralph trying to place ever-increasing numbers of retarded baby-men and displaced older men at ever-diminishing unskilled jobs. Whatever personal suffering Hans's leglessness would cause him, it would be from the vantage

164

point of a well-paying and highly prestigious job. Ralph could hardly wait to usher Hans into his office and hear all the details of who said what.

When Hans did come, Ralph went out with his hand held welcoming before him. "Congratulations."

Hans demurred in his typical way, proud and a little ashamed to be so very proud. "They want me to start on Monday. I—I guess I'll go and get a new suit."

"That'll probably take you all day," Ralph said, thinking about the steadily pouring Christmas rush of shoppers who had been crowding into the downtown area since the first of the month.

Hans looked down at his legs and said, "Oh, no, I can manage them pretty well."

For a moment Ralph didn't understand, and then he said simply, "I was thinking about the Christmas rush."

"Oh, yes," and then Hans looked up. "It is going to be Christmas soon, isn't it? I guess, being so busy, I just forgot."

"You made your deadline, though, with a little to spare—a job before Christmas."

They went in and sat down, and Ralph leaned forward. "Well, what happened? What did they ask you? Did you go through the plant?"

Hans laughed in his self-effacing way. "They asked me a few questions and then a Mr. Mohlencamp took me around. He pointed out some of the machines and asked me if I was familiar with them, and luckily I was."

"Did he try to stump you?"

"Oh, in a very nice, easy kind of way. He asked me if I'd ever done any work with lasers, and I said I'd never worked with them but I'd read about them, and then he said something—well—fantastic, and let me correct him. A few things like that. It looks like a good shop."

"And you start Monday?"

"That's right."

"*Well* . . ." There seemed to be very little more to say.

"Mr. Oakland, I want to thank you for everything you've done," Hans said.

"Just a minute." Ralph laughed. "You're not through with me yet. I'll want to check with you when you've been on the job for a while, just to hear how you're getting along. If you have any trouble getting your relationship with us straight on your tax forms or medical questionnaires, you might want to give me a call. We usually keep in touch with our clients for the first couple of months, and, of course, any time after, if they need our help."

"Oh, I'll be all right," he said. "I have a good job now and the pay is good. I was afraid of more infection, but that's all over with now. Helen's gotten used to me being O.K. We're finished with sickness and handicaps."

"Your job does pay well for this area," Ralph said. "What were you getting out at the field?"

"About the same. Of course, there was less opportunity at the other place—maybe . . ."

Ralph remembered how much Hans had liked that other job. The maleness of it had appealed to him in a special way. Still, electronics instrumentation was hardly invalid's work; it was very much a "man's" job. "I think you'll have good prospects for advancement," Ralph said. He got up and held out his hand. "Thanks for stopping by, Hans, you made my day."

"So long, Mr. Oakland." And he left.

Ralph made the additional note in his records. Then he looked back to the date of the first interview. A year and a half—had it been that long? It was hard to believe. He had always thought of Hans as a "new" client somehow. It must have had to do with the man himself—his independence, his hard work, the quality of his relationship with Ralph. The ideal client sees counseling as a joint effort. With so many of them, Ralph felt it was all sustained on his strength, his enthusiasm, his pleading, defending, consoling, arguing. John Kroll seemed like forever.

He closed the file and looked at his appointment sheet. Ethwald Kittenger. Ralph got up and went out to see Ethwald.

Ethwald Kittenger

(It's amazing; it can't be. Six months ago he was a boy, a terrified, invalid little boy, who went out the door with a little-boy wave.) Ralph must have seen him twenty times since then and every time there was more man and less boy, but perhaps he had always seen vestiges of the first Ethwald, and they must have covered over the man who was really forming to stand there now. (Ethwald Kittenger really *is* twenty; he's a man, a good-looking one, too. I never saw it

166

happening, and it's—amazing.) "How are you, Eth, come in." (There seems to be a hint, only a hint of the—feminizing. What is it? He moves like a man; his gestures—no, it's the clothes: he's too—too *correct*. That's it; the tie is perfect, the collar is perfect, and everything matches almost relentlessly, like—like a store-window man. There's only a hint of the limp, though, and maybe a little hesitancy on the left side when it has to lead. Merry Christmas, Ethwald, and Happy Birthday!) "Well, how are things going?"

"Oh, it's fine at work . . ."

(And he smiled; he's alive. Good. It's good.) "Something not right at home?"

"Mr. Oakland, I need some kind of a job after school."

"Well, I think we can find something for you, Eth, but aren't you pushing it a little?"

"Well, I haven't been paying any attention to my responsibilities."

Well, there it was, a poorly veiled, direct quote from the joy-proof Mrs. Sedges. The boy felt it also and hurried to defend it. "But it's true. I been going to school, and even if I work a little, I still get back to my aunt's about four, and I'm not paying board or for the room or anything, and lately I've even been borrowing some money from my uncle. The guys at school like to get together some of the time for beers or go to the show or dancing, and, well, you've got to have some money for that. I try not to go too often, but sometimes—sometimes it just carries you along, you know? I let off steam that way, sitting around with the guys, and, well, I've been smoking some, too. You can't always be bumming cigarettes from another guy . . ."

(Oh, Ethwald, don't you think I know how much more the cigarettes and the beer and the guys mean to you than you can admit?) The sudden image came to Ralph of 3-Eye Oakland, then a tough and reckless soldier still guarding his little circumscribed independence with too much ferocity. He was reeling down a street in a town near Rome with two corporals, the three of them singing-swearing drunk, but only half as drunk as they wanted to seem, because they had to be men together and men were loud and careless. If it seemed a little comical now, half-touching, stupid, and pathetic, the uncertain face under the helmet-liner, it was because 3-Eye was still more than half-innocent and hopeful as he toasted the whores of the world in the exaggerated obscenity of the Army at leisure. If Ethwald wanted to smoke and drink a beer and say "Oh, Hell" to the fellows in the Clutch-and-Brake class, surely no one could begrudge him two hours now and then, to stand against a whole youth spent in the cloying, false invalidism in which he had been imprisoned. But his aunt resented it. Something threatened her perhaps, in the easy-looking camaraderie, the pleasure, the aggressive maleness, maybe she just resented his joy. The family's finances were certainly comfortable enough to allow Ethwald a few minutes of roistering now and then. If Mrs. Sedges felt that she couldn't give her nephew anything, at least they could wait to be repaid.

"I tell you what, Eth," Ralph said, "why don't you do it this way? Get finished with your training; you can borrow a little for your needs and a few extras. When you are set up on a job, you'll be making enough to pay the money back easily."

"Still, other guys work and go to school. It's quicker advancement."

"But I think you should know that the policy of the agency is against it on two grounds. One, that more students tend to drop programs when they are taking classes and working at the same time; and two, that the students really can't study as hard when they have to split their time. Their marks drop and they are not as readily hired as those students who manage to keep their grades up. I want you to know, Eth, that I don't think that studying and working at the same time is a good idea unless it's imperative. This goes for everyone, not just for you; and you know there's no really desperate need for it."

Ethwald's face relaxed. "I was hoping you'd say that. I told my aunt about it, but, well, she just didn't believe me." He looked down at his cracked and roughened hands. Fastidiousness ended at his wrists; he was proud of working. "I guess I can't blame her. She knew me when I was a—a—just a scared kind of a kid. I sometimes can't believe it all myself, this change, I mean, a job and friends . . ." The words could not express it. He gestured out a little, meaning the whole world.

Ralph was moved by Ethwald's gentleness and the naturalness of his humility.

"Mr. Oakland," Ethwald said, "if only you would tell my aunt, it would seem more—more *important*. I do intend to pay back all the money I borrowed, and for the board and room, too. I do all the yard work and the heavy work around the house. I been painting all the rooms, inside and out."

"I'll do my best, Eth. If worse comes to worst, we can set up a program for you and the state will pay your maintenance by means of a grant. Of course, it's better all around if your family helps you out, but I think that it's way too soon to be thinking about school and an outside job just now. Keep working as hard as you can at school, but no outside job, all right? Would you want me to talk to your aunt in person or do you think that a letter would do it?"

"I don't know if she'd come in . . ."

"O.K. I'll send a letter, and meanwhile"—(They were getting up together.)—"take in the band concert—it's free—and the ice show and the art gallery and the bowling alley and the zoo and the old railroad museum. Paint the house and keep it up and run the errands. There are lots of things to do that don't cost a dime. Maybe you can even take your aunt and uncle to a couple of things. It may help them to see you as you are now."

"I was kind of looking forward to—to learn to dance."

"Why not?"

Ethwald left, and Ralph noticed the secretary's head come up for a moment as he walked. Her carefully trained face showed nothing, but Ralph knew, as he watched, that her mind was registering not *boy* or *cripple* but simply and heartily *man*. He turned back to his office, smiling. It was a good day after all. And he loved this work!

Minnie Cormer

She stood outside the door of the teeming ward. "So long, Minnie, good luck!" Fine, just fine. Good-bye and good luck and a box of tranquilizers and out the door. They knew as well as she did that she wasn't leaving the crazy house; she was taking it with her. She walked down the corridor past this office and that. She had been through most of those offices at one time or another. When they had brought her in from the City Hospital, there was a way to walk—tested and traced and numbered and coded. She talked twice with the psychiatrist, a tall Iranian with not enough English to stay alive by himself, no less to try to understand her when she said, "I tell you, I ain' done no wrong; death-dog ben

169

usin' me fo a rabbit; chase me chase me ever'day. I tyuud o' runnin'; I let 'im run me down."

That wasn't changed. Fact was, nothing was changed. They took her in and now they were putting her out. There was a way to walk; going to see the social worker and the man with the tranquilizer pills and the man with the address of another man she was supposed to go and see. She stopped. In front of her the corridor faded away. She saw the soft gray-blue shadow of a person, and another gray-red shadow, like a reflection. Slowly the two shadows met and combined in meeting and formed a third, a vibrating violet thing. The vibrating shadow had a soft hum. It was her warning. When the hum stopped, she would dark-out, and when she woke up it would be later and she would be sleepy and someone would tell her that she had had a seizure. Now she watched the shadows and she didn't care about the warning. What was the use anyway, what would be—the hum stopped. The sha . . .

"Well, you've been released. We can't keep you, so you won't be sent back to your ward. You've got your medication, so if you want to rest here for a while, it's o.k. You can go whenever you like."

Minnie got up from the hospital cot. "I slep' long?"

"Oh, a few hours. Usually you people come out of the seizures when they are over, but you go right to sleep."

"That make me interestin'!"

"If you epileptics would stick to your medication, you wouldn't have this embarrassment. Maybe you need more work done to find the right combination of medicines," the nurse said. "You check with the county hospital or the city and they'll keep on until they find the right thing for you."

"Lookahere," Minnie said, "I ugly, crazy, and colored. I got two children an no husban'. You think fixin' my fits is goin' fix me anythin'?"

"We don't call them fits; we call them seizures."

"I know uh secret code," she murmured. "I ain' crazy, I got uh 'motional disorder; I ain' got fits, I got uh convulsive disorder; an' I ain' ugly, I plain; an' I ain' black, I dusky; an' my children ain' bastards, they—they *love-flowers!*"

She began to leave, shaking her arm a little to ease the kinks in it. In the heavy sleep after those sudden darknesses, which she had been told were seizures, she often lay motionless, so that she was cramped or stiff when she got up. She turned out onto the corridor, continuing the interrupted walk out to the hospital gate and the world's strange idea of freedom. She thought again of how she had never actually seen a person in a seizure until this trip to the hospital. Her own, which happened once or twice a week and more frequently when she was nervous or coming down with something, were not unpleasant. The blurred shapes sometimes were in lovely colors, the warning hum was soft and comforting. Then, there was the sudden darkness and no more. The only real fear she had ever had from those darknesses was the fear that one might come when she was holding one of her babies, and that in her darkness she might drop the child. But this time she had seen a woman on the ward fall down, writhing and jerking, with her eyes unseeing but vibrating in their sockets in a scary, uncontrolled rhythm. She had gone for help. The nurse had come and done the few necessary things, and then said casually, "Well, we'll have to see about cutting down the violence of these seizures; they're as bad as yours."

She hadn't minded the darknesses before. Now she had medicines to try to control them, and the doctors kept at her about taking them, although they made her drowsy and dull sometimes. But now, since she had seen the violence of the spasms, she had a different idea Why not? Turning on the gas in the rundown place where she lived hadn't worked. There were so many drafts and holes and loose fixtures in the place that it had taken too long and alerted people. She knew she didn't have the courage to hang, choking and gasping until she died, or to jump off someplace, out through a cold night and down, down to be broken to death; but here was one easy, perfect way for her: to throw away the medicines and hope that the fit came on in the middle of a busy street or leaning out a window or resting in a bathtub. Maybe next time, when the soft shapes merged, she could go quickly to a window or a busy street and wait there for the familiar darkness. "Let 'em see if they wants to pull me out o' *that*," she murmured. It was waiting for her whenever she wanted to reach out and take it. It would take no effort and it was her way, for once, all her own special way.

It was bitterly cold. December was riding the winds from the northwest, screaming with the enemy fury of the world. Minnie walked in it, not warm enough and not safe enough. The children were staying in a foster home. If she was going to die, she would have to do something about them first—

and, oh, yes, the last step of the meaningless way. She took the things she had been given out of her coat pocket. The tranquilizer pills, the useless fit-medicine, the receipts for all of it, and a card that said she wasn't officially crazy any more. Ha! But no one would say that she hadn't finished serving the crazy way they had made for her. There was a last thing to do. She came to a bus stop and stood waiting for a bus going to midtown. She had a little money; she would stay in a hotel. When the bus came, she got onto it, paid with a token they had given her, and sat down. Then she began to read the last card:

AN APPOINTMENT HAS BEEN MADE FOR YOU AT 10:30 A.M. Friday, December 14, at the Department of Vocational Rehabilitation: Room 112 Metropolitan Building, 225 East 7th Street.

Scrawled under the city and state in ink was: Ask for Mr. Oakland.

"You bet I bettah ask fo' this big Mr. Oaklan'. It a cinch Big Mr. Oaklan' ain' gone ask fo' me!"

During the past few months Ralph had begun to feel a certain heaviness after he ate. He slept well enough and when he got up, he was alert and rested, but as the day went on he found himself tiring easily and feeling bloated and irritable, and the feeling seemed to persist whether the pressures of the day were heavy or light, whether the wall gave enough to let one of his clients through or whether another layer was built against him. At times he found himself sweating heavily, and when he came home he would throw himself into his chair after supper and fall into a dull sleep. From sympathy, Mary-Ann began to edge into irritation—he could stay up if he brought work home. He countered by arguing that his work was too demanding, that he needed the rest. What about the weekends; there was no special work on the weekends. He found her handling his brief case less than gently if she had to move it, and she put it out of the way as if it were an eyesore.

"What's the matter with it there? I might want to go over a few things later."

"It doesn't belong in everybody's way." And she would pick it up as if it were the national debt and stagger to a corner and drop it down.

"Hey, quit! That's a good brief case. My mother gave . . ."

"I know, I know, but it doesn't belong in the kitchen."

Too much rich food. He went on a diet and began to exercise every morning, reminding Mary-Ann that he was still in pretty good shape ("I did thirty pushups this morning, thirty, and I'm not even breathing hard."), even though it made him feel silly to say it. It sounded like a kid bragging. ("Why, ma'am, I can make this lil' old gun do anything I want.")

The heaviness and bloating got worse. Soon Mary-Ann was becoming irritated only as a matter of form, to cover a gnawing worry. Ralph could see it. He was afraid himself. He was becoming preoccupied and wary, no longer trusting that his food would sustain him or his sleep refresh him. He saw and read about sickness all the time; every client's conscious life was brimming over with his own sickness. Every day was a tide of it washing in and out of the office, rare neurological involvements and plain, straight heart attacks, pain that played with the protesting nerve point-touché, like French fencing, and pain as crude and savage as an attack by bludgeon. Because of the kind of clients that rehabilitation accepted, these sicknesses and agonies tended to be serious and chronic. Ralph's hundred and fifty active cases grew over the four years he had been in the agency to over five thousand people he had seen and spoken to, accepted or denied, tested and trained and counseled, and they all cried to him in one way or another that once sickness settled, it was there to stay. It might lift a little on the good days, but it was always there to lower and lower again, and it never went away. Ralph began to be frightened of his own symptoms, and just as frightened of going to a doctor. His fear began to affect the way he thought about his children. A flushed face and fever and an aching neck might look like a simple cold or flu, but he could name twenty-six cases where it hadn't been a cold at all but spinal meningitis. He knew every complication of the simple. ("Hasn't that sore healed yet?"— fifty cases of osteomyelitis.)

(Oh, hell, everyone gets tired and irritable in the afternoon. Look at the difference between the drivers of the "morning mass" and the "evening mass." And doesn't everyone's eyes glaze at the commercial-splintered mirror that T.V. holds up to nature?) But the tiredness that came at five P.M. in August was coming earlier in September, and by late October it had moved between lunchtime and three. Clients would look up at him from the benches—("Don't walk so fast, so jauntily; I, too, was fortunate.")—and he would wonder whose recitation of symptoms he could anticipate with his own. (Oh, I'll go next time we take the kids to the doctor for something.) He picked up the next file.

Cormer, Minnie Lula. Oh, yes, he remembered. The case had come after Bernardo's was presented at the welfare meeting, when Ralph was ripe with triumph and hanging on his small bough in his own warm little sunshine. The psychiatric caseworker and Supervisor had come with a group of referrals from various mental hospitals. When Ralph saw the record and the workers watching his face carefully he said, "Oh, no, this case is impossible. Look at the number of strikes against the woman."

They told him that it was all the more reason why she needed to find work and get a reason to stay sane. She was coming out of County Psychopathic with no past but misery and failure. She would need something with which to furnish a future. This was the humanistic view. Minnie Cormer's needs came before the profit-and-loss considerations of industries, which would never find a use for her in any of their multitude of needs and jobs. In the social worker's view, to be human was to be entitled to help in finding a purpose in life. Ralph, with a foot in both camps wanted to see it their way, but he couldn't. The woman was a psychiatric case, she got drinking money from casual prostitution, she was a Negro—(not easy to place if they have other troubles; employers seemed to consider it gauche, overdoing the handicaps)—and she was an epileptic and only partially controlled with medication. She had two illegitimate children, who would have to be cared for while she was in the throes of "finding a reason to live." It was impossible; he had told them so. "What's the matter with a welfare grant? She's certainly eligible, and it would mean that she stays home and takes care of the kids."

"That's part of the trouble. When she tried to kill herself, both of them were in the apartment with her and they very nearly died. She's unstable, an influence that's very negative—no, she needs a job on the outside where reality is always there to keep her on the track. In the home situation it's just too easy to drift off. And then, too, there were the men. It just isn't good for her or the kids."

"Look, I know you came in early and heard the plans on the Ramirez case," Ralph had said, "but please don't think
174

that every hopeless one is another Ramirez, hiding a 650-watt bulb behind a ten-cent candle. If you think she's unfit, take the kids away."

That was where he had blundered. They had zeroed in on Ramirez without even losing their modest smiles. "It *is* such impressive evidence about what *can* be done." "Perhaps there's something special here also—all of us in the agency have been following with interest . . ."

He had gone over the reasons. They had said that the psychological trouble was not so serious or long term if only they could . . .

He had argued and countered and explained and the more he did so the more he seemed to be defending an indefensible philosophy. He had given them all the places from which their arguments could spring, and before he knew it, he was cut down and lying in the basket, wreathed in their reasons. It wasn't hard for Ralph to resist doctors or clergymen or anxious mothers, but dedicated co-workers were another matter. Their good opinions, as much as he hated to admit it, meant a great deal to him; so here he sat with the report in his hand and a space with Minnie Cormer's name on it on his appointment sheet. The best he could do, he had said finally, was to see her. He had promised nothing.

Feeling that they had won a concession, they had tried to sweeten it a little. "She's not retarded . . ."

"Splendid," he had muttered, "I'll tell my wife to buy fireworks."

Ralph knew what his trouble was: He sympathized with the caseworkers' point of view, but it was impossible to use a vocational program as therapy when it wasn't therapy for the employer also. No one would be convinced to take a chance on a woman like that, however much it would "serve to give her a necessary sense of reality." Well, it was no use thinking up good arguments now; he had agreed to see her and so he would. He sighed and got up and went out to where she would be waiting.

The switchboard secretary shot him a significant look. Over there, her eyes motioned, and—wow, where do you find them! He looked in the direction of the glance. The woman sat alone on the bench. She was young, his records told him that, but her skin was old and dry and her body was slack. Her eyes opened and closed very slowly, looking straight ahead. She looked as if she might stop breathing at any minute. Ralph went to her and said, "Mrs. Cormer?"

The vacant eyes found him as if by accident. "Miss," she murmured, "I ain' married." Every decibel of sound seemed to be measured in a quantity of energy which she could not possibly pay.

Ralph looked at her and wanted to shiver. She was bringing her own midwinter. Where she existed there was no sun, no rest, no yearning. He had seen many states of depression like this one on mental wards, but how did anyone expect him to talk to this woman about jobs and aptitudes and wages and hours and bus fare? How could they have referred her, glossing over that little word, depression? He had promised to see her and she had come, although he would never know why.

"Miss Cormer, will you come into my office . . ."

She rose and walked very slowly, head down. Ralph sensed the presence of the invisible weight she was carrying. He motioned her gently to the chair and then he sat down. Then they waited. He asked a question; she answered in a flat syllable. He asked another, the same response. Minutes ticked by. He asked another question, and she answered it in a word and then died again. Name, address, age, children, hospitalization, wishes, hopes, desires . . . Everything that he already knew she answered in the dry monotone. Needs? Blank. Possibilities? Blank. Then they stared at one another. We are but dust and shadow. Ralph shifted in his chair. Why did they send her? Once he got up and walked around the little office, trying to break the feeling of great distance that was pushing them apart over that desk. That didn't work either, so he went to sit down again. Unfortunately, he misjudged the rhythm of his motion and he half stumbled back, so that he sat very heavily, his breath rushing out and making him seem to have collapsed in the chair. It was a funny thing to happen in so dignified a situation; any of his other clients would have laughed, but she didn't, and he was surprised that her silence did nothing to diminish his embarrassment at his clumsiness. Accidents often brought some immediacy, some fellow-feeling to the surface in the faces that watched him warily across that desk. He felt tired and sad.

"Well," he said, "here I am. I'm the man who is supposed to rehabilitate you. Is that what they told you when they gave you the slip at the hospital?"

"They say see you. I see you."

"What do you see?"

"White man, clean shirt, big desk ... What you goin' do for *me?*"

"You know, there's always a little part that people seem to leave out when they recommend other people to this office. It's one of those little hitches that always turns out to be the most important thing of all. I want to know you, but I have no way of knowing you without your help. You're going to have to teach me. I don't know what I can do for you or how I can help you. You're going to have to show me. We're ashamed to admit it, about that hitch. We can press a button and shoot a man up high enough to scare the angels, but our social agencies still have to putt-putt along with the same old do-it-yourself system. That's all there is."

"I got enough buttons press already," she said, "but I can't tell you nothin'. I don' know nothin' myself."

"Well, the first thing to do then is to get those seizures under control. That way we won't have to worry about them and we won't have to rush."

"Hell, don' worry about them fits. I ain' pay 'em no mine."

"Maybe you don't, but I can't justify spending my time and the state's money on a one-sided deal like that. If you keep letting yourself have seizures without trying to control them medically, we'll be talking about your seizures all the time. I know about seizures; I want to know about *you.*"

"I don' know if I wan' do all of that fuss, or you either. I wan' think it over."

"That's all right with me. If you want to come in for your second appointment, I'll be glad to work with you. If not, call me and I'll give your appointment to someone else. O.K.?"

She got up and dragged to the door, and Ralph went ahead to open it. He motioned to the secretary and she checked the possible appointment and wrote it on a card. As Ralph waited, looking on, Martenson came out of his office and walked past Minnie, winking at Ralph. Luckily, Minnie finished and left without noticing the wink or the broad gesture. Martenson scowled after her. "Lawdy lawdy, man, wheah *does you dig dem up!*"

Ralph didn't feel like joking, but if he took a stand he would only irritate Martenson, who had often gotten him job leads for Negro clients and whom he would have to ask again. He said, "I send out experts to comb the country. I have contacts in every state in the union. And luck, of course, plenty of luck." But he had compromised himself one more time, a thing 3-Eye would never have tolerated, even if Martenson never looked his way again.

Fatika had come from his office also. It was time for their coffee break. "Another weird client of Ralph's?" he said, trying to pick up the conversation. "What is it this time, a pickpocket with muscle cramps?"

"*I've* got to have a way to get to heaven, don't I?" Ralph answered. Then he was annoyed with his comeback. He kept promising himself that he wouldn't tread on Fatika's special little bunion, but he seemed to keep doing it all the same.

"You have only yourself to blame, if you take these cases," Fatika said. "After all, the choice is with you."

"Of course I have only myself to blame." Ralph laughed. "Do you think that makes it any easier?" They let themselves grin and forgive one another. "Come on, let's get some coffee."

They were turning when Ralph heard his phone ring. "You go on, I'll catch up."

Martenson turned with a gesture, waving Ralph away. "Come on, Bill, you won't see the Lone Ranger there for the rest of the day."

It was kidding and Ralph knew it, but it annoyed him. The Lone Ranger! Did he act like some adolescent defender of the downtrodden? It was just a crack—Martenson being funny.

He went to the phone, promising himself that he would catch up with them and not miss his coffee this time. It was Friday and almost lunchtime. He had seen six people already this morning, fitting in an extra emergency by cutting the other interviews a little short. Cormer had been a tough one, too, and now he really wanted that coffee.

"Oakland speaking."

"Mr. Oakland, this is Hans Marshak."

"Well, hello, Hans, what's up?"

"Oh, I was just woondering if I could drop in and see you this afternoon ..."

Ralph tried to control a sudden impatience. "Well, I'm booked up solid with appointments this afternoon. Was it something special?"

"No, I just wanted to make sure all the details were taken care of."

"Well, they are. Maybe you're a little nervous starting to work on Monday. Don't worry, you won't have any trouble."

178

"Well, I thought I'd come in and just see if there was anything we might have missed."

"Quit worrying, Hans. It's going to be all right. Monday you'll be working. Don't think about anything this weekend. Take a vacation and don't worry about any details. They'll straighten themselves out when you're on the job awhile."

"Mr. Oakland—do you think you can tell? I mean, do you think anyone could tell by looking . . ."

"Tell? Oh, Hans, you've been walking around for a month. You know it's impossible for anyone to tell anything from seeing you walk."

"Well, never mind—I guess I was thinking about something else."

"It's been a long pull, but you've made it in fine shape, Hans, I've got to go now. Look, you check with me on Monday, o.k.? Anything we missed out on we can go over then."

"Good-bye, Mr. Oakland."

He was hurt; Ralph could hear it in the slightly formal "Good-bye, Mr. Oakland." Even Marshak acted like a kid sometimes. Sure, he was anxious about going back to work after a year and a half away from it; but, after all, it wasn't radically different work; he wasn't going to go into an entirely new field; and he had been a top student. He would know the work and be able to succeed in it. It was just the jitters. Ralph tried to relax a little by stretching.

His first client this morning was complaining about transportation to her job. Larrick, the second, was developing more "back pains." Ralph was beginning to realize that Larrick didn't want to work at all. Minnie Cormer was a hopeless case. If she stayed out of the hospital a week it would be a miracle. The welfare staff had been crazy to refer her.

He walked quickly to catch up with Martenson and Fatika. Lone Ranger nothing! "The next one who calls up," he muttered, "is going to get told off. 'Mr. Oakland, I want to be rehabilitated.' 'Sorry, can't take you. Too busy with people who don't.' "

13

"Mr. Oakland, this is Sister Mary Aquinas at the St. Joseph's Home. Perhaps you might remember ours as the one in which John Kroll stayed. I've also called since in hopes that you might consider working with another one of our boys . . ."

"Yes, Sister, what can I do for you?"

"Well, Mr. Oakland, I remembered your telling me that your agency did vocational rather than personality counseling alone, and so, when this problem came up, I felt that you were the proper person to call. The father of three of our children feels that he could keep them if he were able to get work. He has had some sort of back injury for about a year and can't do any heavy lifting."

"Perhaps we could help, Sister, what is his name?"

"His name is Alfred Ritchie. There are three children here and I understand another two placed with relatives."

"Uh—er—Sister, I think I know that man. He's receiving a grant from welfare for those children. He was referred here by welfare, but we found him ineligible."

"Oh, dear, I'd better call the welfare then and make sure."

"I think so. How long have the children been with you?"

"About five months. It's such a shame! I hoped to find a solution for the problem. He seemed to be so devoted to them, so sorry to give them up . . ."

"Well, maybe it's a mistake."

"I pray it is."

"Ralph, this is Etta. You didn't turn in your mileage for this month. I don't know how you think we can keep our books straight when people don't turn in their mileage at the end of the month. Bill Fatika, for instance. Last week he came *running* in here and expected *me* to add up his mileage just because he was late getting . . ."

"Mr. Oakland, this is Mrs. Mercer . . ."

"Yes, Mrs. Mercer, how are you and how are the girls?"

"Mr. Oakland, I'm not a psychologist or some expert, I just started taking in those retarded girls because—well—because I liked them and we got along real well. Oh, Mr. Oakland, it's so terrible, and I feel responsible and I had no idea! You must believe that I had no idea at all!"

"What is it, Mrs. Mercer, what's happened?"

"I called you right away, Mr. Oakland. I just don't know how to start to tell you . . . Oh, it's just *terrible!*"

"Well, suppose you tell me what happened . . ."

"Please excuse me—I hate it when I get to crying and I just can't seem to stop, I'm so upset!"

"Is someone hurt down there? A girl hasn't run away, has she?"

"*Here,* in *my* kitchen, *this* morning. Little Marilee Hutter came down and she looked so sleepy that I just said—I said . . ."

"Mrs. Mercer?"

"I asked her if she had had a bad night, and she said, 'Oh, yes, the noise keeps me awake.' I said 'What noise, dear?' Oh, Mr. Oakland! And then she said, 'All that laughing keeps me awake.' 'Well, what laughing'—I was thinking some girl had a dream—and she said, 'Molly and her boy friend go on whispering and laughing, and then they shake the bed and it squeaks and it keeps me awake the whole night.' *Boy friend,* Mr. Oakland, *boy friend!*"

"Did you ask Molly about it?"

"I was very calm, Mr. Oakland. I didn't break down or anything. You have to remember that they are innocent. It's what makes them so sweet—and trusting—so . . ."

"Please, Mrs. Mercer, could you . . ."

"Yes, yes, I'm sorry. It's just that there's a *path, a worn path,* and it's to *my house!* It's anger that's making me cry—some of it, anyway. I went to Molly, and it was true, every word. A boy started coming to see her about a month or so ago, and after a few times he started to bring his friends! I sent the girls to work today—I didn't want to keep them, so I didn't get all the details. Molly said that they came in by climbing an old set of rungs that my father had built

181

into the side of the house in case of fire. They've been coming two or three times a week, four or five of them! I'm going to find out more and call you back, Mr. Oakland. I'm just so upset. *My house! My beds!* Why—it's—why, it's *criminal!*"

"Ab, this is Ralph. Something's come up that may be quite serious for the agency."

"Oh, God, Ralph, it's not a check mix-up, I hope. If the audit isn't perfect you know that all our funds are automatically frozen."

"It might even be worse than that. You know those five retarded girls who are staying down at Mrs. Mercer's and training at the sheltered workshop? Well, two of them are my cases, one is Fatika's, and one Martenson's."

"Yes, well?"

"Well, you know how gullible most retarded people are. I'm afraid those girls have been discovered by a gang of boys. The boys have been going up and getting in there nights regularly for—well—at least a month now."

"Jesus Christ! Is anyone with you? Oh, God, if anyone finds out, if this gets out, the scandal will kill us! Who knows about it?"

"The landlady found out about it this morning and called me right away. I don't think she told anyone else. The girls are all right. No one's been hurt or anything. She let them go on to work and she says that she'll call me when she finds out any more details."

"You see what it looks like, don't you? It looks like negligence on our part—young retarded kids, defenseless, from out of town and left unsupervised in the big city—*by us!*"

"Don't forget, Ab, the girls *let* those boys in. Even if they are retarded, we couldn't have put them in any sort of custody while they're training; it's illegal and there are no facilities for it anyway."

"Of *course* not, but don't you see how it *looks,* Ralph? I'm going to try to think of something we can do. Call me the minute you hear anything, will you?"

"Sure, Ab, I sure will."

"Could your service find a job for my brother-in-law? My wife made me take him in the store with me and he's breakin' me! I let him do one thing; he gums it up. I let him do something else; he gets it all wrong. You get jobs for people, don't you . . .?"

"Mr. Oakland, my husband works all day and late into the night. The children are grown up and gone and I look around at my clean house and I want to cry. How clean can a house be? I have no trade; I married right out of school. I'm middle-aged, as they say, but I'm not useless. Can't you counsel me and test my aptitudes? I can't be useless in the world. Mr. Oakland, I need to . . ."

". . . I went to Janice and Dee Dee and it's the same with them. As soon as that—that sex fiend found my poor girls, who didn't know better, he made a real block party out of it. The girls didn't hide anything. Bless their hearts, they couldn't even be ashamed. When I asked if they remembered the boys' names, Dee Dee said, 'All of them?' Oh, Mr. Oakland, and right where I was sleeping not fifteen yards away, and I didn't even hear a thing! I sat there and listened to the girls talking, and when I couldn't stand it one moment longer I went up to little Janice and I took her by the shoulders and I said, 'Janice, dear, don't you know that you did *wrong?*' And she said, 'Oh, Aunt Jane, I did at first. Those boys used to come in here and get in the bed with me and there wasn't room for two of us in the bed, and I couldn't sleep. They all acted the same. They would just start hanging on to me and pushing up against me and then they would put that thing in me that they have, and I didn't like it because it *hurt.* I told them it wasn't nice to hurt people. One of those boys I told him to get his own bed to sleep in, but he said he was too poor and didn't have any money.' Can you imagine that, Mr. Oakland, telling the poor girl that story! I said, 'Well, Janice, then, why didn't you tell me that they were coming in there and bothering you?' And she said, 'You know, Aunt Jane, after a while I liked having them and I got glad when they came into the bed.' Can you imagine *that?* How am I going to tell those poor girls about the consequences? I was looking around while Janice was saying those things and there were all the others, DeeDee and Marilee and Molly and Sue just nodding and smiling and agreeing . . ."

"Did you find out anything about the boys? Perhaps there are still precautions . . ."

"Of course I took precautions. I've nailed the windows

shut on that side and I had an alarm wired to those rungs where they won't be able to set a foot on them without me knowing it. And I'll find out about those boys, you can be sure of that!"

"Ralph? Ab. Anything new?"

"No, the landlady called, but it was nothing new. We'll probably just have to wait and see. If there are any pregnancies, it will take time before we know, but she did say that she had wired the place and fixed the windows."

"Call me, will you?"

"Sure, Ab, the minute anything happens."

"Mr. Oakland, you've seen Minnie Cormer, what do you think?"

"I think I made a bad mistake. I'm sorry I agreed to see her. What I hope she will do is to decide not to come in again, because we can't help her. Even if she's not a model mother, it is better that she stay at home and be on a welfare grant."

"But we've shown how unsatisfactory that would be for both the woman and the children . . ."

"But our agency just can't help her. We are a vocational agency, and there's nothing we can do. It's 'society,' but there it is. An untrained white epileptic is hard enough to place. You know, it took me seven months to get my last one working. A white epileptic with an emotional disorder is almost impossible, but a Negro with those handicaps *is* impossible."

"But eighty-five percent of the convulsive disorders are amenable to control."

"But ninety-five percent of the hiring force doesn't know it."

"You could counsel control for the seizures and, with counseling and maybe giving hope for employment, the depression would be eased."

"And then do I counsel her white? Don't you see that I *couldn't* counsel hope because there *is* no hope. She's fighting all of her handicaps and a world whose intelligent machines are making these people obsolete the way buggy whips once were. There just is no hope for employment. I strongly advise counseling for this woman, but not vocational counseling. What she needs is to develop enough emotional strength to get and keep medical control of those seizures. Counsel her
184

into being happier in the home, because there just *is* no possibility of work outside."

"But you have another appointment with her."

"If she keeps it I'm going to say all this to her myself, as gently but as forcefully as I can."

"But you said you would see her, give her a try . . ."

"That was my mistake. I hope she doesn't suffer too much for it, but she should never have been referred."

"We're sorry you feel that way; good-bye, Mr. Oakland."

And he thought: That's the end of the Lone Ranger.

"Oh, Mr. Oakland! What are we going to tell Mrs. Colvin?"

"Mrs. Mercer . . .?"

"You know, I just hung up the phone and it dawned on me—about Andrea."

"But she lives at home, doesn't she?"

"That girl has been over here three times a week at least. She's such a sweet, dear girl and she's so proud of having friends to visit and talk to and they all help me around the house, so I've just let Andrea stay over some nights without charging her anything. When I realized that she'd been over with Molly those nights, I went to Molly and asked her, and it was true. Mr. Oakland, she's the prettiest one, you know, and Molly told me she's had *every one* of those—those—creatures! What will I tell the Colvins? What will they do to *me?* And the disgrace—the whole neighborhood will find out and then there'll be a scandal, I just know there will! Oh, Mr. Oakland, what if one of the poor, dear little girls is *pregnant!*"

"Do you know who the boys are? Perhaps they said something to the girls or, carelessly, to each other, something that we could piece together . . ."

"Who the boys are? Why, *of course* I know who the boys are! Oh, please, Mr. Oakland, don't think badly of me; I'm so upset and these sweet little girls telling me one awful thing after another. Imagine, a boy saying he's too poor to afford his own bed! Lies, Mr. Oakland, lies a ten-year-old would see through. Do you know what they told Janice? They told her they were Army heroes and the government had rewarded them by giving them all their food and clothing free for three years. I asked Dee Dee to tell me exactly what her 'boy friend' had said, and she repeated it and she didn't even know the shame: 'Free bunk and beans on the inside and now I'm getting all the free—free . . . Oh, Mr. Oakland! My girls have been seduced by *monsters on parole from Boys' State!*"

"Mrs.—uh—Mrs. Mercer, please. I'll talk to the Colvins. Andrea is over eighteen and so are all the other girls, and I don't think there will be any legal problems for you to worry about. I'm going to call the Workshop and get in touch with the social worker. I think she'll talk to the girls and contact the parents also. Somebody ought to give the word to those boys. I don't suppose you got their right names, did you?"

"Not unless you can believe they were named Romeo Mineo, King Hercules, and Rutherford B. Hayes."

"What did you say?"

"I said they called themselves . . ."

"That's all right, never mind, Mrs. Mercer. I'll get in touch with the Workshop and call back when I can. Please don't be upset. I know you did the best you could. It was nobody's fault."

"Some people, Mr. Oakland, some people are animals!"

"Ralph, this is Georgia. About John Kroll's hearing . . ."

"Georgia, I've got to have my own little hearing with John first. Someone has been doing a little tom-catting around town for the last month or so, name of Rutherford B. Hayes. I want to find out from John where *he* was on those nights."

"But that was when he was looking for . . ."

"Yes, I know, dear old mother. I also want to know if he worked nights at it. He's said more than once that your locks and bars were no trouble for him, that he came and went as he pleased. We both know, though neither of us will admit it, that he probably stole as well as got handouts, in order to keep himself when he was on Vandalia Street. Did he make a profit out of this search? John has contacts at Boys' State, boys he knew and maybe even admired. Did he meet any of them during those days he was gone? I want to find out."

"Well, if you want to see him before the hearing it might be best for you to go down to Juvenile Hall yourself. His behavior has been good, but I don't want to jeopardize anything by asking for more favors. Oh, and Ralph, I wouldn't take that talk about his 'breaking out of the cracker box any time he wanted' too seriously. I think that if you call him on it, you'll find that it was only four times, and three of those under very special circumstances."

"All right, Georgia, I'll talk to him there, and I hope I can be satisfied with the answers I get. If I'm not, I won't say so in court, but it will change my attitude toward that Vandalia Street sojourn of his."

"Good luck, Ralph."

"Thanks, I'll keep in touch."

"Mr. Oakland, this is Mr. Shaw. I'm in the personnel department at Bracker Electronics. You have a client named Hans Marshak whom we hired in the components department on Friday?"

"Yes, I do ..."

"Well, its—let's see, it's 10:20 now and he hasn't shown up. Is something the matter?"

"No, but there must be some mix-up if he isn't there. Let me give him a call and then check back with you. All right?"

"We have his home number, but I'd appreciate it if you'd let me know."

"I'll check and give you a ring. Thank you for calling."

"Good-bye."

"Ralph? Ab. You heard anything new?"

"Yes, Ab, I have. Another girl is involved, one of mine. Mrs. Mercer thinks that the boys were parolees from Boys' State."

"Oh, no! I've been sitting here this morning watching headlines in future newspapers if this blows up on us. TAX SUPPORTED LOVE NEST—CITIZENS DEMAND INVESTIGATION—UNWED MOTHERS SUE AGENCY—RETARDATES TRAINING FOR OLDEST PROFESSION.

"Second oldest."

"Thanks a lot."

"We may get it in the neck from the paper, Ab, but I think we have a good defense. Those girls are training under state auspices, but they are all over eighteen, and their personal lives are as much their own as anyone else's. We have advised them to be modest and careful; I've tried it often enough myself, but the parents of these kids are bitterly resentful of what they consider interference into their very private business. We can't force them to take our advice."

"Oh, Ralph, for God sakes; I'm not talking about legal rights or even common sense. I'm talking about the kind of thing that will sell newspapers and bring us up before some board or other for endless hearings and destroy any small ounce of public respect we have built up for ourselves. Do you think one of those parents will remember how indignant

187

he was when you suggested that his little daughter might be less easy to seduce than Joan of Arc? From what you said, the parole department will probably get it, too; they're going to have to answer the one about letting rapists go free. I feel for them, but I'm not sorry; it may take some of the fire away from us. Keep in touch, will you Ralph."

"Of course I will. We'll probably have to tell the other guys soon."

"Ralph, this is Etta. You still haven't gotten your mileage report in. Now you've had the whole weekend and all morning to figure it and send it down. You counselors just don't care how much extra we have to do when you hold us up. You may think you're above all these little details, but the state auditors come down *here* and ask *me,* and *I* have to . . ."

"Mr. Oakland?"
"Yes, this is Oakland."
"I am Stephen Marshak. Hans Marshak—is my son."
"Yes, Mr. Marshak, I had meant to call you to ask you why . . ."
"Mr. Oakland, my son will not be at work. On Saturday afternoon my son died."
"What?"
"My son has died, Mr. Oakland . . ."
"Was he in an auto accident? Oh, Mr. Marshak . . ."
"No, Mr. Oakland, it was not . . . On Saturday afternoon, I—ah—asked him to drive me downtown to the Dollarama because we had some Christmas gifts to buy. When we got there, he told me he had to pick up something. Someone doesn't say: Good-bye, Dad, when he is going just next door—I only remembered just now that he said it. Good-bye, Dad."
"Mr. Marshak . . ."
"When I finished with my shopping I went out to the car and I saw him in the car waiting for me. It was my car, you know, but I had given it to him. So I went over and opened the passenger door. His head was against the door frame, but I don't want to speak of that. He had a rifle steadied between his knees and pointed up. I wonder how many people must have walked by and not noticed. There was no crowd at the car, but the streets were full of people shopping. If only someone had noticed him pointing the gun that way. No one
188

even heard the shot. Mr. Oakland, I have to ask you if you know why my son took his life after all that pain and suffering were ended, when he was just going on a new job? I am his father and I loved him and was proud of him, and I can't understand why this was. You were his advisor, you guided him. Tell me why! Let me understand—why he did this thing!"

"Did he discover another sore? Perhaps if he was breaking down with . . ."

"No, it was the first thing I thought of, but there was no sore. I made the doctors check and then check again. It would have been a thing I could understand . . ."

"I—I don't know, Mr. Marshak. The electronics company called this morning—I—I'm sorry, I just can't seem to make any sense out of this."

"I forgot about it being Monday. He was to start the job today. I forgot that."

". . . Uh—how is his wife?"

"Not good. She finds all the reasons to blame herself. She looks and looks for blame. His mother has begun to believe her and that worries me, too. I want to see you, Mr. Oakland, I want to talk about Hans and why—that horrible thing—in that way."

"Would you want to come in now or this afternoon?"

"I think I want to wait until I can say things more—more easily. I don't want to leave my wife alone. In a few weeks, maybe."

"Of course. Would you like to make an appointment?"

"Yes, I think I would."

"All right, Mr. Marshak, let me switch you to the secretary. You can plan to come in whenever you want. Just hold the line and I'll switch the call. I'm so sorry, Mr. Marshak—I—he was a fine boy. Etta, will you make an appointment for Mr. Marshak to see me. Give him priority, will you? Thanks."

"Mr. Oakland, this is Claude Sommers. The school says that my book money hasn't come through yet and they won't let me have any more credit until it comes. Would you call them and tell them it's okay."

". . What . ?"

"Mr. Oakland?"

"I—I'm sorry; I wasn't listening."

They sat around the table with their lunches, eating and talking. Ralph didn't want to be there. His mind kept wondering, finding the voice of Hans Marshak's father, recoiling from it and wandering back to it again. The usual lunch-table talk couldn't keep him from the compelling anguish of that voice, and he didn't want the others to notice his abstraction and ask him about it, laughing. "Hey, Ralph, your can-can dancer slip a disk?" If it had been spring or summer he would have gone to a little park that was three or four blocks away to sit among the bums warming themselves on their appointed round between Plackman Park uptown and the Salvation Army Mission on Vandalia Street. The cold weather had altered their schedule and cut off his escape. It was difficult enough to give his attention to the strained faces of clients sitting before him in his office or their worried sounds on his telephone. Tuna-fish sandwiches and talk about T.V. shows would be even harder.

Bill Fatika was pouring coffee from his Thermos, Bailey opening his poor-but-honest-newspaper wrapping in which his wife always packed his lunch. And it all looked grim and ugly. Even the noise of the other offices emptying endless bureaucrats and secretaries into the crowded cafeteria grated on his nerves and made Ralph wish for his little park in any weather. He walked to the table and the others looked up and said hello.

He sat down with them and opened his lunchbox. Mary-Anne had packed it in a hurry this morning—he could tell by looking at it. She had given him a little container of chicken salad to spread fresh on his bread, but there was no spreader and no salt. He sat and looked at his lunch and thought he was going to cry. If he didn't start eating he would cry, and then Bailey would surely ask why, and then he would break down in great boohoos, sobbing and blubbering, "She forgot to give me a butter knife!" Thinking of it, he passed over into a forlorn smile. Bailey had finished his joke and gone on to something else. Lonigan and Melchior joined them, Ogilvy from the Blind Unit stopped by and said something, and then Lonigan said: "Where's Ab? He missed coffee today, too."

"He's got some kind of trouble; he's been prowling around that office like a rhino with the itch. Hey, Ralph, you're a dozen miles away. Something come up?"

"Yeah, this morning, something pretty rough."

"Client quit training and go off on a toot?" Melchior asked.

"No, it wasn't that . . ."

They saw Ab at the doorway of the cafeteria. His eyes caught them and he came over briskly. Suddenly he was not the easygoing "good guy" of the agency. "Why didn't you check with me again, Ralph, I've been waiting for your call. Did you hear anything else?"

"No, Ab, I didn't. I'm sorry."

"You should have checked again. You know that if this blows up, there's going to be trouble. If we keep on top of things we might be able to forestall some of the publicity, or at least try to keep out of the worst of it."

"I'm sorry, Ab, it slipped my mind. Something else came up this morning and I . . ."

"Slipped your mind? What could come up that's this important? Ralph, sometimes I think you forget who's paying your salary. It's this agency, and if we have trouble it means that you have it, too."

"What?—I'm sorry, Ab, what did you say? My mind was wandering for a minute."

"Ralph, you don't look too good. You sure you're not coming down with something?"

"No, Ab. I had a suicide this morning."

Ab's face changed. "Oh, Ralph, that's tough! I'm sorry. We've had a few cases go like that over the years and I know how they can break a man up. Look, Ralph, why don't you just take the rest of the day off? You can't listen and you can't think with that on your mind."

"I can't. I'm booked up solid with appointments."

"All right, but I don't know how much good you are going to be for clients in the shape you're in. Still, if you want to stay, O.K. I know that this other business won't strike you as being particularly serious right now, but it is, so give me a call if you hear anything, O.K.?"

Ralph knew that it would be difficult to hear his clients, let alone the latest communique from Mrs. Mercer's, but he said, "I'll try, Ab," and gave a weak smile which Ab accepted.

"I've got to work; I'll see you fellows later," Ab said and he left them.

Ralph pulled out his pipe tool and began spreading his sandwich with its little spoon. The others watched him, not knowing how to start asking their questions.

"Hey, Ralph, your wife got up late again this morning . . ."

"I guess so," Ralph said, working uphill.

"This is not your day, boy."

"Suicide—gee, I never thought about a client doing that on me."

"I never did either, until now," Ralph said, and looked at his lunch.

"Well, Ralph," Bill Fatika had not yet set his seal upon the time, "you know that your clients weren't the best kind. I don't mean about being poor; poverty is not a man's fault if he overcomes it. I mean in the moral sense. I don't think I'm telling you anything new, but a client who would do a thing like that doesn't really deserve too much concern, does he?"

"Who does deserve concern?" Ralph asked, becoming suddenly cold and hoping that he wasn't the only one, and that his bitterness would not be lost on the mountain of canonical certainty that he faced.

Earnest Bailey tried to talk between them. "Not now, Bill. Ralph's just gotten the news and it's set him back on his heels a little. After all, the guy was his client, he knew him and . . ."

But Fatika went on. "I'm saying that not enough care was taken to determine the moral character of that client. Taking one's own life is a sin against God; as a matter of fact, it's illegal, and if the state's money . . ."

Ralph knew that he should be quiet, that only an inexperienced adolescent or a fool could imagine himself changing anyone's beliefs on a question like this. The state laws favored Ralph's point of view and not Fatika's. That should be enough, he thought, but it wasn't; and Ralph found himself saying all the foolish, violent things for which he would feel embarrassed later.

"What are your standards, Bill? Your righteousness looks to me like nothing more than unconcern. If God gave my man crosses to bear and didn't give him the strength to bear them, it seems to me that that is a matter between them and not a thing for you to judge at all. Isn't it enough to be a human being? Christ thought so. The only people he lampooned were the so-called solid citizens, the church-going, tithe-paying righteous. Who do we help? People who don't need it or people who do? Oh, hell, Bill, the worst thing is that . . ." His voice dropped because he had turned toward the real source of his confusion and it was exhausting him. ". . . the very worst thing is that he was my best client, even in your narrow, stupid, crazy, ludicrous sense of the word. He was hard-working and decent, a self-respecting, honest man;

192

and I keep wondering if it was something I did or didn't do that was part of his destruction. *Why?* I don't know and I want to know, not why he *shouldn't* have but why he *did*. Why does a bright, courageous guy blow his brains all over his father's car ... *Why?*" He stopped talking and looked at their intent faces clustered in a circle. In some he saw sympathy for his "bad luck." "I'm not good company today . . ." He gathered up the uneaten lunch and left his co-counselors sitting in a little well of silence amid the noontime clamor.

"Hello, Ralph, this is Georgia. I did get that notice you wanted about John's hearing. See what comes of having influential friends ... They've got him held over because of Christmas, and that puts him down at 11:30 on the tenth."

Ralph was annoyed somehow. Did she always chirp like that over the phone? "Okay, Georgia, I'll clear the time and be there."

"You seemed to have had some reservations the last time I talked to you. I do want to say that I've checked out his story pretty thoroughly . . ."

(Why didn't I listen to him when he called? Hans wasn't the kind of man to cry wolf, to ask to see me when he didn't really need . . .)

. . . all kinds of people, not only Captain Sutter, but . . . (Was the clue to be found in the shopping center? Was it some kind of sudden hopelessness . . .?)

. . . to the various places he said he went and they've— (Holidays make everything seem so useless and wasted sometimes.)—put together a pretty logical sequence of his goings and comings—(What threatened him about that new job? Was it something I should have seen and counseled for?)— Juvenile Hall reports aren't bad either, considering— (Because he *called* on Friday and I can't even remember why there was no time to listen.)—and it's definite that he will appear before Judge French, who, in case you don't remember, has called you several times to try to get you to counsel boys that we had sent to him from the Shelter—(He *didn't* say anything. I took him at face value all along. If there were clues or symptoms, why in God's name didn't I see them!)

"Ralph?"—(A fine new life, and it was just beginning for him.) "*Ralph!*"

"Oh, I'm sorry, were you saying something?"

"Well—uh—yes, I was, but I was probably just using you as a sounding board to let me hear my own ideas coming back at me. The hearing is on the tenth in juvenile court with Judge French. 11:30, Ralph—Ralph?"

"Yes."

"I hope you can satisfy yourself about John by then."

"Uh—yes, I'll be there."

"Good-bye, Ralph."

Her good-bye had a special sound. It was sympathetic and kindly. Ralph found that annoying also.

"Mr. Oakland, I'm Mr. Janeway of the Metropolitan housing authority. I just wanted to call you and let you know that I'm going to try to get your client, Ramirez, into our La Placita development if I have to cut all the red tape myself."

"I'm glad to hear it, Mr. Janeway, but why?"

"First let me say, Mr. Oakland, that I've heard about the wonderful job you've done with this man. As I understand it, he was (... Maybe he told someone else his problem. I talked to him on Friday afternoon. Did he say anything to anybody between that time and Saturday, when he ...) but the point I'm trying to make, Mr. Oakland, is that Bernardo Ramirez could be a symbol to a whole group of these people who have never had the example of one of their own making a success in the larger community."

"Well, I'm very glad."

"Half the kids in those projects don't have any fathers at all. A surprising number of the boys and young men don't have the slightest idea what men are really supposed to *do* during the day, and the presence of a man like your Ramirez might give them a (... Good God, I'm tired. I wish I could stop, just stop talking and thinking and working and go home and go to bed ...) and, of course, I wanted you to know about this and if there are any suggestions ... (Only two o'clock—so tired—I wish ...)

14

John Kroll

Ralph sat in the visitor's room, waiting for John Kroll. He had gone through a set of doors labeled:

JUV. DIV.

DEPT. CORR.

BUR. INST.

He wondered how they would ever have the patience to sift small truths and half-truths if they couldn't even spell out their own function on a door. Hans Marshak's death seemed to have left him with a heightened sense of the incongruity, as well as the impermanence, of everything. The love affairs of his youth had ended with a similar feeling. Perhaps he had been in love with his work in a little of the same way, trying for perfection, wanting to see perfection in the work, as he had once looked for it in a series of very human and fallible girls. Now he had to wait and see what the Juv. Div. Dept. Corr. Bur. Inst. was going to make of a boy very like a boy he had once been himself. Nor was he really sure that John was quite the devoted son he seemed to be. He had been looking for his mother, that much was proven fact; but then there was the sudden surfeit of sources answering to the name of Rutherford B. Hayes. John Kroll had seen Andrea Colvin and had been struck with her, and it would be easy for him to learn about the great set-up at Mrs. Mercer's and to find out that Andrea often stayed there.

The door from the detention corridors opened. Temporarily, the prosecution rested.

John Kroll came in first, wearing a white sweatshirt with the letters J.D.F across the front, where Ralph in his time had worn an Army number and afterward the name of a university. John saw Ralph's eyes on the letters, so he nudged

195

Marlon Brando and brought him up to give account. "Yeah, see they didn' get the name right. I told 'em John Dillenger Kroll, but they screwed up ona last letter."

"J.D.F.?"

"Joo-vee-nile Dee-ten-tion Fa-cil-ity is what they tell outsiders, but it really means . . ."

"Never mind, John. Something's come up and I want to find out where you fit in with it."

John looked around. The guard had gone through a door with heavy glass in it and was seated behind it, watching. "You know, the guys say these rooms are bugged." He gave an earsplitting whistle and then sat down in the chair opposite Ralph. "That'll fix the bastards. Guy tunes in on me is gonna *hear* somethin'. Say, maybe that mother-buggin' screw over there reads lips . . ."

"Look, John, what I want to know from you is where you spent the nights of those days when you were down on Vandalia. I'll tell you why I want to know. Some boys found out where there were some retarded girls staying. It was easy to talk the girls into 'putting out' for them. The boys went there almost every night."

"No kidding. Gee, ha! Ain't that a blast?" He sat back, chuckling.

"Well, it finally came out and we have reason to believe that the boys were from Boys' State or were seniors at the Shelter."

"Hey, Oakland, maybe they was provin' they wasn't *antisocial.*" He put back his head and laughed.

"One of the boys, John, was a certain Rutherford B. Hayes."

"Rutherfor—them dirty, lousy stinkin' sons . . . They give my alias name an I didn' get none of the fun. Can you beat that?"

"Were you one of those boys?"

"Nah, Oakland, I wasn't there. I tell you though, I wisht I was. What a soft deal! They didn' even have to pay for it or nothin', huh?"

"Just a second, John, I just want to remind you of one thing. You never were a moron, but remember how it was when people thought you were? Think hard, John, try to feel how it is with somebody who really is so dim that she can't figure out who is telling the truth and who isn't. The boys lied to those girls and made promises to them. If one of the girls

196

gets pregnant, she'll have the responsibility of a baby without even knowing how a baby came to her."

"Look, what do you want from me, Oakland. I told you I didn't knock-up no moron. I didn't like them anyway. I don't like girls that slobber an' look loony."

"Well, then, John, you'll be interested to learn that you know one of the girls involved."

"Don't tell me—somebody finally gave Old Lady Burns the shaft."

"Do you remember the last session you had with me before you took off?"

John nodded.

"Do you remember the girl in the hall, waiting to see me? I think she was there one time before that also when you saw her."

"Andrea?"

"She isn't loony-looking or slobbering, but she was one of the girls. I know you have seen her and spoken to her."

"Them stinkin', dirty rats! She ain't no dummy, she's just— well—she ain't had no *experiences*."

"She's had them now, John."

"Well, what the—I didn't get into her! I thought she was beautiful and she smiled nice and that, but I never went near her or them girls or nothin'. And you may not believe it, but I'm sorry them stinkin' cruds gave it to her."

"You know who they were, don't you."

"Oh, Oakland, I thought you had better sense than to ask me that."

"I do and I won't ask. Oddly enough, there are no charges to bring and no laws were violated, except our own moral ones that say that you don't pick on someone who's too old or young or weak or stupid to defend himself. I'm here for no other reason than to try to be sure of you, and I'm doing that because I'll be putting my own standards and reputation right on the line when I present a recommendation to the court about you."

The thing had a very strange ring in Ralph's memory as he said it. It had been said before, years ago, by someone whom Ralph could not recall. When 3-Eye had heard it, he had let out a long, blistering raspberry, and then shouted into the astonished face, "Well, boil my balls, but don't let the neighbors say I ain't a upright citizen!" Damn you, 3-Eye, Ralph thought, you never knew what reputation can buy. This good name of mine, this prestige, which you and the

197

monogrammed mug in front of us so scorn, buys time for him and a hundred others when they don't shape up right away. It buys services for them from other agencies, *because I* recommend them. It buys time and credit for me and my family. Believe it or not, but I stake my prestige and my job, to a certain extent, on everyone who goes through a program under my guidance. I risk everything a hundred times more than you ever did.

"Hey, Oakland, they goin' to sack you for hangin' around with undesirable and crummy elements like me?"

"That's not the point, John. The point is that if I give my recommendation for you, which is actually a promise that I believe you will make good, I want to know what I'm promising. You see, I might have to take my lumps for that promise, because I won't be able to run away."

"Well, I'll tell you—see it was like this: I seen a bunch of guys from B.S. down there near Vandalia. They got paroled and just were hangin' around 'cause two guys got sacked off of their jobs and a couple of the guys had rabbit deals."

"Rabbit deals?"

"Yeah, you know, there's guys who sign for a guy to promise him a job so he could get on parole, and when they get him squared away, after that, the job kinda disappears. Like now you see it and now you don't."

"And these men get kickbacks from the parolee?"

"Sure, sometimes he has to pull a job to get up the dough."

"You'd think the parole department would catch on."

"Well, there ain't enough cruddy parole officers to check up quick, and there's all kinds of ways to get around it until it's too late. Besides"—and he looked up with an innocence that could have been feigned or not—"they're scared of somethin' comin' out that wouldn't make them smell like no bokay, same as you guys, same as all squares."

"I won't admit that that's not true, but maybe it's partly because a lot of the people we try to help 'ain't no roses' and aren't in a position to influence anyone by themselves. One more thing, John, Miss Burns tells me that there's been narcotics smuggled into the Shelter. I want your assurance that you weren't in on that operation."

John's rage, always so near, burst out again, pulling his face into a sneer and hissing with his voice. "You squares are alla same!"

Ralph got up and the silent watcher behind the door did

198

also. John Kroll turned to follow him back to the detention-corridor. Then he turned around again, half smiling. "It wasn't me, Oakland."

"Okay, John."

"You're still gonna go to bat for me . . ."

"Yes, John, I will."

But Ralph was still wondering, still not convinced, and it made his tone a little distant.

John turned away, muttering, "That lousy, stinkin' dead Rutherford B. Hayes fouled me up twice already!"

John was probably innocent, Ralph thought hopelessly as he left. His own misery and lack of belief were making him doubt that there was any good at all in John, or any hope for him after so good and solid a man as Hans Marshak . . .

Traffic was heavy downtown and Ralph was late getting back to the office. When he passed the switchboard secretary, she stopped him. "Ralph, Ab wants to see you."

"Thanks, Gerry, I'll get up there right now."

He went upstairs to Ab's office and knocked on the door. It was statistics probably. Closures were down or they were up. He realized that he didn't care which. He went in.

"Here—sit down," Ab said. He had been buying Christmas presents during the lunch hour and Ralph had to clear some of them off the chair. Hans Marshak seemed to be standing between him and the ordinary things he wanted to take pleasure in. Perhaps it was Hans also standing in front of the bustle and excitement that blared from store fronts and echoed in the streets. It was nearing Christmas and Ralph hadn't been able to get up any of the necessary enthusiasm. Every year before, he and Mary-Ann had left the kids with friends and gone out shopping together, and had made it a special treat; but this year, Ralph had no heart to go looking over toys, choosing and re-choosing. He looked at Ab's pile of gifts forlornly.

"I had a call from Mr. Colvin this morning," Ab said.

"Oh?"

"That's right. I guess they got the same kind of introduction to things that you did. Andrea stopped by Mrs. Mercer's and Mrs. Mercer tried to question her tactfully, I guess. At any rate, she went home disappointed because none of the boys she'd slept with were really doing work for the government."

"Oh, no!"

"Oh, yes. Mrs. Colvin took her to the doctor and they're

waiting for the tests to come in." The telephone rang and Ab picked it up. "It's Mrs. Mercer," he said, and handed the phone to Ralph.

"Mr. Oakland, this is Mrs. Mercer. I hesitated just calling like this, but I thought you would want to know . . ."

"Yes, Mrs. Mercer . . ."

"Well, I don't want to be indelicate, but I thought you'd like to know it. Molly fell off today."

"What? Where did she fall?"

"You know, she *came in*."

"Came in—I don't understand . . ."

"Oh, Mr. Oakland, she is *menstruating!*"

"Oh."

"Well, I just want to tell you that I'm keeping track of all the girl's conditions."

"Thank you for . . ."

"*Good-bye,* Mr. Oakland."

Ralph looked sheepishly at the phone.

"What was it? What did she say?" Ab asked.

"She's still blushing and I didn't help the situation. She just called to tell us that one of the girls is off our worry list."

"Safe on first. I swear that's the best news I've heard since my kid flunked his driving test. Let's go down and drink a toast to sterility. Only four to go."

"Fine," Ralph said, "I could use a break. I'm sorry I was so dense the other day. That client of mine who committed suicide—well—it just threw me."

"I was so nervous that I couldn't stop myself from going overboard either," Ab said. "I knew that nothing was going to happen right away, that we'd probably have to wait, but, well, when you're in a public agency you have to be very careful about scandal. We've tangled about this before, but I want you to know, Ralph, that there's nothing personal in it. I'm an administrator and I have to be more sensitive to what people outside the agency think. I know that a suicide can bowl a counselor over. I hope you're not letting it get you down."

"Oh, hell, Ab, I look around at my work, my clients, and I wonder if I'm doing any kind of a job at all. That man Marshak was more like what we want to be than most of the others on my books, his values, his ambitions—I admired him and I keep wondering where I was blind, where I missed out and didn't give him the support or help he needed."

"Give yourself time, Ralph. It's too soon to blame yourself

or look for any kind of motive where the shock of the thing is still turning you upside down. And cases fail, too—how many closures have you had this year, men out and working?"

"Oh, about fifty since June."

"And since you've been with the agency?"

Ralph saw that Ab was going to try to get him off the hook with statistics. "It won't work, Ab," he said. "I'd have to be here twenty years to work off one suicide statistically."

"Well, your Ramirez is one in a million, you told me so yourself. I hear he's doing terrific work down there."

"Herb Vinson says that he should be ready for employment by June."

"See? You can't help them all. Relax, Ralph, you did your best. It'll work out." He gave Ralph a serious look and then slapped his arm lightly, and they went down for coffee. Ab's usual ease was something disconcerting to Ralph, but now he let himself be silenced. However Ab or the agency saw it, Hans Marshak's problem would never work itself out. It had been ended; now it could never be solved.

"Mr. Oakland, we're calling about a problem, a very serious problem. We heard that you were the right one to see. I'm Mrs. Hardy. I'm calling for the Altar Guild of our Adventist Church up in Broken Hill. I guess you wouldn't know Broken Hill; it's about thirteen miles from Thompson Creek . . ."

"Are you calling long distance from there?"

"No, one of our ladies had to come into the city today to get her eyes tested and we'll all be going back tomorrow. We wanted to tell you our problem, if you're the right one . . ."

"Well, could you tell me something about the problem?"

"Well, it's quite a long story, but it concerns some people in our community who need—well—they can't seem to get any work and they need to work. I'm speaking for the Altar Guild."

"Do these people know that you are inquiring for them?"

"Well, yes, but it's something we should talk to you about first."

"I can see you—let's see—I'm booked up to the tenth of January. How about the eleventh, sometime in the afternoon. It would give you time to get in."

"You mean you can't see us today?"

"I'm afraid not."

There were whispers at the other end of the line.

"If it's all right with you, Mr. Oakland, we'd rather come sometime in the morning to explain what the problem is. Most of the ladies look forward to a little stay, shopping and all."

"All right. Let me switch you to the secretary and she can give you a time and make the appointment."

"We have to work out this problem, Mr. Oakland, and we will be in to see you."

"Fine, Mrs. Hardy, I'll switch the call."

"Mr. Oakland, we're in a service club, the Busy Beavers, and every year we get up these Cheer Baskets for the poor at Christmas. The problem is that last year the orphan home that we were giving to sort of merged with the state home and there are *so* many clubs giving to *them*. Well, we thought you could tell us about some deserving families that we could distribute our Cheer Baskets to. I'm Mrs. Horner; I'm the basket chairman."

"I'm sorry, Mrs. Horner, but rehabilitation is not a charity-giving agency. I . . ."

"Well, we don't want to work with the welfare if that's what you mean. We don't understand their attitude. They want us to pool all the clothes and gifts and things in that outlet store they have and they won't give us any names of families. *Not one name!*"

"I think the reason for that is that the welfare department wants to keep a strict confidentiality for the sake of the clients. I'm sorry, but rehabilitation has the same policy. I think it's understandable that many of the client families of both agencies . . ."

"But where can we go? Our church keeps telling us about charity and the spirit of giving. Every time we try, some big government agency tells us we can't. We read articles all the time about people on relief and how low their living standards are, but when we try to give them something, why, everybody's all excited and acts like we're *un-American!*"

"Oh, Mrs. Horner, if you really want to help, there is a way, and we need it very badly. Talk to our state senators and tell them exactly what you're telling me about the low living standards of welfare recipients. When the time comes for a referendum voting tax money to increase those grants and get more staff, let the Busy Beavers campaign for *those* taxes, and maybe get out and talk about these problems.

Maybe we should vote money for more aid instead of, say, Christmas lights or decorating that big tree downtown—Mrs. Horner? Mrs. Horner . . .?"

"Ralph, this is Donna Asher at Sheltered Industries. Our crafts-training kids have been earning extra Christmas pocket money this year by making candy wreaths and decorating the little sparkle trees—you remember what a big hit they were last Christmas. They're still only a dollar each and we've put you down for four of each."

"*What?* What am I going to do with all of them?"

"Oh, why don't you give them as Christmas presents; that's what we do."

"Uh—uh—Donna, I have a good idea for you. Call up a Mrs. Horner at the Busy Beavers. It's a service club in town. You might get them to distribute for you."

"We sure could use help. I'll give them a call and thanks for the idea, but it's not going to get you off the hook."

"o.k. I'll eat my way to heaven."

"You'll make a lovely angel."

"How come, with a paunch, pimples, and rotten teeth?"

"But, Ralph, it's for *charity*."

"Mr. Oakland, this is Mrs. Colvin. I hope you will take this in the right spirit—I was going to call you and tell you some of the *terrible* things our daughter came home and told us. You know, my husband has a very quick temper, and he was ready to come over there and give you a piece of his mind. Those *people!* Those terrible *people!* We were certain that our daughter's innocence had been destroyed. She used *expressions*—well—you have an idea, knowing what sort of monsters those—boys were. We took her to a doctor right away. Boys of such a type as that—diseased degenerates, just diseased degenerates! I was afraid that—well—you know what I mean. The doctor didn't find any of those diseases. In fact, he found something else. He found that Andrea is going to have a baby."

"Oh, Mrs. Colvin—I want you and Mr. Colvin to . . ."

"We were shocked at first, shocked. I know that you'll think it unreasonable, Mr. Oakland, but you must realize that it was you, after all, who introduced Andrea to that kind of life. My husband has been very bitter. He was furious with you and that whole agency down there. We had to question Andrea more about—what happened. We found out that by

203

a miracle, bless her heart, she doesn't know how the baby came to her. Of course, when we found out that Andrea's *innocence* had been preserved, well, then there was no reason to think about her future being terrible. My husband was still angry, of course, but when the doctor told Andrea—(he had to tell her, I suppose)—about how she was going to be a momma, why she was just the happiest girl in the world. When she's happy, her father relents. She's gotten us to sign her up to take that Red Cross course, and we're going to go right along with her just to make sure they don't say anything that will upset her. You know how frank those courses are. People have no sense of *delicacy* these days."

"Well—uh—Mrs. Colvin, I'm sure that Andrea will benefit from your acceptance of this, and we . . ."

"I didn't want to take too much of your time, Mr. Oakland, but there's one more thing I wanted to say, and I had to wait until Mr. Colvin left for work because he's still a little irritated with you, and—well—it's personal. When I think about all of this I'm happy, peaceful in my mind. Because, you see, Mr. Oakland, she'll never need to know all those— filthy things. She'll have us and the baby, so she'll never be lonely. Oh, so many of our friends are all alone. Their children go off and marry and leave them and their lives are just, well, just *empty*. I want to set your mind at ease about Andrea, and not keep you, Mr. Oakland. I know you are busy. Merry Christmas now, and I am just going to send you a picture of Andrea. I know she's going to look so sweet in *those* clothes . . ."

. . . (What was it that I didn't see in that woman, or didn't hear? That mother was one of the most conventional women I've ever met, dreams so typical she seemed to feel perfectly within her rights to be rapacious about them. Why do I feel that she has been using me somehow? Something doesn't fit—there was something funny about that very typical dream. . . .) He remembered the three of them the first time they came in: mother and father standing up and arguing and Andrea sitting in the middle of their wrath like some medieval lesson on Holy Serenity. . . .(. . . It was something later. Was it the tight clothes? Yes, but something more, something I saw, a false note, some incongruous thing in a place where—Of *course!* How could I have missed it! That mother and daughter standing in the hall with the full parade of adolescent libido and longing moving past them like history. What does the usual mother of such a daughter do? She

204

buys stout shoes and a great big handbag and she sits up close and lets it be known that there is a witch in the plot, a dragon guarding the gate. She regards these pacing packs of predators with fear and she masks the fear with scorn. They are the enemy. But Andrea's mother sat by quietly while the parade passed and re-passed, not disapproving at all but pleasant and almost dissociated from what was happening. Lots of mothers don't like to let their daughters "know," but then they guard them, they sacrifice their optimism to their daughters' innocence. This one wanted both: the tight dress and the "not knowing." She *wanted* this, one way or another from the beginning; *she wanted that gate taken!*)

Ralph lit a cigarette and then put it out. (Smoking too much—I should cut down. Maybe if I cut out the smoking I wouldn't get this ache in my chest.) He put the cigarette out in the overflowing ash tray. (Why would a mother want this for her daughter, without consciously wanting it, of course? I guess it doesn't matter why. She's got her wish, which is more than most of us ever get. I wonder how Andrea will look when she's well on in her pregnancy. I wonder if—will there be that quietness, that radiance?)

"Ab, this is Ralph. Mrs. Colvin just called to say that Andrea is pregnant."

"Oh, migawd! What did she say?"

"You won't believe it. She said it was wonderful. She's happy, grandpa's happy, and Andrea is taking a Red Cross course in baby care."

"Oh, Ralph, cut the clowning, will you; this is important."

"I'm as amazed as you. Mama is ecstatic. Actually, when I thought about it, maybe I should have known that it was what she wanted—the mother, I mean. She kept that kid in some pretty—uh—revealing dresses. Well, now she has everything she wants and without the entanglement of a man in the picture, no other opinion to have to consider, no in-laws. The girls down at Mrs. Mercer's will probably give Andrea a baby shower."

"I don't believe it—it's too good to be true. Mrs. Mercer's been calling in the last two weeks about the girls. They've all come around. This was the last thing that was keeping me awake nights."

"I wonder why she didn't call me."

"I don't think she trusts your grasp of the language. You are sure of this, Ralph, Mrs. Colvin wasn't trying to lull us while she got a lawyer . . ."

"She meant it all right. I listened to that mother talk, and I found myself wondering why not? The kid will have three parents, plenty of security and love, and Andrea will never have to be a wife or write an income-tax form. She'll never leave home now, and Daddy can have two babies."

"I'll be a monkey's uncle!"

"That's the best theology I've heard in a long time."

"Well, don't let it get you down, Ralph, we're off the hook and home free on a scandal that could have torn into us but good, and I can tell you now that I never thought we'd make it."

"Five different cycles of ovulation, five sets of parents, the complicated interplay of chance and predictable factors, and it's still easier to get than a simple little rehabilitation."

Looking at Georgia Burns's letter, Ralph wondered why he wasn't laughing and dancing. Judge French, perhaps in a fit of holiday spirit, had given John five days juvenile detention and suspended the rest of his sentence. Through the trackless thickets of professional jargon, Georgia's happiness showed shining and strong, like laughter in the archives. She obviously felt that she and Ralph and Captain Sutter, who had testified in his Salvation Army uniform, had saved John's future from sure ruin. Saved him for what? He was still closed from further training, at least until next year, and Ralph was sure that John would never consent to wait that long. He also knew that if John so much as stuck out that famous Marlon Brando lip of his, the whole remaining sentence to juvenile detention or Boys' State would automatically be put into effect, and he would antagonize Judge French, a tough and powerful adversary. These were very bad odds for an intense, impulsive, and willful boy, who wore bravado like a badge. It was supposed to be a triumph for Ralph and for rehabilitation over the punitive forces of the community, but Ralph felt strangely uninvolved; in fact, as he read the letter over again, wondering how he should handle John now, he found his thoughts drifting, tongue on the exposed nerve again. (It was what Hans said about his legs that should have made me stop; a sensitivity like that was too great after a month of walking, the pride was too great. Maybe what I took for pride was a kind of rigidity of ...) He came back to himself staring at the letter. If there was only a place where Kroll's qualities could be used, the lack of caring, the spontaneity, the self-centeredness, the hatred of routine. Fifty or more I.Q. points and he might have made a fine international spy.

Ralph's mind began to drift again. The phone brought him back and he felt put upon. He was always being pulled by bells: telephone, alarm clock, buzzer. He muttered: "Lock-step-lock, tick-tock, tick-tock!" He picked up the phone.

"Bernice, Ralph. Have you forgotten? Miss Cormer is here for her appointment."

"Oh, *hell!*" If she hadn't shown up he could have spent the time getting some of the paperwork out of the way. Now he would have to take the mess home over the weekend and listen to Mary-Ann mutter about it. He got up and went out to show Minnie Cormer into the office. When he saw her, he realized that her coming in at all was something of a miracle. She looked as sick as she had before, as lost, as hopeless. Why had she come?

Minnie Cormer

"Miss Cormer?"

The eye flickered to him. She breathed and got up and followed him, refusing his gesture that she go through the door before him. He had to show her to a seat and then go back and close the door, feeling clumsy and remembering that he had sat down too hard once during their first meeting.

"I'm glad you came," he lied. When he said it, he was ashamed for it. It had come out sounding a little surprised, as if he had not expected her to come back. That was poor judgment and he had to be ashamed of it, too.

"I tell yuh why I come back," she said dully. "I come back because I gone fail uh one thing I try do *my* way. I know whu you think 'o me. Scum."

"That's not true," he said.

"Why not? You any diffrunt res' o' uh worl'? Huccum you ain' in on uh onlies jurgemen everybody agree, onlies thing uh whole worl' agree true?"

"Maybe it's because you're back here. It took a lot to come back here and try to find help for yourself."

"Thousan' good apple in uh tree, you shoots down uh one wormy. I came back here cause I alus have *me* befoa and now I ain' even got me lef'."

"What happened?"

She was mumbling and he could barely make out her

207

words. He had to listen with an intensity that made his head ache.

"Ain' no place fuh me go now. I come out uh crazy house an ain' no diffrent fum when I gone in. Medicine, pill, brown one, blue one—ain' goin' ease me none, hep my babies none. I say to muhself, I goin' wait twell I get picture of my fit, goin' stan er trolly track, train track, out o' winda, jump een uh woadah. That uh fit goin' really fit me. Time gone by. I ain' take none of uh pills. Soon I see at purple-color shadow ats uh woaning. Walk to aidge, I says, flop in uh street, I says. Somepm come up push me back. I come to, middle o' sidewalk, here uh po-lice. Agin one time, an nurrah. Thing won't even lea me die." She stopped abruptly, the long, monotone mumble clipped itself off, leaving Ralph suspended for a moment waiting for an end.

Then they sat and looked at one another, Ralph wondering how he could convince her to live when he hadn't been able to convince so favored a man as Hans Marshak. "The thing that will not let you go; it's not an outside force; it's part of yourself that is fighting and wants to keep you living no matter what. I want to help that part."

"That why I come here. I can' die; I bettah get a job, gone wurk."

He had hoped she would save him by not asking. Now he had to refuse her and do it without equivocating. In her despair, she could feel the noose of a half-truth long before it tightened. "There wouldn't be a job for you now," he said, "there are just too many things you haven't cleared away. You are just not free to work. First you need medical control for those seizures and some counseling to help you in your problems with your children and your life."

"You shuttin' me off wi'out no job . . ."

"*No!* If you can find something, fine. I don't control jobs, I advise. Remember that you're going to have to pay a baby sitter to stay with the children. You'll have to pay the transportation to and from a job, and this I know: without control of your seizures, you won't keep any job longer than a week."

"Whut you gota *lead* me to? You got quota or somethin'?"

"I have nothing making me say what I say. I think it would be best for you to stay on welfare, get medical control, and stay home and bring up your children. Wait— don't say no right away. I know that you have a lot of trouble staying at home. What if we could get you some help, some counseling to get you over some of the tougher parts of being there?"

"I doan know. How anythin' goin' keep me fum recognize uh ole face o' onesome come reg'lar, like pos-man. I don' like hangin' roun' uh bars, git men uh come back with me. Men drunk, mean, dutty—uh men nuthin', but nuthin' bettah—bettah den—nuthin'." She gave a quick, joyless laugh at the language that had betrayed her.

"Don't you think that there could be other ways of being less lonely? Perhaps there are. Whether those ways would work for you or not, I don't know, but I think you might give a little thought to trying to get to the point where you could stay home more comfortably instead of trying to work on the outside."

She got up. "I doan know. I gone home think about it fuh while. Mebbe I get uh fits fix, maybe not. I let you know."

"Call me when you decide either way, please. I want to help and this is the advice I really think is best."

"I know uh rule. You got to close muh case."

She left, and Ralph couldn't help feeling that she was right. It had been his mistake, succumbing to the flattery and reasons of people he respected, over his better judgment; and when he had to come to terms with the victim of his weakness, he wanted only to close her case. He had wished that she wouldn't show up. If she really wanted help of the kind he could offer, it had to be real help, good help. He put in a call to the welfare department.

"There's a special case we should talk over," he said, "but, first, do you have a student who could take on such a case for intensive counseling?"

"We might—who's the case?"

"Her name is Cormer. She's been on welfare, and I think that her only real choice is to get her children and go on a grant for herself and for them. What I want to be sure of is that the student she gets is top flight. She's been through a lot and is quite severely depressed. Any evidence of the High Moral Tone or fake heartiness will be spotted. I know, because she spotted it in me."

"Well, as you know, most of our graduate students in social work have been in the field for a while. If the case presents a challenge, it will be good for a keen student. Suppose I see what's what and call you back."

"Thanks a lot. If she can get fare enough to raise those kids without having them repeat her pattern, it will be well

209

worth the time it takes. I know that she's been referred by welfare as a candidate for rehabilitation, but it just isn't possible."

"I'll call you in a day or two."

It was the best he could do. She needed time and intensive counseling that he couldn't give. A student would have the time and there would be no need to strive for an impossible goal—a job, a steady middle-class existence. Why was he troubled then? He sat behind his professional desk in his professional chair in this familiar office, wondering why this work suddenly seemed so useless and pointless and endless. Was he doing no more than squaring round pegs for a more and more limited number of square holes? He thought of Bernardo Ramirez in that first interview saying, "Jus keepeen' de family . . '" People who played God for a living could, perhaps, envy the one who worked just "keepeen' de family." Something had gone out of the job—and out of the jobholder. What he did was the same, but his excitement in it had withered; his secret pleasure at feeling himself at the center of a great, varied, yet changeless, wellspring of human experience had chilled somehow. He felt himself alone and tired, lost in a meaningless maze of the numbers and money and papers which had been his tools. Perhaps it was his sickness that was grinding the heart out of him. Maybe hopelessness is a contagious disease, and he and all the other workers were in a vast, latter-day plague ward, working against the crushing tides of illness and defeat until they themselves weakened and succumbed.

If this were so, it would explain why there was never any time to take pleasure in a client's successes. The year measured three thousand spilling and falling through the great doors at one end of Ralph's compound, from which about a thousand were sifted to be considered; and from those, another great number leaving by one and one and one, counseled through mental blocks and broken marriages, sent deftly between the meshed gears of agencies, moving hesitantly with maddening slowness through the small exit hatch on the other side. Over the exit was a picture of Adolf Hitler and a sign: SUPERIOR EFFICIENCY: You Will Never Equal My Figures. In the early years he had scoffed at the picture. Anyone can kill. It takes nine months and twenty-five years to make a man, and less than a second to unmake him. Now the same words were said despairingly, and the papers that stated it and the people pleading it raised an answer from him that was a dry, cold parody of the joyful, urgent ambition that had awakened him during his college years.

Ralph had a fairly late vocation. 3-Eye Oakland left for Army service in World War II, where his miner's hard hat became a helmet and his angers and allegiances were not basically changed. He came home alive and a conquerer, having done no more than change his helmet and the objects of his hatreds. He took what was free and what he had coming: a small medal, a luger, two contraceptive kits, and a college education under the G.I. Bill. His first days at the university disabused him of the innocent notion that college was a citadel of the lofty and noble, where all professors were profound and all students reverent. Yet, he stayed, and sometime during that year, in one of the many lecture halls, 3-Eye died and Ralph was born. The angry agnostic had been converted not to God but to man. For mankind and all his causes, he had taken fire with a kind of holy joy. During those years he learned and hungered and learned more, always with the kind of excitement which one associates with a revelation ending: "Go forth . . ."

Now he looked around and saw that he had outrun his eagerness. In all the years of his being Ralph, his joy in belief had lifted him over money troubles, worry, and even the countless setbacks and failures in his work. Now he looked into the grayness of his confusion and heard the clamor of need mounting, and wondered how he could care and hope and counsel clients through it.

15

It had started with Marshak's death, Ralpph thought. That, and the holiday season that seemed so glaringly wrong in the face of the multiple anguishes of Minnie Cormer and the rolls that were full of people who were not simply handicapped but heaped with compounded troubles, that tipped and spilled into one another, feeding the destruction endlessly. For the first time he saw this work as hopeless, and it drove him again and again to his last conversations with Hans Marshak. In spite of his conscious knowledge that it was useless, he kept searching his memory for a key, a clue to the motives for Marshak's suicide, as if finding it would also find the origin of his own loss of hope. There was something in the fierce masculine pride that Hans had taken in his body. To be a whole man, strong and vigorous, had had special meaning for him. Perhaps he couldn't stand the idea of being a little less than physically perfect. Why had he waited then, fighting for almost two years to recover, then to stand, then to walk? Why had he worked so hard to learn how to live and succeed again, only to end himself just as the new life was to begin? Was he afraid? Was there trouble at home that he was ashamed to admit? Perhaps he felt too shy before his wife. He had said, "We're finished with sickness and handicaps . . ." Did that mean what Ralph had taken it to mean, or had it been in Hans's mind to kill himself even before he got the new job? Of course, Ralph now believed that Hans's last call to him, a call he had cut short for some reason that he couldn't even remember now, that that call had been a cry for help. Hans's last words had surprised Ralph even then—why had he not heard them, not caught them? Hans had said something about people noticing him,

212

and then, "Good-bye, Mr. Oakland," in the formal, absolute tone which Ralph had mistaken for an impatience at being hurried off the phone. Had that been the moment when he decided, hoping to have Ralph answer the need, failing, and feeling that he *had* to say good-bye? Over and over the questions went. It was after New Years and still the circle kept turning itself, plaguing Ralph; and the gray hopelessness of his feelings continued. During one of these moments of wondering, between clients, it occurred to Ralph that perhaps it would be better if he quit this job. There was relatively little work with new clients during the Christmas and New Year holidays. Ralph had been able to get by somehow, by quoting himself and acting in the role of Ralph Oakland. His old clients had not seen the emptiness in him yet, but when a crisis came or when the pace got hectic again, the hollowness would surely show through. It would hurt the clients because they would translate it into his hopelessness in the face of *their* indifference, an easy mistake for them to make because of their sensitivity and self-centeredness. Maybe he would talk to Ab; maybe he would go down to Blaunt Components. They had asked him if he wanted to do personnel work there. His past refusals had been because of the dream, the excitement of seeing resurrections and feeling that he had helped in their making. Now, why not? There wouldn't be the feeeling of inundation in seas of suffering, and the pay was better. It would be something to think about. He got up and went out to usher in John Kroll.

John Kroll

In the light, John's hair gleamed greenly. What was that stuff, valve grease?

"Hi, Oakland. How do you like that—I got sprung. Hey, you know who came to the can? My old lady, and she brung me this!" He gestured down at a black-and-white check jacket.

"It's very nice," Ralph said. He was lying. The jacket completed a picture that made John look like a photo on the post office wall. Ralph showed his client in and motioned him to the chair. There was a difference in John that Ralph doubted was the result of Judge French's leniency. He had a springiness in his step and a jauntiness in his manner. It smacked a little of bravado, but at least it wasn't the irritating zombie act that he usually used.

"Well, John, what's new?"

"Jesus, Oakland, I been in the can a couple of times. I was at B.S. till I know the joint better than the friggin' bum that built it, but I never remembered how hot these guys get when they're really gonna send you up."

"How do you mean?"

"Well, they got aholt of my old lady and sobered her up and made her come down, and even, they got her to write to a uncle I got in Minnesota; I never even heard of the guy before. He come down here and said I could go in Minnesota and work for him—he's got a wreckin' business."

"Are you going?"

"Well, yeah, I guess I'll go. Work for him. I won't have to stay in no lousy, stinkin' hole like B.S."

"John, are you sure this isn't one of those 'rabbit' jobs you told me about?"

"Did I tell you about that? Hell, I got a bigger mouth than I thought."

"I hope it's a real job. Oh, John, Minnesota's Juvenile Detention facility doesn't smell any better than ours; their beans don't taste any better. Don't buy yourself out. It's really selling out and ..."

"Honest, Oakland, I never seen this guy before, my uncle. My old lady or somebody wrote and he talked to the judge or somethin'. Anyway, they gave him the O.K. So, I'm goin' out there and I got a job with him."

"When are you going?"

"Jesus, Oakland, you ain't sorry I'm goin'. I thought you'd be glad, the way I loused up your record and everything."

Another of the very few times that Ralph had heard John Kroll consider any problems but his own. Everyone had said that he was totally incapable of caring for anyone or anything. No one had seen what was tormenting him, but Ralph could forgive the others; it wasn't their job to see the invisible and hear the inaudible.

"I just want to be sure that you know what you're doing. If the job peters out, you might find yourself in trouble again. You don't have the education to compete with the crowds of high-school kids coming out to look for work every year."

"Oh, what do I need that crap for; I got *contacts*. He even

214

got my old lady to get me this jacket. We're taking off Thursday."

"All right, John, but look—I want you to do something. If anything comes up, good or bad, let me know, will you. Nothing fancy, just a postcard when you get settled, or—well—if something happens."

"Are you makin' me do that?"

"No, John, I'd just appreciate it and I know Miss Burns would, too. Just a card to either of us."

"Uh—couldn't—uh—couldn't you make me. I mean like if any of the guys found out I didn't have to it would be like I was some kind of a *creep.*"

"Kroll, your case will not be closed unless you keep your Rehabilitation Officer or your Custodial Office informed of your progress."

He smiled quickly. "Thanks, Oakland."

"Okay, John."

"Well, Ralph, I got to be blowin' this town so I gotta pack and all that. Oh, yeah, I brang you a present."

He reached into the pocket of the impossible jacket and took out an envelope. He tossed it on the desk and Ralph picked it up and opened it. It was a picture of John Kroll, checked jacket and lubricated hair, staring out of a three by five white-rimmed card, three poses for fifty cents at the Fun 'n Frolic Arcade.

"I give you the front view," he said. "They give you three views, but I figured you would like the front view better than the side view. I didn' smile or nothin' 'cause lots of the guys get in there and crap around and look silly. I figured if I smiled or somethin', you wouldn' know who it was."

"It looks fine, John. I'm glad to have it."

"Yeah, well, Ralph, I got to get goin'."

"Good-bye, John. Remember your Out-of-State Requirements."

"So long, Ralph, keep it clean."

Ralph had put out his hand. John began to extend his, thought better of it, put it back in his pocket and sauntered out of the office.

How long will that "contact" last if John's ideals and hungers haven't changed? Ralph had a feeling that the penal institutions of the United States hadn't seen the end of John Kroll; but he didn't care, why did he ask John to write? If the work and the people meant nothing, why was he worried about John, John of all people? Well, maybe because he was an old client, a case made and suffered over when the dream was still real and possible and beautiful. Maybe it was no more than a belated good-bye to 3-Eye Oakland, the ghost in a hard hat. Two angry loners. Goodbye, John, good luck.

Ralph picked up the picture again, looked at it for a while, and then put it away in his desk drawer.

16

" . . . Well, it's an uphill struggle, Mr. Oakland, tutoring that Ramirez. It's like breaking granite with a pickax."

"That's strange, Bernardo isn't a stupid man . . ."

"I know, but he is hopeless as a reader. I have a feeling that I'm at fault. You know, our training never prepared us for illiteracy of this kind. We're spoiled, Mr. Oakland. There are voices on the radio and on T.V. that spell out the names of laxatives and drain cures; they may never make anyone literary, but they give hints at the process of translating dead symbols into living sounds. He won't ever read, Mr. Oakland, not really. Maybe we can give him enough to beat out the messages that the school keeps sending home with the kids."

"I hope it's not trouble . . ."

"No, I was thinking about the notice for the Christmas play that he brought in yesterday: January 30th, if you remember. The kids must have been disappointed."

"I'm sorry it's going so slowly."

"It isn't the speed, it's the darkness. English and reading both—it's like a polar midnight to him; there just isn't any light yet."

"But you'll keep trying."

"How do you say Nanook in Spanish? His new caseworker thinks it's a big waste of time, teaching Ramirez to read. I know that communicates itself to him . . ."

"New caseworker? But I thought . . ."

"Oh, didn't you know? Grace Jesperson is leaving—maybe I shouldn't have said anything; I just thought she'd told you . . ."

"No, I'm sorry to hear it. Has she gone yet?"

"Not yet—she's sort of clearing up this week, and they

give them a party, I guess. I think she mentioned going to work as a paid companion. Well, Mr. Oakland, I won't keep you. You told me how important you felt this reading was and I felt that you should know."

(Another one gone. Another good one somehow unable to stay on and be dedicated. How much of the pride in a job is spread out to include the company a person keeps on it?) Ralph was aware that he resented his title, the Lone Ranger. If he had been teased as one of the Three Musketeers, he would secretly have been very proud. In this work the telephone wasn't a means of communication if the ear at the other end was deaf. The law was not a means of help if the co-worker used it only to separate, as Fatika had, good from evil—and now, hearing, daring, compassionate, pretty-and-young Miss Jesperson wasn't going to be Evers to his Chance any more. (If only some good ones will stay, maybe just ten good ones, maybe only nine . . .)

"Excuse me, ladies, I don't take calls during interviews except from caseworkers whose time is as crowded as mine. Well . . . ," and he leaned back, "where were we?"

"We were talking about what's brought us in to see you. We had it all down in our minds to say to you, and then having to cancel out because of the big snow, well, it just seemed to fly out of our minds. Broken Hill's a small place, Mr. Oakland, and we're still small enough to give a thought to our neighbor. Well, Thrysa, why don't you tell about it?"

"Well, as Dorothy said, we're from the Adventist Church in Broken Hill, the Ladies' Altar Guild. I hate to say this, but—well—our problem sort of started when Church of Christ came to Broken Hill. I hate to say this, but ever since they came it's just brought out the worst in everybody. You see, there'd been a kind of competition between the two churches in Broken Hill over the years, and when the Presbyterians moved their church down to Thompson Creek and the Church of Christ people came, why, I guess they just felt they had to prove they were as good as we were—felt *inferior,* don't you know."

"Well, Mrs. Hardy—if you'd . . ."

"Yes, well, I am. I won't go into the things that happened—picnics got bigger and bigger, tryin' to outshine—and we were to blame, too—don't shake your head no, Ellen; Fay Rountree and those others just made it worse and you know it."

218

"Mrs. Hardy, if you'd just tell me what the problem . . ."

"Well, I'm coming to it right now. Things did go too far, and well, the Altar Guild got carried away, and, well, we—well, we took those *Cubans*."

"What?"

"It was my fault, Mr. Oakland, at least part of it; but part of it is a hoax, Mr. Oakland, hoax plain and simple."

"What happened, Mrs. Hardy?"

"Well, it was Harold who suggested it; he's been going down to those Great Discussions meetings Thursday nights down at Thompson Creek. Well, somebody down there got to telling how different churches were sponsoring these Cubans to come out to different parts of the country and settle. The churches pay part of their ransom and their fare out here from that jail, you know, because of the dictatorship. Well, it sounded like a real wonderful idea, our church bringing a family to freedom like that, and it shut up Church of Christ good, too. Well, we got them on the 13th of December—paid their fare and everything. Fixed up the Crile house for them and got started making Christmas plans. Went down to Thompson Creek to pick them up at the station, and you know, Mr. Oakland, you know those people didn't speak one word of English, *not one blessed word!* There was a man and his wife and four children and the man's brother, that is, he palmed himself off as his brother. But come to find out, he's not related to any of them. Come to find out, Mr. Oakland, we had to get the Spanish teacher all the way up from the Consolidated school and interpret, and her Spanish isn't all that strong. Well, she found out that he was a deep-sea fisherman, *a fisherman,* in these mountains, one-thousand and five-hundred miles away from an *ocean!* The worst part of it is that we feel we've been deceived about the whole thing. That—Cisneros man doesn't even belong to our church, but we were *supposed* to get people who were good, God-fearing tithers of our own belief. Others don't fit in, Mr. Oakland, you know that. Now with this Or-tiz, he says he's of our belief, but with that other one, we just feel we've been taken in. Yes, I do, Ellen, I think those people over there in Cuba just palmed him off on us to feed and keep. The whole crew of them just stay in that house there and talk in Spanish all day and don't even keep the place up."

"I gather that you want to know if the state can help to get work for the men . . ."

"Well, *we* can't afford to keep them; we just bought them
219

out. And then Miss Frink—that's the Spanish teacher—she started to ask for pay, and someone has to drive her up and back all the time. We had food and clothing for them for a week and then, of course, Christmas things, but we can't support them much longer. Broken Hill all together's no more than two thousand population. They seem grateful and all, but what are we *going to do?*

"You see, Mr. Oakland, we wanted to show them the American Way, bringing them over and letting them be free, but if they can't do for themselves, well *that's* not the American way at all."

"Well, ladies, I can't promise to do anything right away—suppose you arrange to have the men here in my office, say on the 16th. I'll take care of the interpreter. Then we'll find out what's what."

"The 16th, why, that's over two weeks away."

"Well, that's when my schedule opens up."

"Oh, dear—oh, very well, but please, please try to get something for them to do."

"Mr. Oakland, I'd like to ask you something."

"What is it, Mrs. Hardy?"

"Please don't take offense, Mr. Oakland, but I want to tell you that my grandfather came here from Germany in 1887 and he landed without a cent. He worked at all kinds of jobs until he got enough money together to come out here to mine. *He* had a wife and children, too, just like this Mr. Or-tiz, but he never was on any dole. He got right down and worked and then he came out here, and when the bottom dropped out of the silver, why he farmed a little and mined a little and that man kept going and he was a respected man in Broken Hill, and when he died he was the equal of any one in town. Now this Or-tiz is no different, why doesn't he just take hold?"

"1887, Mrs. Hardy, when a man could work and have his courageous kids and faithful wife working, too, right along beside him."

"They certainly did."

"And they took any kinds of jobs, too, didn't they—working way into the night . . ."

"That's right."

"Well, child labor is illegal now, and neglect is illegal, too. Even if your grandfather was illiterate, there were hundreds of jobs he could hold. Even working himself across the country, like my grandfather did, camping along the road.

That's illegal now, too. Now that we know about vitamins and balanced diets, could we trust to the old standbys: sourdough, beans, and parched corn? My grandmother used to go to the back doors of restaurants and pay a couple of cents for the uneaten food. She never considered it charity because she paid for the food. That's illegal now, too. And what were the old standby jobs, jobs you could do from town to town across the country?"

"Well, they used to paint people's houses and do repairs ..."

"Union—he'd have to be in a union."

"Well, my father did loading."

"Union, too, and it's automated now; they need one man now where they once used thirty."

"What about making deliveries? My grandfather walked through four feet of snow on his deliveries!"

"Would you wait two days for a man to go up to Broken Hill with medicine? Deliveries today are made by car or truck. It's faster and better. There has to be a driver and that means that he has to be licensed and belong to a union."

"Well, why don't they *join* a union?"

"The dues are stupendous and he would have to be a citizen. There's also an age limit. It would be hopeless even to apply."

"But—well anyone can do a little honest farming!"

"Yes, the farming. Somehow there's always the idea that a man can do a little farming. Your grandfather was a squatter, wasn't he, Mrs. Hardy? Mine was too. There was nothing dishonorable about being a squatter then. After a number of years, a squatter could earn his deed because he'd endured on his land. But the land is owned now—and there are taxes to pay on it."

"That's what I always say, Mr. Oakland, it's the government interference that's ruining our American ..."

"Mr. Oakland, this is Janeway of the housing authority again. It's about Ramirez again, too."

"There's nothing wrong, I hope."

"Well, not for him. What's wrong is the way things are here. You see, the family's been in our La Placita project since the end of November. It's mostly Spanish-speaking, mostly illiterate, as you know. The kids on the project are some of the worst juvenile offenders in town. I'm not saying that this Ramirez is any kind of a fireball, but since he's moved in, he's been limping along to school every morning. At first the kids made fun of him, but the way I understand it, he's become quite an influence in the place. Seems the heating plant went on the fritz one day, and this Ramirez just kind of shuffled down there and looked at the thing and said he could fix it—you know that slow way of his. A flick of the wrist—that's the way I heard it—and everything is going like a million. Well, before long the families in the project start calling him in to fix this or that. The kids quit laughing and started waiting for him to come home from school. Last week he took them to his school; eighteen hostile-aggressives yes-sirred their way through four floors of Central Auto without lifting a thing."

"You're not looking for some new kind of social worker are you? I just don't know if he has that kind of talent."

"Oh, no, Mr. Oakland. There's still lots of glue-sniffing, tire-lifting, and seat-slashing out of La Placita. I'm not expecting a new division of General Motors to open there, either, don't get me wrong. It's just that some kid, just one maybe, or two, might see some kind of future in that every morning walk to school. Just to know someone with a Spanish accent who is with it in the Anglo world—oh, the hell of it is that he's likely to get out the moment he gets a job."

"Well, that's not going to be for a while."

"I went up to see him yesterday. He was beating out the first part of *Dick and Jane*. He was up to the part where things really get going between Spot and Baby. He was all scrunched up in his chair, clutching his handkerchief, and his face was contorted as if he was *having* Baby. He told me that Central Auto had put him ahead again. He's working on the stuff they usually give in the middle of the second year. That means he'll be ready for a job soon. What all this is leading up to, Mr. Oakland, well—can't he go further in training before he has to work? The way low-income housing works, the projects tend to get stripped of successful people. No wonder the people who are left feel that they've been dumped, left in a new kind of ghetto."

"I'd like to help you, Mr. Janeway, but the next training that Bernardo could take would be at the college level, and they wouldn't look at him with his *Dick and Jane* background. I'm sorry, I wish things could be changed. You might try to get him to stay at La Placita for as long as possible."

"I've tried time and again with so many of them. Every time something good happens, the family it happens to

222

leaves. You never get stability or community pride that way. Well, you must be busy. Sorry I bothered you."

"Uh—Mr. Oakland, this is Alan Devereaux."

(Don't come back, please, don't come back on the load! Don't you people understand that there are six others in your place, that there are two hundred and fifty of them now!)
"Well, hello, Alan, what can I do for you?"

"You remember I'm at Wings Barber Shop out at the field? Uh, well, Mr. Swan asked if maybe you have someone you could send because we're going to put on another man."

"Oh. (Thank God!) Well, that's just fine, Alan, I haven't got anyone trained right now, although there are a few in barber school. We have a bulletin board out here, though, that the counselors refer to. I'd like to put up a notation so that the other men could see if any of their clients could fill the job."

"o.k., Mr. Oakland. I wanted you to get first crack at it."

"Come in, Ralph, I've been meaning to ask you to come by," Ab said.

"Is something the matter? I didn't forget something . . ."

"No, it's about the Ramirez case. I know he's not working yet, but from what I hear that won't be much of a problem. Anyway, we'd like you to work the case up for presentation at the next regional conference. The men down in Indio county might send some more cases up here for training if they . . ."

"No, no Ab, we don't need more trainees. Let's keep Indio county as slow as we can. We need more trade schools and more jobs. We've got ten times the number of people we can service . . ."

"Well, I'd like you to write it up anyway. If you have any comments about the case, you can put them in also."

"A decent training school in Indio county? Never."

"Oh, they won't get one, but you can write it in if you want to."

"I guess I can."

"Uh—Ralph, you asked if something was the matter with your work. It isn't, but something has been troubling you. Even Fatika notices it. You've been letting him win all the arguments lately, and it's making him uncomfortable. What is it, Ralph?"

"I don't know, Ab. This morning some women came down to see me about a stranded fisherman. One of them started to
223

go on about self-reliance and the old pioneer virtues, and then a man from city housing called up about Ramirez—well—they want him to stay in city housing, but he's bound to move. Last year, or six months ago, or even after that, it would have been a chance for me to get in and stir around and see if something could be worked out . . ."

"Oakland Against the System."

"*Yes*, and I was glad when I could get it to work for me and for the guy whose trouble I was wearing at the time, but this morning I just told him how things were and that was it. When I hung up, Betsy Ross was still waving her petticoat about individual self-reliance and the encroachment of government. I lost my temper. I probably blew up because I worry about laziness and dependency more than I'll admit. I know that there's something wrong with Bendemeer, for example, who would rather sit on welfare than learn a trade. There's something wrong with our system, too, for letting five years of dependency build up before we get around to trying to help him. No, Indio county won't get the trade school either, because the Bernardos who need it have no power. The thing that riled me about this woman was her self-satisfaction with it all. Her grandfather made it on luck, pluck, and thrift in an unspecialized agrarian community, so why can't the modern counterparts get lucky, plucky, and thrifty and succeed in a mechanized, specialized, overpopulated community?"

"Are you sure you were so upset about that? Isn't it that suicide that's still bothering you, that client of yours—what was his name, Marshall?"

"Marshak. What's happening to my resilience, Ab? I've heard nonsense before; I've seen stupidity and made mistakes, but now, somehow, the nonsense angers me more than the stupidity makes me wonder if all of this is worth it?" He leaned over and put his cigarette out on the ashtray on Ab's desk, noticing that it was clean. An empty ash tray at this time of the day meant that Ab wasn't smoking, and that meant that his ulcer was bothering him again. (Is that what is happening in my own insides; is that the trouble—making me feel sick every afternoon and groggy in the evenings? Is that why I spent all my wasted leisure time feeling bloated and dull? Is the ache going to become a burn . . .?) Ralph suddenly was consumed with hatred for his own limitations, and himself for being bound to them. Ab was bound, too—sharing a trouble is dividing it, some modern homily says.

224

Not here, buddy, not now. This work demanded too much from everyone, and half of infinity is still infinite.

"Let me tell you something, Ab. Marshak was one of the few I didn't have to take through the program on my own guts. I never had to plead with his teachers or beg the world or beg him to keep at one more day in training or one more chance on a job!"

"Do you have any idea why he killed himself?" Ab asked.

"No. The more I think about it, the more I wonder about my place in it—I might have fallen down. It was a very masculine job, the thing he did before the accident; there was a lot of pride in the activity of it, going over those planes and climbing around in them. There was a lot of camaraderie, too, noise and bigness and male fun. It was the part of the job he liked most; it meant a lot to him, being 'one of the "real men . . ." ' "

Ralph suddenly thought of Ethwald Kittenger and his terrible hunger to belong, to be a man at last, one of the "real men" with men. How terrible it would be for Ethwald if something happened to take away that definition from him in his own mind. It had happened to Marshak. Had his counseling contributed to the loss somehow? "I can't help feeling that I should have made more allowance for—well—I put him in an electronics place as a technician . . ."

"Hardly a Pollyanna type of a placement."

"Maybe it was cut up into cubbyholes with too little contact between the men. Perhaps I didn't go deeply enough into the conditions on the job . . ."

"Ralph, I want to tell you something. Stop being egotistical. It is, you know—yes, it is. You're giving yourself quite a starring part in this suicide. If I remember what you mentioned about the case, he never even gave the job a try. You don't take over a client's success; why damn yourself for a client's failure."

"You know as well as I, Ab, although most people can't admit it, sometimes it's the subtle things about a placement that make it a success or failure—a year and a half of terribly grueling work, physical rehabilitation and adjustment, testing, training. Even if he was conscious of what the trouble was, could he come and tell me after going through all of that? Hans was a proud guy. I know that he could never have faced me and said that he didn't like a program without giving a damn good reason. He was too proud of being logical and rational to admit to being put off by some subtle 'atmosphere' on a job."

"Ralph, the more you talk about this case, the more it reminds me of one I was in on—do you have a minute?"

"Sure, Ab, but I never knew you had a suicide."

"The—uh—the case was a young kid, fourteen years old. He climbed a tree to get a neighbor's cat out. He fell. Woke up in a hospital broken up so bad that nobody thought he'd live. Legs broken, arms, back. His skull was fractured too, and for a while it looked as if there was considerable brain damage. He didn't die, though. He came along little by little and pretty soon the picture seemed to be that he would live, but with a permanent paralysis."

"I guess it wasn't total, though, if he was your client."

"No, he had some motion in his left hand and he could wiggle the toes of his left foot. He was a friendly, outgoing kid in a small, neighborly town. People came to see him, schoolmates, friends. People would just drop in when they had a minute or were passing by. The hours were very long and the pain was very bad. He knew that if people were going to keep visiting, he would have to be mighty brave and mighty damn cheerful. In the spring, when baseball practice took all his school friends away, he began to fight that stubborn brain to make it give him back his body."

"He had to retrain it then, or else get another part of the brain to take over the functions of the damaged part—I've seen it happen with stroke cases sometimes. It can be rough going."

"It's like climbing a mountain. You know, you don't often hear people say it about that kind of thing, but it was a selfish life. His whole concern was in nothing but his hand, his arm, his leg; to lift the hand, clench the fist, bend the knee, pull the foot, day after day, every day after every day. A month, two months, he could move his arm and bend his knee. Six months, he could move both arms and one leg. He doubled his hours of exercise and then tripled them. A year, he could play and interplay all those dozens of nerves and muscles that go into sitting up. Two years, and he stood."

"Wonderful!" Ralph said. "Wonderful."

"Yes, it was. The doctors and nurses said they couldn't believe it. His bravery and courage made people look at him in a special way. It—it humbled people. He was sixteen then and he swore that he would walk into seventeen. He did, too. Took him eight months, crutches to braces to cane, and then

226

to his two legs. He walked and then he ran. A week after he walked for the first time on his own legs he stood on the edge of Faxon's Ravine and got ready to jump."

"Did he . . .?"

"No, my brother saved me. He'd followed me up there."

"It *was* you, then."

"Yeah, it was me, but don't go blabbing it around. I wouldn't want Bill Fatika telling me I wasn't a good Christian."

"If you know why you wanted to die, Ab—*why?*—please tell me *why?*"

"Didn't it come to you in the way I told it? I tried to make you see, Ralph. When they tell the Christmas story with the shepherds and the three kings, it always gets me. The two ends of a miracle are commonplaces, ordinary days, Ralph. I keep thinking and remembering how dark the night will seem to those kings and those shepherds trying to live on December 26th, when the light is gone. I climbed a mountain, sweating and straining and trying to get above the pain, hand over hand, all alone. I climbed a mountain with no rest and no holiday because of the immensity of the job. Three years, almost. It was like Everest. At last I got to the top. You know what I found there? I found the rest of the world, strolling and chatting and littering up the summit and picking their teeth while they looked at the view. I wasn't Hillary when I got to the top of that mountain, just an average kid again and three years behind everybody else."

"But why didn't you tell the doctors or your parents or your brother? Why did you have to keep being so damned cheerful and courageous when things were bad? Why did you have to close them out of your disappointment when you found out what was on the mountaintop?"

"That's the worst part of the whole thing, right there. Every word of encouragement and admiration fed my isolation, while I was climbing. Don't get me wrong—I needed those words of encouragement, they were right for the time, but, I guess I began to live in them, to hide in them."

"I don't understand what you mean."

"Oh, hell, Ralph, I was nothing but a breathing pulp at first. Later I was so ashamed—a boy fourteen who wets the bed, who can't even wipe his own behind. I had to sneeze and lie there with it all over my face until somebody came and wiped it off. When you're like that you feel broken and ruined. You want to cry all the time, cry and give up. You lie in bed and feel all your past self—expectations and skill, strength, hope eroding away. Can't you see how easy it would be to begin waiting for the praise you get when you come through on something? Remember, Ralph, this is over a period of time that's not lived like ordinary time."

"But they were kind, they were friendly—people visited and talked and helped, didn't they?"

"Exactly, and the only feeling of self-respect and confidence you can get is from them—the visitors, the nurses and doctors, and their good opinion comes to mean, well, maybe more than it should. I remember when I started on the exercises. With my legs broken and months of inactivity, it really hurt to get them moving. I pushed and pulled until I fainted, but it wasn't because I was courageous; it was because I was cowardly and had to make them say that I was no goof-off but a man, a man with guts."

"Did they?"

"The student nurses came in and had a beer party in my room that night. It was a small hospital and everybody knew. It was a terrific honor. Of course, everybody made out as if it was a big secret. I needed that beer party, even they never knew how much it meant for me to drink that shot glass full of beer, but their salutes to me were what kept me from being able to talk to them honestly about the fears I had and how dependent I was getting on their praise. I was the brave kid, the good kid, the cheerful, uncomplaining kid. If I broke the image, I was afraid I would lose everything." Ab sat back, took out a cigarette, and put it between his lips without lighting it. Then he smiled. "I'm tapering off."

"Ab, let me try to go on, then. When you finally walked, you must have been at your loneliest; and when the big letdown came, you found out that you had cut the lines between yourself and the world. Is that it?"

"Well, sort of—and there's one more thing. It's the hardest thing to face in some ways, and that is simply that people get tired. My family and friends had had years of my pain, my muscles, my legs, my—difference. They were just simply tired of it. I was getting over it, getting well, so why fuss about it? There had to be a letdown; it was only natural. Even Peg feels a little let down after she has a baby—nine months and a spectacular moment in the delivery room, and then, well, it's just a baby. But nobody *told me* about the letdown. I guess they were just tired of encouraging."

"Maybe. We're supposed to be happy with success. Not to

228

be happy with success is—well—it's un-American. People have to believe that success is unqualified, and not to be happy with it sort of puts dirty footprints all over their own dreams."

"You really think so? I always wondered why I felt so guilty about saying how—how it was back then, how bad it was walking around town, *walking,* mind you, and seeing my best friend in an Army uniform and hearing about another in college."

"Let's come to my part, Ab. How did your brother know to follow you when you went up to that ravine?"

"Well, I think he was free to hear me call for the help I needed. We'd always been close, but he wasn't as involved in my 'rehabilitation' as the rest of the family were. I know what you're thinking, Ralph, but you're not being fair to yourself. You think that you should have been the 'brother,' the 'outsider' who heard Marshall's call for help."

"Marshak's."

"Don't you see—he had to keep up the image for you, too. You weren't in the position that my brother, Steve, was; an outside-insider both nearer and further from me; you were a professional and that counted against you."

"But, Ab, he *called.* The day before he shot his fine, proud brains all over the inside of his father's car, he called me and I gave him some quick pats on the back—'you'll be fine' sort of brush-off. It was Friday, and I was rushed about some damn thing or other, but I told him it would all be fine, and now I wonder how I could have listened to him for a minute and not heard what he was trying to say to me."

"I've told you about my cowardice, Ralph, and now I'll tell you about the bravery, o.k.?" Still fighting the cigarette, he took a piece of gum. "I had to tell my brother in a way that he could hear. It involved sacrificing some of that proud, cheerful image I'd built up. Your boy wasn't brave enough to call in the kind of words that would let you hear it as a cry for help. He wasn't brave enough to give up that extra-stoical pose that you'd held him so high for. You're not stone, Ralph; if he'd have said it halfway, you'd have heard it."

"God, I wish I could believe that." Ralph got up. "I've got a client due," he said. "Thanks a lot, Ab. I'm going to think about this again. Funny, I just fell in so easily with the picture he painted. I just thought of Marshak so much as a hero, I guess I assumed that he couldn't be anything but a hero."

"Thank *you*," Ab said. "I'd kind of written those years off. They meant no more than a deferment from the Army and occasional nightmares now and then. If they can help anyone, well, maybe they'll pay for themselves yet."

Ralph opened the door and turned around to look at Ab again. He had forgotten that he wasn't the only one carrying parts of a boy around. Ab was getting paunchy and he was having trouble with his ulcer. Being on the first rung of the administrative ladder made him supercautious and overconcerned about "making a fuss," but he had let his "boy" come out to Ralph, and Ralph would never be able to see him so flatly again. Nor would he forget the slight twitch of the man's cheek muscles that remembered involuntarily the wincing of a boy in pain.

"Watch out for the giants, Ralph, the smartest or bravest or quickest. They have far to fall and hard to land, and don't show up late again at tomorrow's staff meeting."

When is a hero not a hero? When he can't be a coward too? That makes half a coward of Hans Marshak and maybe half a hero out of—out of a punk like—like John Kroll.

"What a jerk! I known it alla time!" said 3-Eye Oakland.

"Mr. Cafarde, this is Ralph Oakland at rehabilitation . . ."

"Oh, yes, Oakland, what can I do for you?"

"Well, the last time I was up to see you, you mentioned that you had an opening in your personnel department. I wanted to check with you to see if the job was still open."

"Well, we can always use good people. Frankly, I didn't think you would ever quit down there; your enthusiasm was one of the things I liked about your work. Well, you state fellas probably don't get much pay—that's why you're looking around, isn't it?"

"Well, the bills do add up." (The pay is fine; it's the long vacations I can't stand!)

"Don't be ashamed of setting your sights higher; come on down and we'll talk it over. Oh, by the way, how old are you?"

"I'm thirty-eight, sir."

"Oh—uh—I didn't know that. You see, we don't hire anyone over thirty-five. It's company policy. I'd sure like to bend it for you a little, but our insurance rates would go up and the rest of the departments would get their noses out of joint. You see, we have to pay quite a generous compensa-

230

tion. Your forty-five-year-old man, he gets a heart attack and . . ."

"Well, Mr. Oakland, I'm sure you know how desperately the center needs rehabilitation personnel. We're privately supported and it makes things look bad for us when we do such beautiful corrective surgery and physical therapy, fit limbs, and have all of the latest equipment, and then just watch it all go down the drain when the patient goes home and has nothing to do. They end up taking the brand-new arm off and setting it in the corner and going back to the T.V. We'd be glad to have you come with us—of course, I've heard about your work, Vidabeck and Henkin. Yes, you'd be the man we'd want, but there is one hitch."

"What's that, Mr. Barr?"

"Well, how much are you making down there?"

"Eight thousand."

"Yeah, I was afraid of that. You see, we couldn't possibly pay more than six-five to start, and it probably wouldn't ever go over seven. You wouldn't be happy taking a pay cut."

"Well, Mr. Barr, I'd like to come down there and talk terms with you. The center is near where I live and it's quite possible that the cost of commuting will . . ."

"I know this sounds very crass to you, but it's policy here and at every other place I know not to hire men at cuts in pay. You've been an eight-thousand-dollar man for a good while, and you just wouldn't stay content as a six- or seven-thousand-dollar man . . ."

(I'm a *priceless* man! A priceless man. And unless I save myself, I'm going to go under. I must look like one of them now, as if I was sitting on the other side of this desk. They keep drowning, and they see me, so comfortable and wise on the shore, very rationally discussing the birth dates of their grandfathers. I know the look, and now . . .)

"But the pay might actually be more, considering . . ."

"Nobody does it. It's been tried, but it never works, take my word for it. It does something to a man's self-respect. I'm sorry, Oakland, but it just wouldn't work."

"Ralph, I've got some good news for you."

"What's that, Ab?"

"Remember back in August, Marshall put in for that pay raise? Well, it was okayed by the legislature, almost half of what we asked for."

"It's the same raise for all of us, isn't it, Ab? If we're competent or incompetent, if we take tough cases or glide through on clients who just need the state's money, if we try to spend that money wisely or go through it like confetti—it's all the same, isn't it?"

"I don't know who pulled your plug this morning, Ralph, but it's a raise for you, and you know yourself that you deserve it. This hike makes us one of the top-paying state jobs."

"That's nice, Ab. With the ivy growing so green and thick, you can hardly see the bars."

17

The School of Social Work had called Ralph about their student counselor for Minnie Cormer. The more he heard about the student, the more misgivings he had. The best graduate students were usually well beyond college age, long-time caseworkers or juvenile officers who were going for advanced degrees. Many of them were canny and perceptive and they knew the ropes. At first Ralph had hoped for a Negro worker who could understand Minnie's problems fully and be frank without arousing the suspicion of prejudice on Minnie's part, but as he thought more about it, he became less sure. It would take an exceptional Negro worker not to look at Minnie with the special horror that all minority groups have for "their" failures. Minnie Cormer would not be helped by being somebody's living badge of disgrace. Perhaps a Jewish or a Spanish student, cousins in isolation but not sisters. When the supervisor of the student field assignments discussed Barbara Winston and her background, Ralph felt disappointment overwhelming him again.

The student was a cute, bright, white little co-ed right out of college. She had been raised in a strict, Fundamentalist home in a tiny, insular, middle-class farm town. Her church was the same as Bill Fatika's. (Its adherents referred to themselves as The Righteous, thereby needling Ralph into calling them The Self-Righteous.) What possible point of meeting could there be between an innocent, unsophisticated, small-town girl, whose deepest personal experience with sin was probably no more than a secret, guilty belief in biological evolution, and a mentally tormented Negro epileptic whore? Ralph had no control over these assignments. He could only hope that there had been some mistake. "You

233

know the case I mean, don't you? You do have my records on it . . ."

"Oh, yes, Mr. Oakland, they're all here and in good order. If you want reassurance about this girl, I can tell you that she has something quite special and an enthusiasm for this work that brings results."

"But, Mrs. Holland, this client is the closest thing I've seen to the embodiment of human suffering. I'm afraid that it might be too strong a mixture for a little co-ed like Winston."

"I said we thought that she had something special. It seems to be a hunger to understand anything and everything that there is in the world." The tone became a bit stiffer. "We pick the student assignments which we believe will be beneficial to *both* student and client. If you'd rather suggest *another* client . . ." The Supervisor had felt a toe testing into her corner of authority.

Ralph needed the counseling services of the students, so he withdrew the toe and smoothed over the surface. "Oh, no, this client needs help desperately. If you feel that your student is competent to give help, I'm sure she is. I'll be glad to meet with her and talk the case over . . ."

"I think we have enough material here. Of course, later in the counseling process . . ." They were doing the subtle minuet of delicately balanced steps by which they defined the relationships of people in different agencies, something like a mating dance between a male and a female bureau.

"I'll be interested in the progress of this case."

"We are certainly going to inform you when the case comes up in our meeting . . ."

"I'd like to be there also when the student is introduced to my client."

"Oh, yes, I think we can arrange that. I think it would be very useful."

He had tried—there was nothing for him to do but hope. Minnie needed all the wisdom of an unprejudiced saint—and the patience. He got up, sighing, and went to see the next client.

Stephen Marshak carried many marks of his dead son, although, because of his age, the pride and silence looked more like stiffness. He held out a thin, strong hand. "How do you do. I am Stephen Marshak."

"How do you do, Mr. Marshak. Will you come into my office."

Ralph noticed his walk as they went toward the door. More than anything else, Mr. Marshak's carriage reminded Ralph of Hans. Was that graceful and dignified bearing so important to Hans that the possibility of its being altered was enough to make him kill himself, or was it that "letdown" that Ab had spoken about? They sat down and Ralph began, hoping to put Mr. Marshak at his ease. He found his speech suiting itself to the reserve and dignity of the man who faced him. Had it been that way with Hans? Had he reflected such a stoicism, leaving his client no place that would yield, no place that could receive an admission of fear, a despair? When Ralph was finished with the useless small talk, he watched the man who sat still, measuring his back against the invisible ramrod. That spine would never sag!

"Mr. Oakland . . ."

"Yes, Mr. Marshak."

"I think maybe I shouldn't have come. You'll think I'm cruel and I don't want that. You'll think he had a father who didn't love him, and that isn't so."

"Why should I think that?" It was the standard thing to ask, part of a once-learned "technique" that was only used to keep the thread of the interview, but Mr. Marshak seemed to open into it almost gladly.

"In the first days, Mr. Oakland, the first days and nights both, I sat up, just sat in the chair because the whole world was shaking so bad I was afraid I was going to fall down if I tried to stand up. And afterward, I said: He was a good boy, such a good boy, with a good future, and starting over again. Why did he do it? And I started asking everything in my life *why?* Now I come here and sit and talk to you and I'm mostly just angry."

"Are you angry at yourself or at him?"

"What right does he have, that fine son of mine, to turn over all the years on top of us, his mother and me, and his wife? It was like he blamed us, that he made us keep saying to ourselves: Where did we hurt you? How did we fail you? And there's no answer. It isn't honest. It isn't right to call everything like that in question and then go where nobody can answer." He motioned to the closed office door. "Out there I left some tools he had when he finished school. What did he think I would do with them? How did he think I was going to look at those tools that we all talked about and hoped over? It's not—it's not what a man does!"

(What a *man* does! God, what an echo!) "I think he had his own reasons . . ."

"Maybe he did, but they're dead, those reasons. Why should I have to hear them after what he did! No, Mr. Oakland, I'm going to give his clothes to the Salvation Army, and I'm going to give his car to the junkman, because I don't want other people to have it where there's marked in the lining the blood and the brains of my son. He did this to me, Mr. Oakland, and all his education to make fancy reasons won't reason that away. I don't want those reasons after all!"

Ralph wondered why he had come, if not for some logic to be born between them that might make Hans's death believable to them. He was a deliberate man; it showed in the way he wore his clothes. Perhaps this was to be the final, fitting visit—An End to the Rehabilitation. But all at once Stephen Marshak put his scrupulously cleaned shoemaker's hands in front of his face and began to weep soundlessly.

Ralph picked up the dead phone and said into it, "Don't buzz me, please, I'll be right out." Then he left the office.

When he came back again, Stephen Marshak was sitting with his fists in his lap, very pale. He began to apologize. "It comes over me and I can't stop. To be a man, and cry . . ." And he breathed out heavily, and Ralph heard the man—man echoing.

"Mr. Marshak, whatever the reasons were, I don't think that we were as great a part of them as we think." Ralph let himself feel the words to see if he really believed them, and found that he did at least a little more than he didn't.

"He couldn't talk to me," Marshak said. "I wasn't crazy about his wife, you know, and she didn't like me too much either. If I would have made myself like her maybe . . . Oh, look at me now. *If.* His mother all the time, 'if this' and 'if that.' Now the *if* goes all the way back. Yesterday she says, she says, he goes to the toilet on the floor when he was three years old and we hit him for it. *If* we didn't hit him—can you imagine that?" He sat awed and helpless, like a witness describing a train wreck. "His wife and my wife got close after the accident. I used to think it was one good thing happened from that mess. Now they look at each other sideways, because there is blame somewhere, and they think if they give the other one the big mess of it, then the smaller mess will be for them." He sighed again. "A man doesn't stop loving, Mr. Oakland, never. But—I can't forgive him what he does to us every day."

236

It was probably the longest single utterance that the reticent man had ever made, and it had been an effort. At first, Ralph had almost looked forward to Marshak's visit, because he felt that at least part of what Ab had said to him was true for Hans also. It gave a meaning to the wild, extravagant act, which the family might need as he had needed it. Now he saw that with all their ifs and their reasons, his reasons wouldn't help; and Stephen Marshak, for all the anguish in his crying "why," didn't want to know why.

"Uh—the tools," Ralph said, "are they out in the waiting room?"

Marshak's face eased. They were back on familiar ground. There was no horror to be faced there, only the safe, ordinary landscape—and something to do. "Why, yes, they are. I put them under the bench there."

They went out into the waiting room and Marshak pulled out the small metal box.

"I just opened this to check if it was the right one." He flipped the square catches down and opened the box.

Everything was arranged with scrupulous care. There were a few large tools but most of them were the delicate gauges and instruments of the fine, elaborate electronics equipment on which Hans Marshak had been trained to work. Were these instruments too delicate, too "feminine" a work for someone who gloried in the big, rough maleness of his world? Oh, hell, Hans had plenty of time and there were the many, many chances offered by his re-occurring infections to change the training program, if he didn't like the work. Maybe he couldn't have spoken in the closest terms about his needs, but there were lots of ways to say what he wanted without losing face and before the stakes got so high. But—could it be . . . ?

"I think all of them are in there; it's the complete set," Marshak said.

"Well, Mr. Marshak, I think this is the set that the school gives the men to work with, and they keep it afterward as theirs."

Marshak's hands came up for a moment, defending. He didn't want the tools. "Well, we have no use for them. Someone poor perhaps, who could use them . . ."

"All right then. Thank you, Mr. Marshak. We'll be glad to have them."

That, too, was a lie. The tools were part of a kit, the other materials of which had been used up. They would gather dust in one records storeroom after another, and when somebody remembered, they would be given to the Salvation Army for the next highly trained electronics components technician to pick up, if they weren't obsolete by then. For a moment Ralph felt a little dizzy. In modern wars men die in millions and their costumes and agonies look quaintly old-fashioned to those in the very next decade. The evanescence of men and things never seemed so immediate as it did now. Were there people in the world who still planted a tree at the birth of a child in the innocent hope that in a distant time that child, grown up, matured, and aged would sit in comfort beneath the green and mellow shade of the tree, a triumph of prudence and forethought?

The old Stephen Marshak turned to Ralph. "I better be going home. Lately she doesn't like to stay alone in the house, so she works in the shop. If I don't get back, she'll begin to worry."

"Good-bye, Mr. Marshak." And they shook hands. "Good luck. Give my regards to your wife—and my sympathies, of course, to her and your daughter-in-law." He wanted to say something more, but there was nothing in the world that would not hurt the straight old man. Ralph picked up the box of tools and went back into his office.

Agipito Cisneros and Erminio Ortiz

Then, there were the women from Broken Hill again. They came with their hats of spring and innocence; their perfumes called Jungle Savage, Dark Intrigue, and Lust; and the politics of William McKinley. Behind them was a small, coffee-colored man wearing a suit which was obviously not his. He had a small mustache and he was timorous behind it, a frightened stranger. Ralph's interpreter was late and the ladies were afraid of the silence, and so they spoke to one another over the head of the small man. As each one entered the conversation, the stranger would turn his head politely and incline it toward her, although it was clear that he did not understand a single word.

At last the interpreter came, a young, somewhat scornful man, nominally attached to Judge Moonhoven's district court. His name was Bundy. The young man took a long look at the stranger, spoke, listened, and spoke again.

"He says his name is Agipito Cisneros."

238

After a few sentences given and taken, like a warm-up, the young man turned to Ralph again.

"This one is a cut above the ordinary. Some of them you get are so ignorant even in their own languages that it's impossible to communicate with them."

It seemed to Ralph like a terribly cold exercise. He didn't want it to be run like a field trial, so he motioned the ladies out into the waiting room and settled them on the mourner's bench. They told him that the other man, Ortiz, was sick in bed with a cold, but he had agreed to abide by any decision that Ralph made for them. Ralph sighed. He had explained the purpose and the process, but apparently they hadn't understood. Before he attempted to explain again, he might as well see Cisneros.

He went back, hoping to see the stranger relieved that at last, at long last, he was being understood in the familiar and trusted words of a native tongue. But there was only silence. Why didn't Bundy unbend!

Ralph said, "First, I think we'd better tell him just what this procedure is about. This is the office of the State Department of Rehabilitation and I am Mr. Oakland, a counselor."

The Spanish echo followed the English recitative. The little man's head snapped up when the translation made the meaning clear to him.

"Department of the State?"

"Oh, no," Ralph said—Bundy translating rapidly—"it belongs to the state, but it is not the Department of State."

But the man had come quickly to Ralph, smiling broadly and shaking his hand and saying something with great vigor. Bundy began to argue, gesturing against the other man's gesture; the man countered to Bundy and back again, until Ralph came between them and caught the word midair.

"What's he saying?"

"He says he also is of the state—was of the state—that you are thus a brother, that you would understand. He says, at last, the time has come. He says he will now make his statement."

"What? His what?"

"Apparently he thinks you're some kind of State Department representative. I've made it clear to him, but he says he wishes to make a statement."

"A *statement!* About what? Are you sure he understands that this isn't a legal proceeding?"

"He just keeps saying that now he will make his statement."

"Well, tell him—no, wait a minute. He obviously has something to say, so why don't we let him say it? There's no use arguing with him; we'll only lose the contact we're trying to make here. But, Mr. Bundy—you know, it just occurred to me. This guy was probably taken out of that Cuban jail, brought over to Miami, put on a train, and taken two thousand miles inland and one mile up in the mountains, given a suit of clothes and a handshake—all without ever having told anybody anything."

The translator looked around the small office. "You're not in a position to *do* anything about it. Are you going to *do* something about Cuba?"

"No, that's the whole point. Nobody is, so nobody has heard the man out. He is a bureau man, he says, one of my own, and he wants to go on record; and, by God, he's *going* to go on record." Ralph went to the door and called the secretary officiously. He suddenly felt better than he had in a long time. "Miss Hanrahan, I have some dictation . . ."

Head up from typewriter—"What's the matter with *you*, Ralph? Put it on the tape and I'll get to it when I get to it."

"This has to be done right away," he said. Whether it was the presence of the ladies on the bench or a special tone from Ralph, he couldn't tell, but it brought her over with her pencil and pad and a guarded look.

"Miss Hanrahan is our secretary," he said to Agipito Cisneros, and it ran drily over the mouth of the interpreter. "She will take the statement. It is the word of Agipito Cisneros. This is his interpreter, Mr. Bundy."

The secretary sat down.

"The official statement."

Miss Hanrahan didn't know whether to laugh or not. Bundy sat as rigid as a shock victim, but Agipito Cisneros was sitting forward in his chair, intent, serious, and every inch a man.

"Esta es mi declaration . . ."

"I make this statement," Bundy droned, "without fear and with no promise of reward. It is my own true statement, my cry, my testament out of my heart—(You know how these people go in for the whipped cream.)—in an utter and complete belief in my innocence—(I'll tell him to get on with it.) . . ."

"No," Ralph said, "let him say it his way. Take it all down, Bernice."

"I was in the government service of my beloved country, Cuba, from my youth. My father was before me, and his father before him. In grain statistics, they were; I was an accountant. I was an accountant for the Department of Excise and Import Taxation."

"They told me he was a fisherman," Ralph said, looking toward the closed door.

"I worked during the years of the reign of President Batista, it is true, but my job had nothing to do with revolution or counter-revolution and in my heart I said to myself, I work for Cuba. In my job I have never seen any of these things they say were cruel to the people. I do not say it is a lie. I say only that the accounting office of the Department of Excise and Import Taxation is run in a good and decent and honest way. When the government changed, we all go on working in the same way, now for the new government. Always, always for Cuba. Over us, the head accountant is the same and the people in the Department of Excise and Import Taxation are the same and do the same work." His voice stopped, his expressing hands went up; the interpreter paused, waiting, and Miss Hanrahan's pencil stopped eating across the green lines. In the office of the State Department of Rehabilitation there was an afternoon slowness to listen to until the quick brown hands flashed down again like teeth, or knives, cutting the strings of his believable past.

"I am arrested. One night—in my night clothes—just—arrested. They search my house; they frighten my wife; they take; they destroy. They pull me to jail. Who accuses me? I cannot guess. It must be that I am the victim of a mistake. It will all be made right at the hearing. Cisneros is a common name. Days and days—days go by. We are hungry. We come out in sores—(Bundy was beginning to pick up; his words moved faster across his mind; his tone was less cynical; Bundy was no longer bored.)—I remember—I remember one man, Calderón, who was in the Tobacco Division, and one day he was just gone, and they had a rumor he was arrested. You see, I did not—*I did not know then!*"

He shouted suddenly, and the pencil tore paper and broke, and Bundy's voice cracked between the outrage on one side of his head and the rational afternoon of the office. Miss Hanrahan rose like a ghost and left and returned with another pencil. Cisneros began to make profound apologies, which

241

were easy to understand without Bundy's benefit. He regretted deeply his loudness; he was upset; it was not his nature to be a man of violence; it was only the passion of the moment. Please to accept his most sincere—Miss Hanrahan took her seat again and read in her light voice: "I did not know then . . ." And for a moment they couldn't remember what he had not known.

"Oh, yes, I had not known that there was simply—to be gone. I had thought of Calderón, since I knew the man and liked him—ah, it is a mistake. Then, when he did not come back and the office closed all around where he had sat, so that he was really not to be remembered any more, I thought: Oh, poor Calderón, he must have taken something on the side. In such days as I had—crowded together with the other prisoners, all of us in the cells and some taken away and shot and some beaten up, some making confessions and giving the names of people, hundreds of names of people to be arrested, and to disappear. Señor—in this time, many months all together, my wife and my family are not told of me and they know nothing. Then, one day, they are brought to me and I am told there is to be a trial. Thank God, at last. I am going to be cleared. At last my name and honor are to be restored, *and my house, also, which was taken away, will be restored to me!*" He paused, hesitating between his indignation and the faces of his wife and children. "They have to leave the neighborhood, you know, because of the shame. Police come all the time. I told her to go back to the place of her father—it is a village, but the family is known there and it is safer than the city. We all weep. I tell them I will join them when I have restored my name to honor. They say it is not important in this country to have honor. This is sad to me, for it means much to us . . ."

"Tell—tell him . . ." Ralph said.

"Never mind," Bundy said. "Let him go on."

"Then comes the lawyer to see me. I begin to tell him what I tell you now, and he says I must be still and listen to him. He says that it will go most easily, most well with me if I say I am guilty and have been made a traitor by associations with traitors, which came because of a—liaison that I have with a woman. This is the best I can do, he says. It keeps me a *macho*, a virile man, and shows that I was acting beyond my control, a kind of insanity of love. He says he makes much study of this. Convincingly, a man telling this story, he says, got only three years imprisonment at a trial

242

yesterday. Indeed, because it had become an expected thing, the judges are easier with it. The malefactor does not stand out; he is only one of many, and no one to single out for special punishment. At this I cry and shake my fist. I am innocent! I am not a sinner! I am a man who thinks of the name of his sons and the affections of his wife! It is indecent! I tell the lawyer it is indecent.

"In the morning trial I am named with people I have never known and in places where I have never been. I say I am not guilty. They tell me to confess more names and it will go easier for my case. Or perhaps to prove my loyalty, let me name other men I know to be spies. This word makes my soul cry out. Who, now, will follow me as I have followed someone, through this night of terrible dreams? My barber? The old lady who collects the papers? The man beside me at the bureau? I say to them I know nothing but my own heart, and that I know is innocent. The judge does not listen. The judge says only, 'Shoot him'; just 'Shoot him'; just—that. They take me away. Excuse me."

He took out a handkerchief and began to wipe his face. He was full of agitation; he seemed barely able to keep his hands or body still.

Perhaps he wonders, Ralph thought, if we can sit here in this office and conceive of a despair like that. Cisneros took a deep breath and went on.

"Then began a time—you will think I am insane still, if I tell you that it passed like they say it passes for the insane. You must understand they do not tell you: such a day you will be shot or such a week or even such a month. Every night the fear grows bigger; it must be tomorrow since it was not today. Every footfall of a guard—*Dios!*"

He cried into the room, sounding and sounding again in the unconscious reflex of Bundy's "God . . ."

"Every day another man, five men, ten men, were taken away, not missed because there are too many others, and others always brought in. I would not be missed; we were a river of men. And for me every night and every morning were like an overflowing of fear without an end. Fear will dull a man six months, seven, eight—and the others, I do not any longer remember. I would be insane truly if not for the providence of God, that He sent me into the prison Erminio Ortiz. Erminio was a fisherman, arrested like myself. Early we came together in the crowded and stinking cell. He is a good man, he has the strength of a saint. In the dark hour of my fears he talks to me. We share food, water. We trust. He, too, was condemned, but with him things are a little better. The government that is supposed to be so for the poor people—it doesn't like to show itself to kill a simple fisherman. Also they are more eager to let him go for ransom. They give his name to the charities in the United States."

"I don't understand," Ralph said.

"Neither does he, probably . . ." Bundy started.

"Years ago, a certain religious man came preaching where Erminio was, and this man healed Erminio's family of their illnesses and was a good man, and Erminio took his church, when the numbers were few, out of gratitude to that good man. So the people of this church in the United States remembered his name, and by his miracle, I was saved. He told them I was his half-brother, that we were one family and wanted to be brought out together. I still do not know if the government is so confused that they believe us to be brothers or if they themselves are not tired of the fear and the killing and the dying. But we were taken out, both of us, and Erminio's family with him, out of the prison, out of the mad-house-country that was once my country, and into America. Two days, two whole days, we ride on the train, until I become afraid this country is too big to understand the nature of the small prison room in which we were standing so long. Now we are so far away—I tell you that even the stars look different in this place . . ." His voice trailed off and then returned. "My brother-friend, Erminio Ortiz, and I are grateful to the good pious ones who free us and take us so far and give us food and safety. I do not know how I can ever repay them. Does somebody wish, anywhere, an accountant with knowledge of the excise system, but speaking Spanish? If I can work, I wish to pay all those expenses which the people and the churches have taken on themselves for us. Erminio Ortiz, with whom I have ofen spoken of this, himself agrees most strongly. How can we tell you? It was never to be believed—as we are innocent—that we would one day be called traitors. We never dreamed that we would, Ortiz and I, be crying out our innocence in the rooms of another country, before men of another language. The great country of the United States has heard us and taken us, deep, deep into the middle of itself. From Broken Hill I make this statement for Erminio Ortiz and with his permission. I am myself, Agipito Cisneros, and I speak this out of Broken Hill in the United States of America, and it is true, as God shall judge me on the Last Day."

He put his handkerchief in his pocket and sat down. The now weary Bundy, who had risen with him when they were standing together in the crowded cell of a Cuban prison, looked around. Miss Hanrahan just sat. It was to her that Ralph spoke first.

"Make three copies of this statement, one to the office of the President of the United States, one to the office of the Secretary-General of the United Nations, and one for our files. Just for the record. You might as well make an extra copy of that for the ladies out there. I think they should have one also."

"Cuba's what you saw a couple of years ago on T.V.," Miss Hanrahan murmured. "It was important because it had a dictator and the Russian bases and all. But about jailing all these people—it was all *true,* wasn't it?"

"It was really true."

"I didn't convey it all," Bundy said quietly. "I didn't convey the confusion, the complete strangeness of it all . . ."

"We got the message, loud and clear," Ralph said. "Bernice, will you type this up when you get a chance . . ." Then he said to Bundy, "Don't go yet. He's made his statement, but I haven't made mine. The first thing we are going to have to do is to find out if he is eligible for our program."

STATE OF MINNESOTA
DEPARTMENT OF PROBATION & PAROLE
Bureau of Prisons
Department of Institutions

TO: Ralph Oakland, State Department of Rehabilitation
RE: Kroll, John, White, Male 17.

Subject has been charged with a felony in this state. The Probation Department is requesting that you send to us any pertinent information concerning Subject's background and schooling, juvenile record, training, employment, etc, in order that we may present these to the Judge in the event of a conviction as a guide toward fixing sentence. We would also appreciate the names of any other agencies having had dealings with Subject. Copies of this inquiry have been sent and records requested from Boys' Shelter, Office of Judge French (Juvenile Detention Facility), and the City-County Department of Welfare. Please reply and send all appropriate records at your earliest convenience.

L. L. Runciman,
Probation Officer

For a moment Ralph's hand hovered over the letter and his mind over Captain Sutter in his safe world of good or evil. His defense of John wouldn't help much—Georgia would use it and maybe Ralph would use it—but all of their reasons and meanings would be blown away like dust against the wrathful wind that was sure to come from a seldom generous juvenile judge who figured he had been taken. No, let Captain Sutter go on thinking about a John Kroll somewhere out in the clean, farm-dotted landscape of his mind's Minnesota. The hand drew away from that part of the letter and went back to the top, where it noted an immediate answer was requested.

Under the signature of the probation officer was the "release" signed by John, a standard form which gave Ralph permission to disclose the appropriate parts of John's misery to the appropriate agencies. Ralph recognized the signature, but he didn't feel angry or bitter, only tired. By dint of work and testing and persuasion, he had been able to prove to the world that John Kroll was not a moron. That was all very well, but John would never be superior in any trade or craft or business, and average was becoming not good enough. It was a shame—it was a great shame, but Ralph could feel very little of its tragedy penetrating. There was only disappointment and a quiet thought: On somebody else's guts. Now John Kroll will ride on somebody else's guts and time and allocation of money and energy and reputation and burned out hope. Ralph folded the letter and went on to the next one. The phone rang. It was Herb Vinson, sounding concerned.

"I've been giving this Ramirez problem a lot of thought, Ralph. We could keep him on until spring, but he doesn't need it, not really. I'd love to have him stay on as a teacher, too, but he's got eight kids and I couldn't pay him what he could get in some shop. He's a top mechanic now. Uh—Ralph, I know that he doesn't make too good a presentation of himself. I mean, if you don't know him, it's hard to see him as a mechanic, certainly not as a machinist."

"Oh, do you think so?" Ralph said, trying not to sound sarcastic. "Then, I hope you are going to ask me to give you as reference, I mean to let the employers call you."

"Well, I thought in this case that instead of having the secretary look up the applicant's record, it would be better if I talked to the employers personally. It's better if they can call and hear me tell them that the man they are considering is top flight."

"Well, his background is going to chill some of the employers, and his being on welfare is going to put a crimp in some others. We don't mention it, but the employers usually can guess when a man is on the county rolls."

"Why do you have to mention that he's Spanish—I mean, when you call for an interview."

"Well, Herb, I didn't in the beginning. It seemed to be playing into the hands of the prejudiced people, to make a thing of it when the client was colored or Spanish, but a couple of my clients got pretty badly hurt. A bigot won't care what he says in front of his victim, but I do care, and it makes for bad feeling all around when the employer feels he's been used by the agency. It will take work, but I think we can get a few shops to give Bernardo a trial."

Bernardo Ramirez

But after all his calls had been made, there were only four shops left. None of the employers had been very enthusiastic, but the sifted four on Ralph's list had said at least that they would be willing to meet Bernardo and talk it over. Well, they would try the places one by one.

Ralph picked Bernardo up the next morning in front of La Placita. It was cruelly bright and terribly cold. Bernardo got into the car, tears running from his nose and eyes.

"I coun' unnerstan' col' like dis col' here. You think col' like da goo' for people liveen'?"

"Oh, it just takes getting used to, that's all. We dress heavily and we heat our houses, but mostly it's just getting used to it."

Bernardo fingered his leatherette motorcycle jacket and pulled the Homburg hat down. "You know, i' cost a lot more bein' poor here . . ."

Ralph laughed.

They came to the first place. It looked good. They got out of the car and went in. The owner took one look at Bernardo, turned away, and left them standing in an empty shop. At the second place the boss was out. They went on to the third.

Bernardo sat quietly in the car, passive and still, as if this job was for a total stranger, and Ralph wondered how he could ever convince Bernardo that such accepting, such infinite compliance was working against him in this new world. Passivity was still such a great source of comfort to him. Surely Bernardo was not suffering in this as much as he. Bernardo's comfort irritated Ralph. His was a gift that hundreds of men would give a decade off their lives to have, and he didn't seem to *care*. Now he sat there like a mottled statue in the uneven heat of Ralph's old car, not angry at the first rebuff nor expectant but only in that maddening surrender to the greater powers of the world.

They had pulled up at Ridley Motors and Ralph watched the fat Prometheus get out of the car and waddle along the sidewalk. Bernardo was the lucky one. He worked with machines, man's pride and joy—gears and bolts that responded directly, caused effects, reasons that didn't change in front of the worker's eyes. Ralph had to work with *him*—and with the other illiterates who were not geniuses, and with the misery-loving mothers, and the suicides. It suddenly came, all at once, where he had been going when Hans Marshak's last call for help had come and he had shut it off. He had been going to drink coffee with Bill Fatika! They had called him the Lone Ranger, baited him, made him feel ridiculous, and so he had been short with Marshak at what he now knew to have been a critical time. No wonder he had forgotten—a stupid, petty, meaningless reason, a further blow to himself and Hans Marshak's despair. He looked again at the peon dreaming before the door of Ridley Motors, and sighed. In fixing motors, at least the victories were pure and had no flavor of defeat. Bernardo was lucky, so lucky, and he didn't even know it.

"Open the door," Ralph said.

They went in.

Ridley was a no-nonsense man; Ralph could see it and that he was proud of it. He had passed the hurdle about Spanish-Americans; he had passed the one about handicapped people; but he gave Bernardo Ramirez one look and began to stiffen with incredulity and anger.

"Mr. Ridley," Ralph began.

"Look, mister, I know the state hires you to find jobs for these guys," his voice dropped a little, "cripples and that, but get that guy out of here, this kind of job isn't for—*him*." He shot a look at Bernardo, who had tactfully wandered a little away from them and was looking at a mounted motor.

"He's a moron," Ridley said.

"How do you know?"

"One look at him, just one look'll tell you that."

"I'm not sending him here for his *looks*. He's Central Auto's top man. Call Herb Vinson and he'll tell you himself."

"Hell, I don't want to call around and make a fool of myself. In school, with teachers fixin' up the mistakes, maybe it's different . . ."

"Everybody knows Central Auto's boys; they are top men. So this one is not a fashion plate and he's not Robert Taylor, but he *is* the best student Central has."

Ridley looked at Bernardo again. His eyes narrowed. "This isn't a joke is it? One of them quiz shows or hidden microphones or nothin' . . ."

"Give him a chance, right now. This is no trick and he can prove it."

As if to refute the phrase, Bernardo had turned and was ambling slowly toward them. They dropped their voices and then stopped talking, embarrassed. Ralph could see that Ridley didn't want to hurt Bernardo. It made him even more irritated with Ridley's stubbornness. Bernardo came up to them and stood very close. Ralph knew that closeness meant human contact to most Spanish-Americans, but it meant crowding to Ridley.

"You haveen' trouble wi' da motor," Bernardo said, looking back at it.

"Yeah," Ridley said, backing away and trying to ease into the subject of not needing any help. "I'm not gonna work on it here though; I'll send it back to the factory. Parts out of alignment."

"I cou' fixeen' da here, if you wan'." A step forward. (Why do *Anglos* run away?)

Ridley began to wave him off—he didn't need any help with the motor—but, now, Ralph couldn't give up without a fight, not after Bernardo had spoken up for himself, that first word of independence that was reaching to span four centuries of Ramirez' enduring under the sun. He had come forward.

"Oh, do you think you can fix it?" Ralph asked conversationally.

"Of course not!" Ridley interrupted, probably sensing that Ralph was trying to lead him against his will. "I told you it was out of alignment." He was becoming irritated because he didn't want to have to throw them out.

"Wha' you say is true," Bernardo said pleasantly, again striking that lovely balance between respect and self-assurance all but lost to the ears of modern blue-collar employers. "Bu' I been lookeen' here, an', see, you cou' grine dis one down, see?"

"Yea, well you saw that just by looking, but what would you do on the other side?"

"Oh, you cou' fit in one more beareen', an' here, here, come up wi' fiteens'. Fitteen' here, you won' get no shakeen'."

"Aw, hell," Ridley said, going for his tools. He came back scowling. "Maybe you talk a better job than you can do. Well, go ahead."

Bernardo looked gently at him. "Cou' I show you here?"

Ridley shrugged. "It's crazy, but go ahead and let me see you work. I want to see how you'll allow for pressure buildup there."

"See, wit de fiteen' *here,* de pressure na' gon' come much *dere* no more."

"Yeah, but it's only taking the problem to the other side—here."

They were both over the motor, intent. Bernardo had the wrench going.

"Is more easier fixeen' dere, see . . ."

"I have another appointment at noon," Ralph said, "we should . . ." He became aware that they were no longer listening.

Dear Mr. Oakland,
   It gives us great pleasure to inform you that you have been elected to the presidency of the State Rehabilitation Association for the maximum (4-year) term. Congratulations and our best wishes for a fruitful and successful term as President. . . .

It was a genuine honor, a real, honest-to-goodness vote of respect, and it seldom went to men on the counselor level. By a simple write-in vote of everyone in the Association, the officers were chosen. The votes were not bought or campaigned for or given for favors. A good many must have come from counselors in distant parts of the state, whose clients he had supervised three or four or five years ago when they were sent to the city to be trained. It was a clean honor, cleanly come by, the kind of prestige that even 3-Eye would have been proud of and might secretly have yearned for. Now it seemed to Ralph that it was coming not as a sign of success but as a compensation. Now, because the dream was gone and the work was piled up over his head, because Marshak was dead and Kroll had failed and a hundred others every month were not even capable of taking training to be hired, The System, without even realizing it, was attempting to comfort him by the giving of raises and prizes.

He suddenly remembered his aunt, a lonely old lady who used to wear pounds of rhinestone necklaces and a heavy ring on every finger. He had laughed at her. He saw now that her weight of jewelry was only a compensation, really, the once wished-for luxury that was at last possible, and just at the time of life when it was no longer a symbol of love or conquest or power. He would have to thank the State Association. He began to make a note about writing. Mary-Ann would be very proud.

The phone rang. Then there was another client. In the afternoon he called Central Auto School.

"Herb, this is Ralph. I thought you'd like to know that Bernardo is working down at Ridley Motors."

"You're kidding! Ridley is a man-eater; he's famous for it. His rate of turnover is something—hey—but you know, maybe he's been getting so many of the sassy rod-jockeys lately that a polite guy like Bernardo would look pretty good . . ."

"Well, he hardly *looked* good, and the first meeting was a little bit of a shock—Bernardo had to rebuild a motor practically before he made the job."

"What did I tell you! Say, Ralph, I've been thinking about Bernardo. What it boils down to is that I want him back; not right now, but after he gets going at Ridley's. I want him back part-time or, maybe say, two nights a week to teach. I'll pay all I can, because I want to see that he gets more—more experience."

"But Herb, why? Is there some special need at the school?"

"It's two things, Ralph, one for us and one for him. Hell, college-trained teachers can talk down to trade-school men and make them feel stupid and second-rate. We have a lot of the kids right off the hot-rod circuit come in here to be mechanics. Bernardo being the way he is, the kids figure that, by God, if *he* can do it, so can they. Only a guy like him could convince those kids that it's just as manly to work careful and neat as it is to wrench and jab and cuss. Bernardo works like a surgeon; he's clean and polite and the difference shows on every motor he's ever touched."

251

"But, Herb, it's going to be an awful grind. I doubt if he has the drive for that kind of a deal: working days and teaching, and 'fixeen' theen' ' for the neighbors, which you know he'll have to do, too."

"That's why I want it for *him*. He's got it in him to engineer motors, to invent, to make something new. Don't you see, Ralph, today he hears and learns, and tomorrow he knows, and the next day, what? Soon he's going to start to go, to think something new, to—to—bust out of the old ways and go beyond us. He should learn as much as he can right now, because the more he learns, the bigger his new way is going to be."

"Well, Herb, I'll ask him."

Ralph made the note on the case record: Ramirez, Bernardo, sex: M, age 30 The world is beginning to need you, Bernardo—it was true. Ralph smiled. The complex, foreign, literate, hurried world was giving the still-strange, still-illiterate Bernardo a place in which to root himself and grow. This need for Bernardo's special gift would bring him pride, too. The hunger for such a pride in Americans—maybe in others, too—was a sharp lure, sharper than the hunger for social prestige, perhaps, or wealth; sharper, perhaps, than the need for freedom . . .

Freedom . . . "I speak this out of Broken Hill in the United States of America . . ." Ralph sat back in his chair and thought about Agipito Cisneros, bureaucrat, "traitor," and, someday, American; and about Bernardo Ramirez, the gentle genius. Is it still true; can it still be true today?

America was made in the beginning by outcasts; it was born in the same shock and agony that had cried out of Agipito Cisneros; and it had found in itself hope and had brought forth genius. "My God," Ralph murmured to himself, "it is still happening . . ." He suddenly realized that it was happening in this job that he so loved and so hated, between boy-convicts and retarded girls, brain-damaged professors and tragic suicides, and that he was being permitted to see it and, now-and-then, to help. The resurrection was not with the protected or the wise or the well-educated, who don't need miracles, but with the wretched and wronged and seemingly unfit. Well-favored men like Ralph might shape the dream of justice under law and the sacredness of the individual. Pious men like Fatika might envision the Peaceable Kingdom here as well as There, but it was over Cisneros, Ramirez, Kroll, and Cormer that these rainbows come to

ground and were tested in squalid reality. In spite of conferences and agencies, bureau gears and budgets, incompetence
and ignorance, the children of Lincoln might still welcome
forth the children of Lazarus.

"July fourth," Ralph murmured, "and I almost walked
right past it."

18

"Mr. Oakland, this is Barbara Winston. I'm the student who is doing the counseling with Miss Cormer . . ."

"Oh, yes, Miss Winston. I've been wanting to call you about when we could get together."

"I've had about four sessions with Miss Cormer. Her case is really interesting—I mean, I've never met anyone who lives the way she does . . ."

"Oh?"

"I just wanted you to know, Mr. Oakland, that I think we can work together and that I think she may agree. I was as surprised by that as anyone else. I hope I can come to understand her; I have a feeling that it would take someone like me to sympathize with what society must be doing to her . . ."

"Frankly, I don't think I see how, Miss Winston, but I wish you would tell me."

"Well, unless you've grown up in my faith, it would be difficult to understand how a person could get the idea that he'd fallen short no matter what he did. You grow up being prayed over. Oh, Mr. Oakland, it's so hard to be prayed over! The whole society does it to Minnie, and no wonder she can't feel easy in the places ordinary people go to get a little fun. I don't understand her—not yet— but I don't pray over her and I think she appreciates that."

"Barbara, call me Ralph."

(Could a compromise like that be a success? How am I going to save myself in this tragedy-mill without becoming indifferent? The miracle of resurrection is their miracle, not mine. Maybe all I get is a kind of backward-looking pride. For five years, five whole years, I've been somewhere near

254

the top of this vocation. I can't figure that hard any more; I haven't the youth or the strength; but maybe I was one of the few who determined the heights of this art for one little space. Is that enough? If so, I guess it is. There will still be clients and battles. Maybe less complete, maybe relinquished more easily, but I had five years. Five whole years . . .

"Ralph, this is Ann Ellison. There's a problem here that I think you might be able to help with—a man about forty. His name is Jeromes, a telephone lineman. He's been one for years, but there was a freak accident while he was fixing a line and he took the charge of that live high-tension wire. Of course, it would ordinarily kill a man; but the charge got him first in the left foot, burned its way into the bone, and ran upward, burning up the nerves in the leg and across the trunk and up the right side of his body through his arm and out at the fingers, leaving them burned to the bone. The hand, of course, will have to come off, but he'll have one hand and the opposite leg. The real problem in the case is that he's horrified of being permanently disabled as far as working. The power company people that I spoke to said he was one of their best men, competent and steady, but the psychological . . ."

"No, I don't care if he's blind; can he get from Harper to Thompson Creek, at least? Our men can get from Broken Hill to there for their English lessons, if your man can make it from Harper. I'd like it to be every day; it's vital. The state will pay a fee plus transportation. I don't want them coming to the city, not yet. They'll end up in the Spanish ghetto and be lost. We have to surround them with America . . ."

(Maybe it's just to know that hope is as relentless as despair. I've got to go to that doctor soon; my stomach is burning up. I know what it is now, nothing more romantic than an ulcer, as grinding and chronic and unresolving as this damn job . . .)

"Mr. Oakland, this is Dr. Steinhagen. You were recommended to me by Dr. Finch. I'm a heart specialist also. To be blunt, I've had some problems with three of my patients. One of them is a roofing contractor, two are truckers. All of them have serious heart conditions and shouldn't be working in jobs like those. I found that they had returned to their jobs

255

because they didn't know anything else, and, of course, the increased pressure of new bills to pay. I've come to realize lately that you can't just tell a man to quit the only kind of work he knows. I want to send these men to . . ."

(It's hardly the American Dream. I wonder if it's true; if hope really does wage as hard a war as despair. If it's true, can I live with it? Even if I'm not in the Dream, at least it's still there—if not mine, then someone else's.)

"Ralph, this is Georgia. We have two boys, brothers, who just came to us last week. They're hostile and aggressive, but it seems a shame just to let them go, because there's potential there—Ralph?"

"I'm not taking impossible cases any more Georgia . . ."

"Have you gone out and gotten drunk over Kroll yet?"

"I wish I had. I may not be able to do that either any more."

"These boys are bitter, too. I'll not deny that, but they have potential, both of them. What's the joke?"

"My answer. I don't know whether it's a laugh or a groan. What were the names?"